Hidden Treasures

ALSO BY MICHELLE ADAMS

Little Wishes

If You Knew My Sister

Between the Lies

Hidden Treasures

A Novel of First Love, Second Chances, and the Hidden Stories of the Heart

Michelle Adams

HARPER LARGE PRINT

An Imprint of HarperCollinsPublishers

HarperCollins books may be purchased for educational, business, or sales promotional use. For information, please e-mail the Special Markets Department at SPsales@harpercollins.com.

FIRST HARPER LARGE PRINT EDITION

ISBN: 978-0-06-311749-5

Library of Congress Cataloging-in-Publication Data is available upon request.

21 22 23 24 25 LSC 10 9 8 7 6 5 4 3 2 1

For Lelia

Hidden Treasures

Prologue

The Cotswolds, Winter 1982

The car was there again. Red lights pierced through the darkness and thick smoke chugged from the exhaust. Frances had seen it parked there last night too, and once the week before that. In her little street in a quiet Cotswold's village, it was unusual to see strange cars. The first time she assumed the people inside might have been tourists, hikers lost up a dead-end street and unsure where to pick up the trail. She would have stopped to offer the two men directions if it hadn't been so cold, but she was keen to get Harry back inside after a blustery afternoon walk. Later that evening when she'd looked out the window the car was gone and she'd thought no more about it. But now they were back, and that changed things. Even from that distance she knew it was the same men, those who had left cigarette butts on the frozen ground. They were here for her, because of what she had in her possession.

They were here about the Klinkosch box.

Hearing her son whimper, she turned away from the window and hurried across the room. Still asleep but restless in his cot, Harry's mouth was open, his lips suckling at chilly winter air. Frances pulled the blankets toward his chin, retrieved the lost pacifier from under a cuddly bear, before carefully inserting it back into Harry's gummy little mouth. Distracted by her son, for a moment Frances almost forgot about the car outside, but the thought was soon back with her, reminding her that they weren't safe. If it wasn't five in the morning, she might have called Mrs. Gillman from next door, asked her to come over. It would seem easier if she wasn't alone. They could have a cup of tea and a slice of cake, and for a while she could fool herself into thinking that everything was fine. But what good would Mrs. Gillman be against two men if they decided to cause trouble? The only person who really could protect them, who she wished was there in that moment, had chosen not to stick around.

With Harry settled she edged toward the window, pulling the curtain back for another look outside. They were still there, just as she knew they would be. Frances knew that she had to do whatever it took to keep

Harry safe. It had been easy to make promises the year before, offering to take the box, to hide it, to make sure it was never found again. But things had changed, and it was different now. Back then she couldn't have imagined anything more important than Benoit or the safekeeping of the valuable antique entrusted to her care. But now there was Harry, and he was more important than anything else. More important than Benoit. More important than a stolen box. There was nothing she wouldn't give in order to keep Harry safe.

Moving slowly so as not to wake her sleeping boy, she pulled a small step across to the wardrobe, then climbed up so that she could reach to the top. She knew what she had to do. From the hiding place behind the hat boxes, her fingers found the cool metal of the Klinkosch box, and slowly she pulled it forward. It was heavier than she remembered as she lifted it from the edge, but still just as beautiful. The detailing was marvelous, the filigree around the edges, the cherubs on the side. Stepping down she held it close to her chest, thinking of the moment when she first saw it, and of Benoit's face when he handed it over.

"I took it because I loved you," she whispered to herself, remembering what Benoit used to say to her. "But I must hand it over, because now I love Harry so much more."

The decision was made. She would take it to them, give them what they wanted. But as she took one last look at Harry resting safely in his cot, an unexpected thought came to her. What if the return of the box wasn't enough? What if they wanted revenge for its theft in the first place? Perhaps handing it over would no longer be enough to keep her and Harry safe. What if they hurt her, leaving Harry alone? Or worse still, hurt Harry? It was an unbearable conundrum. Unwilling to risk his safety, she set the box down on the side, moved to the cot, and scooped Harry up. Sitting down in the corner of the room she held her son close to her chest when he started to whimper. A tear streaked across her cheek, unable to see a way out of the mess.

"It's okay, there, there, my precious boy." Bouncing him against her chest, she realized that she was stuck. Keeping the box put her at risk, but so did handing it over. "Mummy will find a way to keep you safe," she whispered, even though she had no clue how she might be able to do that. "I'll never let them hurt you." And then, kissing his head, she made her son a promise that she had no idea how she would be able to keep. "I promise to do whatever it takes, Harry. They might find the box, but they will never, ever, find you."

Chapter One

Nook Cottage, The Cotswolds, Summer 2022

In the same little cottage down a dirt track lane, Harry Langley was sitting on the edge of the threadbare chair where his mother had spent the best part of the last ten years. Every muscle in his body ached, the position awkward with his tall frame bent almost double, his legs too long. By that point he had been there for a couple of hours, still dressed in the black suit that was one size too small and made him feel like a schoolboy still in last year's uniform. Scrunching his eyes tight, he tried not to think about the chaos all around him. Standing up, he loosened his tie, shook off his jacket, wishing that his mother was there to help him with the massive task ahead. But she wasn't, and he was alone, because they had buried her ashes at three p.m. that afternoon.

With the last of the day's sunlight glinting from the mirror that hung on the chimney breast, Harry glanced around at the rest of the mess. Nothing about what he saw was new to him because he had been living within it for the last ten years. But still it came as a shock. His mother's collection extended around the circumference of the room, the door to the hallway frozen somewhere within it, leaving just a small passage through which he could walk to the front door. Just as bacteria colonized an agar plate, the volume of possessions multiplied into the kitchen and up the stairs, a lifetime of hoarding staking its claim on every available surface. It had claimed the walls, the carpet, and in places even the ceiling. And now, following his mother's death, it was his job to try to sort it out, so that the house could be sold. He didn't know where or how to begin.

"Come on," he said to himself, private thoughts verbalized as had become customary. Without his own voice, the silence would have been suffocating. "We're going to have to do this eventually. Might as well be now." Kneeling, he lifted the flap of a nearby box, labeled *Spare Parts*. A metallic scent hit him, an iron edge to it, sharp like the taste of blood. After fishing about inside he pulled out what he thought was a spark plug, and after that something obscure that could have been some sort of pump. Black grease stained his fingertips, which he wiped on the suit he knew he'd never wear again. The obscurity of the items only served to reassure him that his house was packed like a can of sardines in every possible corner with useless possessions. "Jesus, Mum. You really did keep everything."

Well, almost everything, he thought.

From his position on the edge of his chair, he stared across the room to where his mother used to sit, the empty cushion dipping in the middle, as if expecting her return. Memories of the evenings when a balmy sun would bathe the room in pink light, bringing life to her cheeks and warmth to the drafty house, came to him then. As she would doze in the chair, he often used to look at her and wonder. Wonder why. Wonder when. But most of all he would find himself wondering how she could have done it. Had she found it difficult to let him go? Did she ever wish she could go back to that moment when she walked away, when she left him on the shopping center bench, and undo what she had done?

Did she ever wish she'd kept him?

How old had he been then? Old enough to remember the ice cream that the guard brought him while the police were called, and the note she pressed into his chubby hot palm. Almost ten years had passed since they had reconnected, since he had found her, and during that time he had done everything he could to be a good son, even living with her in the hope of getting the answers he needed to his questions. Now she was gone, and he was alone again, left in her house, and he still couldn't explain why she had given him away.

Outside the summer's day inched toward eventide, the gray opalescence of clouds forming overhead and bringing the promise of rain. The air thrummed with the need for a storm. When it rained at River View, the care home where he had been working for the last ten years as a nursing assistant, the water levels of the river would rise to cover the part of the garden where the flowers bloomed. Worry grew then, over the thought of Margaret in room three, and whether somebody in his absence would deliver the flowers to her room as he did every other day. Joseph too would be missing him, no longer able to read but with an indisputable appetite for the newspaper each day. Harry would always find the time to read to him, but would any of the other staff do the same? The value he added to their lives seemed minuscule in comparison to what they added to his; they made him feel worthy and beneficial in a way little else could. How he longed to go back to that. Being in this house almost exclusively for the past couple of weeks was getting to be unbearable.

That afternoon, as runnels of sweat had trickled

down his back, Harry had glanced at the faces of those at the funeral. Besides Victor, his boss at the care home, and Mrs. Gillman, the old lady from next door, there was just himself and the four pallbearers, who had stayed for the service to make up the numbers. He suspected upon Mrs. Gillman's instruction. But twenty orders of service sat idle on the pews, as if Frances Langley had slipped from the world causing barely a ripple on life's surface. A few weeks shy of her fifty-sixth birthday when she died, it was no age to have suffered a rogue DVT that got stuck on its way through her lungs. Harry had hoped the funeral would mark a turning point in the road for him, but the journey ahead was undeniably difficult, and he didn't know how he was supposed to get through it alone.

When he heard the unmistakable squeak of his garden gate, followed by footsteps on the cobbled path, he felt sure he must have fallen asleep and was now lost somewhere in a dream. But moments later came the tapping of knuckles against the peeling paint of the front door. He wasn't expecting anybody, and it was a bit late for visitors.

What time was it? Gazing down at his wristwatch was a habit, even though it had stopped long before the day he began wearing it. It was one of the few things his mother had given him, strapping it to his wrist before she left him on that bench. Although he had no idea of the truth, he had always felt sure that it had once belonged to his unknown father. He had always liked to believe that as a child, but when he had asked his mother, all she ever told him was that it came from somebody who loved him. Unprepared for guests he sat upright as the knocking resumed. From the corner of his eye he caught a glimpse of his reflection as he stood up. His hair was almost black, and his skin like pale honey, but his face was lined in a way it never used to be, his eyes darker and shaded. Turning away, he edged toward the hall. The truth was, he didn't like to see just how much he had changed.

"Just a moment," he called, edging past the junk. Perhaps it was Mr. Lewisham, the lawyer in charge of the sale of the estate, who had told him in no uncertain terms that he better stop messing about and sign the necessary paperwork. Hoarding, it seemed, was almost synonymous to unpaid debts, and the cottage, like it or not, had to be sold. But what would he be doing there at that time in the evening? Harry had three weeks before the auction was due to take place. With some urgency this time, the knocking started up again.

"All right, all right," Harry said as he slid the chain from its bracket. On second thought, it was probably Mrs. Gillman. She had promised to plate him up a dinner, even though she herself was inching toward her nineties and in no physical state to be taking care of a man who was heading into his fourth decade of life. But she was that sort, always trying to help where she could, or solve any issues with a kind of wartime spirit that Harry admired. No doubt she would have been great at helping clear his mother's house, if it wasn't a near impossibility to negotiate the mess with her walker.

"It's taken me all day to find this place again," Tabitha said as Harry opened the door. Her face was cast in a gentle silhouette yet there was no mistaking it was her. Golden hair streaked by fire pooled on her shoulders. Shadows sketched a slim face, the chiseling of age that made him think of old photographs, of youth, and how it could be lost. That softly pointed nose, not as straight as he used to imagine it. Her body was the same, her frame slight, her skin pale, as if not a day had passed since he had last seen her. His breath caught in his throat so that he could barely speak.

"What are you doing here?" he said, his voice croaky and clipped. Whip-fast thoughts of his appearance quickened his heart rate. What would she make of him, and how he had changed in the decade they had been apart?

"Honestly?" she asked, her lips pursed. "I have

literally no idea." Razor sharp, her voice had an edge to it that he recognized, as if they were fresh off the back of an argument and nowhere near finding a resolution. Seeing her again, the same person changed by time, the person whose touch he once knew so well and whose musky scent he could muster just by thinking of it, had rendered him mute. Standing before him was the woman he had lost, and the woman he had never stopped loving. Eventually she took another step forward, but still he didn't move. "Aren't you going to let me in?"

Contemplating the proximity, so close he could reach out and touch her—and oh how he wanted to reach out and touch her—it was as if time had bent back on itself. Ten years ago, he had watched her walk away from this house, but now the scene was playing out in reverse. She was back, and for a moment it was as if nothing had changed at all, as if she was returning after just a few short, angry hours apart. As if they still belonged to each other. But then he remembered how much his reflection had changed, how time had moved on, and how life, for some at least, had been lived. How Tabitha, no doubt, had moved on. Glancing to the floor, he took a step back.

"Sorry, yes, of course." He held himself firm as she

shuffled past. Birds sang in the trees outside. Water babbled, the surrounding land rain-soaked and soft. As she moved past, he caught her scent, and goose bumps shivered up his arms. Fingers flinching, he moved to touch her, just to find out if she was real. Pulling away at the last moment, he realized he was too scared to break the mirage or do anything that could cause her to leave. "I can't believe you're here," he managed to say as he closed the door.

For a moment she said nothing as her eyes scanned the mess. "Neither can I. And it's worse than it was before," she said, tapping a brown envelope against her leg. Shame enveloped him like a curtain drawn, that she was witness to the way he had allowed himself to live.

"I know," he said quietly. "There's been a lot going on, I suppose," he said after a time. "I'm trying to clear it. But as you can see, it's quite a big job."

"You can say that again. Look at it all," she said, shaking her head. "I assume you weren't expecting me."

"No." He paused, not sure where to even begin. "Don't get me wrong, I'm glad you're here, but why would I be expecting you, after all these years?"

"Ten," she said. "Ten years." She motioned to the living room door. "We have something we need to discuss." When he didn't move, she said, "Can we go through, sit down?"

"I'm sorry," he stuttered, "it's just . . ."

"Just what?"

"Well, I didn't expect to see you."

"You said that already."

"I know, but now you're in my hallway, and you look, I mean, you always looked, but then we were young, and now, well, you're a woman and, well . . ."

"Oh, just spit it out if you've got something to say."

"Well, I have," he said, aware of the heat in his ears, the flush of his cheeks. "I was going to say that you look great. Beautiful. That's what I was going to say." He took a deep breath. "I'm sorry. I'm rambling," he said then. Pointing to the living room door, he beckoned her on. "Please, go through."

Weaving between boxes and bags stuffed with secondhand clothes, he led her through the wedged-open door to the living room, then offered her his mother's chair. His skin prickled at the memory of her body as she moved past him, of the way she used to hold him, and how they used to fit together. Of what it felt like to touch her. It might have been ten years, but he wanted her still as if it was yesterday. He had never stopped. As he stood near the window, she took a seat.

"So, where is she?" she asked then.

"Who?" For a moment he had forgotten anybody else existed in the world.

She tutted, let her gaze drift to his face. "Your mother, of course."

His assumption had been that Tabitha's arrival was symptomatic of his mother's passing, so her question threw him a little. He stumbled through an answer. "Well, she's not here."

"When will she be back?"

"Er, she won't be," he said, stumbling a little. "She, um, she died."

Tabitha stopped tapping the envelope, her nervous fidgeting eased by the new information. "Died?" she asked, her eyes finding his, the first time her voice betrayed its softer qualities. The gray blue of her irises drew him in, like pools in which he could swim toward something better. "When?" she asked with a degree of suspicion.

"Couple of weeks ago."

"I don't understand," she said. "That's not possible."

He shrugged. "I'm afraid it is. We interred her ashes today."

Tabitha looked to the envelope and noted the postmark. "But she wrote to me two days ago." Leaning across the room she handed the envelope to him. "She told me I had to come here, that you needed my help."

For a moment everything seemed to freeze, no breath for him to take, no sense of his surroundings tangible to touch. It was as if two worlds had collided, and he was in that moment right after impact, just before the explosion destroyed everything he once knew. He could never have imagined any situation in which his mother and Tabitha could have ever been brought together, and now Tabitha was here, saying that his mother had engineered it, that she had brought Tabitha back to him. It was too much to take, and he sat back in the chair as he finally took a breath.

"That can't be right. She couldn't have."

"But she did." He took the envelope at her indication. Scrawled across the front was Tabitha's name, and an address he didn't recognize. The top had already been torn open. Italic letters bore all the traits of his mother's hand, the swirling consonants, the rounded vowels. He reached inside and his fingers found a second envelope. Pulling it out he saw his own name written on the front.

He looked at Tabitha for an answer. "I don't understand."

"And you think I do?" she asked, sitting back in the seat, crossing her legs. "Look at the letter she sent me. It won't take you long." Pulling out the folded paper, he read the brief message.

Dear Tabitha,

Ten years ago, when Harry came home, I didn't understand what he was losing in leaving you behind. Although I didn't ask him to, I know it was my fault that he ended your relationship. He didn't know how to be my son, and thought in trying to be so, there wasn't the room to be anything else, and I wasn't strong enough to show him how. Please go to him now, deliver this letter, and help me put the wrongs of the past right again, and help him save his home. I'm afraid you might be the only person who can.

Frances

"You see," she said when it was clear he had finished. "What are these past wrongs I'm supposed to help you put right?"

That was about the size of it. Turning the envelope over he saw that indeed the postmark was from two days before.

"I've got no idea," he said after a while.

"And the bit about me being able to save the house. What's that about?"

"I don't know that either."

"Are you going to lose it or something?"

"Yes, in three weeks' time. My mother rang up a

lot of debts, and I've got to cover them. I don't have a choice. It's going to be sold, and I don't know where I'm going to go."

"Then you'd better open your letter. See if it makes any more sense than mine."

He nodded, and sliding his finger under the flap, he tore the envelope open. Reaching in for what he expected to be a letter, he was surprised to find the thick edge of a Polaroid photograph. It was of a jewelry box, something ornate and silver. Maybe tin, he supposed if it was old and not worth much. It was quite beautiful whatever it was made of, cherubs on the sides, olive branches fashioned into handles. The bottom was rippled as if surrounded in flames. On the back of the photograph his mother had written something else.

Harry,
Many years ago, I hid something very precious to
me. It was the most precious thing I possessed in all
the world. Look for this box. It is here, hidden in the
house. As you search through the things I've kept,
and once you find what's hidden inside this box, you
will have the answers I could never bring myself to
give you.
Now I'm gone, I must give you this chance to
understand who you are, no matter the repercussions.

*Tabitha is the only person I can think of who might
be able to help you do that.
I know you doubted that I wanted you here, but all
I ever tried to do was keep you safe.
Forgive me, please.
Mum*

Harry set the photograph on his knees. "I don't
understand," he said. The mess towered over him as
he looked up at it, and then to Tabitha whom he still
couldn't quite believe was there with him. She reached
toward him with an outstretched hand, so he offered
her the picture, their fingers just inches apart. "Among
all this?" he asked. "I'm supposed to find that in all
this mess? I just don't—" he began, but she cut him off.

"Oh my god," she said, leaning forward. Seconds
later she was on her feet, staring at the mess.

"What is it?"

"She wants you to find this box. Is that what she's
saying, that it's somewhere in this house?"

"I think so."

Unexpected laughter snuck from her lips. "But it
can't be," she said to herself. "How could it end up
here?"

"How could what end up here?" Harry asked, still
unsure. Tabitha's reaction was putting him on edge.

He could feel his heartbeat quickening, her excitement infectious.

"Don't you recognize this box at all?" Shaking his head, his confusion growing, he saw a smile forming on Tabitha's lips. "Jesus, Harry. Didn't you pay any attention at school? You've really got no idea what this is?"

"No, Tabitha. I've never seen it before in my life."

"Well, at least I understand why she thought I might be able to help. Because this is a piece of history, Harry. When I received her letter, I could never have imagined this. This is called The Klinkosch Box, and it is an antique that has been missing for almost eighty years. One of the most famous artifacts looted by the Nazis during the Second World War. Nobody has any idea where it is. There must be thousands of people looking for this in some shape or form, and your mother's telling us that it's here, in this house." Shaky fingers covered her mouth to stifle the excitement. "Harry, do you have any idea how important this is? How much something like this is worth?"

Hope rose in his chest like a child's balloon. A future where he could pay his mother's debts, stay in the cottage that had become his home. "Would it be enough to save this place?"

For a moment her face softened, and he saw the same woman with whom he'd once fallen in love. Whom he still loved. Ten years apart had done nothing to diminish his feelings for her. Seeing her again had confirmed that. Turning away, he glanced in the glass at his reflection, the tired eyes staring back at him, the lined cheeks etched during years they'd spent apart. Could she see him, as he once was, or did she see only what was left of him now? Back then he'd had no choice but to leave her behind, but now she was here again he realized how much he wished it had been different.

"No," she said, shaking her head. "This box would be worth enough to save your home ten times over."

Chapter Two

A hidden box worth enough money that he could save his house? Something meaningful left by his mother, a taste that she cared all along? It seemed absurd, impossible to be true. How could something of such value have come into his mother's possession and be lost among all that mess? Feeling sure that his mother was wrong, he was almost ready to dismiss it, yet to his surprise Tabitha seemed less convinced that it was all the delusion of a woman who had long been less than well.

"This is why she wrote to me," Tabitha was saying. "She knew I would know what this is." Every now and again he found her attention drawn by the mess, wonderment perhaps that such potential could be buried within it. Yet Harry found his attention drawn not by the prospect of a valuable trinket box, but instead by Tabitha herself. After ten years apart, here she was, in his house. Each time she stopped talking he found himself waiting for when she might speak again. The initial glimmer of anger in her voice had dissipated, replaced by soft intonations that reminded him of just how safe he had felt while they were together. How passionate she was about the things, and people, that she loved. How she would always find a way to touch him, and how she always seemed to know when he was lost in thoughts of his unspoken past. But also, those remembrances stirred realizations of how he had let her down when he left, how he let their relationship fail in the hope of reconnecting with his mother. It was hard to recall his own failings. But what right did he have to those feelings, when it had been his choice to leave?

"I can't believe you've never heard of it," she was saying. "I suppose you're going to tell me next that you've never heard about the Amber Room either? Or *The Lady in Gold*? Gustav Klimt?" He shook his head and she stood up and took the photograph from him, pointed at it. "Okay, well, they were all pieces that were stolen during the Second World War. Looted by the Nazis. This," she said, pointing to the photograph, "is The Klinkosch Box. Taken in France when Paris fell." Pacing back and forth before him she seemed to swing between shock and laughter. "I can't believe it's been found."

"Well, it hasn't actually been found, has it?" he said, trying to stay focused. "How the hell would a piece of art lost in the war turn up in a cottage in the Cotswolds?"

"I don't know," she said. "But what if it *is* here? That would be incredible."

Her excitement for the box was infectious. Threads of the same enthusiasm were beginning to weave through him. Although the larger part of himself was certain there could be no chance that the box was here, another part of him couldn't help but be seduced by the *What if?*

"Okay," he said. "Suppose it really has been found. That it's here in this house. Why would my mother tell you about it when we haven't seen each other for ten years?"

Just for a moment everything was still. "Okay," she said, as if readying herself, her fingers pressed together. "Your mother knew I worked as an art historian, didn't she?"

Harry shifted in his seat. "Of course she did." He spoke quietly. "I told her everything about you."

"Then she would have known that I would know that this is one of the most famous items ever plundered by the Nazis. It was thought to have been lost forever, melted down and changed into something else. Maybe lost during a bombing raid. There have been rumors about it ever since, but this photograph is the first categorical proof that it survived the war. It's an absolute miracle."

"How can you be so sure?" Harry asked.

Leaning in, she pointed to the photograph. "You never were much of a detective, were you? Look at the background." Taking another look, he saw that alongside the Klinkosch box was an old broadsheet newspaper, and the box was roughly one third of the size. "Look at the date," she said. "That newspaper is dated 1981, which means the box was undeniably in existence some forty years after it was previously known to be. This is a major development."

"That's the year before I was born." He could barely believe it, but neither could he deny it with the same certainty he could moments before. "But how would my mother have it? That newspaper looks to be written in German. And why would she wait until she had died in order to tell me about it?"

Tabitha eased back into her chair, seemingly lost in thought. "Well, I can't answer either of those questions. I can only tell you what I know."

It seemed surreal to Harry. Ten minutes ago, he was alone in a house full of rubbish. Now he was sitting with the woman he once thought he would spend the rest of his life with, talking about stolen art of significant monetary and historical value. All those days when his mother used to sit at the window, staring out to what he assumed was nothing. The way she had left him on a bench in the shopping center and disappeared from his life. Now he couldn't help but wonder if there wasn't a much bigger picture that he had always failed to see. Moving his right hand, he placed it against the wrist-watch.

"Okay," he said. "Tell me."

An hour or so later when Tabitha finally left, the house had never felt emptier. For a while he drifted through the space, nebulous and loose, fussing at the mess in a half-hearted effort to search for the box. As if such a lost piece was likely to be found sitting under yesterday's newspaper. But he couldn't concentrate, couldn't even relax to sit. Tabitha was still there with him, like a ghost or a shadow, following everything he did.

She had told him what she knew about the box's history, its seventeenth-century creation and subsequent journey through Austria, before its eventual theft during the Second World War. Then, just like that, as unexpectedly as she arrived, she was gone. And in her place, Tabitha left not only a physical void, but a mystery about who his mother really was, and what secrets had been buried in her past. Finding the Klinkosch box, he began to think, might help him understand her in ways he had never managed before. Perhaps it might even be able to silence the questions that had always gone unanswered, such as the identity of his father, and why he had been given away. But after a time, physically exhausted from the day behind him, he eventually fell asleep in his chair, dreaming about his mother, Tabitha, and, of course, what might have been.

At the tail end of a long night, sunlight bled through the windows to bring dawn, rolling in like a wave to the shore. He had been awake for several hours by then, too wired for rest, unable to shake Tabitha or her visit from his mind. Every time he closed his eyes, he saw her face, the love notes she used to leave him, her smile when he held her hand. But the box too was something he couldn't let rest. If it was here, and it was worth what Tabitha said it was worth, then he might be able to save his home. Using his phone—his mother had never allowed a home internet connection—he trawled the internet for information. Sketchy as the signal was, he managed to confirm roughly what Tabitha had told him. Tapping on the calendar icon he counted the days; he had just less than three weeks before the house would be auctioned off. Would he be able to find the Klinkosch box in time to save his home?

When the doorbell rang he was already shoulder deep in dust and paperwork. It was going to be like looking for a needle in a haystack. But as he opened the door and saw Tabitha standing on the other side, it gave him some hope that perhaps he wouldn't have to search for it alone.

"Oh," he said, his shock evident in the shiver of his voice. "You're back." Beauty stared at him, the face he had missed. Taking a few cautious steps into the hallway, treading carefully over the mounds of paper and boxes, her eyes moved from one object to another. Over piles of newspapers, dolls' heads, and finally to him.

"I know. And believe me, I didn't expect to be here at all, let alone twice in two days." Some of her initial anger had returned; it couldn't be easy for her to be in his presence after the way he let her down so badly. Choosing to live with his mother had, by default, been a choice to leave the relationship he shared with Tabitha. Ten years ago, it became obvious that his mother had needed almost constant care, her hoarding and depression tipping over into the realm of unmanageable. Tabitha had wanted a life together, a family, a home filled with love. He couldn't be there for his mother and give Tabitha the life she had wanted. Still, he had never been able to leave the sense of guilt and regret behind.

"Well, it's wonderful to see you again so soon."

"I had to come. Finding the Klinkosch box is historically important. I thought maybe you wouldn't even bother to look," she said, her eyes still scanning.

"No," he said, ushering her forward, amazed he had been granted a chance to spend time with her. "Come and see. I already made a start, but I admit the progress is somewhat slow." In the shade of the stacked paperwork he sighed, as if seeing the mess for the first time. "As you might imagine."

Arriving in the doorway to the lounge her mouth opened wide. "I had no idea it was this . . ." she began, searching for the right word. "Complicated. I couldn't see half of it when I was here last night. It's like each piece is holding up another piece. Like that game we used to play."

"You mean Jenga."

"That's the one." Slumping against one of the boxes to sit, she angled her head toward the ceiling, taking in the sheer mass of it all. "You've got your work cut out for you, that's for sure."

Was there a chance she was regretting her decision

to come back? "It's okay if you've changed your mind now that you've seen it in the light."

"I haven't changed my mind," she said, her left hand at her throat as she took a big dusty breath. "Nothing lost to history is ever found easily. There's always effort involved. And I'm here because I'm a historian. We have to find that box. It might be the most important thing I ever do professionally." That was the easier story, much simpler than admitting she was there for him. "So, we'll meet here each day, do what we can by getting rid of what we must." She sighed again. "It's not going to be easy, but we'll go room to room, and if the Klinkosch box is here, we'll find it."

"You're offering to help me?"

"Yes. If you'll accept it."

"Well, I could do with all the help I can get." Just then the doorbell rang. "Did you organize reinforcements?" he asked.

With some relief for the interruption, she said, "Nothing to do with me."

Harry stepped back and opened the door. "Oh, good morning, Elsie. Is it Friday?"

Elsie Gillman, once tall but now hunched with a bit of a stoop and a shock of gray hair, moved slowly with her eyes to the ground as she negotiated the step. A walker guided the way. She always popped over for a cup of tea on a Friday morning. She had been calling in and seeing his mother regularly even before he was living there, and was, Harry suspected, one of the main reasons his mother had remained well for as long as she had. Harry always looked forward to her visits. Her wit was sharp, and she didn't miss a clip. Plus, she was the only person his mother let into the house, so she was one of the few people with whom Harry had had a regular conversation in the last decade.

"It's not, but I saw you had company, and I knew you wouldn't have anything to offer her." Elsie moved close to Tabitha as she pulled a used ice cream tub from a basket attached to her walker. "Cheese scones," she said. "I assume you've got some butter."

"I have," Harry said, "but it wasn't necessary."

"Oh, would you stop that. I didn't make them just for you. They've been in the bread bin since my last visit." She placed a hand on Tabitha's arm. "Hello, my love."

"Hello," said Tabitha with a smile.

"Or," Harry said, smiling, "you thought you'd find a reason to call by and find out who's here."

"Well, yes, that too," Elsie said, seemingly without any concern at being caught out. "So," she said, gazing at Tabitha. "Put me out of my misery, wouldn't you? Who are you?"

"Tabitha," Tabitha said. "I'm an old friend of Harry's."

"Tabitha, eh? Not *the* Tabitha?" she asked, looking back to Harry.

"I think that's quite enough from you," Harry said, taking Elsie by the shoulders and gently steering her away. "Thanks for the scones, but we have got a lot going on this morning. I'll pop in later with your box." Once they were by the door, he ducked down so he could whisper in her ear. "Sorry, but it's a bit awkward."

"It must be. You can't get rid of me fast enough."

"I'm sorry. I'll tell you all about it later. I promise."

Nosing back over her shoulder, she said, "She's lovely, though. I can see why you always liked her."

"I know she is. But you're not being very subtle. And you're absolutely rubbish at whispering."

"There's no time for subtlety when you're ninety next month, Harry. Sometimes you just need to be straight with somebody." And moments later she was heading up the path, closing the gate behind her with a smile on her face.

"So," Tabitha said once the door was closed. "You told her about me."

Harry gazed down at his feet, wished his sock didn't have a hole in it. "Might have mentioned you, once or twice." He wanted to tell her then that he had told Elsie everything about her, about how he had lost the most wonderful person there was, who had taught him how to enjoy the world in a way he never had been able to before. But he couldn't say any of that. "Why don't we make a start, and then have a break for one of her scones."

"Sounds like a plan. Where does that lead to?" she said, pointing to the crawl space that ran parallel to the stairs. Above it was a mound of paperwork that had formed a tunnel when it toppled over a couple of years before. It was all held together by forces of tension, no supporting structure to speak of, yet it had held true since the day it formed.

"The kitchen," he told her.

"And that's the only access? You have to crawl on your hands and knees to get there?"

"It's not so bad. It's been like that for years. It's quite safe."

Bending down, she made a rudimentary assessment. "Well, I'm no engineer, but I don't suppose we've got much choice. I think it's unlikely that the box is in among all that paperwork, but we should start here. I don't want to die because I got buried under a pile of newspapers from the seventies. And we're going to need the butter for the scones anyway." For the first time since they were back together, he saw a hint of that smile he had first fallen in love with a decade before. "Come on, I'll let you lead the way."

It took them the best part of the morning but working just one item at a time they began to clear through the pile. They pulled newspaper after newspaper from the extremities of the tunnel, along with enough junk mail to open a small recycling plant.

While they worked, he thought of the box, and the answers it might contain. His mother's past had always been a mystery, but now he felt as if an explanation was within touching distance. After filling eight black bags, they stacked them outside in the back garden. Harry took each one and positioned it alongside the house in a rare spot that was clear of mess. On the final journey he stopped to check on his pigeons when he heard Tabitha coming after him.

"Harry, I need you to help me with . . . Oh," she said, pausing to look at the birds. "What are they?"

"Pigeons," he said, poking his finger through the wire mesh, smiling to himself as one of his flock pecked at the tip. "I've got six."

"Why?"

Nobody had ever asked him why he kept birds before. Nobody but his mother had seen them. Life in the Cotswolds in his mother's cottage was a lonely affair. He had thought to acquire a cat or a dog for company, but knew it wasn't a safe environment for an indoor pet. Then, by chance or luck, he found a pigeon in the garden one day, lame with what to him looked like a broken wing. Charging himself with the task of nursing it back to health, feeding it titbits and dripping water into its beak with a syringe from those that his mother inexplicably had, it had felt like serendipity. Trapping the second bird seemed entirely justifiable as company for the first. Tending to their daily needs became a reason for his presence, a way to justify it, and the birds became something that was just for him. In a life where his identity had been whittled down to little more than hopeful son, the birds gave him back part of himself. Plus, a daily conversation with a flock of trapped birds was better than no conversation at all if his mother was having an off day. Before long he had built a coop out of old pallets and had collected over twenty birds. Right now, he had six, following a few deaths and a handful of escapes. He felt Tabitha's gaze upon him, still waiting on an answer.

"I just like them, I guess. I like taking care of them."

The brief silence felt charged, vibrating between them with things left unsaid. "Well, there's still quite a lot to clear inside," she said. "And those scones aren't going to eat themselves. Come on, let's take a break." As Tabitha headed back inside, Harry turned to follow.

They stood in silence alongside each other while the scones heated in the oven. Harry could sense a shift in mood, although he didn't understand it or know what it was that had changed. He had a feeling that it was something to do with the birds, and his eyes were continuously drawn to a tattoo on her shoulder, a new addition to the body he once knew, and no longer did. It was a bird, the image like a splash of variegated watercolors, purple on orange on yellow.

"We've made good progress," Tabitha said, breaking the silence as she took a bite into the first scone.

"I can't believe how much we've already cleared. But I bet you wish you'd ignored that letter, don't you?"

"Not really," she said, taking another bite. As she licked her lips, she said, "It was worth it just for this. It's really good."

"Baking is her superpower," Harry said. "She could probably end a war with her hot cross buns."

"Ha," Tabitha laughed. "Not one for beating about the bush, though, is she?"

"Er, no. Sorry if she made you uncomfortable."

"She didn't. It was kind of nice to think she knew who I was. It means you hadn't forgotten about me."

"Forgotten about you? Are you kidding?" Should he do it? Should he tell her that he still had feelings for her? Perhaps in ten years she didn't feel the same way as she once had. But if he didn't say it now, apologize for how their relationship ended at least, he might not get another chance. "Tabitha, I want to . . ."

"Sshh," Tabitha said. "Did you hear that?"

"Hear what? I can't hear anything." This was it. He was going to do it. He was going to tell her that losing her was a mistake. "I want to say . . ."

"No, Harry, wait. I can hear—" she began, but then cut her sentence short as a heavy rumble vibrated above them. She looked up toward the stairs. He saw her eyes widen. "Harry, quick, move."

Bursting into action she pulled him back toward the kitchen, and only seconds later, panting from their position of relative safety, they watched as the paperwork from the stairs began to shift and slide. The overhanging mass avalanched toward the hallway. From their position at the back of the kitchen they watched as the paperwork settled in a dusty heap, a few solitary pages still drifting to the ground like clumps of snow from a warming roof during a period of sudden, unexpected heat.

"What the . . . ?" she said, taking a step forward.

Harry made to follow but realized after a moment that he was struggling. Tightness gripped his chest, his inhaler on the other side of the mess. Dust circulated like thick fog, and his lungs were about to give in to it, wheezing as they did. Leaning down as he knew to, hands on his knees, he desperately fought to stay calm, and not to chase the breath that was trying to leave him.

"Harry, we're going to need some professional help here. I don't think we can do this on our own. Harry?" she said, turning, wondering why he wasn't responding. But by the time Tabitha turned around Harry was on his knees, bent over double, wheezing as his chest rocked back and forth. "God, Harry," she said, rushing toward him. Grappling at his pockets while he struggled to breathe, she screamed, "The dust has set off your asthma. Where's your inhaler, Harry? Tell me where it is."

Gasping for one good breath, he managed to say, "Living room. On the table."

Without a second thought she bounded toward the hallway and Harry had no choice but to listen as she stumbled over the shifting mass of paperwork. Watching as she disappeared into the haze, he felt the return of the fear that always came with the fight for breath.

But moments later there she was, his inhaler in her hand. Prepping it with a shake, flicking off the cap, she handed it over ready, as if she had last done it only yesterday.

"Hold it in," she said, as he breathed on the inhaler, sitting at his side, rubbing his back. Once his breathing settled a little, she was back on her feet, and before Harry could stop her, she was calling for help.

"I would have been fine," he said as she arrived back alongside him, his condition almost back to normal.

The look on her face didn't suggest she was open to changing her mind. "You've just had an asthma attack, Harry. You don't have a choice about it." For another moment he couldn't breathe again when she reached down to take his hands in hers. "The ambulance will be here soon. Until then just sit up straight. And take another puff. Come on, Harry, just do as I say. I remember what to do."

In that moment it was as if he never left, that Tabitha was still his, and that he was still the man she called hers.

"You gave me quite a fright," she said later that day from a chair beside his hospital bed. "It's been a long time since I had to deal with an asthma attack."

"Me too," he said. "I don't remember when I last had one."

"Then it's all the better that you stay here tonight like the doctors said. You can't be too careful with something like this, Harry. Don't worry about the house for now."

The tension that had simmered between them, the weight of what had been left unsaid, all seemed to have evanesced in the aftermath of his asthma attack. Perhaps not gone, but certainly assuaged. "What about the birds? They'll need feeding."

"What the pigeons need is to be set free," she said. Captivity was not something she could get along with. Her free hand reached up to her shoulder, her fingertips brushing the tattoo. It was one small way in which their lives had changed. Walls had been built between them, each formed of a different shape and size. One happened to be the size and shape of a pigeon coop. Only then had he begun to recall the tender way she cared for animals, the hedgehog she nursed through the winter, the spiders she would carefully trap, before returning them to the wild. One day he had suggested a trip to London Zoo, and she had spent the next two hours educating him on the inhumanity of keeping animals, in her words, hostage.

"I'm sorry. I'd forgotten your feelings about that."

"They're wild birds."

"I take good care of them. I promise."

"In the wild they could take care of themselves. But I suppose for now I could stretch to feeding the poor things."

"Thank you," he said then. "I appreciate it." Trying to picture himself letting them go wasn't very easy, but once the house was sold he supposed he'd have to anyway. Still, he could cross that bridge when he came to it. "But I don't just want to say thank you for your help with my birds. Also for coming when she wrote to you. For being here now."

"It's okay," she said, as if this was nothing, as if it hadn't been unthinkable only a few days before. "But I think we've established the house is going to be more work than we anticipated. We should call a clearance company."

His chest was still feeling tight. "No," he said, determined. "I have to do this. It's what my mother wanted, and it's my . . . my last chance to . . ." he said, stumbling over the truth.

"To what?"

He owed her this, didn't he? He owed Tabitha a chance at knowing the truth after all this time. "To prove that," he said, clearing his throat, "I could have been a son worthy of being kept, if I'd have been given a chance."

Her silken fingers slipped through his. "What do you mean?"

"I'm sorry I never told you ten years ago, because I know you never understood my reasons for staying with her, and for leaving as I did. But I only found my mother as an adult. I grew up in foster care. Mum couldn't look after me, not the way she was. She gave me up when I was little."

"Oh, Harry. Why did you never tell me?"

"I didn't want you to think badly of me."

Filling with tears, her eyes glassed over like snow-drops at dawn. "Badly? Why would I?"

"I thought maybe you wouldn't want to stay. That there was something wrong with me."

"Wrong with you?" Pausing, she looked away for answers in thin air. "You thought that you weren't good enough?"

"Maybe. It wasn't always easy to understand, because I never knew the reason she gave me away."

"Oh, Harry. Is that why you decided to stay in that awful house with her? To try and understand?"

The pulse of his body shook under the weight of his honesty. "I suppose so. And this is why I have to find that box. I need to know who she really was, so that I might understand why she couldn't keep me. Maybe this box can help me answer those questions, or even tell me who my father was."

"You never knew?" she asked, and he shook his head, glanced down to his wristwatch. Moments later he felt her hand on top of his. She could still do it, ground him and make him feel safe with just a touch. "Then yes, we really must do this ourselves," she said, as if taking a decision. "In which case, if it's that important, I'll stay and help."

"What?"

"Until it's done. I'll stay."

"No, I couldn't ask you that."

"You didn't," she said, smiling. When he turned to face her, he found pale eyes without the dark punctuation of mascara. It was as if he was looking into the past, and that made it impossible to look away. "I offered. And anyway, she wrote to me too, remember? Plus, if Elsie Gillman is going to come over with her baked goods every once in a while, that's got to be worth the effort alone."

"Thank you," he said. The words didn't seem enough somehow, but he didn't know what else to say.

Reaching down into her bag she pulled out a slip of paper and a pen. "Now, there's no fridge for me to pin it to like I used to, but the idea is the same," she said, pressing a folded piece of paper into his hand. How many little notes had she left while they were together? Hundreds, maybe more. Unfolding the note, he read what she had written. "I promise you it's true." Fighting against tears, he read the words and held the paper to his chest. *You have always been enough, Harry.* "And I mean it. Just like I always meant it. If she wanted us to find that box together, that's what we're going to do."

"Tabitha, I don't know what to say. Just the fact you are here and helping, it's . . ." His words caught in his throat.

"You don't need to say anything, Harry."

His feelings were too big and confusing to navigate in that moment, but perhaps he could focus on the practicalities. "I don't even know if it's worth your effort. I've lived in that house for ten years and I've never seen it. It could have been lost years ago."

"Nothing's ever really lost, Harry," she said, standing up to leave. "It's just that sometimes things are so well hidden that you stop being certain they exist anymore."

He slept soundly that night, remembering what she had written on her note. It was his first night in a comfortable bed in years. Since the stairs had become impassable, he had taken to sleeping in the chair pushed back in the reclining position. Now he was stretched out, comfortable, with a soft pillow and warm covers. He'd rather hoped that Tabitha would be there when he woke up, but as he looked across to the chair the next morning, in her place he saw another little note, promising to pick him up when he was discharged later on that day. But perhaps what he didn't realize then was that there was no such thing as a simple note exchanged between two people who had once loved each other so much.

Chapter Three

Mirepoix, France, Summer 1981

Frances awoke to a cool breeze and the bleating of sheep coming from the farm about one kilometer to the north. To the south was the village itself, a place to which she walked each day, and which felt so far removed from her quiet village life in Bibury back at home in England. In the mornings, when the air was still hazy and the southerly wind slipped from the distant shoulders of the Pyrenees, it was hard to imagine ever leaving this place. She had spent the last seven summers here, and this was her third week of staying with her aunt at the artist's retreat just outside the town of Mirepoix. The previous summers had been shared with her parents, and she had endured the relentless car ride with Bach on repeat, only because of what she knew to be at the other end of it. But this year she had arrived alone by train. Oddly enough, as the carriage rocked through the expansive French countryside, she had found that it felt very much to her as if she was returning home. When the taxi turned onto the long private track and she had seen the barn spreading out before her, the painters dotted across the endless fields, it had, she realized, felt like relief.

For a while she lay there in the giant bed, watching the gauzy drapes shudder in the breeze, smiling at her most recent collection, seashells that she had dotted along the windowsill. Voices echoed from the terrace below, the clinking of teaspoons and the lull of relaxed chatter. Some days she was up early, eager to get on with her day. But today she wanted to lounge, thinking about the night before, the kiss she could still taste on her lips. Men in England could never taste that way, impossible to replicate the heat of summer, the slick of salt on a top lip. Cigarettes and stewed tea, that's what it would be like at home, she imagined, like her father's breath when he used to lean down to kiss her when she was a child. The thought made her shudder. It was just one more wonderful thing that was different in France. In England she felt lost, unsure about most things in her life. Yet here, although it was possible to struggle with the simplest of tasks thanks to a language barrier that she was yet to fully cross, she felt in every way as if she was right where she was supposed to be.

With the lure of breakfast and an empty stomach Frances pulled herself from bed and dressed in a light cotton dress, perfect for the weather, and slipped her feet into her sandals. Arriving in the kitchen, she kissed her aunt on the cheek.

"*Bonjour, mademoiselle,*" her aunt Henrietta said. Her greetings were always warm, as if she was always pleasantly surprised that Frances was there. Her aunt's style of care allowed her to feel free, like herself, and she loved her even more for that gift. Without breaking her attention on the pan of sizzling eggs, she handed Frances a plate filled with croissants and bacon. "What wonderful things does life have in store for you today?"

"Erm, not much," Frances lied, selecting a croissant and taking a bite. Aunt Henrietta was so kind, always touching her hair, taking her in for a hug. It was so different here, and Frances wished she had not created a barrier of mistruth between them. The lies felt awful, but what choice did she have? "I'll just head to the market, I think. Maybe the bookstore, and see Amélie."

"Ah, Amélie," her aunt said. "I haven't seen her

once since you got here. Last year you were joined at the hip."

"I think she has a boyfriend," Frances said, knowing that would be a reasonable explanation. Nodding, her aunt seemed to buy into the possibility.

"That I don't doubt. There's not much else to do around here." Plating the eggs, she handed them to Frances. "Well, don't forget your duties in the barn before you go. I need everything set up by twelve."

"No problem," Frances said.

"Unless perhaps today you might choose to stay. It wouldn't hurt would it, to give it another try?"

Frances smiled, but her body caved. "Oh, come on. We tried already, Aunt Henrietta. I was useless."

Her aunt scoffed as she cracked another egg into the pan, this time fried, sunny side up. "Your problem is that you have no appreciation for art." Fat sizzled as she cracked a second. "I have one son who is a lawyer, and a daughter who does nothing but make money for other people. You, my dear, were my last hope."

"Well, I'm sorry to disappoint you, but I think that ship has already sailed. You can't force somebody to like something or to be good at it. Just ask Dad."

"I know, I know," she said, rolling her eyes. "You want to be an archivist, not a doctor, and apparently not even a painter. You know I'm only teasing you."

"Dad isn't teasing," she said, taking another rasher of bacon. Her father was in a constant state of distress over her becoming a doctor, and they had argued repeatedly before she left for France. A worse fate, she could not imagine. Her place was in a museum, archiving the past, restoring paintings, protecting treasures. That was what she wanted to do. Frances motioned to the eggs. "Which table?"

"The one with the Swedish couple," her aunt said, kissing her on the forehead. And then she whispered, "Your dad will come around. He loves you. Just give him time."

"I've already given him all the time he's going to get. You can't force somebody into something, can you? I'd make a terrible doctor."

"No, my love, you can't. And yes, I'm sorry to say that I'm quite sure you would. But at least you know what you want."

Oh yes, she really did. Frances knew exactly what she wanted. But she didn't want to talk about her father or his determination she become a doctor. Picking up the plate, she moved toward the door. "I better get these to the table before they go cold."

"Don't forget about the barn," Aunt Henrietta called as Frances left.

Frances knew she would never be able to. Not since Benoit had kissed her there the night before.

The view from the terrace was something that Frances often conjured to her mind's eye during the winter months of drudgery in her home country. The light trickled through the mature trees that bordered the garden, allergens and ground dust picked out in the sun's rays. Packed earth scorched by the sun was cracked underfoot, but nestled as they were in a valley, greenery stretched out all around them, like giant ripples on a pond. Closer to the farmhouse, roses tangled around each other, pink and white, so intertwined it was impossible to tell where one stopped and where the other began. The mountains were there in the distance, their summer caps, gray and craggy, just visible through a mist of cloud. In the dark of night, picked out by a full moon, it was their silhouette that formed the backdrop to last night's kiss.

Frances had first met Benoit the summer before, when he moved back to Mirepoix. Lured back to his provincial roots by the business of antiques, he was a collector and dealer, and he fascinated her. Of course, she didn't know any of that when he first spoke to her, when she had walked into the village with her aunt on that balmy July evening to attend the book festival. The summer before, bored by the poetry readings in a language she couldn't properly understand, and feeling a little light-headed after drinking a warm pastis, she wandered over to a table of old books.

"That's an interesting choice." Hearing her native language startled her. Nobody but her aunt or Amélie spoke to her in English. But this voice was male, gravelly. "For you, or a gift?"

When she turned around, she saw a tall man with a slim frame, dressed in a baggy pair of chinos with the cuffs rolled up at the ankle. What struck her was how different he looked to anything she knew from back home. His hair was neatly styled in a side parting, his sunglasses clipped in the open neck of his shirt, despite the grayness of the evening. A crescent scar punctuated his cheek, giving him a permanent dimple. When he smiled his lips drew wide, big and plump, the shape of a heart. Like nothing she had ever seen before, she lost all sense of what to say. He seemed to gaze at her, as if there was nothing else to see.

"The book," he eventually said, pointing to the one in her hand. "Is it for you?"

"I don't know." His upfront approach had stunned her, his intense stare almost uncomfortable. She wanted him to look away, but feared if he did she would simply stop existing. "How did you know I was English?"

"I didn't, but those red shoulders were a good hint." He laughed, taking the book from her. "You know this?" he said, holding it up.

"No." The truth was that she had barely even registered the book in her hand, was holding it by chance. She looked across and saw the cover, read the title. "Is it any good?"

Turning to rest against the table, he stretched his legs out before him with his feet crossed at the ankle. Sighing, he opened the cover to read something on the inside before closing it again with a snap.

"I am going to bet that nobody knows this book is here." Before she had picked it up it had been sitting in a suitcase along with close to one hundred others. "You know Edouard, who runs this bookshop?" He motioned to the shop behind him and she shook her head. "Well, let me tell you that he has no appreciation for historical items, or the value of books. He only cares about making money to keep his wife in designer clothes." He laughed at his own joke, and so she did too, although she tried to hide it the best she could. "This book is a first edition. Printed in 1925, New York. You know the story?"

"No."

"It is of a man who loves a woman he should not." His hands brushed the cover, the darkest black leather, fine gold gilt down the spine. "It all goes wrong, of course. It always does. But he had a damn fine time along the way." Heat blushed her cheeks, and she could feel him beside her as if the air was charged, pulling her in like a magnetic field. Cicadas vibrated in the trees as he lit a cigarette, offered her one that she didn't accept. "You should take this with you," he said after a time. "I have a feeling you will appreciate it more than Edouard."

She shook her head. "I was just looking. I don't have any money."

By then her heart was beating fast. Each time his gaze rested on her she felt her cheeks grow hotter. What was it about this man that had reduced her to this? She focused on the book as he patted the spine against his hand.

"Let me share with you a secret. Just for you, okay?" She nodded and leaned in closer as he beckoned her forward. "If you were to take this to the counter with the intention of buying it, and our poor, simple Edouard realizes what he finds in his possession, you would not have enough money in the pockets of that beautiful strapless dress to buy it." Her hands reached to her bare shoulders. "I doubt that if everybody here pooled all the money in their pockets together that we would have enough even then." He shook his head and shrugged his shoulders. "Nobody here cares about this book. A book like this should never be left in a pile like that. Nothing of such beauty," he said, his voice lowered to a whisper, "should ever be hidden among such, such . . ." He paused, his face crumpled with confusion. "I forget the word. What I mean is that something so special should be treasured. Kept safe, by a person who loves it." By then he was leaning toward her, and she felt herself leaning into him. Their faces were only inches apart. "It is a great book, worthy of something more than a tatty old suitcase. Deserving of a keeper who would care for it, don't you think?" There was a chance in that moment that she would have agreed to anything, perhaps even becoming a doctor. Nodding, she showed her approval for the idea. "So," he said, pushing the book toward her. "Edouard is busy over there, watching the performance." On a nearby stage somebody was reading another poem, a crowd clapping. "I think you should walk away with it."

"Steal it?" she whispered.

"Why not? Won't you look after it?"

"Of course I would, but . . ."

He interrupted her. "Better than Edouard, I bet. You would be doing history a favor."

The way he dropped his *H*s made her mouth dry. "But it belongs to him."

Benoit smiled then, beckoned her forward. A scent simmered from him, something woody, unlike anything she had ever smelled before. The book was still in his hands. "If it was always supposed to be yours, how can anybody accuse you of theft?" Pulling a pen from his back pocket, he opened the first page of the book and wrote something, before handing it back. "Now it belongs to you. It's got your name in it."

"No," she insisted, looking around to see if anybody was watching them. Her aunt was, but she didn't notice that at the time. "You just said it was a first edition. You don't write in a first edition." He smiled. "Anyway, I couldn't take it." Then she realized what he'd said. "Wait, how do you know my name?"

He threw his cigarette to the floor and stamped it out. His cheek was close to hers as he whispered in her ear. "Let me show you how it's done."

He took the book from her hands, tucked it under his arm. With a quick smile and a wink of his left eye he turned to leave, moving quickly away. Just like that he was gone, leaving nothing but a memory of his smile and the scarred dimple in her mind.

"Who was that you were talking to?" Aunt Henrietta asked when Frances returned to her seat, her skin slick with sweat and her heart still pounding.

"I don't know," Frances said then. But in her head, a thought gained ground. *But I want to.* So later that night, when she arrived home and climbed the stairs to her bedroom, she was pleased to find that book waiting on her bed. Picking it up she sniffed the cover, leafed through the pages. He had been there, in her room. There was that woody scent again, as if he was still right there with her. She locked the door, as if she had a secret to keep. In that moment it felt as if he could do magic. Whoever he was. "*The Great Gatsby,*" she read aloud as she sat back on her bed. Opening the cover to see what he had written inside, she found the proof that he had been real all along.

Dear Frances. You cannot steal what is already yours, B.

The moon shone brightly through her window, so light she couldn't sleep that night. Warm under the covers she didn't stop once until she had read the whole of the novel, and even after that, when her bones ached with fatigue, when she closed her eyes, sleep remained elusive. All the while she was thinking about the initial signed in the book and wondering how it was possible that he knew her name. And although she had no answers as to how, what she did know was that she was glad he did.

The most eager of the painters were already at their easels when she left the barn behind. The track that led away from the barn was long, dusty underfoot as she walked toward the road. She was still thinking about that night when she had met Benoit for the first time. It was hard to believe that evening at the book fair was over twelve months ago. They had spent most of that time apart, but they had written often. Sometimes she thought it was only his letters that got her through those days at home, the countdown until she was able to return to France.

Less than one kilometer from her aunt's retreat, tucked behind the hedge of the neighboring farm, she waited for Benoit just as they had planned. It wouldn't do for them to be seen together. Aunt Henrietta would never understand what they shared, would surely revoke the freedoms that allowed her to live and love as she did. If she was just a few years older the age difference wouldn't matter. But she wasn't, and so it did. Sitting down on the small boulder onto which *Ferme des Bonnets*—Bonnets' Farm—had been engraved many years before by Benoit's grandparents, she waited. That kind of coincidence, that her aunt would buy the property next to his family farm, made her believe that their meeting was little more than destiny.

The whir of his Citroën 2CV grew louder. Pulling up at speed just as he knew she liked, so that for just a moment the dust from the summer ground fogged the car, she could see him laughing as it cleared. Nerves beat through her as she skipped to the car, the excitement of seeing him getting her every time. But today that feeling was even stronger, bolstered by the memory of the kiss from the night before. As she pulled the door closed Benoit was leaning over, his hands on her body, leaning in to hold her. As he pulled her close her heart quickened, everything right as she felt his hand caress her face, her waist, then her leg. His hand moved quickly under the edge of her skirt and brushed against her thigh. Her skin shivered as he pulled it away.

"I have missed you," he whispered as he kissed her. "Now you are back in France I do not want to be anywhere but with you." With his smooth hot hands on her skin and his breathy whisperings amid kisses and gentle touches, she could imagine her whole life before her. It all looked just as perfect as that moment, where everything seemed possible. It all looked like Benoit.

"You only saw me last night," she giggled.

"And I will see you again, every night. How could I not? But is that ever enough? How am I not supposed to miss you when we're apart?" He kissed her again before turning to the wheel. During a brief pause in his touch, she looked to the back seat and saw the picnic basket from which they had eaten the previous night. A subtle smell of warm cheese filled the car. It could have been unpleasant, but it wasn't at all.

"Do you have to work today?" she asked as he began to drive.

He nodded, his lips pouted. "I'm afraid so. The march of real life continues on."

When he didn't work, they would often spend the day together. Last week he even took her to the beach, Gruissan-Plage, just outside of Narbonne, where they swam and ate fish and drank wine. By the time she got home she was tipsy, her head dizzy with the secret of their connection as she placed the seashells on the windowsill of her bedroom. They had walked hand in hand, unafraid and in full view. Magical moments she knew she would treasure forever. They had visited a beautiful old antiques shop and he talked her through the value of old books, how to spot a first edition as he had given her the year before.

"Then I guess I'll go to the town," Frances said. By then they had already reached the outskirts of Mirepoix, the houses steadily multiplying, the scent of the countryside fading. Lavender replaced by cooking and fuel. "I'll go to the bookshop and find something to read. Edouard lets me read as much as I want."

He smirked. "He wouldn't if he knew."

Her breath caught at the truth, just thinking about the night he took that book. It was still on the bookshelf in her room, and she would often get it out just to look at that message he wrote to her, finger the letters as if they were part of him. It was the first thing she did after arriving in France this year, yet the thought of how she had acquired it left her with a sense of shame. It made her want to hide away, close the door on the world.

"Don't. I still can't believe you took it."

He winked as he pulled the car over into a narrow side road just before the crowds began to gather at the market square. "I might have taken it, but you chose to keep it."

That was true, she supposed, but he hadn't left her much choice once her name was written in it. Perhaps it was a test, she wondered, and smiled to herself to know that she had passed. "What was I supposed to do?"

"Exactly what you did," he said as he reached over and kissed her again, but with less urgency as the thrum of the town beckoned just over their shoulders.

"Maybe we can meet at lunchtime?" she asked as he pulled away, his hands still in her hair.

He grimaced. "I'm sorry. I cannot today. I will see you tonight, I hope."

"You hope?" she asked, in a way that was anything but hopeful.

His lips curled into a pout. "It is a busy day. Work cannot wait."

He kissed her cheek once more and she knew that was her sign that the meeting was over. As she stepped from the car, he opened the little window. They had spent so much time together that she felt sure she could read his face by now, knew he was truly sorry.

"Tomorrow will be different, not such a quick meeting. Tomorrow," he said, pointing his finger in an official fashion that reminded her a little bit of both her father and school, "I will take you out. What do you say to that?" Without hesitation, her smile widened. "You know how hard that is for me, right? A whole day just for us." She nodded. "But I do it, for you. Because?" he asked, waiting for her reply.

It was their own private joke. He asked the question and she gave the answer. "Because you love me."

"Because I love you," he said, so sure of everything. At the beginning she too had been so sure of what they had, but as time moved on things seemed to be getting harder for her rather than easier. Why was it so hard to keep something so important a secret? Surely there was nothing to be ashamed of if they loved each other. Yes, there was the age difference, but she wasn't a child. People would understand. And yet when she thought this way, she couldn't help but acknowledge her own secret, the thing she had kept from Benoit. If people would understand, why had she lied to him? Would he love her the same way if he knew the truth? She couldn't bear the thought that he wouldn't, and so each time she had tried to be honest, the chance had come and passed like a firework that failed to explode.

"I love you too, Benoit," she said in place of the truth she wanted to share. "And I would do anything for you. You know that, don't you? That I'd do anything at all."

His lips curled into a soft smile. "And I would do anything for you, my sweet."

She leaned into the car. "Would you really?"

Letting his head drop to the side, he stared intently, as if he was perhaps the first person to ever really see her. But it was a look of pity, she knew, as if she was too stupid to understand; sometimes she felt so ridiculous in front of him. Like the child she felt so sure she was not. When she felt like that she wanted to run, and not just away from Benoit, but from everything. But then she would remember that sometimes the way he looked at her made her sing inside, as if the very business of being alive gave off a vibration that could be heard as song.

"I would do everything within my power," he said. "Now go and give Edouard my regards." He drove away laughing to himself, as if he had just told the best joke in the world.

As the car curved around a bend in the road, one arm waving out through the window, she watched him disappear for another day. It was quiet then, save a couple of birds singing in the willow trees above. What should she do now? Go to town, sit in the shade of the oak trees in the marketplace, reading a book and sipping *chocolat chaud*? Go home and mope, as her father always said she did? It all felt pointless, standing there on the road, Benoit nowhere in sight. Her mind drifted to all those letters he had sent her in the buildup to her return. Her parents had called her maudlin for months, couldn't understand her mood that waxed and waned with the tide of his secret communication. For close to a year all she had wanted was to be there in France with Benoit in the shadow of those beautiful mountains, in fields that gave off a scent that smelled of kisses and skin and whispered promises of a future that seemed impossible if she thought about it for too long. Mirepoix, with Benoit, was the only place she felt truly at home. And now she was there, doing what she had craved for so long. Or at least, she told herself, something close. But it didn't feel as she had expected. At least not at moments like this, alone at the side of a road, her feet covered in dust, with no company but her own.

The town lay ahead of her, Edouard and his bookshop from which she would always consider herself a thief. When she did buy something, she always made a point of telling him to keep the change, even though she would never be able to buy enough books to cover the value of a first edition of *The Great Gatsby*. It still felt wrong to keep it, but not so wrong she was prepared to give it up. That stolen book belonged with her, that's what Benoit had said. And she belonged with him. When you knew something was right, you just had to treasure it, keep it safe.

The sounds of the busy marketplace filtered on the breeze, the commotion of trade and life. Somehow there seemed little point in going there. So instead she reached up, picked a few blackberries from a bush by the side of the road, and turned to head for home, the juice of them sweet in her mouth. Sometimes, especially moments like this, she thought about how little she knew Benoit, or the things he did, and the places he went. The company he kept. But she'd always tell herself not to worry, that he loved her, and today was no different. He would do anything for her, he had just said so, and she knew she would do anything for him. *Like lie to him,* she heard the voice inside her head. She did her best to ignore it, couldn't let silly childish thoughts ruin what they had. He was hers, and she was his, and nothing that was already yours could ever be stolen. But did that also mean that it could never be taken away? As she walked back to the retreat with sweet blackberry juice on her lips, she realized that was one thing she didn't know.

Chapter Four

Tabitha reached into her pocket and pulled out her mobile phone. Breath quivered through her lips as she saw that she had another three messages from Daniel. Part of her was desperate to know what he had to say, but she was in no doubt of the vitriol they contained, so she clicked delete without reading them first. It was now over forty-eight hours since she had seen him. Turning, she saw Harry coming in from the garden, his cheeks flushed with effort on what was another scorching day.

"I'll do some of the stuff in here," he called without looking up. "Might as well make a start on the kitchen."

"Okay," she called back. It was so good to be back with him. Beside his gray temples and unfashionable hiking clothes, he was the same old Harry; that cheeky smile when he couldn't quite meet your eye, and his inexplicable affiliation for old people. How she loved that. He rarely made friends while they were together, but when he did it was always with somebody at least thirty or forty years ahead of him in terms of age. Back then she had thought it was something Harry saw in others that he liked, to help them in whatever small way they needed. But now she wondered if perhaps it wasn't the other way around. Perhaps they had an affiliation for him. Only this morning he had swept the garden a few doors down and replaced a blown lightbulb for the retired couple in another cottage, and had arrived back at the cottage in a flap about wasting time when he should be looking for the box. He was still that same person she loved, who always made her feel calm. Harry always could make her forget the rest of the world. Now, though, she wondered if that wasn't because he was simply too scared to live within it himself.

"Harry, come and have a look at this," she called through from the living room a little bit later. It seemed that Frances Langley had been a lover of mail order, although quite just how much and for how long hadn't been evident until her death, when the layers were peeled back to reveal periods of a life that had remained a mystery until then. Tabitha heard him stand, then the rhythm of his gentle footsteps on the hallway tile, a sound that calmed her as he approached. When he arrived in the doorway his cheeks were flushed, his hair all ruffled.

"Did you find it?" he said, slightly breathless.

"No, sorry," she said, realizing his desperation. "But I did find this." Handing him a small black book, Harry turned the pages.

"What is it?"

"I think it's an inventory. Look, it's got a description, dates, where she bought something. She logged it all, and there are loads of them." Tabitha pointed to a small pile of notebooks.

"All like this?" Harry asked.

"Looks like it. Some of them appear to log the dates and time she saw people outside. She even recorded number plates. Maybe we can try and find an entry for the box."

"That would be great."

"And look," she said, holding up a large black case. "You'll never guess what else I found." After lifting the lid, she turned it around so that Harry could see inside. "A trumpet." She laughed. "Your mother sure knew how to collect a range of stuff. I've seen less variety in flea markets and museum storerooms." At the sight of the gleaming instrument his face softened, then hardened. "What is it?" she asked.

"I can't believe it," he said, careful hands reaching for the instrument. "I used to play one of these."

"I never knew you played an instrument," she said. "So, is this yours?"

He smiled but shook his head.

"It can't be."

"Then what was she doing with it?"

"Who knows?" he asked, his voice alluding to the impossibility of such answers. "What was she doing with any of this stuff?" He brought it to his mouth, pressed his lips against the unpleasant cold of the mouthpiece, enjoying the familiarity of the foul taste. Taking a good breath in he produced a resonant C that vibrated through his whole body. Tabitha smiled, savoring it.

"Play me something," she said, sitting back and crossing her legs. "What do you know?"

Without another word he whipped his way up the C scale, his fingers remembering the notes. Even if it didn't sound as fluid as it might have on account that the valves needed a good oiling, it did leave him feeling somewhat pleased with himself that he could still remember how to play. Feeling himself blush as she

applauded his effort, he recalled the sense of content-
ment roused by the presence of somebody in the crowd
who was there on his behalf. Foster parents who'd
said they were proud. For years he had grieved for his
childhood, regretted it as if it had been a catastrophe
that he himself was responsible for creating. But the
sight of that trumpet had reminded him that along
the way were people who had loved him. He wished,
then, that he could remember the names of the couple
who had sat in the audience and clapped his performance of "O Fortuna."

"What's wrong?" she asked as he set the trumpet
down. Noticing a tear as it skirted his cheek, she moved
to touch his arm. He turned away, hoping to hide it.

"Just takes a lot of puff, that's all, and I'm out of
practice. I had better take my inhaler, otherwise I'll
set off my asthma."

"Do you want to talk about it?" she asked as he set
about looking for the inhaler.

He hid his face, shook his head. "Not really."

"Maybe that's the reason why you should," she
suggested. "It might help."

As he felt the emotion getting the better of him,
his lips began to quiver. This time there was little he
could do to stem the flow of tears, and the first slipped
hot and fast across his cheek.

"I'm angry with her, Tabitha. And with myself. Seeing all this stuff I just feel like, how could she have lived like this? How could *this* be my life?"

"It can't have been easy," she said, rubbing at his arm. "But I think she was sick, Harry. Maybe she didn't even realize how bad things were."

"I know that, but I wish she had. I spent my life away from her, never feeling like I was good enough for anybody. It wasn't fair, Tabitha, and neither is the fact that I'm the one who is left to clear this mess up. I lost everything because of her."

"You didn't lose everything, Harry," she said, pulling him close. A barrier between them had softened. "I promise you that you still have more than you even know."

That evening they managed to clear some more space. The living room had been transformed from a couple of meters squared containing two chairs, to a small corridor that permitted access to a window, the fireplace, and enough space to spread out on the floor. After deciding to call it a day around nine that evening, they agreed that they were hungry, so Tabitha ordered a pizza. While they were waiting for it to arrive, they carried some boxes out into the rear garden. They had come across piles of his mother's clothes, dolls, jewelry, some of which Tabitha thought might be of value, and more sheet music for the trumpet than Harry thought might be possible to play in his lifetime. Inventories of collections, filled with pictures of rocks, shells, and leaves, but not one single entry about the Klinkosch box or how they might go about finding it.

"So, what are you going to do first?" Tabitha asked as he returned with a steaming cup of tea once they had finished eating.

He sat back in the chair. "About what?"

"Rebuilding your life. You'll need new hobbies to fill your time. Any ideas?"

"You mean after finding somewhere to live if we don't find that box. Oh, Tabitha, I've got no idea. All I can think about at the moment is finding it."

"I'm not asking you to commit to a space mission, Harry." She pointed at the trumpet. "What about that thing? Wouldn't you like to play it again?"

"You mean in public?"

"Yes. What if I could find somewhere you could do just that? Would you do it? To try it, at least?"

He eyed the trumpet case suspiciously. "I would. I don't know if I'm good enough for that, but I would like to give it a try."

"That's good enough for me." She looked down at

her watch. "Oh god, look at the time," she said, standing up. "I have to get a wriggle on." Disappointed that she was leaving she watched his demeanor shift as she put on her jacket. Something familiar returned to her then, the thought of returning to the life she lived without him. It sat heavily in the center of her chest, making it harder to breathe. "What time should I come back tomorrow?"

"Whatever time. It's not like I have work to go to. I'm still on compassionate leave."

"Perfect," she said, then feeling awkward about the enthusiasm, added, "I'm sorry. That's not what I meant."

He looked at her through soft eyes. "I know what you meant."

"Then I'll be here as soon as I pass by the museum. And I'll organize an appointment to get that jewelry valued." They had come across quite a haul, most of it costume but some pieces she thought might offer him some monetary value at auction. "Not sure how much it's worth, but I would have expected that all together you might be able to get at least a thousand pounds."

He stood from the chair. "How much?"

"Honestly," she said, registering his surprise. "I told you already some of the pieces are silver with precious stones."

Snatching up the bag in which they had placed the items, he pushed it toward her. "Do you want to take them with you now?"

"No, keep them," she said, pushing his hand away, but he was already shaking his head.

"No, please, you take them," he said. "And once you get them valued, we'll decide what to keep and what to sell. They might be some of the last things of hers that have some value."

"We'll decide?" she asked quietly, taking the bag. It felt ridiculously heavy in her hand.

"Yes," he said. "We."

His voice tremored as he spoke, and she wondered how much courage it must have taken for him to assume that she would be around long enough to take a joint decision in an unknown future.

"Then it'd be my pleasure to help," she said. Breath rippled from him as he relaxed. "I'll bring them back as soon as I can." They walked toward the door and he waved as she left.

"See you tomorrow, then," she called as she closed the gate behind her. And as she glanced back for one last look at him before turning round a corner, she found he was still there on the doorstep, still waving even though she was halfway up Awkward Hill. So much had changed since he told her their relationship was over, so many decisions had been taken that she could never undo. And yet somehow, looking at Harry watching her as she left, he made her feel as if she was still the woman who had fallen in love with him all those years ago. For a moment, alongside Harry, it was as if all the mistakes of the last ten years had never even happened. She had missed him, she realized. Perhaps too, she understood, she had missed the person she was when she was with him.

Chapter Five

Her car was parked at the end of the narrow road that led all the way up to the small village green. The pub where she had stayed for the last two nights had bookings for the weekend and she couldn't stay there anymore. There were other hotels nearby, but she needed to pick up some clothes anyway, and now was as good a time as any. It was late, and Daniel would be at work. If she was going to go home to collect her things, she was unlikely to get another opportunity as good as this one in the next few days. Closing the car door, she realized that Harry already felt too far away.

As she drove to the place she called home, she thought about what life used to be like when she was Harry's girlfriend. Simple things like how he had her favorite prints framed and hung, and how he had once ordered a glass display cabinet for the collection of fossils she had been curating since childhood. How, when she explained what each one was, he never said they were just rocks like some people once had. How, when she woke up at night, he would already be awake, checking that she was okay, ready to listen to whatever was on her mind. That because he spoke so little, everything he said seemed vital. There had been so much to unite them then, that even now, ten years after he had left to take care of his mother, it seemed inexplicable that she was married to another man.

After a short drive back to her house she climbed the steps, standing at the door of her home. Everything seemed quiet as she listened for the sounds of life coming from inside. Pushing thoughts of Harry aside, she reached into her pocket. There it was again, that tightness in her chest, the one she always had when she reached this door. That voice in her head, the one person still on her side, who believed in her enough to try, shouting for her to run. Trembling, she held on to her key, wondering how a place so familiar could invoke such a sense of fear. How had she lived this way for so long?

She couldn't hear a thing coming from inside. Moonlight shone against dark windows. At this time in the evening he had to be out, didn't he? She pulled the key from her pocket and inserted it into the lock. But as soon as she opened the door, she heard his footsteps on the wooden boards they had sanded together, quickening toward the door as she fought to retrieve the key. *Turn around,* that voice implored her, but logic was usually ruled by fear, and she froze. For a moment when he pulled the door wide open, he seemed so pleased to see her that she almost let herself believe it. But common sense prevailed, and she pushed her left hand into her pocket to fiddle on her wedding ring before he could see that she had taken it off.

"Where the hell have you been?" he said, pulling her into a tight embrace. "I've been worried sick." Held tightly in his arms, his fingers brushing her shoulders, needling into her as they always did, she realized that he had been waiting for her. It didn't matter the day, or time. Whatever time she dared come back he would have been there, waiting to claim his possession. Knowing there was no choice but to see this through, already aware he was reaching out to close the door behind her, his eyes resting on her face, she dropped her bag onto the ground. The door gave off a clunk as it closed, and with it she felt herself shrink. They were alone, behind closed doors, something she promised herself would never happen again. She wondered if she smelled of Harry's house, whether Daniel would be able to smell it on her, like pheromones, or the scent of betrayal.

Clues sparked in her sight line like spurs of fire from a lit log. That beer bottle in his hand; was it the first? The fifth? Were his shoulders relaxed, or wound with energy waiting to be expended? Was his jaw soft, or tight with anger? How this reunion might play out depended on factors like that. The simplest of things could turn a pleasant evening sour, but there was always a clue. They had been together long enough for her to realize that.

"I've been working," she lied.

Tipping the bottle back he took a long slow swig from his beer, draining whatever was left. It rang out like a warning bell as he dropped it against the tile floor. Taking a step closer to her he sighed. What thoughts were going through his mind, she wondered. What did he expect from this meeting? Glancing past him then, she saw a few more bottles on the floor of the living room, scattered like bodies after a massacre. Only then did she realize the slight stumble in his gait, affecting the hairs on her arms, rising vigilant and ready. Her heart rate quickened at the realization he was on his way to being drunk.

"Have you seen the time?"

Of course she'd seen the time. She'd been very careful not to come home before ten. The idea of this house being empty, the certainty of it as a chance to claim her things, was matched only by the disappointment to realize it was not.

"Yes, I know. I'm late. Sorry," she said, angry at her apology, her words scratchy because her mouth had run dry. "You know how it's been with all the new pieces and the new collection." Angered by her trembling fingers, which attested to her fear, she clenched her fist shut tight. How could he do this to her so easily? Why did she feel so helpless in his presence? Why had it always been so hard to leave? "There are so many demands on my time, and I had to travel to bring back a really important piece." Sometimes she did this with him, spoke when it wasn't necessary, and she knew all the extra details shook the credibility of her defense.

Reaching up he brushed her hair away from her face, his touch cold yet firm. "And you couldn't call?"

"Sorry," she said, shrugging. "It was a last-minute thing."

"That place doesn't deserve you." Peeling her fingers loose he took her hand, pulling her into the hallway. Following his lead, she tried hard not to think about the irony of his statement. "You know, I called the museum." Letting that information linger for a moment, he let his fingers weave in and out of hers, almost gently, a trick to confuse her. "That girl Jenny on reception said she hadn't seen you."

If she had been thinking clearly, she would have thought of that. Harry had made her forget herself, as if the last ten years hadn't happened. Like the rest of the world didn't exist. Four days with him and her strategy for Daniel was slipping. "I've been working out of the office," she said, unable to look at him. She went to pull her fingers away only to find them locked in his grip. Mustering all her courage she looked up to find he was smiling. "You know how that can be."

"No," he said, his grip tightening. Or was that just her fear she could feel? Perhaps *she* was tighter. She wasn't sure anymore. "Actually, I don't."

She couldn't tell where this conversation was going. The door was still in view, and she couldn't shift the idea of the road, the cars, the thought of the other houses nearby filled with people that could help her. *Run,* she heard that voice say again. *There's still time.* "Aren't you going to be late for work?" she asked.

"Took some time owed to me," he said, beginning to lead her into the house. "Wanted to see you once you got back. I knew you'd have to come back eventually. All your stuff was still here."

With her hand held tightly in his he led her to the

settee, through the littered bottles. Inviting her to sit, he patted the cushion beside him. But as she went to sit down he shifted, so she landed in his lap, him laughing, her smiling to hide her discomfort. It was automatic now, she didn't even have to force it. Strong arms that had once given her a false sense of security slid around her waist, beneath her jacket, and up the length of her back. A love bite that she hadn't given him blushed like a plum on his neck as she felt his fingertips bobble down each of her vertebrae.

"It's been a while, hasn't it?" he said, moving in close. "All this work you're doing, paving your way to heaven." Just for a moment he stopped, his fingers woven into her hair. Gripping it, he turned her head so she had no choice but to look at his face. Their eyes met, his breath stale as it brushed warm against her lips. For a beat he said nothing. "You're such a good person." How was it that the simplest of sayings could sound to her ears like a threat? He kissed her cheek and stroked her hair. "You make me a better person just by being here with me. I've missed you," he whispered in her ear. "Have you missed me?"

"Of course I have," she said, her voice frail and small, and as the last words slipped from her lips he pulled her down and rolled himself on top of her, all in one fluid movement. His hands began moving across her body, his lips along her neck. He kissed her and she kissed him back. *It's not the first time,* she told herself. *It's just like it was before.* But this time the truth didn't help. Because now she saw another face in her mind's eye, and the one before her felt wrong.

"You're back now. Back where you belong," he breathed hard into her ear. But then Daniel stopped. His hand brushed her side to the jangle of jewelry. Reaching into her inside pocket he pulled out the small plastic bag that Harry had given her. He sat up, peered inside, and then began to smile.

When he pulled his hand out of the bag, a tangle of necklaces dripped through his fingers. Appendages of rubies shone red and bright. "What are you doing with these?" When she didn't answer he rummaged in the bag again, his eyes widening along with his smile. "Someone's been a very naughty girl."

"I didn't steal them." A thousand explanations came and went, out of reach like stars in a night's sky. "They are pieces ready to go on display," she finally said. "I've only got them because I've been asked to get them valued tomorrow. Insurance purposes."

"And they let you take them all knotted together like this, in a cheap old plastic bag?" he said, never once taking his eyes away from the contents of his hand.

"Yes," she said, although she realized the implausibility of her ruse. "If I don't take them back to the museum, they will notice they are missing." Close to ten years together, she could read his thoughts easily enough.

"Didn't before, did they?" The 1940s Rolex on his wrist was a classic. Every time she thought about taking that watch from a passing collection, she felt sick. He had been to the gallery, seen the timepiece, and then spent the duration of the exhibition convincing her to ship the collection back minus the piece he wanted for himself. She had wanted to impress him, that was all. At the last minute she had agreed and spent every moment since regretting what she had done.

Just for a second, she felt a false sense of relief as he stood up and his weight disappeared from her body. But reality was soon racing toward her as he stuffed the bag into his back pocket. He cupped her chin in a firm grip, just enough so she understood. "I'll get them valued for you. You work hard enough already, not back here until half past ten at night." He stepped back, grabbed his coat. "You put your feet up instead."

"Are you leaving?" she asked as he moved toward the door.

"Going to head into work," he said, smiling. He moved back, kissed her once more.

"I thought you had some time off?" It was a strange

balance. The worst thing was being near him, but now, with those necklaces in his pocket, the idea of him walking out that door was unimaginable. "Please stay."

The sneer that she once took for a smile crossed his lips. "You wouldn't have a clue what to do without me, would you?" In just a few steps he was standing over her, his hand on her chin, moving her face so they were looking at each other. "This time, don't go disappearing on me again, all right? Next time you go," he said, a finger tapping her chin, "I won't wait so long for you to come back. I'll come and find you instead. Wherever you are." Just moments later she was back in the house, alone.

Not that it made any difference, but she rushed to the door to pull the security chain across. His exit, the sound of his feet, the heavy, imposing tread of his movement, made her long for the simple, easy steps that Harry had taken earlier on that day. Everything about Daniel made her feel weak. Small. But this time as she lay against the door, panting through a mix of fear and apprehension of what could have but ultimately hadn't happened, she found herself hoping for the first time in a long time that he would come back.

She thought of the note she had left for Harry on the fridge and wondered now how she could ever return if she didn't get those necklaces back. No, she said to herself. That wasn't an option. First, she would get the necklaces back, and then she would leave for good. It didn't matter where to, because anywhere was better than that house. But then a possibility filtered into view, something that felt right and secure. She'd go to Harry, because she knew he would keep her safe. He always had when they were together, which was why it was so hard when he had left. Ten years ago she had tried to save what they had, but had lost it anyway. Now she knew about his secret history, it was almost possible to reason what had happened before. It wasn't necessary to like something first, in order to understand. But was there now a chance that this time he could save her? Then, as she really thought about the idea of leaving this house for good, of leaving to stay with Harry, she wondered whether, just maybe, there was a chance they might be able to save each other.

Chapter Six

Mirepoix, France, Summer 1981

L ast year, while Frances's parents were there, they liked to enjoy the downtime, space away from two busy careers, where more often than not they were on their feet. As a cardiothoracic surgeon, her father rarely sat down, and spent most of his time staring at a person's inner workings through the open mouth of their chest. Sometimes when Frances spoke to him he seemed surprised by her wakefulness, as if during his working life it was possible to forget that people could speak and move and have opinions. Frances figured that if you were used to holding somebody's life in your hands, perhaps it was only natural that all the other things that made a person who they were had the tendency to sound like little more than trivial background noise.

Often Frances would reason that this was why her father couldn't understand her desire to work in a museum. When she had first suggested it, they had gone along with it, took her to visit countless collections, to let the fantasy play out. But the longer it had gone on, and the closer it came to choosing subjects to study at school, her parents, and her father in particular, began to raise their concerns. It all felt so very staid to him it seemed, the idea of dealing with artifacts all day long, turning pages of an ancient book with soft cotton gloves in the search of history. It was dead information, stuff that had already passed. Working in a museum, he said, would have been the equivalent of operating on a corpse; pointless, tiresome, and with no obvious landmarks of success. Perhaps that was why the knowledge of that secret book, hidden on the shelves that somebody had built into the eaves under her window, excited Frances every time she thought of it. Finally, she had found another person who could revel in that which she loved. Somebody who saw her as more than a strange anachronism. To leave that book on her bed, to sneak into her world to leave his mark, made the things she loved real, and more than an idea to be stifled and surpassed.

At that time last year, with nothing more than a book in her possession, she knew nothing of the man who left it, or where she might find him again. When she thought of his size, his loose clothes and the sunglasses dangling from his shirt, the casual way he held himself, he seemed almost like a fiction she had crafted in her mind. He was so different from the boys she knew, in their tracksuits and scuffed trainers. Was he really that good-looking, or was she imagining it? Had he really winked at her before he turned to walk away?

A month before that night she had kissed a boy, and it hadn't left much of an impression. At least not in the same, positive way. Peter Jenkins had been a boy in the year above, who, at the time, had seemed sophisticated in comparison to the rest. Moving differently, he held his head high with his hands in his blazer as he sauntered along, a satchel slung over one shoulder rather than down at his knees like the rest of them. She always had liked different. They had arranged to go to the park that Saturday, and he bought her an ice cream. He had less to say than she had expected, asking about safe things like which subject she preferred and whether she thought the rumor about Mr. Bolton and the blond girl in year twelve was true. When he asked where she normally went on a Saturday and she replied "the library," she knew it had been the wrong answer. Still, before walking her home he had kissed her, their mouths spread wide with his tongue poking in and out like a piston while they hid from view behind the boating shed. Afterward he had rested his arm across her shoulder and she had tried to be excited about it, even though in truth she felt a bit stupid, walking along at a funny angle so his arm didn't pull her hair. How pathetic that all seemed now.

One afternoon not long after receiving the book they all traipsed down the lane toward the market square. There, her parents, aunt, and uncle ordered small, strong coffees to while away the next few hours with various interludes for cheese, wine, and cigarettes. Not long after she arrived, Amélie appeared. They had become friends years before, when language barriers were insignificant and all that was required for friendship to bloom was an earnest willingness to try. Amélie beckoned her over to a merry-go-round and they rode the horses for half an hour because Amélie's dad owned the ride, even though their ages were beyond it. While they were out of view of their families, Amélie pulled the cigarette from her sleeve; slim, white, and contraband.

"Where did you get that?" Frances whispered, slipping from her horse. By now Amélie's English was better than Frances's French.

"My papa. He never notices. Come on," Amélie said, taking Frances by the hand. They ran from the merry-go-round of garish colors that continued to kaleidoscope behind them. Unseen in the shade of the cloisters, they ran until they were out of sight, where they tucked themselves around a corner, secure on a set of steps to a long-abandoned shop. Amélie sat down and Frances huddled in alongside her. She was taller than Frances, mousy brown hair, a face that Frances always thought seemed particularly French in characteristics, which probably arose from her disinterested nonchalance rather than any particular facial feature. Frances would never have tried a cigarette with anybody else, and yet suddenly it seemed like the only thing she wanted to do.

After they exhausted a few broken matches they managed to get the thing alight. Amélie held it between awkward fingers, her joints unsure and rigid. Frances wasn't entirely sure what looked wrong about it, but something about the picture wasn't right. Amélie drew in a long breath, before doubling over to cough.

"Give it to me," Frances said, laughing. "You're not supposed to swallow it." Taking the cigarette she mirrored her father, the slack fingers, the gentle curve, the slow way he took in the smoke. It took her all her efforts not to cough, but she managed.

"Let me try again," Amélie said, taking the cigarette back. This time, with more poise, she managed a full, if somewhat shallow breath. "It was just the first time, that's all," she said, making excuses. "I know what I'm doing now."

Their relationship was one of discovery, first experiences, and subtle lies. With Amélie, Frances fit alongside her in ways she never could with her peers at school back in England. Her interest in museums and artifacts did little to spoil her credibility with Amélie, guaranteed because she was foreign and interesting and different. The same applied to Amélie, like the fact she liked to swim naked. It must be the French way, Frances always thought, and so that's just what they did. In England somebody would probably have called her a dyke if she suggested getting naked to swim together, and the girls would have likely avoided her even more than they did already, but it didn't seem to matter here.

"So, did you do anything else with him?" Amélie asked, reinstating the conversation that had been cut short by Frances's mother yesterday lunchtime. Telling the story about Peter Jenkins had been something Frances had been anticipating for weeks.

"No," Frances said. "Well, not much anyway. I guess he touched me a bit."

"Where?" Amélie asked, her eyes narrowed with voyeuristic excitement. "You mean up here, or down there?" Amélie hovered her hand around her belt and moved it up and down like a barometer moving with the weather.

"Give me the cigarette first, and then I'll tell you." Reaching across, Frances moved to take it, but it was then that she heard a bell, and felt the draft as the door opened behind her. Both frozen to the spot, Frances said nothing as the man from the book festival crouched down behind them. Frances couldn't breathe. It was him. There she was talking about Peter Jenkins, and all the while *he* was behind her. He reached out, took the cigarette from Amélie, and drew in long and hard.

"Benoit," Amélie said, and nudged his leg, as if she knew him. Something else followed in French that Frances couldn't quite catch, but it seemed good-natured enough because they were both laughing. They did know each other. They were . . . friends?

"She is angry at me, because she says I have spoiled your fun," the man she now knew to be called Benoit said as he took another drag on the cigarette. "You are here talking about boys and smoking cigarettes, and I am just an old man, getting in the way. At least that's what Amélie thinks. Do you think I am an old man?" he asked, his eyes on Frances. She felt her cheeks flush berry red.

"No, I don't."

"Good. But these are strong," he said, turning the cigarette as if to appraise it. "Where did you get it?"

"Her father," Frances said, not wanting to take any responsibility for the acquisition.

"Well, you can't smoke this. Amélie, go and get something better." From his pocket he pulled a money clip, fingered a twenty-franc note, and handed it to Amélie. "Go to George, on Rue Delcasse, and tell him they are for Monsieur Benoit." Snatching the money, she was on her feet and turning to leave.

"Francis," she said. "Are you coming?"

"You can go if you want," Benoit said, his voice quieter, as if he was speaking just for Frances. "But I would love to show you the shop. I think you will like it. Amélie can meet you back here."

Behind her a narrow window gave a wink as to what was inside. Up against the glass she could see stacked books, knickknacks, and oddments of a time gone by. A grand clock ticked on the wall.

"I'll stay here, wait for you," Frances said to Amélie. With a roll of her eyes, Amélie headed down the street.

"Come on," Benoit said, stamping the cigarette on the ground. "Let me show you inside."

Ducking through the doorway, Benoit led her into a narrow room, dark from its position under the cloisters where the sun couldn't reach. It was a relief, the day hot, the atmosphere close. Wooden floorboards sloped along a gradient, giving everything a slightly off-center appearance, making her steps feel unbalanced. In the center of the shop was a wooden table, stacked high with boxes containing unknown items, and along the walls were empty shelves, thick with dust from decades past.

"I only got the place recently, so it's a bit of a mess. And this is just the back room," Benoit said. Pointing to a doorway, he stood aside to let her pass. "The front of the shop opens to the square. What, you don't want to see?" he asked when she made no move to go through.

Whatever he had at the front of the shop could be seen another time. There was something much more pressing that she knew she had to ask. "It was you who left that book in my bedroom, wasn't it?" she said.

Folding his arms across his chest, she was sure she saw him blush. "I did. Was I wrong to leave you a gift? I'm sorry if you did not like it."

"I liked it. I was just surprised."

"No man has ever given you a gift before?"

"Not one like that," she said. "And not by breaking into my bedroom."

From a shelf he pulled a pack of cigarettes. Holding them out, he offered her the box, but she shook her head even though the pack was full. Moments later he lit one, balanced between his teeth, and he sat back on a stool just a couple of meters away. He held it differently from her father, down in the place where one finger met the next.

"You are the same age as Amélie?"

"No, I'm older," she said, sure that those additional months mattered.

Nodding, he took another long drag on the cigarette. The smoke stung her eyes. The space was too small for them both. "I thought so. Amélie is childish, but you are not. So, you must be studying, right?"

"Yes," she said.

"And what is your subject?"

There were so many different things she had to learn that seemed so irrelevant to her. School was full of things she took little joy from, like math, German, geography. None of it useful. Only one subject came to mind, the only thing she really loved. "History."

"Ah, a woman after my own heart."

That evening when she went home, she would play that conversation back over in her mind time and time again, and it was always the use of that word that got her. Woman. He didn't see her in the way that anybody else did. Had she lied when she said she was older? Had she misled him by claiming only one subject? She knew that she had let him believe something that wasn't true, that she was older, available. It was at that point that she had sat down on the other wooden stool, had leaned in close, her movement bringing their faces just an arm's length apart. She had chosen to ignore her lie, because more than the truth, she wanted to be seen by Benoit in exactly the way he saw her. From beneath his shirt where it gaped with the weight of his glasses, she noticed the hairs on his chest.

"So, what period of history are you interested in?" he asked then.

"All periods," she said, not wanting to say the wrong thing. "I don't just like dates, but pieces of history. I like the objects. The things I can touch and see. Touching something that somebody last held centuries ago. Like pots, say, or paintings. I've got a collection of plates back in my aunt's barn."

"I would like to see that. And paintings, eh? I like paintings too." He sat back and ran his hand through his dark hair. Smiling, the little scar on his cheek creased, making his face asymmetrical. She wondered what it would be like to touch that scar, whether it would be soft, or hard like a knot. "Myself, I like the neoclassical period of the French Revolution. *Liberté, Egalité, Fraternité.* This is something you know?"

"No," she confessed, but was eased when he didn't seem put off.

"My favorite of the three is *Liberté*. Liberty, Frances. A man's right to choose for himself. To do what he thinks he must. To be free to be himself." Everything he said made her feel as if she knew nothing, yet when she spoke he watched the movement of her mouth as if there was nothing more important to be said in the whole world.

"I like that one too. The freedom to be who you are." Thinking of her father just a short distance away, she realized that he was trying to stop her from being who she truly was, trying to guide her down a path she didn't like. Medicine, law at a push; this was not who she was. Why didn't they want her to be herself?

"You know," Benoit said then. "Amélie will be back soon."

"Yes, she will."

He drew long and hard on the cigarette. "Before she comes back, can I tell you something?"

"Yes."

After stubbing his cigarette out in a small china dish, he leaned in close, his voice dropped to a whisper. "I wanted to say that I overheard your conversation on the steps, about that boy. That he had kissed you, and touched you. No, no, please do not be embarrassed," he said when she felt herself blush. "But I wanted to give you a little advice. About men, and how you should look upon us. May I?" She nodded. "You see, there are a lot of men who will like you. Your hair . . ." he began, his fingers trailing through from her face, all the way to where it skimmed down her back. "I love dark hair like this, and your eyes are so bright. I have never seen a blue like it. You are the most beautiful woman I have ever seen in my life. Everybody can see it, I am quite sure. Perhaps everybody except you. Perhaps that is what makes you even more striking. So, before you let a man touch you, you must first make sure he is worth it."

Her next question was formed before she could do anything about it. "How will I know he's worth it?"

"How to know if a man is worth it? Hmm," he said, as if he was contemplating the very meaning of life. "That is a hard thing to know. Even harder to explain. Perhaps you cannot know, until he touches you."

Floorboards creaked as he shuffled closer. The smell of coffee and cigarettes met her as he leaned in. Then he took his fingertips, their touch as soft as silk, and beginning just behind her ear, let them slip slowly and softly along the side of her neck. Goose bumps shivered across her arms, her stomach turning in knots. A pressure built between her legs although she couldn't have explained it at the time. Across the knot of bone that marked her shoulder his touch descended, before his fingers meandered onto her chest. All the way down he moved, across her nipple, until his hand cupped the entirety of her breast. His touch grew intense, and then just a moment later his hot lips pressed against hers. How long did that last, that moment when they were connected? What would they have said if Amélie had walked back in?

"When this other boy touched you, did it feel like this?" he whispered, his breath tickling her cheek.

"No," she said. "It was nothing like this."

From the corner of her eye she caught sight of Amélie running down the street, just a few seconds away from the shop. "Then that, Frances," he said, standing up from the stool as the bell rang to announce her friend's arrival, "is how you know."

Chapter Seven

By the time morning was breaking across a warm summer city, she knew she couldn't go back to Harry's without first getting the necklaces back. So instead she went to work the next day, tried to focus on the current acquisitions she had in progress, and sat in on two meetings about finance to which she paid little attention. For most of the morning her focus remained on the cheerful messages she was sending to Daniel, the whole show of it making her feel a bit sick. Telling him that she missed him created a hole inside her, a sort of void. Who was she now? What was real anymore? If she played nice, she hoped he might come home that night and bring the jewelry with him. But the whole process left her feeling as if she had eaten bad food, a taste in her mouth and a sense of dread in her guts. By lunchtime, when she stood at the sink to wash her hands, she couldn't bear to look at her reflection in the mirror.

Daniel didn't come home that night, never answered any of her messages. Tabitha waited, sitting in the chair they had recovered last year, choosing the material together. Another Band-Aid on a gaping wound that opened up on the day he first hit her. Three days passed like that without a word, barely working, calling and messaging in an attempt to find out where he was. But despite her fears for the jewelry, in Daniel's absence her confidence surged, along with a sense of hope, and when she packed a small bag with some clothes and her passport, which she hid in the back of the linen cupboard, she felt stronger than she had in years. But most of the time she spent thinking about Harry, and about how she had failed to keep that promise she had written and stuck to the fridge before she left. How on the very day she promised him that he could trust her, she had let him down.

Friends called her but she didn't pick up. Running at the gym killed some time, but she left without breaking a sweat. Even books seemed to hold little more than ants crawling across the pages in the place of written word. In the end she started flicking through the channels on the television, anything to while away the time. When she came across a show about bridal dresses, she settled on that. It was harmless enough, but after missing so much sleep in the previous three days, eventually she dozed off. Waking up a few hours later, a different show was playing, one that followed families who hoarded. The old man in the house was in such a poor state, crying in the arms of the visitor from the council who was trying to explain why it was unreasonable to keep fifty cats, why keeping as much stuff as he had—it was even worse than Harry's—was so dangerous. Within moments of waking Tabitha had burst into tears. Built up emotion spilled out, for everything she had lost years before, and everything that kept her away now. But most of all she was crying for Harry, and the thought of how she had abandoned him when she promised that she would be there to help. Ten years apart had done nothing to limit what she felt for him. Shoving her feet into her shoes, she grabbed her keys, and before she could change her mind she was on the road to Harry's place.

By the time Tabitha reached the entrance to Awkward Hill she was out of breath and hot with sweat despite the fact she had done nothing but drive. The sun had long set, but the ground was hot, heat trapped in stone. Flying through the rickety gate, smacking it into the wall, she was relieved to see a light on in the window. Paint crumbled as she banged her fist against the door. Hinges creaked as she poked her fingers through the letterbox and called his name.

"Harry," she shouted. "Harry, open the door." Still nothing. There were boxes blocking the hallway that weren't there before, the route through to the kitchen almost blocked off again. He'd been bringing things back inside. Oh god, what had she done leaving him alone as she had? "Shit," she said to herself as she scanned the ground for something that could break glass. Her fingers found a rock, small enough to handle with some dexterity, large enough to put through a window. With her hand drawn back, she was just about to strike it against the window when she saw a shadow move in the kitchen. Was that him?

"Just a minute," she heard him call, and the relief was instant. Opening the letterbox again she saw the lower half of his body trying to shift a box, then heard the shuffle of paperwork and grunting as he hauled things out of the way. It took several minutes before the door was opened, and even then, it was only enough for a visual.

"Harry, what the hell's going on?" He glanced at her face, surprise, confusion all fighting to work out what she was doing there. His gaze flicked to her hand,

the rock; reminded of its presence by Harry's attention, she tossed it down to the ground. "Are you going
to let me in?"

"Well, it's a bit difficult. I wasn't expecting company." It made her sad to think that in such a short
space of time he had stopped expecting her. Or maybe
that was normal, she wondered, and that it was only
she who held on in desperate hope. "There's a lot of
stuff in the hallway now. I don't have any more room
to move things. This is all rubbish."

A sense of relief and pride flooded her. For a
moment she had thought everything they had done
had unraveled. "What about round the back?" she
suggested. "I could jump the fence."

He shook his head. "Garden's full of brambles,
remember? It would be a disaster." She was starting
to wonder whether it was just an excuse, but then he
said, "You could try the window to the living room.
I'll go and open that if you like."

An overgrown rosebush formed the only remaining
obstacle in her way, but as Harry drew back the curtains and pushed open the window, she saw he had a
plan. Flakes of rotten wood showered away as he threw
an old blanket toward the bush, covering it for the most
part with a protective layer of material.

"Do you think you can pull yourself over it?" he asked.

Tabitha nodded. "Just get ready to pull me in." With one foot braced against the sill, she reached up to the edge of the frame, hoping the rotting wood would hold. With a one, two, and three for momentum, she pulled herself forward, levering her weight on her foot. Two hands reached for her shoulders, and with a bit of effort and ungraceful clamoring she fell forward into Harry's arms. The sense of relief of being back inside that house was so overwhelming she could feel it like water rushing all over her skin. Like she'd broken through the surface and could finally take a breath. Breathing in, she caught a scent from many years ago. The essence of Harry, unchanged.

"You didn't hurt yourself, did you?" he asked as they came to a stop.

"No," she said, still holding on to him. His body felt the same too, and she wasn't keen to let go. Then she got a thought about the lost jewelry, so stepped away and brushed herself down while Harry closed the window and drew the curtain on the rest of the world.

As she looked up, she took in the changes that had taken place in Nook Cottage. Gone were the orderly boxes and neat corners. The columns that once seemed as strong as the Parthenon had been all but destroyed, as if Christian raiders had taken umbrage to the icons and had wrecked them as an affront to an ancient religion. From where she was standing, she could no longer see the sitting chairs, or the route to the kitchen. There was only one small space on the floor where it seemed Harry might have taken to sleeping if the rolled-up quilt was anything to go by.

"What happened?" she asked. Despite the honesty of her question it seemed to her an entirely obvious answer.

"Mr. Lewisham called," he told her, without realizing she had no idea who that was. "The auction has been brought forward, and now there's a definite date. The house is going to be sold, repossessed if I don't cover the debts. I have to sign the papers. After that the house will be gone and I'll be homeless." He raised his arms in exasperation and then let his hands slap against his thighs. "He says he thinks it will fetch a good price, and that these sorts of places sell well at auction. I was banking on the mess putting people off, but it would seem that's not the case." He shook his head in disbelief. "I have to find that box, Tabitha, and time's running out."

"Well, to be quite honest, it looks like things have gone from bad to worse," she said, while avoiding having to explain where she had been. Thinking of that beautiful jewelry lost to Daniel, she felt so guilty. And what if he did come looking for her? Would she be putting Harry at risk just by being here? Always quick to temper and handy with his fists when jealousy stirred, what would Daniel do if he found her with Harry? Focusing on the most pertinent task was a way of ignoring her own failings and the risk of Daniel for now, so that's exactly what she did. "I'm going to assume you didn't find the box so far."

He shook his head. "No, but I found this. Take a look."

Handing her a crumpled old newspaper, it was a copy of Le Monde. "I don't see what you mean. What am I looking for?"

"Page eight. I saw it by chance." Waiting, he gave her the chance to locate the article. "It says that the Klinkosch box was sighted in Munich, but then lost again. And later in the story there's a mention about some art thief from France, and that maybe he took it. Look, there's a picture of it from before the war."

"I never knew you could speak French," she said, skimming the article.

"I can't." Reaching to his back pocket, he pulled out his telephone. "Translating it took me close to an hour."

"When is this from?" she asked, turning to the front page.

"Nineteen eighty-five," he said. "Doesn't help us much, I suppose. The picture Mum had was from nineteen eighty-one."

"No, but your mother kept a newspaper with a story about it. That has to mean something, even if only that she was following the story. And if she did have it since nineteen eighty-one, then this story was false. It could never have been in Munich four years later."

"Exactly. So, who started the false story?"

"Your mother?"

Harry shrugged. "I don't know about that, but I think I'm starting to understand it's importance. People really were looking for it, weren't they?" She nodded. "It's amazing to think that Mum might have had it. And now, seeing this in her house certainly makes me want to believe it could be here, among all this rubbish, of which I can assure you there's a lot. I must have found a copy of every *National Geographic* magazine ever printed. *Kerrang* too." Picking one up, he handed it to her as proof. "Why did she keep all this stuff? Why did she even have it in the first place? I just really wish I could understand her, and what made her live like this."

"I guess we might never know the answer to that

one," she said, setting the newspaper and magazine down. "I don't know how you managed to live like this."

"Honestly, I've no idea. I tried at first to put things right, but I suppose I got overwhelmed by it too." Relief flooded him when she nodded to show her understanding. "I tried to focus on helping her, but that wasn't altogether easy either."

"I can imagine. Well, maybe it's not our purpose to question, but instead to find just one thing." In a grand show of readiness, she pushed up her sleeves. "Let's start in this room and get everything that we don't want out into the hall. Tomorrow morning I'll head to the museum and pick up the van and we can start clearing stuff out."

He was quiet for a moment. "There's still the stuff in the garden too."

It was unavoidable. Her disappearance was the elephant in the room, and the truth was there was no space for anything else. "I said I'd come back, didn't I?" He nodded, and she thought of those items Daniel had taken from her. From Harry. Could she tell him the truth? No, she decided. It was too big a risk, even the thought that he might ask her to go was too much. That this kindling fire of friendship between them could be stifled and snuffed out by her terrible mistake of judgment in going home. She hated Daniel then perhaps more than she ever had. How was she ever going to be able to confess that she had lost them? "I'm so sorry. I let you down. A few thing's came up, and I was waiting on the valuation for that jewelry." The lie was out before she could stop herself. "Still hasn't come back."

"Oh, that's okay," he said, digging into another box. "These things take time," he said, pulling out another *National Geographic* magazine. "I think I might have read that one as a child," he said, gazing at the cover. He tossed it to the floor and turned to her. "How could you think that you'd let me down? You can't be here all the time helping me. I've heard you on the phone, talking about your work. You have an important job." Harry seemed to get embarrassed then too for a moment, opening his mouth a few times without any sounds coming out. Eventually he found his voice. "And anyway, I found your note."

"You did?"

"Yes."

"What did you think when you read it?" she asked, her heart pounding, wondering how long it had taken him to find what she had written. She had really meant those words, as scary as it was to admit. Realizing she still had feelings for him despite her marriage and a decade spent apart was as confusing as it was complicated.

Without glancing up, he struggled to stifle a smile. Or perhaps the smile stifled him, made it impossible to say what he truly wanted. "We better keep working, Tabitha." With that he picked up a box and took it into the hallway.

That evening they managed to remove at least fifty percent of the mess from the living room. They ended up with five bags of baby clothes, twenty framed prints of naval ships, and several different editions of children's encyclopedias. They stumbled across more of his mother's inventories, but after close to an hour working through them, they still found no mention of the box. Hidden in the corner of the room underneath a molding inflatable mattress they also found a small box of handwritten letters, all in French.

"They're addressed to your mother," Tabitha said, handing him an envelope. It had been ripped open, torn with haste, and the paper was brown, the ink faded.

"When's the postmark from?"

"Not sure. The ink is all rubbed away."

Harry reached into the box to retrieve another letter. "This one looks like nineteen eighty. She'd have been what, like fifteen or sixteen then?"

"Who do you think they're from?"

Harry was already into the third letter. It was all in French so he couldn't understand, but each letter was signed in the same way. "There's no name."

Leaning over his shoulder, Tabitha gazed at the letter. "It's signed *B*. Is that family?" Tabitha asked, trying to decipher what was written. Relying on her high school French, she tried to translate some of the sentences. "I think this bit says, 'I've been to the marketplace again and the shop is . . .'" She paused, squinting. "Oh, I'm not sure." In places the cursive handwriting was almost indecipherable, with too many sweeping loops and deep tails. "Let's try another one."

"I'll go and make us some tea," Harry said. Returning with two mugs, he resumed his position on the floor. As he sat, he looked around at the space they had created in the room, realizing that it almost looked like a normal lounge. Almost. "There you go," he said, handing her a mug, a faded letter still in her other hand. "Any luck with that one?"

Harry was surprised to feel such disappointment when she shook her head. "I'm struggling to make out some of the letters. Your mother could obviously speak French well enough, though."

"I guess so, yes. I didn't know that about her. She

must have known what was written in that newspaper article too."

"I would say so. Because, Harry, although there's a lot I don't understand, I think these are love letters."

He moved closer, gazed over her shoulder as if he could understand what was written and needed a closer look. "Love letters? In French?"

"Yes. Could your father be from France?"

"I have no idea. I don't even know if she ever went there."

"Based on what's written here, I'd say she did. And look at what we know so far: the Klinkosch box was from France, there was the article in the French newspaper, and now these letters. Harry, none of this can be a coincidence. The answers are all here somewhere. We're getting closer, I can feel it."

Earlier that evening they had found a couple of suitcases filled with old coats, and so in need of a chair they opened them out and sat inside. They weren't very comfortable, but they were good enough for two people otherwise engaged and with nowhere else they would rather have been. The actual armchairs were stacked with paper. Rhythmical ticking from a clock drew his attention, and when his eyes glanced at the hands, he couldn't believe what he saw. "Oh gosh, I hate to tell you, but it is two a.m."

The deepening of night on the other side of the flimsy curtain hadn't escaped Tabitha's notice. Daniel might have been home by now, would have dropped his bag by the door and after pulling a beer from the fridge he would be wondering once again where she was. Would he search for her? She had parked out of sight, most of the vehicle hidden behind a bush. Would he spot it, if he drove past? What would happen if she were to go home now? Would she stay, settle back into that life, waiting for the next time he found fault in something she had done? Would she get the jewelry back? Years of trying, and still she couldn't quite predict the course his behavior would take. The only thing she could ever be certain about was the demise. It would always come, she just didn't know when.

"I guess time flies when you're having fun. I think we've done a pretty good job," she said, pushing thoughts of Daniel and his threats aside as she looked up to the piles of bin bags and the space created. "This room is almost clear."

"Except for those skateboards." There were six of different sizes stacked up in the far corner, a tripping hazard they decided was best left far out of the way.

"I used to skate when I was a teenager. I wasn't very good, but I was fast."

"So many things I don't know about you, Harry."

"No, there aren't that many things, not really."

Something was on his mind, evident in a hint of melancholy. All it took was a look, a slight tremor in his voice, and she could sense the basic rudiments of his emotion. Ten years apart and there had been no deterioration in her ability to read him. There was no hiding from a person who loved you, and Tabitha did love him. Whether she wanted to or not, and perhaps even more now than she had while they were together. Ten years apart could whittle away at a life, at confidence, integrity, or conviction, but it couldn't touch love. It was as boundless as the infinitude of the universe, an emotion beyond the realm of time.

"What is it?" she asked.

Without the hint of a wheeze, he took a deep breath, and she thought for the first time that night how the dust hadn't bothered his asthma once. "It's just, we've cleared this whole room essentially, and we haven't found it yet."

"The Klinkosch box?"

"Yes." He set his tea aside. "I've barely slept these past few days and . . ." He paused, fiddling with a button on one of the coats beneath him. "Without you here to keep me motivated I get sidetracked by the things I find, wondering if they might be important. Thinking about who my mother was, and who my father might have been. What life would have been like with them. And . . ."

"And what?"

"Well, you'll have to go again soon. It's already the early hours of the morning, and tomorrow I'll be all over the place again."

"You know," Tabitha said, speaking slowly, unsure even in the moment what she was going to say. "I don't have to go to work tomorrow. I could stay to help you."

He shook his head. "That's kind, but there's always the next day, and the day after that. All the days lead to selling this house and having no idea where to go." He thought of the note still stuck to the fridge and wondered if she really meant what she had written. "You can't just stay here with me, can you."

"Who says I can't?" A tremor in her voice betrayed her nerves. "What about if I stay until this is done? I said I'd stick around before, but I hadn't really meant continuously. But I could, if you wanted me to. I could stay here," she said, swallowing. "With you."

"You mean, stay here, stay here? Like not leave at all?"

"Yes." Had she overstepped a boundary? Part of her wondered if she should retract her offer, say it was silly. But that thought seemed so wrong to her that she pushed on, committed. "That's what I wrote on the note, isn't it?"

From his pocket, he pulled her note loose, handed it to her. Noticing her handwriting, she read the words: *Turns out we really were inseparable after all.* It was a thing they shared, something he used to say to her every night. In the moments before sleep he would whisper in her ear, "We're inseparable, you and me. That's how you make me feel."

"You kept it," she said, and he nodded. "I always believed you when you used to say that," she said. "I think part of me always knew I'd see you again one day."

"It was just the way I always felt. Like we belonged together, and that we always would." He was pleased to see her nodding. Was it to show that she remembered, felt the same, or something else? Whatever it was, he thought that probably it was something good. "Well, if you were to stay, I don't know where you'd sleep."

Pointing to the folded quilt, to the spot alongside where it seemed he had bedded down the night before, she said, "I can sleep there."

"But that's where I have been sleeping."

"It wouldn't be the first time we've slept with each other." Almost choking, he spat out some of his tea. "I mean in the same bed, Harry. Alongside each other. And, to be honest with you, I'm exhausted. Why don't we get some sleep before we start again in the morning?"

Watching as she stood up without even waiting for his answer, straightening the quilts and coats into some sort of order, he wondered if it was really possible that she was just going to stay. Whether they really were inseparable. With her here, it was possible to believe that they were.

So when she beckoned him to join her, he did. Settling down in the makeshift bed, she smiled at him before turning out the little lamp he had been using at the side.

"Night then," he said.

"Night, Harry. Sweet dreams." It was the same whispered wish she always used to offer him before sleep, and it made him feel as if she was still in some way his. And he found himself hoping desperately for that to be true. Because he knew now, realized the fact as if it was a physical part of him that had surpassed all possibility of denial, that being without Tabitha was a situation even more terrifying than being alone.

It didn't take long before she heard the gentle whistle of his breathing. It was strange to share a quilt with Harry again, to sleep in her clothes, and yet she felt calmer than she had in months. Years, even, there alongside a man who wasn't her husband but who was at one time the man she had intended to marry. The mattress of coats wasn't as uncomfortable as she thought it might have been, but knowing that she didn't have to go home came as an even bigger relief than she'd expected. There was no way Daniel could find her here. Just no way.

Eventually she sat up and reached to the box of letters they had unearthed deep in the living room detritus. Pulling a random envelope from the pile, she opened the folded paper, brown at the edge and with a smell that wasn't unpleasant. Using her fingers to open up the envelope, she peeped inside to find a single stem of dry lavender, the tail end of its aroma lingering after all those years. Slipping from their ersatz bed, she settled back into one of the suitcases and used her phone to illuminate the page. Most of the text remained elusive. But there was one short passage that she could understand. She read it over and over.

> *I fell in love with you for your kindness, the goodness of your soul, even though I was not a person deserving of such love. All I can think about is the warmth of your touch, and the way you fit so perfectly, wrapped in my arms. No two people who fit together so well could ever be considered wrong. Don't you think?*

She looked at Harry and thought perhaps he wasn't so different from his mother. He was kind. He was good. Sitting there, watching him sleep, she knew it was entirely possible to fall in love with those qualities. To remain in love perhaps, even when you told yourself you weren't.

Comforted by his proximity, she watched him sleeping until her eyes began to tire. Then, without too much thought for the consequences, she let her body move until it was positioned against his. Warmth flooded her as she inched closer and closer, radiating from his form as she let her arm drape across his chest. He was always too warm where she was forever cold, and even in summer she used to press up against him, their temperature together balanced in a way they never were when alone. They fit together, complemented each other, like his mother had with this *B* signatory.

"We still fit together, Harry, just like we always used to," she whispered, but it was more for herself than it was for him. "We've always been inseparable." Why had she come back here? For herself, for him, or was it possible that she was here for them both? Did she know that this was how it was always supposed to be? When her eyes fluttered shut no more than a few moments later, she slipped into a deep and restful sleep, knowing without doubt that Harry would never harm her. Those instinctive feelings she had learned over the last decade had no place here. For the first time in years, she felt absolutely and unquestionably safe.

Chapter Eight

Traffic thrummed past as they lingered outside the rear stage door. The first sounds of the brass instruments were already trumpeting out through the doors. For the last ten minutes Tabitha had been doing her best to encourage him inside, but he was shaking his head.

"I can't do it," he said. His hands fiddled one at the other, his gaze locked tight to the floor, avoiding the trumpet case that was resting at his feet. Tabitha looked down to see his hands were trembling.

"What do you mean you can't do it? I've heard you play. You're good."

"It's not the same," he protested, glancing again at the doors. "Playing at home is one thing, playing in there is another." His stance tightened and he shook his head and folded his arms like a small boy who wanted to make his point heard. There was no doubting that she had cajoled him into it, but when Tabitha had broached the idea, she had made it sound easy. And he had wanted to do it, had even washed the instrument through last night, oiled the valves before practicing for three hours straight. Eventually Elsie had come over to tell him to pack it in. But certainty was infectious, and it was easy to get carried away by somebody else's confidence, like watching a TED Talk on YouTube and thinking you could take on the world at the end of eighteen and a half minutes. "I don't think I can do it, Tabitha. I'm not ready. I should just be back at the house, looking for the box."

Disappointed, she let it go, a simple nod of her head to show understanding. One thing she had learned about Harry was that there was no point in pushing him. If he wasn't ready, it would have to wait. She knew that about herself too, that sometimes you needed more than one attempt before you were able to execute a correct and necessary step.

"What about just going in and saying hello, without any pressure to actually play?"

He pulled the flyer from his pocket. "It says here

that they meet on a Tuesday and a Friday," he said. "We could come back on Friday when I'm feeling a bit better about it."

"Okay, that's a great idea," she said, hoping it sounded as encouraging as she intended. The last thing she wanted to sound was sarcastic, a lilt that, she had been informed since she married, often decorated her voice. "And you can practice some more in the meantime. That way, you'll feel better prepared too."

"Yes. I suppose so." He picked up the case and together they walked away.

By then it was late afternoon, the lazy sun stretching the shadows across hot pavements, the air still thick and oppressive. It had rained briefly last night, but not enough to break the atmosphere. They had sat and watched the storm together, the flicker of lightning rippling across the sky through a thick mass of cloud.

"I'll tell you one thing, Harry, I'm really hungry," Tabitha said as they headed toward the bus stop. Being off work because of a fake sickness meant she didn't have access to the work van, and Harry had lost the keys to his car somewhere in the disarray.

"We can pick something up on the way back. Cook in the newly cleaned kitchen." The back garden was filling up with rubbish, but the benefit of that was that the kitchen was almost clear. "Whatever you fancy."

"Or we could eat out," Tabitha suggested. "What about going to a pub?"

"A pub?" Harry didn't seem convinced. "I think we should stop wasting time away from the house."

"But cooking will take just as long," she said, gazing up and down the street at what might be available. "We can't search every moment of the day, and well, frankly, I'm hungry now," she said. "By the time we shop and get home and then cook something it'll be at least another hour." The way she used the word *home* softened him, and he felt himself relenting. One of her hands rested on his shoulder as she pointed the other toward the pub across the street. "Let's go there instead. We can eat quickly and still have the rest of the afternoon and evening for searching. And while we are in there, I'll try to do some searching on the archives online, see if I can find anything more about the Klinkosch box that might help us."

"Okay," he said. "If we're quick."

"We will be. Come on, this will be my treat."

They chose a booth in the far corner, and Harry sat his trumpet down on the leatherette bench seat like it was a guest at the table. Just a short while later Tabitha was heading back from the bar with a pint of something brown, a glass of red wine, and a ring of plastic with the number twenty-three written on it.

"Should be about fifteen minutes. I ordered you the fish and chips." For a moment then she wished she hadn't been presumptuous, wondering if perhaps she'd overstepped the mark. Daniel hated it when she made decisions on his behalf. "But I can go and change the order if you like. If it's not what you want. Or," she said, her anxiety growing, "you can go. I was silly to order. I didn't think. I'm sorry, I just didn't think."

"No, no," he said, oblivious to her anxiety, waving his hands for her to sit down. "It's fine. It's what I would have chosen anyway." Whether that was true or not, she liked the sentiment of his agreeability. It was an echo from the past, when she would try to help and it wouldn't be misconstrued. How she had missed him, and his sense of easygoing kindness. In a show of appreciation, he smacked his lips together after a sip of beer. It used to drive her crazy when he did that. Such a simple thing back then seemed so important, but now the way she judged another person's flaws was set against a very different standard.

"I suppose we needed to get out for a bit," he said then, relenting.

"Yes," she said. "We needed a break from it, I think." Opening her phone, she began to search for information on the internet.

"And it's years since I last did something like this."

Dark walls surrounded them, lights over the booth making it feel as if they were both on show, and yet somehow alone in the world. Her screen glowed between them. Only the background chatter of the other guests reminded him that they were surrounded by strangers. "Can't even remember the last time I've been in a pub."

"Really?" she said, pausing. He nodded. "Well then, I'm glad we stopped. You have missed out on so much in the last ten years, Harry."

"Yeah, I guess so." That idea made him think about his mother. "Oh, by the way. Did you get any news about the necklaces?"

"Not yet," she said, not looking up, not wanting to linger on the thought of her lie. "Hopefully it won't be too long. But in the meantime, when it comes to rebuilding your life, you just sort of have to try and get back in the saddle, so to speak. Try new things. Do old things again."

His shoulders curved in. "You mean like going into that theater."

"Well, it would have been nice."

As if weighted, his head lowered toward the table. "Next time. I promise."

Pausing, she realized it wasn't easy for him. "Don't make a promise for me, Harry. Do it for yourself," she said, reaching to touch his hand. Harry felt the hairs on his arm stand up as her fingers brushed against his. "You have lived for too long in that house. You need something else in your life. Something for yourself. You'll have something in common with those people. They like what you like."

"I know, but you have to remember, for the last ten years I haven't done much. I'm out of practice with these things. I don't think I know how to talk to people anymore. I know you hate the fact I've got those birds cooped up in a cage, but I've had more conversations with them in the past few years than I have with anybody else." With his fingers in a damp ring on the table, he drew a figure of eight. "I'm out of practice with a lot of things, Tabitha. For ten years all I've known is my job at the nursing home and my mother. Unless you count Elsie as a friend, I haven't really had anybody to chat to."

"Elsie counts for sure. Don't you remember that old man who lived above us in the flat? What was his name?"

"You mean Eric?"

"That was it. You always used to be up there talking to him."

"I used to like chatting with him. He survived the Normandy landings, you know."

"Why did you never hang out with people our age?"

Harry shrugged, but he knew the answer. "I never thought they had much to say. Older people had experience, had better answers to questions I had. In my foster homes, they were the constant, the people who helped me understand what I was doing there. I guess I just liked their company more. They never criticized Mum either. The kids at school never had anything nice to say."

"So, what was she like?"

"Mum? Well, you met her. You know."

The pub was filling up, and the background noise gave her reason to lean in. A sip of velvety wine loosened her words. "Not really, Harry. I only met her once, and to be honest, at the time, I was more interested in the fact that you were telling me you were never coming home." He glanced at his hands, took a sip of his drink, and then a big breath in. "I guess what I'm really asking is, was it worth it?"

For a while she wondered if she had pushed him too hard, because for a few moments he didn't say anything and his gaze hung limp, his eyes staring at some invisible scene from the past. "I don't know whether it was worth it, to be honest. But she was a good woman, I think," Harry said then. "Eccentric, definitely, not entirely well mentally perhaps, but she was a good person."

"You think she had mental health problems?"

"Other than the hoarding, at the time she died she hadn't left the house in months. Wouldn't even see the doctor. I kept telling her that she had to go, especially toward the end because her leg was swollen and red. They knew it had a clot in it, but she refused, and even when I organized a home visit, she wouldn't let the doctor in. She was supposed to be taking something to thin the blood, but she wouldn't even take that. I was supposed to be doing the injections. The nurse trained me and everything, but she wouldn't let me give her a single dose." Eyes snapping shut, Tabitha could see how hard it was not only for him to recount the memory, but to accept that he hadn't been able to help. "She said she didn't deserve their care, and that when it was her time she would go without fanfare or protest to the contrary."

"You did everything you could for her, Harry. There was nothing more you could have done."

"Sometimes I feel like I should have forced her, injected her while she was asleep. I thought about it."

"It was her choice. You gave her ten years of your life. That was more than she gave you."

"I'm not sure about that." When he looked up Tabitha was surprised to see the immature hint of a smile. "She gave me you, didn't she? She brought you back into my life. I have to be grateful for that."

Harry's last comment made her think about the letter she had received, and how it might have been possible for Frances to send it when she hadn't left the house, and when she died before the postmark was stamped. But beyond those discrepancies, she had to admit she was grateful to have received it.

"Yes, Harry. She did. But it must have been hard, all this time with her. Don't try to convince me it has been easy."

He shrugged. "It was what it was. Family is family, and you get what you get, right?" She could relate to that. "What about yours?"

"Still not talking to them. Nothing's changed for me." Diverting her attention back to the phone, she resumed her scrolling.

"Why not?"

"Because they're . . ." she began, but her stock answer, the one she always had ready when somebody asked, no longer seemed enough after the conversation they'd just shared about his mother. To tell him that they didn't care and neither did she, seemed trite and inaccurate, childish somehow. It's what she told him ten years ago, but a lot had changed since then, for both of them. "I don't think there's a way back from the troubles we've had."

"I'm sorry about that."

"Don't be." She shrugged. "I made choices they didn't like. They acted in ways that hurt me. I did try to smooth things over after . . ." She paused, sipped more wine. "You know, after you left, but it fell apart again. I met somebody they didn't approve of. I thought I was in love."

"Oh?" he asked.

She wondered whether it mattered that she hadn't told him about Daniel, or that she was in fact married, or that she had seen her husband only days ago. Either way, he should know the truth. But putting anything of Daniel into what she shared with Harry felt so wrong, and she didn't want to talk about the lost necklaces, only get them back as soon as she could. Trying to piece the story together, to create a way that she could tell Harry, she went over it in her mind. But it didn't make sense even to her, so how could she risk telling Harry? She couldn't even begin to imagine what she would do if he didn't want to see her anymore.

"Yes. All a big mess really," she said, letting the chance for the truth fade away. "We're not together anymore, and I haven't seen my parents in years."

"I'm sorry."

"Don't be. But look here at what I've found." Turning the phone toward him, he saw the Klinkosch box fill the screen, and next to it was an ornate key, the handle a twisted olive branch. "Apparently the key was found in Austria in the nineteen fifties in an old apartment. It was returned to the last family who owned it in a gesture of goodwill, the Ellison family, who it says here used to live in Paris, before they eventually moved somewhere south."

"Do they still have it?"

"Doesn't say. But it does say they had to move because people kept breaking into their home to try and steal the box. That a person was attacked for it."

"Bloody hell," Harry said. "Are we in danger if we find it?"

Tabitha shrugged a little, but the look on her face suggested she thought they might be. "Maybe we shouldn't make too much noise about it if we do. Items like this are heavily sought by many."

"Where did they move to exactly? This Ellison family."

"Doesn't say that either."

They were interrupted as the meal arrived, two oversized plates with a small piece of fish, overdone chips, and a bowl of unappealing tartar sauce that seemed dry around the edges. It was his first meal out in ten years, and all he could think was that he hadn't been missing much. They shared a look of mutual understanding before picking up their knives and forks.

He took the first bite. It tasted better than it looked. "Did you ever think about going back to see your parents? Maybe you could still put things right?"

Over the years she had come up with hundreds of excuses why she shouldn't. But now she began to wonder whether there really was a good reason to stay away, except for the fact she was still technically, and in perhaps many other ways, married to the man they hated. "I don't know," she said. She couldn't tell him the truth. To do so would be to reduce her presence in Harry's house to a necessity when she knew it was so much more than that.

"I guess when you don't have something anymore, you just get used to it not being there," he said.

She reached over and touched his hand then. "I'm not sure you ever get used to it." The moment of sudden, charged emotion left him with a raw panic, desperate to change the course of the conversation. Was this when he was supposed to tell her how he felt, about the fact that he had never stopped loving her? Did she feel the same way as he did? At first he had intended to tell her how he felt, but he had since come to understand that to do so was to risk being knocked back, and that was too big a gamble to take. If she didn't feel the same way, she would undoubtedly leave, and that would be it. Gone for a second time. Lost because of his own failings. No, he had to keep his feelings tight to his chest. He couldn't bear the thought of losing her again.

That night when they arrived home, they did some more clearing. They arranged for a man who Tabitha knew to come with his pickup truck the next day to take everything from the back garden. But first they had to clear the hall so there would be space for the removal team to work. They were nearly through the mess when Harry stopped and sat back on his heels.

"What is it?" She checked her watch. "Come on, don't flake on me now. I know it's nearly three a.m. but we've nearly finished."

"I was just thinking."

"About the box, yes, I know," she said, knotting another black bag. "You're thinking about it even more than I am."

"No, not that," he said. What he wanted to say had been on his mind since that afternoon, and although he wasn't ready to admit how he felt about her, he did want to tell her how grateful he was that she had chosen to be there. "You know, you're the first one . . . the first person to, um . . . the first person who has ever stayed with me through choice."

"What?" she whispered.

His head turned to face her then, and she saw that his eyes were wet. In that moment the world around her faded into oblivion. Even the walls of the room retreated. It was just her, and him. Two people in love, and both too afraid to say it. "You're the first person who made the decision to stay with me, and you did so at a time when most would have run away screaming. I guess what I'm trying to say is, thank you."

"You don't need to thank me." There were so many things she wanted to say. She should be the one who was thanking him, for giving her an escape from a life she was desperate to leave. But that would have negated everything he just said, so she held it back.

"And I need to say sorry, because I keep letting you down. I still have my birds locked up outside that I know you hate, and I keep holding on to things that you think I should throw away. I can't even go into a room full of strangers and blow a bloody trumpet when you've put so much effort into organizing it, and when I said I'd do it. And I wanted to, really I did."

"If it makes you feel better, I only made a phone call, Harry."

"No," he said, firm now. "Don't try and minimize what you did. You bothered, and I'm so thankful for it." He took a heavy sigh in and let it go, staccato through his lips. "And all after I hurt you so much ten years ago."

Instinctively she knew where his hand would be, so she reached out, her fingers finding it alongside his hip. For a second, she felt them flinch, before they relented to her touch.

"Nothing that happened ten years ago matters anymore."

"It matters to me. I shouldn't have abandoned what we had. Not for anything."

"Well, I'm still here, aren't I? You didn't lose me."

"I did for a while."

"I'm not going anywhere, Harry." All those conditions, the variables that she had at first tried to ignore, peeled away then. She wasn't there because she had nowhere else to go. She wasn't there because she was buying time until she could get the jewelry back, or any of the other things she had wondered over the last few days. In her heart she knew that while she might have been there for all those reasons to begin with, she was now there for one thing only. For him. With Harry she felt like herself, rediscovering all those hidden feelings that she had never quite been able to deny.

Deciding to leave the letters that evening she closed her eyes as they slipped into their makeshift bed. Only moments later she felt his breathing deepen as he slept with her in his arms. She thought to herself then how she had been lost all this time, but not just from Harry. She had also been lost from herself. Now she was only grateful, that here beside him, she felt as if finally she'd been found.

Chapter Nine

Mirepoix, France, Summer 1981

After that day in his shop when she lied about her age, Frances didn't see Benoit again before she had to return to England. Yet every remaining moment in France was spent thinking about him, lost in thought about what he was doing. "Why are you so quiet?" Amélie would ask, and Frances would just laugh and say, "Never you mind," and that was the end of it until the next time she would ask. What was there to tell? A brief touch, not much else. Their lips had met, but that was all. What they had shared was barely even a kiss. Still, thinking about it made her mouth curl into a smile she seemed powerless to prevent.

Now, a year later and back in France after months of desperate letters and promises of something more, she was without him again. His first letter had come as a total surprise not a few weeks after she had returned to England. For months she had been picturing her return to France, had imagined them spending every moment together, but now she was there she found herself stuck in a cycle of torturous days without him. Where was he? Had she done something wrong?

On that first night after arriving back in Mirepoix she had gone to his shop just as they had arranged in their letters, although she had to admit now that it hadn't been what she was expecting. Longing poured from his letters, yet that first night they had struggled to even touch. It had taken them until the following day, when she had reassured him that she wanted to, for him to kiss her in his car, pressed into the seat by his weight with the seat belt straining at her neck. It hadn't been how she imagined it, but still it had filled her with that same rush as the first night he had touched her over twelve months before. But now, after three wonderful weeks of seeing him every day, he had simply disappeared.

The best-case scenario was that he had become stuck on a work trip. It was the only possibility she allowed herself to entertain. He'd told her about one such trip in his letters, after he'd dashed to Munich on the trail of a Matisse. *People will do a lot to acquire such a masterpiece, my love. Munich was beautiful, but this time I regret it was a false lead. That beautiful painting will find its home again one day, be returned to the people with whom it belongs.* She had asked Benoit to show her the painting he had been chasing after she arrived in France. "You remembered," he had said, seeming coy as he hurried to find a book. Falling heavily on his knees, he set the book down, then leaned over her, turning the pages with careful consideration. "Ah," he said when he found it, his fingers brushing the image of a woman sitting in an armchair, a fan in hand. "Such a beautiful piece. What is she thinking, this muse of his?" Frances found herself fighting back tears as she stared at the woman's face, such melancholia in her expressionless gaze. It was almost as if the woman in the painting had known right from the moment she sat for the portrait that at some point she would be lost. Would end up somewhere she didn't belong. "I thought the lead was good, but we were not able to find it. Perhaps next time." Then he had turned the key in the lock, kissed her mouth, and they didn't talk about the painting again.

Without his company, Frances walked to the village, moped around the market, always making sure to check Benoit's gallery, that was now a fine shop filled with myriad trinkets. There was no little sign in the window to explain his absence. To kill time, she browsed the shelves of Edouard's bookshop, eventually buying a copy of *Anna Karenina*, a book Benoit had suggested she read. Once again, she told Edouard to keep the change, all the while wondering if her guilt over the first edition theft could somehow be intuited as they exchanged polite conversation.

Frances was sitting on one of the benches in the shade of the farmhouse when she saw Amélie for the first time since she had arrived in France. Clematis dripped from the wall above her, and the aroma of basil was tickled free from the nearby pots by a warm breeze. It was before noon, and she was in the full glare of the sun's relentless ascent. While the light was bright enough to blur the features of the oncoming girl, there was something so familiar about the way she skipped along, that same gait she remembered from their time together the previous summer. Frances reached for the glass of fresh lemonade at her feet.

"Have you seen him?" Amélie asked as she arrived before her. It was their first meeting this year, and Frances couldn't help but wonder about the three weeks she had already been in France, and how she could explain her lack of communication. Bringing her hand up to shield her eyes from the sun sharpened Amélie's features. They had changed, chiseled by another year's maturity, but that alarmed her less than her friend's question. Did Amélie know about Benoit? "He is, how you say," Amélie continued, pausing to find the correct English, "dreamy?" She sat down on the bench next to Frances and reached for the glass of lemonade, as if they had been together only the day before.

"Who?" Frances asked.

"They say he is from Toulouse," Amélie continued with a sigh, staring into the distance where a small group of painters sat around their subject. "That one day he will be a famous model in Paris. If he goes, I will ask him to take me with him."

Frances breathed a sigh of relief. Amélie wasn't talking about Benoit, but rather the naked man on the grass about ten meters away. He was lying with his arms outstretched as if he was sunbathing, his legs splayed out so that everything was on show. Twenty or so busy artists worked intently and tried their best to capture what they saw. The truth was, Frances had hardly noticed him.

"Yes, he's nice, I suppose."

Amélie scoffed. "You suppose? Do you not see what I see?" Frances supposed she didn't. "So, tell me. How is it that you have not written to me in so long? And how now that you are here in France you tell me nothing of your arrival? Have I done something wrong?"

Frances felt her insides swell with guilt. "No, of

course not." For six years they had spent their summers together, always writing letters between visits. It had been Amélie she had told when she first got her period, when she first kissed a boy, and when she first got a job in the local library back home. "I've just been really busy helping my aunt."

"You forgot me."

"I didn't," Frances protested.

"Don't worry, I forgot you too for a while."

They were quiet for a moment. Frances knew that Amélie was hurt, but she hoped time would allow it to pass. It was impossible to undo what had been done, and she couldn't tell her about Benoit. She wouldn't understand even if she did. In that moment she wanted to, but she knew it would have been a mistake. Benoit was adamant they were to be kept a secret.

"I saw your aunt on the way in," Amélie said. "She told me that he is going to be there for at least another hour. I could sit and watch him all day." Frances glanced over, took in the curves of the model's naked form. Thoughts of Greek gods came to mind, the expertly carved bodies rendered in marble that Benoit had shown her in one of his books. The model was what people would think of when asked to describe the perfect man. But still, Frances felt nothing, no spark, no flame of heat that she felt when Benoit was near.

"I'd rather do something else," Frances eventually said. "I'm not sure he's my type."

"If he is not your type, I don't even want to think about what you might like." She pointed at the naked man and sighed again. "That is the perfect man. But anyway, if you don't want to sit and stare at it, let's do something else. It's a beautiful day, and so hot still." It was true that the recent storm hadn't cleared the air. "We could swim if you like?"

Last summer Amélie and Frances had been inseparable. Even after the brief liaison with Benoit in his shop, she had remained by Amélie's side. A couple of times Frances had suggested they sneak round the back of the market square to smoke cigarettes, hoping they would bump into Benoit again, but never once had he been there. Although she thought of him it was easy enough then to slip back into her childhood customs. By then Frances knew every inch of Amélie's body, the way it looked, smelled, moved. They had ridden bikes alongside each other, swam naked without a second thought in L'Hers river not five minutes away. Now, after Benoit, the idea of swimming naked alongside her felt a bit strange.

"I haven't got my costume," she said, feeling self-conscious to even consider it now. What with her body used for other things that she only did with Benoit.

Amélie rolled her eyes then poked her in the chest, the tip of her fingers prodding into the soft flesh of Frances's left breast. "You have not changed so much, and neither have I. We have seen each other before, non?"

Arrogant in her certainty that Frances would follow, Amélie stood up and headed for the trail that would wind all the way down to a soft grassy bank by the river. Just as she disappeared behind the first line of trees Frances took one last look to the gate, and when she saw no signs of Benoit's little 2CV, hurried to catch up with Amélie.

"The water is so warm," Amélie shouted as Frances stood on the bank of the river, the point at which L'Hers succumbed to topography, relenting into a natural curve. At this point the course of the river took two routes, parting like a smiling mouth with a treelined islet between. Their side was shallow, rocky in places, which kept boats away. They had never been disturbed while swimming, not even once. Glancing down to the sloping riverbank Frances saw Amélie's discarded sundress. Her sandals and underpants were kicked off there too, partially covered by long grass. "Come on, what are you waiting for?"

Amélie called once more, before dipping under the water and coming up with a splash.

Self-consciously, Frances slipped off her clothes, taking her time with her laces. Then, once naked, she hurried into the water, cool enough to relieve the heat of the blistering summer day. Amélie smiled, reassured that their friendship was unchanged, and proceeded to splash Frances with copious amounts of water, just as they had six years before. And once she was in the water Frances found that her anxieties and apprehensions faded into the shadows, left on the grass with her clothes in the shade of the towering conifer trees that kept them safe from view.

Frances had no idea how long they had been in the water, but her skin was pruned and her stomach rumbling by the time they scrambled up the bank. By then her nudity had ceased to be a problem, and so they sprawled out on the long grass as they had during summers before, her skin itching as the soft blades bristled against it. Carelessly she picked at the petals of a daisy.

He loves me, he loves me not.

"Do you remember that boy who used to walk around with a placard on his shoulders?" Amélie asked after they had been sunbathing for a while. "The one who sold dry baguettes?"

Frances wrinkled her nose at the memory. "The one that smelled bad?"

"Yes." Amélie nodded. "His name is Gaspard and, well, we did it."

"Did what?" Frances asked, but even as she finished asking the question, she knew the answer from the smile on Amélie's face. Her mouth stayed open, her words unfinished. "Oh my god. You did it? With *him*?"

"He doesn't smell anymore," Amélie reassured her.

"Still," Frances said, half horrified for Amélie, and half for herself that she was yet to do it. Benoit had promised that he was happy to wait. Now the thought that Amélie was doing it with Gaspard, the boy they had ridiculed the year before, made her feel like a childish prude. Maybe, she thought, this was her chance to settle her concerns. "What was it like?"

"Perfect," Amélie said, but even as the words left her lips she was already correcting herself. "Well, that's not really true. I guess it was okay. It was all over pretty quickly."

"Did it hurt?"

"No," she said, shaking her head, and breathing heavily at the memory. "Well, maybe a little at first, but then not at all. Maybe he has a small, how you say . . ."

"Amélie!" Frances slapped her with one hand and

used the other to cover her mouth to stifle her giggles as she rolled onto her back. Amélie was giggling too, so much that her sides began to hurt. Of course, Frances was no stranger to the male form; it was impossible to remain uneducated in that topic while living at her aunt's retreat, La Muse. But her only information regarding that particular part of the anatomy was aesthetic, and even though she had felt the hard, knotty lump of Benoit's body when he suggested she touch it through his trousers, she didn't really know what it did or how it felt. That was when her heart began to beat to the rhythm of panic. Was that it? Is that why he had left?

"You have to tell me everything, Amélie," she said, the panic still there on her face, the frown etched vertically between her eyes. "I have to know."

Amélie sighed with the pride of a girl with one foot into adulthood. "What can I tell you? It was all over in about two minutes." Then suddenly shy in a way she had not been before. "But I liked it. We did it a lot by now."

Frances looked at the grass and suddenly felt unsure about wanting to be lying there. Benoit was out there somewhere, and she had to find him. Very suddenly she had to find him and show him. The air was cooling, a cloud passing overhead, as if giving her a nudge in the right direction. Reaching for her dress, she slipped it over her head and got to her feet.

"What are you doing?" Amélie asked.

"I have to go."

"Where?" she said, sitting up. "Why such a rush?" Frances hurried her feet into her sandals. "Do you have to go and meet Benoit?" As soon as she heard the name Frances stopped lacing her sandals and stared at Amélie. "It's okay, don't worry. I didn't tell anybody."

Frances's mouth had gone dry. Peeling her tongue from her gritty palate she spoke, her words crisp around the edges. "What do you think you know? Benoit is a friend of my aunt's."

Amélie shrugged. "You don't have to lie. I saw you together. I was walking up the road toward the town and I saw you climb into his car. I stopped, watched for a moment, and then he reached over and kissed you. It was just a few days ago."

"Who did you tell?" Visions of people who knew, like the gossiping women in the café, raced before her eyes. Was Edouard quiet with her the last time she was in the bookshop? She had thought it was her guilt over the book, but perhaps he knew what she had been doing with Benoit too. That was why he had disappeared, then; he had been cast out, or her aunt had driven him away, or told the . . . No, she couldn't even allow herself to imagine it. Jumping to her feet, she scrambled about for her second sandal.

"Why are you being like this?" Amélie asked. "I didn't tell anybody."

Frances shook her head. "I don't believe you. You told people and that's why he's disappeared. That's why he's gone."

"He hasn't gone. He went away on business."

Frances stopped in her tracks. "What?"

"He went to Paris and he's coming back tonight or tomorrow. Anyway, why are you getting so upset? It's not like it's something serious. It's barely even real. People wouldn't even care if they knew. This is not England, you know."

Frances wished she had something to throw at Amélie then, but she had already laced her second sandal. With her heart rocketing along she took a deep breath, tried to calm her rage. "It is something serious. Benoit loves me." It felt magical to say it aloud. There was no point in denying it anymore.

Amélie shook her head. "The only time that what is happening between you and Benoit becomes something serious is when your aunt finds out." As if they were discussing nothing more than a television drama, Amélie rolled onto her back at the same time she rolled her eyes. "That's if she doesn't know already."

Frances ran as fast as she could until she was back in the gardens of the farmhouse, Amélie's words sounding in her head. By then the artists were gone, and she was close to tears. Her eyes were all hot, like they were when she fought with her father about her studies, when he insisted she become a doctor. Tears were going to leak out all over the place, she knew it. The idea of somebody seeing her and asking what was wrong terrified her, as she wasn't altogether sure she wouldn't just tell them the truth. So instead she headed to the artists' barn, bursting in, panting and wiping the first tears from her cheeks. Before she even knew what she was doing she had snatched up the nearest pot, filled with brushes and speckled in paint, and launched it at the dusty ground with a shout, watching as it shattered into hundreds of pieces. Still she felt no better, so she grabbed a second pot and was about to launch that too when she heard a shuffle behind her. Standing there in a pair of jeans and a white T-shirt was the life model from earlier. With his clothes on she barely recognized him at first.

"Why don't you put that one down, eh? Breaking it won't help."

It felt heavy in her hands, ready for smashing. Sometimes she did that, broke things to feel better. Never changed anything when she did, though. It never helped. Carefully, her hands trembling, she set the pot back on the side, the model nodding his head as if he agreed with her course of action.

"Want to talk about it?" he asked, and she shook her head. "Are you sure? Sometimes it's just what you need."

Perhaps it would help her to talk, she thought. Perhaps she could find somebody who agreed with her, who would tell her that things would be okay. That Amélie was wrong, and that what she shared with Benoit was as serious as it could get. But how could she talk about Benoit, or the way she felt? How could she tell this stranger that she loved a man almost fifteen years her senior who had told her that they must keep what they had a secret?

"And sometimes it doesn't," she said, deciding against it.

Racing away, she fled through the other side of the barn without another word. Out in the open she ran across fields, through the door and into the farmhouse, before rushing up the stairs. Once she was safely in her room she flung herself onto the bed and cried, Amélie's words still ringing in her ears.

Her aunt called her downstairs shortly after that, and that evening they ate their way through a cassoulet with a rich tomato sauce and great big hunks of rabbit. Her aunt complained about cats in the barn again, breaking her pots, and Frances wondered if that was the conclusion she had reached or if she knew the truth and was angling for a confession. Had the model told her aunt? The very idea of it added fervor to her concerns. If Amélie knew about Benoit, it was more than a possibility that other people knew too. The food was too heavy, too rich in her stomach, and it stuck like bones in her throat.

"Auntie, I'm not feeling very well."

"What's wrong?"

"Time of the month," she lied. "I'm not hungry. Mind if I go and lie down?"

Moments later she was back in her bedroom, under the covers. All she wanted to do was shut out the world, forget that any of this was happening. It all felt so unfair, so messed up, in that special way the whole world rotates on your own personal axis at sixteen years of age. Yet despite the predicament she found there was only one thing that settled her.

Thinking of Benoit and the things he used to tell her made everything else fade out. There was a moment the week before, where they had pulled in at the side of the road after leaving the beach. Breathless and sweaty, he whispered in her ear, "It all feels so easy with you,

Frances. Life is so simple when I think of how I love you. Do you know how many hours I spend thinking of you? How I long to touch you, kiss you, listen to your sweet voice? You are the best form of escape from real life, Frances. All I want is you."

Feeling better at the memory, her heart rate began to slow, and the sick feeling that was lingering in her stomach settled. Because there was no denying it; she was his fantasy. Surely, she thought to herself then, alone in her bedroom, waiting for him to return, there could be nothing more real or important than that.

Chapter Ten

They worked with what felt like carnival spirit over the next few days. The things they continued to find amazed them; more baby clothes, magazines, and broken models of naval ships, enough that they could have opened a specialized eBay store. Even the phone calls from Mr. Lewisham, reminding him about the auction and how he still had to go down to his office and sign the transfer papers, couldn't dampen their mood. Harry put it down to the van arriving, getting rid of what they had decided was junk. There was something about the development of space, the freedom to move around in it. Even Elsie could move around freely now and popped in often with biscuits and steaming dishes of stew to keep them nourished, brandishing her walker to highlight the changes. Physical weight seemed to lift from Harry, a lacuna in which he could rest in place of what his mother had chosen to keep. It was almost like permission, to both move on and to stand back to take a glance at the woman his mother once was. To hold items she had lovingly kept, and to gain insight into periods he hadn't known her. Photographs were littered like fossils through rock, and told the story of a beautiful girl who collected since she was small, items like flowers and leaves, then tins and dolls, who eventually became a woman, and who for a period of time at least, took very good care of a child. Those were the only photographs in which she smiled.

But what also played a huge part in creating the joyful spirit of those days were the little notes Tabitha had left him on the fridge. The latest read *stop snoring* with four exclamation marks. It was easy, simple, and intimate. It was everything they used to be.

Almost.

Because there was one very obvious part of what they used to be that they had not revisited. Passion had stoked their relationship the first time round, and he couldn't fail to notice the response of his body when he had woken not three days before with Tabitha in his arms, the tightness in his trousers when he felt her head pressed against his chest in the little nook by his armpit, sleeping just as she always used to. But physicality aside, it had been no more difficult when he woke a day later to find her already awake, eyes wide and smiling, staring at him while he slept. That morning she'd been holding his hand too. Along with that realization came an avalanche of feelings he couldn't outrun or control, tangled like the silver necklaces they'd found that could never be recovered as individual pieces in their own right.

With all that whizzing about in his mind he burned through piles of junk like wildfire could tear through cities. He tossed dolls, coats, electrical cables, and Walkmans and CD players, some of which were still in their wrappers or boxes. Endless numbers of vinyl records appeared beneath other objects, along with four turntables on which they could be played.

"Shall we put one on?" Tabitha asked him as she sifted through the titles. "There are some real oldies here."

"Sure," he said, not paying attention. But when the music started it took him straight back. Sinatra sang out, and they listened to "Strangers in the Night" while working through the wreckage of his mother's life. The song transported him to the first house he ever stayed in as a foster child, where that night he must have heard the song ten if not fifteen times. Maybe it was only once, and he just remembered it differently. Who knew? But what he could remember with certainty was the question that wouldn't leave him that night. Where was his mama? Where had the life he knew gone, and the people he loved? It had been a question to which he had never really received an answer.

After a while Tabitha stopped again. "Hey, Harry," she said, appearing from behind a pile in the dining room, the door to which they had forced open the day before. "Come and look at this. I think I might have found something of yours."

Harry hurried to the dining room, thoughts racing toward the box. In her hand he saw an old sticker album from the 1986 World Cup in Mexico. Leafing through the thick pages he found that it was almost complete, just a few faces missing. While he hadn't thought of it since the day he last touched it, it was in that moment a simple and precious treasure. Something he had loved and cared for still in this house, found after all that time. It was filled with childhood hopes and dreams, a testament to the hours of anticipation and effort he put in at the time. But not only that. It was also proof of the time he spent with his mother. Every day she would take him to the village shop and buy a pack of stickers, and they would work on it when they got home, sorting through the repeats, filling in the gaps, sorting out the swaps for friends he didn't have because he was yet to go to school. But the memory was bittersweet, because he knew that by the time the final of that World Cup was played he was living somewhere else, where Frank Sinatra provided the soundtrack. At some point in those weeks of sporting celebration something happened so terrible that she had left him to somebody else's care.

"You remember doing this?" she asked as they sat on the bottom step of the stairs.

"We did it together," he said, turning page after page, remembering her hand on his, helping him place the stickers corner to corner. The scent of her lavender perfume when her face was close to his. "I can't believe it's still here." Besides the photographs, it was the first piece of irrefutable evidence they had found that he had ever existed there at all. "I want to keep this," he said, aware that his words sounded broken, his voice cracking.

"Then let's put it somewhere safe so it doesn't get lost again." Carefully taking it from him, her fingers brushing his, a thought began to form in her mind. Tabitha knew what it was like to live with promises from the past not being fully realized. She didn't want that for him. Their attention was interrupted when the doorbell rang. Turning to Harry, she saw that he was as surprised as she was.

"Did you organize for another pickup?" he asked as he stood, wiping the corner of his eye.

"No," she whispered, aware that her hands had begun to shake. Butterflies swarmed in her tummy. Had Daniel found her? Gripping the bannister, her heart was thumping as Harry moved past her. It was the same feeling she always had when Daniel arrived home, when she wondered if she had done something that day to upset him.

Just before he opened the door, Harry caught a look at Tabitha. There had been foster homes in which he had been afraid, knew that if he did the wrong thing, he could expect a good clip around the ear. He remembered the feeling of fear, and he was sure that was what he saw crossing Tabitha's face now. But what about the doorbell had made her so afraid? Who did she think was there? Not wanting to raise attention to it, he reached for the handle on the door. He was sure he heard her take a sharp intake of breath as he opened it.

Cast in the soft light of a cloudy evening, before Harry stood a man in his late fifties, maybe early sixties. A tweed jacket and a V-neck sweater gave him the appearance of a weary professor. His hair had thinned at the top, was straggly around the sides, and strands of what remained wafted back and forth in a light breeze. The man took a step back, taking one last look at the nameplate on the side of the house.

"This is Nook Cottage, Awkward Hill, isn't it?"

Harry nodded and Tabitha joined him at his side. "You look so young," he said, shaking his head. "I thought for a second I'd got the wrong place."

Harry looked to Tabitha for an answer, and he noticed that her composure had returned.

"Who are you?" she asked then.

The man smiled, let out a little chuckle. After pulling a handkerchief from his pocket he mopped his sticky brow and wiped the end of his nose. "Well, more importantly, who are you?" the man said, looking to Harry. "I'm rather hoping that you are Harry Langley, Frances's son."

"Well, yes," he stumbled. "I am."

"Ah, fabulous." The man shoved his handkerchief back in his pocket. "At last I have found this place. I thought at one point that I might not. I'm Steven," he said with a smile, holding out a hand. Neither Harry nor Tabitha took it. Eventually he let it fall. "Steven Bradbury. I'm your late mother's ex-husband."

Several moments passed when Harry could do nothing but stare into space. Facts he had known his whole life seemed set for a collision with some extinction-level event. As far as he had known his mother had never been married. But if she had been at some point, had she married his father? Gazing at the stranger's features he began searching for familial characteristics in the lines around the man's eyes, the curve of his lips and structure of his bones. Could he find the genetic traces of his roots in the pink pug nose, or in those green eyes that shone deep and steady like flickers of jade on a cavern wall?

"It really would be better if I could come in," Steven Bradbury eventually said. "I appreciate that this must have come as a bit of a surprise, me turning up like this, but I have some very important paperwork for you. I'm sure, deep down, your mother would have wanted me to give it to you now that she has passed."

Harry nodded and stepped back. Tabitha felt for his hand and gripped it tightly in hers, but she noted this time that his fingers didn't respond to her touch. "Come through," Tabitha said, pulling Harry out of the way and closing the door behind them. She was glad, on some strange personal level, that they had made the house a bit more presentable, because she could see from the wide-mouthed look on Harry's face that Steven's reason for being here was as unexpected as his presence. But she wasn't sure whether she trusted Steven yet. After all, lots of people knew about Frances's death. Could he be a chancer, here to take advantage of a person stuck in grief? "Head through that way, Mr. Bradburn," she said, wondering if he would catch her trick. He did.

"Bradbury, dear. Steven Bradbury."

Even still, she was going to check him out online as a matter of priority. Scam artists were always working their way out of the shadows and into the homes of vulnerable types. Harry certainly didn't seem like he knew who he was, and she wasn't about to let Steven scam the man she . . . Well, it just wouldn't be right. Harry was vulnerable, and she was the only person likely to stand a chance at protecting him if Steven had undesirable intentions. But then she remembered the jewelry that Daniel took and wondered if he hadn't already been exploited.

"Take a seat, Mr. Bradbury. I'm going to put the kettle on." Harry's eyes widened at the idea of her departure. "I'll just be a moment," she reassured him, before disappearing into the kitchen.

After flicking the kettle to boil she grabbed her phone and did a quick search on Facebook. It took a couple of false starts and some frustration with the signal, but there he was, Mr. Bradbury's smiling face alongside another woman who looked nothing like the pictures of Harry's mother. Listening to what sounded like a one-sided conversation, mumbled voices making small talk, Tabitha hurried some tea bags into cups while she absorbed as much information from the profile as she could, like birthdays, a holiday he had been on, and which town he lived in.

"Harry was just telling me that you have been helping him clear a few things out," Steven said as she walked back through with a tray. "Frances always was a bit of a collector."

"Yes, a few things," she confirmed, and handed him his tea.

"While we were married, we lived in Poole, Dorset. I was born there, you see." That was one fact he had right according to his online profile. "We were only married for a few years, at least in the truest sense of the word, but it took me an age to get rid of the things she collected over that time. In the three years we lived together she must have purchased more than one person could use in a lifetime." Harry thought of the volume of things they had cleared out and realized he could understand that. "Ten years and one new wife later and I am still finding things your mother had left behind. She even had things up the chimney."

Harry looked to Tabitha, and she understood that was one place they were yet to look for the box. "When were you married?" Harry asked.

"Oh," Steven said, sitting back in his chair, taking a

sip of his tea. "It must have been late eighty-six, until the early part of ninety." Was that why he was given away? Because she wanted a new life with this man? He was abandoned for a new marriage? "All a bit of a whirlwind to be honest with you. We met one weekend in Blackpool, when they'd got the illuminations up, and we hit it off. She was quite good fun, your mother, when the mood took her. Had the sort of character that made you think anything was possible and that nothing really mattered. We were married within the month. I went from single bloke to having a wife in the space of three weekends. My parents thought I'd gone bloody mad."

"What about Harry?" Tabitha said, looking down at Harry from where she was sitting on the arm of his chair. He looked away, didn't know what to say. All Harry could think about was that Steven couldn't have been his father. Tabitha turned back to Steven. "Didn't you know anything about him at the time?"

"Not a dot," Steven said, a smile on his face that spoke of a tender sort of kindness, as if he knew things should have been different but understood he was powerless to change the past. "It wasn't until years later when I found all the paperwork that I discovered the fact of your existence. But I can tell you that I did wonder then whether if we had been raising you together, things might have been different for us, and I certainly wish she'd given me a chance to try.

"You see, I couldn't work out what it was at first, what was wrong in our marriage. Some days it was as if I was a king, and other days she treated me as if I was nothing. Her mood could change faster than the English weather. I used to enjoy the ups at first, but then I realized she was just as ill during those fun moments as she was when she could barely get out of bed. Manic depression we called it back then, but it's got another name now I suspect."

Tabitha looked to Harry, wondering what he had experienced in the ten years they had been apart that she was still to learn. Harry did nothing but shrug.

"Then one day she just told me it was over. It had all been so chaotic for a year or so before that, I can't say there wasn't a part of me that wasn't relieved. After she left, I cleared some stuff out, and I came across a lot of important things. I tried to reunite these documents with your mother at the time, but she was a bit elusive, and I had no way of tracing her. I even came here once but she wasn't living here at the time." Tabitha looked down to Harry, who was sitting with his hands in his lap, his head bowed. "Or maybe she was and just didn't let me in. I did think about posting them through the letterbox, but I remembered the mess she created in my home and I just couldn't risk them getting lost. So, I hung on to them. When she died there was a joint insurance policy still in our name that we had both forgotten about, and so the legal firm called me to deal with it. That was when I remembered all this," he said, patting the paperwork in his lap, "and I knew I had to try and find you. They might not be addressed to you, but you have always been the true owner of these documents. It's only right they are returned to you now."

It seemed a struggle as he reached across with a pack of paperwork as thick as *War and Peace*. Harry didn't make to take it, so Tabitha took it instead, making a thud as she set it on her knees. Paper crinkled as she leafed through the first pages. Before her she saw letters written over thirty years before, by social workers, doctors, and then others that looked to have been written by his mother. Copies of court documents and a ruling that said something along the lines that Harry was better off remaining in foster care.

"It's all in there, Harry," Steven continued. "Every letter she ever wrote. All the while she was with me she was asking for information. Although she never asked to bring you home, she never forgot about you either, and always wanted the best on your behalf. The truth was that she was in and out of hospital so frequently that it would have been impossible for her to care for you properly, especially after she left me. While we were married there was some semblance of normality, but I'm pretty sure that faded with time. But she never could let you go, Harry. You've got to realize that. Never, not for one moment."

Tabitha looked down to Harry to see him curling in on himself, like the petals of a beautiful flower at night. "Harry, are you okay?"

When he didn't say anything, Steven spoke. "Look, this is a difficult thing, and I don't want to intrude. I've no place here in a discussion like this between a man and wife." They both looked up. Such an assumption could have been funny in another situation, but at that moment the humor was lost on them both. Another reference to what could have been. "I've no idea what it's like to be left like that, or how it might make a little lad feel. But if knowing what's written in there," he said, pointing to the file, "and that she always regretted what she did might help you understand, then what's in that file might be just what you're looking for. And on the top, that's about the insurance claim. I don't need it and you are the heir to your mother's share. All you need to do is let Mr. Lewisham know." He stood up and made to leave, and Tabitha attempted to follow. Harry didn't move. All Harry could think was that Steven seemed like a nice man. He wasn't his father, but he wished maybe he'd had a chance to try to be. Steven held out a hand, palm up, and patted thin air. "You stay there." He let his head fall to the side as he took a final glance at Harry. "Looks like you two have a lot to discuss."

Less than ten minutes before, Tabitha had been sure that Steven Bradbury was there to stir up trouble. In a way that was exactly what he'd done, but not quite how she had expected. Now, with the door closed behind Mr. Bradbury, she was standing in the hall-way trying to remember just what exactly Harry had told her. The fact he had lived away from his mother wasn't new, but what was it Mr. Bradbury had said? Something about being left? She had assumed that the decision to place Harry in care was carefully made, involving all the right authorities. Now she wasn't so sure.

Harry was still in the chair, his head still low when she returned to the living room. The file that Steven had brought with him was in his lap, and his fingers were gripped around the edge like an eager little boy holding a present at Christmas.

"I don't mind if you want to go," he stuttered.

After a quick rearrangement of the furniture, shift-ing the chair in which Steven had been sitting so that it was right up close to Harry, Tabitha sat down. "Why would I want to go?" His hand was hot and sweaty when she took it, and although his fingers didn't curl around hers like they had before, there was the tiniest flicker of his muscles, and that minimal response was enough for her to know that space wasn't what he needed. "I'm going to stay here with you, like I already said I wanted to. Nothing has changed. And if you want to explain what is in that file then you can, and if not, it doesn't matter." Their eyes met, his mouth opening as if he wanted to speak but had lost the words to express how he felt. It was as if he couldn't believe anything of what had happened in the last few minutes, least of all her willingness to stay.

"Don't you want to know the truth?" he asked. All of it was there in that file no doubt. All the details, the history that made him question everybody's intentions and believe that nobody could ever genuinely love him. The reason even now, when he knew that he was in love with Tabitha, that he couldn't bring himself to believe that she could ever really love him in return. "Don't you want to know the way I ended up in care?"

She smiled. "Of course I do. But it's your truth to tell, so you should only tell it when you're ready."

The tightness in his expression softened then, a relaxing of the fine lines that framed his eyes. Something was leaving him, a fear perhaps, an easiness grown between them that neither could have expected to root so deeply after ten years apart. Harry felt it too, knew in that moment that if he were ever going to tell another person the truth, he would never get another chance as good as the one he had right then. He would never be with another person who would make it so easy for him to be himself. And he wanted so much to be. Trust in another person was something that had always evaded him, an elusive idea left for other, more fortunate people. But he wanted to know what it was like, to trust somebody with all the little details that made him who he was. Losing Tabitha was a terrible thought, but no worse than the realization that if she didn't really know him, she wasn't really his in the first place.

"It might take a while."

"Take all the time you need," she said, leaning back in the chair. "I'm not going anywhere, remember." So, while he told his story over the next couple of hours, she didn't let go of his hand once. Everything he had held back, the secrets about his past were all laid out on display. Harry waited for her to flinch, to pull back, to wonder how she had ended up there, with him. But she never did.

Tabitha had always believed there were moments

when feelings changed, events that solidified choices and emotions. With Daniel it had been his offer to live with him when she complained about her parents, when he had promised to never let her go when she was so hurt that Harry had. Now, there with Harry, he was offering her a glance into the unedited version of his true self, the version so many of us keep hidden from the rest of the world. A moment of true vulnerability through choice, instead of fear. He had chosen to express the hardest parts of his emotional history, and there was something infinitely more precious about that than anything anybody had ever given her before. Truth was being unearthed right before her eyes, like an ancient roman villa appearing through soil, revealed in all its truth and beauty and broken fragility, and she was the first person to witness it.

As he finished retelling his story, she shuffled over to his chair, took him in her arms. It felt right to her then to place her lips on his skin, to kiss him, to let him know that she felt just as she always had, only more deeply in love than ever before. Her hands were shaking but that was as sure a sign as any, she thought, that what she was doing was right. The most important of things always made her feel nervous, no matter whether they were good or bad. Right or wrong. The first kiss was innocent enough, the taste of his skin sweet like vanilla. When he didn't flinch, she dared a second, her lips trailing as she pulled gently away. Her breath bounced warm from his skin. But as she went in for a third, he shifted. His body tensed, then moments later he pushed himself from the chair.

"I should feed the pigeons before it gets too late," he said.

Then for a moment he paused. Was he looking for her to convince him otherwise, or to give him permission to leave? Choosing the safer option, she said, "Okay, Harry. I'll wait for you here." Then she watched, feeling helpless, as he walked away.

Half an hour passed before she ventured out. With enough room on the little wall in the back garden, the night balmy with a clear star-filled sky, she took a seat alongside him. His inhaler was at his side, and she supposed he had taken a puff. The patch of mud behind him might once have been a lawn but now the dry grass sprouted like Maldivian islands from a sea of soil. It was like the rest of the house, forgotten and uncared for. Harry was holding a pigeon in what looked to be a tight yet caring grip, stroking its little head while it cooed. He had it nestled against his chest, whispering soft caring words that Tabitha couldn't quite decipher.

"Are you okay?" she asked as she sat.

"I don't know." He took a big breath in and kissed the pigeon on the head before popping it back in the coop. Tabitha thought perhaps she understood why he kept them now in ways she couldn't have hoped to understand before. "I'm sorry I didn't tell you the truth about being abandoned." For the first time in his life, he had revealed the full extent of it, all the details; how his mother left him on a bench in the hope that somebody would find him. "I didn't want you to think less of me."

"I could never think that way about you, Harry. What happened when you were small isn't your fault. You didn't do anything wrong."

He nodded as if there was a chance he might agree. "But that's what I always thought. That was how I felt." She reached up and placed an arm across his shoulders. "Seems like maybe she was ill for a lot longer than I realized."

"It looks like it. If she was ill like Mr. Bradbury said, it must have been very hard if she was on her own when she had you, managing an illness as well as a newborn."

"I think so," he said. Although he had always loved his mother, and wanted nothing other than to make her happy, there was always a part of him that remained angry with her. Every day it would surface, that negative feeling like a trusted old friend trying to guide him back to an earlier chosen path. That voice seemed quieter tonight, and in its place, there was a kinder version of himself, one that wondered how hard it must have been for her. "Perhaps if I'd had other family members it would have been different. Somebody who could have helped, or at least helped me understand. Her parents died on the night I was born, but wasn't there anybody else?"

"You mean cousins or something?" He nodded. "We could search if you like."

"Yeah, maybe," he said, but from the absent way he picked at the mud, she doubted he was certain. "For a while I thought maybe she had died, you know? Like she had always intended to come back, but something awful stopped her. Then I would dream about her coming back, reclaiming me. It wasn't always easy being a foster kid." He looked away then, up at the sky and into some unknown fragment of the past. He closed his eyes, and she realized there would always be things she didn't know about Harry, no matter how long she stayed with him.

"How did you find her?"

"By chance. I'd just started at the care home, and one of the residents who'd been there for rehab was being discharged. Her transport hadn't turned up, so

I offered to drive her home. That was Elsie. When I drove into the street, I just knew it. I stood there looking at this house, and I knew that was where I'd lived. I knocked on the door, and she answered, and that was the day I came home, told you. I know you think I was looking for her and kept it from you, or that I'd known all along, but it wasn't the case."

"She must have been so glad to see you."

"I have no idea. I wanted so badly to make things right for her. I just wanted to commit, you know, to being her son. To helping her when she so obviously needed somebody, but I never really managed it, and in the process I lost you too."

"Don't say that. I'm sure she must have been pleased to have you back, even if she couldn't express it. Look at what Steven said, that she was always interested, always writing letters to Social Services for updates and wanting to know how things were. And you haven't lost me. I'm here now, aren't I?"

"I know," he said, revealing just a hint of a smile, although he struggled to believe it. In the gray light of dusk he gazed at her face and thought how it had changed. How time had slipped them by. He had told her the truth, but rather than feeling closer to her as he had hoped he might, he felt raw and exposed, as if he had been scrubbed all over until his skin was pink.

How could she love him, as he wanted her to, now that she knew? It wasn't possible, was it? "I just wish she'd managed to tell me all this before she died. I wish I knew why she'd kept all this stuff, when she couldn't keep the one thing that should have been most precious to her. Why couldn't she just tell me the truth?"

"Some of the most important things are the most difficult to say," she said, and then both of them were quiet.

After Harry complained that he was tired they went inside and stretched out on their makeshift bed, both slipping under the covers. It was only seconds before Harry closed his eyes, yet Tabitha couldn't settle. So instead, she watched him for a while, wondering what he would do if she reached over and kissed him again. But no matter how much she wanted to, she knew he was vulnerable in the wake of Steven's visit. Now wasn't the right time, no matter how much she wished it was.

His breath soon slipped into a resonant burr, so she crept from underneath the quilt and pulled the box of French letters close, fingering one from the stack. Trying to piece together a story with her broken French, a story that she knew belonged to Harry's mother, felt like a huge responsibility. But perhaps between these letters and the file Steven had returned to Harry, they could build a picture of who Frances really was. Maybe it would give Harry the answers he so desperately needed. His mother's story had no end yet, and Tabitha had no idea whether the love spoken of in those letters ever had a chance to flourish. Love, she thought then, should always be given a chance.

Once she was sure she wouldn't disturb Harry, Tabitha curled up behind him and let her arm rest over his body. With her front pressed along his back, she thought of how many nights he must have spent in his life, wishing he had somebody to cradle him in his sleep. Perhaps both as a child and as an adult. What she wanted to do was to reach back through time, hold him when he was scared or lonely, and tell him things would be okay. That somewhere in the future she was there waiting for him, and that if he would let her stay, she would ensure that he would never be alone again. Then, almost without warning, as big a shock to her as it would have been to Harry if he had been awake, she found herself whispering in his ear. "I'm falling in love with you again, Harry. I don't think I've ever really stopped. If that's not what you want, you better find a way to stop it, because I already know I can't."

Chapter Eleven

A light wind bothered their hair and chilled their fingers as they stood outside the theater, the trumpet case swinging at Harry's side. Standing at the top of the steps, flyers fluttered on a nearby notice board and a can rattled along the pavement. The stage door was propped open with a chair, and they had seen a few people coming and going, all of whom had raised a smile and uttered a brief hello as they passed.

"You see," Tabitha was saying while Harry nibbled on his lip. "They seem like nice, normal people." He nodded, but he didn't seem very sure. He looked down at the case, as if he couldn't quite believe what he was doing. "You promised, remember?"

"I know I promised."

"So, are you going to go in there or what?"

He wanted to, really he did. To renege on his promise a second time was unthinkable, especially in the shadow of what they had become since Steven Bradbury's visit. To wake up with her next to him, often her hand in his, was magical, gave him a sense of hope for the future that he would never have been able to imagine before. Never had he established what he did wrong to make people leave, but he was sure that not doing what they wanted was a strong contender. The thought of Tabitha leaving him after coming back was unbearable. He had to go in. Yet even though he had spent all last night tootling on the trumpet and oiling the valves in preparation, his nerves beat loudly in his chest today like a cry for a battle that he was in no way ready to face.

It was just then that a woman climbing the steps to the theater stopped in front of them. Wearing a dark pair of trousers and a light cream blouse with a floral scarf draped about her neck, Tabitha thought she was probably in her sixties.

"Judging by the size and shape of that box," she said, pointing at the case in Harry's hand, "I'd say that's a trumpet." He nodded, tried a smile that he was relieved to see reciprocated. "That would place you right in front of me, yet I don't know your face. Maybe I'd recognize the back of your head. Give me a twirl." She laughed, and Harry wondered whether she was serious. Motioning then with her finger, as if using it to swirl paint, he did as instructed, while at his side Tabitha struggled to stifle a giggle. "No. Never seen that shaggy mop of hair in my life. You must be new. Are you planning to join us?"

Harry hesitated but Tabitha saw her chance. "Yes, he is. Hi," she said, stepping forward. "I'm Tabitha, and this is Harry."

"Pleased to meet you, Tabitha," she said, shaking her hand. "You too, Harry. Well, I'm always ready to strengthen up our brass section." She gave a bolstering punch to the air in front of her. "Give the woodwind section a run for its money. You'd never believe how many flautists there are in there, and how they drown us out. Play well, do you?"

"He does," Tabitha said.

"Good. Then let's get a move on. The bandmaster doesn't take kindly to latecomers." She reached for his hand. He let his slide alongside hers and they shook. "I'm Polly."

"Harry," he said.

"I know. Your friend here already said. Now come on, you might as well come in, unless you want to get wet." Angling her gaze to the sky Harry followed, and saw that overhead the clouds were turning black. "Oh, damn it," she said, when they heard voices coming from inside. "If we don't go now, we're going to be late."

With a friendly shove from Tabitha he found himself following. Listening out for Tabitha's footsteps behind him, he was reassured by the rhythm of her walk. As she hurried along, Polly explained how the band had formed over twenty years ago, and how they had traveled far and wide doing performances. Up the stairs and through the foyer, they passed a set of double doors into the shadow-dark auditorium. But ahead the stage was lit, an early star in a dusk sky, and something told him that he was going to be okay.

As he stepped inside, he felt some of the magic of those past performances return. The idea of stepping up onto the stage and putting on a show . . . how he loved it. Yet the theater was beyond anything he knew from his past, the space almost regal with the red velvet seats and huge drapes half open on the stage. Heading down the aisle he forgot about Tabitha for a moment as the thirty-member-strong orchestra came into view. There were violins, cellos, a couple of saxophones, and an obscene number of flautists just as Polly had told him. Then he spotted the brass section. He could hear somebody running through the C scale on a trumpet, echoed on a tuba just behind.

"You better go and introduce yourself to John,"

Polly said, breaking the spell. She pointed to a man who was wearing a red blazer and had all the formality of an army major. A little baton already in his hand. Polly gave a roll of her eyes. "He takes it all very seriously but he's a nice enough chap." Harry turned to see Tabitha taking a seat in the front row. "I'm going to go and get set up. Go on, then," Polly said, giving Harry a little shove. "Go and make yourself known."

Harry soon found himself sitting in a spot alongside a boy in his late teens, facing John the bandmaster, who indeed, he established, was not there to welcome time wasters. Reassured to see Tabitha smiling and flashing him the occasional wave, it reminded him of one of his foster mothers, the pride on her face, and the wonderful comments she had made after a performance before one Christmas. "Exceptional," she had said, lamenting on the way he held the notes, and the way he didn't even have to look at the music. "You brought such feeling to the piece." Would Tabitha say something similar today?

Reaching down he flicked the clasps on the trumpet case, lifted the lid. Although his trumpet was there, just as he expected, it was not the gleaming brass instrument, bright under the stage lights, that drew his attention. Instead it was the note, poking out from between the keys, a little scroll of torn paper. Carefully, as if uncovering something precious from the earth, he prized it out, unfurled the message. Tabitha's writing. *You only have to be scared for as long as you tell yourself you deserve nothing more.* Placing it on the stand, he read the words over and over, until it was time to bring the mouthpiece to his lips. For the first time, even though he was still scared, with Tabitha's message right there before him, he did it anyway. Because in that moment he thought to himself that perhaps he really did deserve something more.

Remarkably, he thought as they played through a few numbers, he could still do it, his fingers finding the right notes as he followed along. Punctuating the merits of his performance were a few mistakes, and they didn't seem to go unnoticed by John, who cringed each time he heard a note out of tune. Reading the music was harder than he remembered, and he kept missing the sharp notes, making his part sound flat. But anytime he was feeling uncertain in his abilities, or that perhaps he wasn't cut out for this, Polly gave him a tap on the shoulder and whispered that he was doing great. At some point, after nipping outside for a phone call, Tabitha returned with wet shoulders and damp hair, and dare he say it, there was something reminiscent in the look on her face that gave him permission to hope she was proud of what he had achieved.

After the practice finished, while rain drummed the rooftop, John informed him that he had put in an admirable performance, and that he was welcome to come back the following week. That they had a show in six weeks' time that he would love Harry to take part in. By then Harry felt exhausted, beaten almost, but despite all that found himself agreeing to join. His muscles ached and his teeth were sore from where he had been pressing against the mouthpiece. Yet he felt alive and strong. After a quick chat with Polly to confirm that he would see her next week, he hurried, almost running down the aisle to where Tabitha was sitting.

"Well?" he asked as he arrived alongside her. "What did you think?"

"I thought you did great, Harry." They hadn't discussed their growing closeness, or the way he often found her skin pressed against his, but when she reached down and took his hand it felt entirely natural to walk out of the theater that way. "I know a little place nearby where we can get something to eat. Let's go there to celebrate, and you can tell me all about it."

So that was how they left, Harry holding his trumpet in one hand, his other clasped firmly in Tabitha's grip. Rain drizzled, the might of the earlier storm passed, but they didn't seem to notice it. They walked along the river, through the park, while she listened to him talking about the pleasure of playing in the band. Stealing small glances her way, he looked for confirmation that she had really enjoyed it, and that she was proud of him. But his gaze was never reciprocated. Instead she seemed attentive to her surroundings, as if looking for something she'd lost. Was he boring her? Had he blown it by talking too much about himself?

"I'm sorry," he eventually said. "I'm going on and on."

"No," she said, stopping on the pavement. Shaking loose from his hand, she turned to face him. For a moment he was panicked, thinking that perhaps she had already changed her mind about something they hadn't even discussed or agreed upon. Was it the revelations in his file? But then she smiled, stroked his arm, and it reassured him a little.

"Yes, Tabitha. I haven't stopped talking for a moment. I'm out of practice, and don't know when to give somebody a break."

"It's not that, Harry. I love listening to you tell me about it. I'm sorry if you think otherwise. It's just . . ." Words failed her, blocked by the pain that was forming between her eyes. "Just, um, look." She paused. Then she crossed her arms across her chest and although Harry was no expert in body language, he could sense something had changed, and that he didn't like it.

"About this," she said, moving her hands back and forth between them. "I don't know what this is, and I don't know what to do."

The minute Harry sensed where this was going the fear gripped him. His gaze became turbulent, chaotic glances going this way and that. He wanted so much to tell her how he felt, but the risk was so great. What if he pushed her away?

"Do about what?" he asked.

"About us, Harry. Maybe I'm wrong, but I know what it feels like to me, and I have no idea whether you feel the same way as I do, or whether I'm just being crazy or whatever or . . ." She paused to catch a breath. "Now *I'm* going on and on."

"It's okay," he said, desperate for her not to stop because if she did, he might be expected to fill the silence himself.

"It's just, I don't know what to say or do. I don't know what's right, or whether I'm just being stupid." Pressing the base of her hands at her eyes, she let out a little grunt. "Jesus, Harry. Say something, wouldn't you?"

"I don't know what to say. I'm scared to say the wrong thing."

Her loose arms slapped against her legs. "Just tell me how you feel? Am I the only one who feels this is becoming something? That we could be something to each other again."

What did she say? That they could be something? So, she really did feel something for him after all? Even after everything she had learned, was she telling him there was a chance she loved him? If ever there was a moment to tell her the truth of his feelings it was now. After everything she said, surely he couldn't have got it wrong.

"No, Tabitha, you're not the only one."

A held breath whickered from her lips, and smiling then, she began almost laughing. But something was holding her back. "Phew," she said, mock-wiping her brow. Or was she sweating? He thought maybe she was, and he thought then of how she always used to sweat when she was nervous, like when she took her driving test and came back with great big puddles stained dark on her dress. Every muscle in his body was shaking too, his tongue so dry he could feel it cracking. Yet he was smiling too. Tabitha felt something. She really did. And more than that, he had been honest about how he felt, and she was still there with him. "Finally, we've said it. I thought maybe I was misinterpreting something, but I'm not." She sighed, touched her head. "So, now the next bit."

The relief seemed transient at best. "The next bit?" Harry asked.

"Yes," she said, her smile faltering. "I want this, really I do. But it means that I have to tell you something. I mean . . ." She trailed off again. "Look, I have something I need to explain. Something really important. Why don't we just go to the coffee shop, and I can tell you everything."

"Okay," he said.

Telling him about Daniel wouldn't be easy, but he had been so honest with her that she had to share the truth with him. Not just about her marriage, but also about what she was beginning to assume, in light of Daniel's silence, was the permanent loss of his jewelry.

They continued on, hand in hand, all the while Tabitha trying to get the story straight in her mind. But just then she felt the resistance as Harry stopped. He shook her loose, and headed back up the street.

"Harry, what is it?" she asked, but he said nothing. Instead she followed, until just a few shops back up the road he stopped again, staring into a window. Moments later she arrived at his side, and she felt her heart sink as she saw what the shop was, at what he had seen in the display. Three necklaces that once belonged to his mother, sitting in the window of a grotty pawnshop, a place that she had never seen before in her life.

"Oh my god, Harry," she said, her hand rushing to her mouth as if she was going to be sick. "Harry, you have to let me explain."

"My mother's necklaces," he said, his hands against the window. "One of the last things of hers that I remember her having." Slowly he turned to face her. "How could you, when you knew what they meant to me? They belonged to her. To me. I thought you understood how . . . I don't know, but I thought . . ." He searched for something else to say, but nothing came. A sense of foolishness washed over him, and he wanted to run, get away, consumed by an urge to disappear. As the picture of what had happened became clearer to him, he found he was gripped by a deep sense of shame, as if he was responsible for what he saw before him. As if his own inadequacies had facilitated it. Shame had followed him around his whole life, and he had long understood that once it got its grip on you, the slightest slip could feed it. It came rolling in like a storm, bringing the conclusion that he had let his mother down again by somehow not being enough. He didn't know how exactly, only that it was the truth.

Tabitha took a step back, brushing her wet hair away from her face as the rain began to fall hard. Unable to articulate what she wanted to say with any certainty, she began to cry. The explanation was too big in the face of the jewelry in that window. It would have been possible if she had the time to paint the correct picture, but with the evidence before her she had reached the final scene of a tragedy before she even had the chance to introduce the characters. Just a moment longer was all she'd needed, but now the chance to do this properly was gone. Now it was too convoluted, like the knot of necklaces she hadn't been able to untie.

"I'm sorry." It wasn't good enough, but in that moment it was all she had. "I'm so, so sorry, Harry. I can explain this, I promise you."

"Is this why you brought me here?" he asked. "Is this your way of confessing?"

"No, Harry, I didn't know. It's not what you think. It's my husband, he . . ."

"Husband?" He staggered backward, his hand on his head. His face began to crumple, as if he was about to cry, then it morphed into something altogether scarier. He was devastated. "You never said you were married. You said you felt something for . . ." With tears in his eyes he looked away. He had been foolish; he knew that now. He'd been right all along. Creating a life with Tabitha was nothing more than a dream.

"It is over with him, Harry. Or at least I want it to be. It's just very complicated. You don't understand."

"Wanting it to be over is the same as saying it's not

over at all. You're still married. I've been so stupid to think you could feel something after all that time. You only stayed because of the box, didn't you? Because you think you can find it for yourself?"

"No," she said, trying to sound firm.

"You want to pawn that too?"

She was shaking her head, pulling at his arms. "No, Harry. No. You've got it all wrong. This is not what you think."

But he wasn't listening, not even looking at her. "I'm so stupid. All this talk of feelings and what we might be and all along you've got my mother's things in that place for money. Why did I trust you? Why did I let myself believe in something that could never happen?"

Reaching forward she gripped his arms. Rain struck Harry's face, but he barely flinched. "You trusted me because you love me, and because you know that I love you. This is not what you think it is. Please give me a chance to explain." She reached out to hold him again, certain she could put this right. But he was already pulling backward, unable to look at her. "Harry, don't do this," she said as the distance between them grew. "Please give me a chance to explain." Moments later he broke out into a sprint down the road, desperate to put as much distance as he could between him and the woman who had almost made him believe it was possible to rectify the past.

Now he knew it was not.

People always left. People always screwed you over and abandoned you. He was better off on his own. Maybe he really didn't deserve anything more than what he already had. And that night when he arrived home, exhausted from walking for miles in heavy, wet clothes, he locked the door and sat in the dark. Shivering, the sound of a swollen brook struggling outside, he thought of his mother. He had so much love inside him for other people, and yet it had led him nowhere, a beautiful trail to an impasse from which it felt impossible to return. All those emotions wasted because they hadn't made a scrap of difference to the course his life took. You couldn't escape who you really were. So instead he picked up his trumpet case and threw it at the mirror, sending it smashing into jagged chunks on the ground. Standing over it he saw himself, distorted as Picasso might have painted him, should he have been worthy of a portrait. It had always been impossible to escape his own identity, but as he gazed down at his altered image, he began to understand that not even he really knew who he was.

Chapter Twelve

Mirepoix, France, Summer 1981

E ngland always faded like a bad memory over time while she was in France, yet during those days without Benoit, it seemed as if she was living two lives. In England she was Fran, could speak the language of her birth without thought or stumble. She didn't exactly fit in, but she did the things her peers did, and tried to get along. Nothing remarkable, unless you were troubled by her love of collecting innumerable curiosities and an occasional bout of the blues. That was what her father called it when she struggled to get out of bed. But in France she was somebody else, and that person she became when she stepped across the threshold of her aunt's farm had no restrictions. It was that version of herself that she wanted to be. Not just on holiday, but all the time. Fran loved that girl, welcomed her in.

The French version of Frances never lingered in bed for days, unable to find the will to get up. At least she never had before. But without Benoit, that strong, capable girl was slipping away.

"Try not to smash any of those." She turned upon hearing the voice she didn't recognize, to see the face that she did appear in the farmhouse kitchen. "They are nicer than those dirty old jam pots in the barn."

Setting the soapy plate back in the sink, aware her face was flushing from the reminder of her behavior yesterday, she forced a smile. It was the life model who had seen her smash the pot in the barn. "I wasn't planning to," she said. The model stepped forward and picked up a clean cup and poured himself a coffee, moving with a casual nonchalance, a look of disinterest that was at odds with his effort to speak to her.

"That is good." His accent was stronger than Benoit's. She liked it, a reminder that she was far away from home and not the girl she was there. "Because plates work better when they are whole."

"Was it you who told my aunt that the cats broke those pots?"

Without looking her way he sat down at the table and helped himself to a leftover croissant. The wait for an answer was agonizing. "They are everywhere," he eventually said. "Crawling all over the fields. Madame

Henrietta came out to the barn, saw the broken glass. She made some assumptions and I let her believe it. I wasn't sure that it would have been a good idea to tell her that you smashed it on purpose."

When she sat down next to him his gaze finally met hers. Up close she could see that he was quite attractive, just like Amélie had said. His face still had the softness of youth, yet had also crossed the threshold into manhood. Although she couldn't see it now, she knew his stomach was well defined and his shoulders broad, his form like the men she had seen on the covers of her mother's romance novels. Knowing what his body looked like underneath his clothes made her conscious of her own body. Was he wondering about her in the same way that her mind was considering him? But her thoughts centered around one thing, and it wasn't how attractive he was. Instead, all she could think about was how much less wrinkled his face was than Benoit's. How soft it looked. How young.

"I'm Alex," he said, and held out his hand. "It is nice to meet you." She reached for it and they shook.

"Frances."

"Yes, I know. I heard your aunt calling you yesterday. You are not French, *non*?"

She shook her head. "English. I'm here for the summer."

"Your family?"

"In England. My father doesn't like to travel."

He seemed surprised, as if it was the most ridiculous thing he had ever heard. "And your mother?" Alex seemed confused by the arrangement, his head bobbing to the side, waiting on an answer.

"She works a lot too." She was glad of that truth. Her home life wasn't easy, her father obsessive with his rules and regulations. He liked order, straight lines, and didn't seem to like very much at all the things that accompanied being a teenager. Homework was to be done in the bedroom, and even there the little rubbed filings left behind from an eraser could stoke his moods. Their jobs were very stressful, her mother often reasoned, which meant that by the end of the day there wasn't all that much left for Frances.

"So," Alex said, licking his fingers as he finished the last morsel of pastry, "I suppose that means I can ask you to go out with me without having to worry about what your parents will say?"

The hot flush of embarrassment raced to her cheeks, made worse by the intense summer heat that rippled from the baking ground. Instinct told her to shout no, and to tell Alex that it was because she loved Benoit. But she couldn't say that. It left her wondering if it wasn't for Benoit, would she say yes? Alex was very attractive, just a little older than she was. This almost-man before her should be exactly what she wanted. Only, she realized, he wasn't. Not at all.

"Like on a date?" He nodded and she had to stop herself from laughing. Amélie would be so disappointed in her. "I don't think so."

"Just one date. Come on, you might have fun."

Her laughter got the better of her. "I don't even know you."

"That's the idea of a date." He shrugged. "To get to know somebody. Come on. Why not?"

"Because she is no more likely to be interested in the likes of you than she is the likes of me, Alex."

They both turned around at the same time. There stood Benoit, his face more serious than she had ever known it. A deep crease cut vertically through his forehead, skimming the top of his nose. He looked remarkably handsome, she thought, that little scar on his cheek, the flop of dark hair across his face. He was wearing a pair of glasses, and she thought he looked smart and intelligent in a way a man as beautiful as Alex never would. Dressed in a pair of white trousers, a light blue shirt, with a gray twill jacket thrown over his shoulder, he looked like everything she had been missing. He had a high forehead that shone in the sunlight and seemed to lend him an air of importance.

A brush of stubble across his chin a stroke more casual than usual.

Alex stood up to greet him, moving back from the table, putting distance between himself and Frances. *"Of course, Monsieur Bonnet,"* he said, slipping back into French. *"I'm sorry, I didn't even know you were back."*

It was as if he had forgotten Frances was even there. Benoit made him nervous, she realized, something that for the first time today she could say they had in common. All her fears over Benoit's absence came simmering to the surface.

"That is obvious. Now, why don't you get back to the warehouse," Benoit suggested. *"The new shipment is in, and it needs sorting. Plus, there is another delivery due later this afternoon. It is coming from Austria, and it is very important. Be sure to deal with it straightaway."* He looked down, smiled briefly at Frances and for just a moment she felt as if the whole world was looking at her. *"Well, what are you waiting for?"*

Without so much as a wave Alex headed from the kitchen and toward his bicycle on the far side of the courtyard. Frances watched as he pedaled away, dust kicking up behind him. When he disappeared from view Benoit sat down at the table and placed his hand on top of hers. Instinctively she looked around for her aunt, uncle, or anybody. They were alone.

"Mon amour," he said, but it did little to settle her fears.

"Where have you been?" she dared herself to ask. Trembling, she linked her hands together, forced them into her lap. If she didn't she would have jumped from her chair and into his arms.

"I'm so sorry. I wanted to call but I didn't feel it was right. Too risky." He motioned toward the house, and she understood that he couldn't have risked calling. Realizing that she had hoped he would only made her feel young and stupid.

"Yes, it would have been a risk," she conceded. It was a reminder of what they really were, something hidden, of which other people would disapprove. It was a reminder that she had sold him a mistruth, allowed him to believe she was older than she was.

"I wanted to, though. You must believe that."

"I want to." Amélie's words rang in her head from the day before, the insinuation that what they had wasn't serious. "I just missed you, that's all."

"And I have missed you, which is why I have canceled all work for this morning." Her lips curled into a smile. All her fears shed like an unwelcome skin. Nothing had changed, Frances could see that now. "I have a lunch I must attend," he conceded, "and I'm afraid I really cannot get out of it, but until then I am all yours. Meet me in the same place? I have something to show you. Two things in fact?"

That made her smile. "What?"

Chuckling to himself, he stood up when he heard somebody coming. Breath brushed her skin as he leaned down and whispered in her ear, "You'll have to wait and see. But don't be too long. I might die if I don't get to touch you soon."

Runnels of sweat ran down her back as she ran all the way up the road. Arriving at the abandoned farmhouse halfway between her home and the village, she quickly found him, parked in a small clearing not visible from the road. As had become customary she opened the door and climbed into his car. A song was playing that she'd heard before, that sounded like summer and spoke the words of her heart. *Is this love that I'm feeling?* Gazing across to Benoit, she wondered if there was anything but love that this could be.

"You look so beautiful," he said, leaning over and kissing her on the lips. The unfamiliar scratch of stubble brushed against her cheek, the conversant softness of his lips. His hands were strong against her, moving up and over her arms and into her hair. "I have missed you so much."

"I've missed you too," she said, smiling, feeling like things were right again in the world. "Where do you want to go today if we only have a couple of hours before your lunch?" His promise of a full day came to mind, but she pushed the thought aside.

That was their usual routine, taking a narrow country lane toward a strange village, somewhere they were unknown. Sometimes they would park in a secluded spot and do things that made her blush by the time she arrived home, and other times they would walk, or sit in a café, where he would ask about her life and the things she liked. Those were her favorite times, even though she often had to lie; she couldn't talk about school. On those days she felt the same heaviness that hovered above her in England, that fog she could never seem to shift, but she always tried to hide those moments the best she could. Benoit had never asked about them, but her aunt did. She always knew when the fog was coming. "Is it happening again?" Aunt Henrietta would ask. "Can I do anything to help?" To which Frances always said that it wasn't and that she was fine. Sometimes she thought that was the truth, but other times she knew it was a lie.

"I don't want to go anywhere," he said with a chuckle. "Today I want to show you things, remember?" He pointed toward the farm gate. "It is usually closed, *non?*"

"I guess so," she agreed with a shrug, failing to see the importance of the change and having no clue whether the gate was usually closed or not.

Reaching into his pocket, he pulled out a key and dangled it before her. "This farmhouse has been in my family for two centuries. It will be my new home. I want to share it with you," he said, starting the engine. Her breath caught in her throat, and she felt her hands tingle as she gripped the hot leather of the seat. Share it with her? Share his home? The little 2CV chugged into life. "Let's go."

They followed the driveway all the way to the back of the property and parked. As she stepped from the car, she saw the tall building rise before her. It was narrow, and must have been relatively untouched for the best part of fifty years. The blue paintwork on the window frames was peeling and rotten, some of the plasterwork damaged too, exposing sections of old wattle and daub that made up the skeleton of the building. Swathes of lavender grew wild outside, and somewhere in the distance she could hear the gentle trickle of water that reminded her of home.

"What do you think?" he asked as he arrived alongside her.

"I think it's beautiful," she said, and she really meant it. But despite the sight before her, her mind was on what he had said just a few moments ago. He wanted to share this place with her. What did he mean by that? Did he want to show her, or share a life together within its walls?

"There's a lot to do," he said, taking her hand, "but we have plenty of time for that. Let me show you where we are going to be spending our time from now on." With his hand hot in hers and their shoulders brushed together, they ran giggling from the car toward the house. He turned the key in the lock and moments later they were inside.

Dust and debris littered almost everything she could see, but it was clear that somebody had been in there ahead of them, making a degree of effort to clear it up. A grand oak table punctuated the center of the room. The surface had been wiped clean and a vase of cut lavender sat in the center. Had he done that for her?

"I missed you so much," he breathed into her ear as he backed her against the closed door. Pushed up close against her body, he reached to turn the key in the lock. "Four days away from you is too much. I won't do it again. I can't."

Moments later his lips brushed against hers. He

kissed her hard at first, eager and rushed, before he slowed down, his touch gentler as his mouth caressed hers. His hands moved from her face to her chest, and over the curve of her backside. Nerves kept her touch centered on the small of his back, because the first time she had done that he had groaned, and she had taken it as a good sign. Soon, she knew, he would move under her dress, slip inside the edge of her underwear. Only once had she said no to him, and after that he had pulled away and whispered his regrets, lamenting his foolishness that she could ever feel for him what he felt for her. Feeling stupid then, she had spent the rest of that day wondering if she had messed things up. It had taken another three meetings before he had tried again, and that time she had let him, just like she did now. Only now she was thinking of Amélie, and the fact she had already done so much more.

"How can I go without this?" he whispered again, before scooping her up, her legs wrapped around his waist.

Unbalanced, they staggered through to the lounge where there was a small table and a settee. Setting her down on the sofa cushion, he knelt before her, pushing her knees apart with his size and moving in close. The weight of him made it hard to breathe, and she felt trapped. But she knew that she wasn't, could have left at any moment. Sometimes it surprised her how much she wanted him, but other times it was as if she was suspended above her own body, looking down on herself, with the need to stifle an overwhelming urge to get up and run.

Benoit pulled away. "Frances, I feel that you are angry with me today," he said as he sat back on his heels. "Either that or your mind is somewhere else. It's okay," he said, when she went to disagree. "Perhaps you have every right."

"Do I?"

"Of course," he said, using the skirt of her dress to cover her legs. You know how much I want to be here with you, but sometimes work forces me to leave. It will always be that way I'm afraid to say." Again, Amélie's words came to mind, the insinuation that this was not serious. "What is it, *mon chérie*? There is something wrong with you today. Do not hide how you feel. Tell me."

"It's nothing really."

His hands slipped from her legs as he pulled back, and her body moved instinctively toward him. It was terrifying to her, just how much she wanted him, and just how out of control he made her feel. Just moments apart and her body missed the weight of his, where only moments ago it feared it.

"Then tell me. If it's nothing serious there is no reason for concern."

"It's exactly that," she said, almost annoyed with him for his choice of words, and herself for being childish enough to let her emotions get the better of her. "We're not serious, are we? We're nothing, not really."

He knelt up. "How can you say that?"

"Because it's true." Pushing past she moved toward the table. When she looked up he was still on his knees, facing the wrong way. Where she had found the courage to tell him what she was feeling she didn't know, but she had to make the most of it before it peeled away and left her for good. "You say you want to be with me, but you already know you have to leave for a lunch. You want to come here, kiss me, and go." Dust clouded her body as she slumped in another chair and spoke with more sadness than she had intended. "Back to your real life."

He crawled over to where she was sitting, arriving between her legs. He opened them out, and after kneeling up between them his face met hers.

"*Mon amour*, but kissing you is all you will let me do." He stroked her hair from her face and kissed her cheek so softly. "You told me you are not ready for the love I have for you." His lips moved down to her neck, his words little more than breathy whispers. "And I respect that. I do not want to push you."

"Maybe I need to be pushed."

"No," he said, shaking his head. "When you are ready to move forward you will know."

"What if I told you I was ready?" Angling her hips toward him, she sensed his body tighten with desire. "If I said I wanted to do it now? Right now, here in this place."

His breath was short, his voice shaky. "Then I would ask you if you were sure."

"And I would tell you that I've never been sure about anything in my life, until you. I would tell you yes, as many times as you wanted to hear it."

With that he pulled her close, and with one fluid movement he scooped her up. Charging toward the stairs she felt her hair tumbling over his shoulder, the thud of his heart against her chest. Heavy feet led the way up the staircase, the wooden treads creaking with urgency. Kicking open the first door on the right, she saw a bed, crisp white sheets with lucent drapes drifting at an open window. The room smelled freshly cleaned, but then it could have been the lavender simmering from the garden below.

"Is this what you wanted to show me?" she whispered, her words catching against her dry tongue.

"No," he said, placing her feet on the ground. Moments later he was standing behind her, his arms around her waist. He produced a small broach, the stones inside gleaming and bright. It was of two birds sitting on a nest, one with its wings cocked ready for flight. "This is for you."

Her fingers shook as she touched it. "For me?" He nodded. "It's beautiful."

He turned her around and pinned the broach to her dress. "They are lovebirds." His hands caressed her face as he leaned to whisper in her ear. "Like us, lovebirds can never be separated." Then his fingers moved toward the strap of her dress, letting them slip beneath. Just a second later he brushed it from her shoulder. Smiling gently, he waited for permission. Her smile gave it, and this time she didn't try to stop him. Her dress fell to the floor, weighted down by the broach.

During the act he was gentler than she anticipated. His earlier kisses were rough and eager, but now it was as if they had all the time in the world. He kissed what felt like every inch of her, even in unmentionable places that she had never expected him to go with his mouth. Time disintegrated around her, and as she roused from an unexpected sleep not an hour later, she found him sitting at her side, stroking her hair, wearing just his pants and a necklace.

"I have to go." She nodded, smiled into his hand as it moved to cup her cheek. There was a chill in the air, but his skin was warm and soft against hers. "Thank you for trusting me. All those letters and I think only now do you understand how I feel for you."

"I always knew," she lied, but it was a good lie, one she wanted to be true. Glimmering against his skin was a low-hanging necklace. Reaching up, she took hold of the pendant. It was a Magen David, the star of which brushed low against his abdomen. Attached to the star was a key. "What's this?"

He took the necklace from her hand and looked at it as if he was seeing it for the first time. "Something dear to me. I never take it off."

"I've never seen you wear it before."

He winked. "You've never seen me naked before."

Her cheeks reddened, and she pulled the sheets up higher. "So, are you Jewish?" she asked, recognizing it as a religious symbol.

Their eyes met as he let go of a heavy breath. He shrugged his shoulders.

"Maybe in one lifetime I might have been, but not

really. My parents were, and it was their faith that made me who I am today. Their beliefs, and the things they experienced have shaped my journey."

"And therefore brought you to me?"

He smiled, lay down next to her. "I suppose so." He kissed her then, let his hands trail the curve of her body. "We can come here whenever we like. It is our home now."

"Okay," she said, unable to stop smiling. That fog that sometimes caught her had never felt so distant. Amélie was a stupid girl, she thought to herself then. They were as serious as could ever be. It was undeniable. "Do you think this is where will we live forever?" she asked, and she was so happy when he smiled, because she knew then he really wanted it too. Oh yes, Amélie, she thought. She could shove her silly ideas right where the sun didn't shine. Benoit made her feel as if she was the queen of the world.

"Forever and ever, and we will live happily ever after like a fairy tale." He kissed her once more on the lips, smiling and laughing. "Now come on. We must get going. I'm already late for my lunch meeting."

By the time she arrived back at the farm the painters were already focused on their subject. Yesterday she had felt shy to see Alex reclining on the lawn, but this time when faced with the anatomical parts that set him apart as different from her, she felt changed from the girl she was the day before. Now the way bodies fit together was no longer alien to her. She had given part of herself to Benoit that day, she knew that, and in doing so she had loosened herself free from her childhood. Benoit too must surely be changed by her. If there was part of her that belonged to him, surely there must also be part of him that belonged to her.

A while later she saw Alex approaching the bench on which she had been sitting for the last hour. Unprepared for questions, she reached up and pulled the lovebirds broach from her dress. His body was a tangle, his arms fighting for space as he pulled his shirt over his head.

"Sorry about earlier," he said, scratching the back of his head when he arrived before her. Gazing anywhere but at her, she realized that Alex was embarrassed, perhaps humiliated that his agency had been brought into question by Benoit. "I had to help Monsieur Bonnet with his delivery." He sat down on the bench alongside her, scratching his feet back and forth in the dirt. Reaching into his pocket he pulled out a pack of Gauloises cigarettes. When he offered her one she considered taking it, but she didn't. "You should have seen what came in."

It felt strange to hear him speak of Monsieur Bonnet, her Benoit, who only that morning had been lying naked in a bed alongside her. Thinking of it that way, as if she was in on some sort of secret, made her feel powerful.

"Oh really? What was it?"

Thick cigarette smoke clouded around her as he stood up and beckoned her away. "Not here." Moving away from the courtyard and from where people could overhear, she followed, sitting as he had on the stile that marked the start of the trail that led to the river where she swam with Amélie. From his back pocket he pulled a Polaroid photograph.

"What is it?" she asked as she took it from him.

"He got it on his trip to Paris. It's called The Klinkosch Box. You know it?"

"No," she said. The box was metallic, silver in color, and decorated with cherubs and filigree. The base of the box looked as if it was molded like flames.

"Well, this has been lost since the Second World War. This photograph proved its existence. Look, see the date." Alongside the box was a newspaper, and the date was from just a few months before. "Monsieur Bonnet has been looking for this piece for years. Now it has been found. Worth thousands on the open market."

"So, he's going to sell it?" she asked, wafting the photograph back and forth.

"No. It is almost impossible to sell it."

"Then why does he want it?"

He shrugged. "I guess because it belongs to him. This piece has come home. You see, when . . ." he began, before being interrupted.

"What are you doing?" The sound of Amélie's voice surprised them both. Alex motioned to the photograph, and then to her pocket, so she slid it away, out of view. *"What are you hiding from down here by the river?"* Amélie asked when she arrived beside them. When they were in company, Amélie always reverted to her native language. For the most part Frances could keep up, but she always worried there was something she was missing. *"Not from me I hope."*

"Of course not from you," Alex said, continuing in English. "Why would we be?"

Amélie arrived alongside Alex and smiled. "Oh, no reason. *Sauf si vous avez un secret?*" Frances did have a secret. Biting her lip, she just about managed to stop herself from smiling about it.

"Amélie, *nous ne sommes pas des enfants,*" said Alex. "Only children keep secrets. We were just talking."

"Hum," Amélie scoffed. "It is too hot for that. Too hot for anything but swimming."

"You want to go swimming? Perhaps *you* are a child," Alex said, rolling his eyes. Frances wondered when they had become friends. Only a few days before it was as if Amélie had only just met Alex. "You must be crazy. The pool is too far, and I do not have a car."

"Ah, but you do not need a car where I want to swim," Amélie said, pulling off her sandals. "You see, Alex, you are wrong. We all have secrets, even Frances, *non*? And I bet Frances is not a child anymore, right, Frances?"

"Amélie," Frances said. The hot blush of shame flushed across her cheeks. Did Amélie know what she had done? How could she know?

Moments later Amélie slipped into the cover of the trees. But just before she disappeared from view, Frances and Alex watching as sunlight glinted from her tanned skin, she pulled her dress over her head to reveal her naked body. Bones and muscle flexed gracefully under her skin as she walked, a lure and certainty in her movements that Frances envied.

"Where is she going?" Alex asked, unable to take his gaze from the trees, from the idea of something that was slipping just out of reach.

"To the river," Frances said. "I think you're supposed to follow."

Alex nodded, turning back to Frances. "Shall we go together?"

"No. I don't feel like swimming." Showing her body to Alex was the last thing she wanted to do today.

"You know," Alex said then, gazing to the ground. "I don't have to go with her." Reaching out, his fingers brushed against hers. "We could go somewhere else, together if you liked?"

"No, no," she said, pulling away. "You go." The way he looked at her reminded her of Benoit. It was how he had first looked at her when they met at the book fair, as if there were things he wanted to say but was too unsure about saying them. "I'm going for a lie down."

Turning to walk back to the house, she sensed that Alex was still standing there, uncertain whom he should follow. Frances stopped, then turned back.

"Alex," she called. "What did you mean about that box coming home?"

"I meant into Monsieur Bonnet's family. It was taken from them, and now he's taken it back. But it must be kept a secret as there are some people very unhappy about that fact."

"If it's where it belongs, why are people unhappy?"

"Because ownership is nothing more than perspective, Frances. Not to Monsieur Bonnet's mind, but to some other people." He inched toward the trees. "That box will stay in his new home," he said. "He owns the farmhouse just down the road."

"Yes," Frances said, smiling as she thought of the photograph in her pocket. "I did know that."

Lying down on the bed for a while, she thought of the morning behind her. It was impossible not to smile at the thought of what she'd done. But the memory of Amélie saying she wasn't a child anymore made her concerned. It was as if she knew what they had done, as if it was written all over her face for all to see, or simmering from her, the scent of a childhood lost. What if other people found out? What if her aunt discovered the truth? She would make it harder for her to see him. She had to ask Amélie what she knew.

Sweat dripped from her skin as she hurried through the trees toward the river. But when she arrived at the water's edge, her skin clammy, cicadas buzzing all around, Amélie and Alex were nowhere to be seen. Certain that she was alone she pulled her dress over her head and slipped into the water.

As she swam, she thought of the house, the broach Benoit had given her, and the box from the picture that Alex had shown her, and that she still had in her pocket. The thread of doubt that lingered at the back of her mind was still there, but this time it was not over Benoit's whereabouts. This time it was her own lie.

We all have secrets, even Frances, non?

What would Benoit do if he was to discover her lie? Her real age. He thought she was nineteen, almost twenty, but she had only just turned sixteen. It was just a number, she told herself. But if that was the case, why had she kept it a secret?

Earlier that day, when their bodies were no longer separate from each other, he had whispered in her ear that he wanted her over and over again. Eventually she had said, "I'm yours, Benoit," and she had felt him grip her harder then. "Say that again," he had begged, and so she did, over and over until they couldn't breathe. *I'm yours, I'm yours, I'm yours.*

After that, while his body was still on top of hers, he had whispered in her ear that when he woke in the morning it was her face he wished he saw alongside his. "You are everything, Frances. My greatest love and my hardest secret."

Plunging under the water she felt the cold swimming all around her. Submerged, a kaleidoscope of light flickering through the surface to her skin, she felt her breath swelling in her chest. Bursting from the water when she couldn't stand it anymore, she dragged herself from the water gasping for breath, burying her face in the grass. Perhaps her age didn't even matter, because things were serious now, all right. They didn't get more real than this.

Stupid, stupid Amélie.

Chapter Thirteen

That afternoon, while thunder grumbled through the sky and lightning colored the edges of clouds, Harry found two more messages on the answerphone from Mr. Lewisham. The instruction was clear, that he should go to sign the paperwork as soon as was possible. There were three other messages too, each from Tabitha, which he deleted as soon as he heard her voice, without listening to what she had to say. He had to shut it out, the hurt, the betrayal, the foolishness. How had he become so stupid?

All he wanted to do was sleep, to slip into that void between life and consciousness where he didn't have to think about what she had done. Yet every time he closed his eyes he saw her face, making it impossible for him to rest. It was only now as he paced around the freshly cleared space that he realized the ludicrous nature of what he had begun to hope for. Even though she had tried to tell him she still felt something it hadn't really made sense to him. Believing she could love him was difficult at the best of times. Did he really think she was there to help him after ten years apart? What she had done was understandable, he realized now.

In short, this was less than he deserved, for stealing the future she had once thought they were going to share.

Knuckles rapping against the door woke him from his daydream. Outside, backed in gray cloud, he saw Elsie from next door, standing underneath an umbrella.

"Can I trouble you for a spot of assistance, Harry?"

It was bad timing. He wasn't in the right frame of mind, and his sigh surely gave it away. "Sure," he said, reaching back for his coat. He stepped out into a fine drizzle. "It's no bother. What is it that you need me to do?"

Half an hour later he was sitting on her second armchair drinking a cup of tea, a towel around his neck because the dripping pipe had turned out to be more of a problem than he realized. The shoulders of his T-shirt were drenched. The water supply was currently off at the mains, and a plumber was on the way.

"I'm so sorry," she said, offering him a biscuit. He took one, a custard cream with a spicy kick from where it had been sharing the box with the ginger nuts. "I didn't anticipate the thing falling apart." The pipes were rusted and crumbling. He should have known better than to try to tighten the joint. That was the thing with these old cottages, and for that at least he supposed he should be glad to see the back of his mother's. There was always something that needed fixing or replacing.

"It's okay," he said, setting his tea on the side. Gazing around the small room, it was like looking into the past, the carpet pink and well-trodden, the furniture mid-century and not at all modern. On a nearby dresser he noticed a collection of framed photographs. Moving across he picked up a frame. Could it really be?

"Lovely strapping lad, you were," Elsie whispered.

"Is this me?" he asked, already knowing the answer. Elsie nodded in case any further confirmation was needed. He'd been in her house hundreds of times, always with a job to do. Never once had he noticed it before. "You knew me then, before she gave me away?"

"I did, and you were the apple of my eye, weren't you? When you and your mother disappeared, I was heartbroken, and I missed you terribly. My Alf had died the year before you were born, and your grandparents had been ever so good to me, God rest their souls. I loved helping your mother when you came along. She struggled a little bit with her moods. We called it the blues back then, but together we managed to get through it."

"What about my father?"

"I never asked, and she never told. That was what we did back then, brushed things under the carpet. It was our way in my generation. But when she came back, I asked after you. I was desperate to know where you were. Never got a proper answer as to what had happened, but I had my suspicions. I figured you must have been adopted by a new family, that she hadn't managed on her own. When you turned up ten years ago, well, I couldn't believe it. Who'd have thought that nice helper in River View Care Home was the little lad I'd bathed and changed? I couldn't believe it."

"Why did you never say anything?" he said, sitting back down.

"Your mother asked me not to. I don't think she found it easy to look back, come face-to-face with her mistakes. The only thing she used to go on about was how she had ruined things with that girl of yours. She wanted to try and put things right, and she said that she felt sure that Tabitha would be the right person to help you. She felt terribly guilty too, about you ending things with her. When she developed that blood clot in her leg, it was as if she knew the way it would end up, and, well, she wanted to make sure you knew the truth, whatever it was. She wanted to try and bring you and Tabitha back together. That was why she left me with that letter. I was more than happy to post it for her."

"It was you who posted the letter to Tabitha?"

"Least I could do, wasn't it? Your mother and you had given me a reason to keep going when I lost Alf. I always wished I could have done more to help her, really I did. I was over the moon to see Tabitha here the other day."

"Yeah," he said, thinking of their argument earlier. "Not sure she's coming back."

"Where did she go?"

"Home to her husband. She never told me about him."

"Oh, I'm sorry, love."

"It's not just that. I gave her some stuff to get valued and she pawned it. Says it wasn't her fault, but I don't know."

"I thought she seemed like a lovely girl if you ask me. You sure there can't be some sort of misunder-standing? She was married, but still she was here. How did she explain it?"

"I didn't really give her a chance."

"Oh, Harry. Sometimes the truth isn't all that easy to spit out."

"Well, anyway." Thinking that Elsie was probably right, Harry tried to move things on. There was something more important to ask. "So, did she . . ." he began, nodding toward the picture, before he realized he didn't know how to ask it.

"Did she what?" Elsie probed.

"Did she ever tell you why she gave me away?"

Elsie shook her head. "I did ask. I even offered to help get you back, said you could both live with me, but she said she couldn't bring you back here, that somebody was looking for her. That they were after something."

"After what?"

"I'm not sure exactly, but she said it was some kind of box. I didn't really understand it." The Klinkosch? Was his mother on the run with it? "I don't know if she was in some kind of trouble. Often she didn't make much sense. She always just said she needed to keep you safe. But she was a good mother, Harry, at least at first."

"And you think that she loved me? When I was a baby I mean. You think my mother cared?"

"Harry, love," she said, reaching across to pat his

knee. "Your mother loved you more than anything else in the world."

After the plumber arrived and got the situation under control, he headed back to his cottage. It was strange, but the more evidence he had that his mother did care for him made him want to be there without her even less. He picked up the phone and dialed Mr. Lewisham's number before he could change his mind. The phone rang a professional twice before somebody answered.

"Lewisham and Beale solicitors, Pamela speaking."

"I would like to speak to Mr. Lewisham, please."

"I'm afraid he's not available right now. Can I arrange an appointment for you to come into the office?"

"Yes. I need to come in and sign some paperwork."

Listening while she was quiet, he heard the leafing of pages. "Well, his schedule is full over the next couple of days, but I can offer you an appointment for next Tuesday."

He sighed, not even caring that it was audible down the line. That was too far away. He needed to sign this place over and the sooner the better, get it off his shoulders. Tuesday was a whole weekend away. He had the time to lose his nerve a thousand times over before Tuesday.

"No, that's no good. It needs to be today."

More leafing. "Well, I'm afraid that just isn't possible. The earliest appointment I can schedule you in for is Tuesday, perhaps Monday afternoon at a push, but that will need to be confirmed with Mr. Lewisham himself. I'm sorry, sir," she said, her voice becoming stern as if she had predicted his negative response, "but that is the best I can do."

Harry took the provisional Monday appointment and made himself a cup of tea. That was when he saw another of Tabitha's notes pinned to the fridge. The sight of it ripped through him, stealing his breath. Evidence that she had been here and was now gone made him feel broken, the fight within leaking away like water from a burst balloon. As much as he tried not to look, to pretend it wasn't there, once he knew it was it was all he could think about. Snatching at the note he forced himself to read what she had written. *You still look adorable when you sleep*. It crumpled like a dry leaf in his hand, and he tossed it to the floor as he slipped outside. He needed air, space from the house. A cool breeze brushed against his skin while clouds passed overhead. Setting his mug of tea on the ground he took out one of his pigeons while observing the others scratting around in their coop.

His birds had been one of the few joys in his life

over the last decade, and yet now to look at them he felt shame over their captivity. They seemed happy enough, sure, cooing just as he expected and pecking when he gave them food. But although he hated to admit it, Tabitha was right. It wasn't fair to keep them. They didn't belong in a cage. Tabitha had wanted him to set them free, had told him that all birds desire their freedom. Now he thought maybe he could understand that, because for the first time in his life he realized that he wanted it too. Like never before, he wanted to shake off the chains of everything that held him back. Staring down at the little bird, its beady eye wide and alert, he wondered how he might feel if he let it go. Would it feel like a loss, or that he had gained something in its place? After giving it a kiss on the head he set it down on the damp ground.

"Go on, then," he said, watching as it pottered along, pecking at the soil. Using a soft finger, he gave it a gentle shove. "Go on if you want to go." The bird carried on pecking, made no attempt to leave. Eventually Harry picked it back up and returned it to the cage. Maybe there was a time and a place for everything, and even birds had to be ready within themselves before they were able to accept their freedom.

He drank his tea in two giant swallows and headed back inside like a fighter ready for confrontation.

"Right," he said to himself. "Enough is enough." Grabbing two rolls of the black bags Tabitha had brought with her and starting with the remaining piles in the living room, he began shoving whatever he could find into the sacks. There were clothes, old photographs, black-and-white ones of people he didn't know or even stop to consider. Endless boxes of baby toys. Dolls. Kitchen utensils. Vinyl records. It was all going, every last bit of it. Only once when he chanced upon a photograph of himself when he was no more than three years old, sitting in the snow with a ramshackle excuse of an igloo behind him, did he stop to pay notice. It was his memory, documented. Wasn't it? He was alone in the image, but somebody had taken that picture. His mother, perhaps? Had they built that snow house together? He allowed himself a moment to enjoy the accuracy of his own recollections, the pictures painted in his mind, before he tucked the photograph in the file that Mr. Bradbury had brought him.

By the time he had finished he had twenty black bags stacked in the hallway. Remembering what Steven Bradbury had said about the fireplace he even reached up the chimney, but other than a few photographs and scraps of paper he found nothing. By the time he finished even the stairs were half cleared, the light in the house had improved, and the smell seemed somehow fresher, man-made and plastic rather than the musty scent of persistent decay. He had a lot of work left to do, he knew that, but he was considerably further ahead. Adapting to the method of detached indifference really got the job done. But he also knew that clearing the house was only one small step. Leaving it behind was another thing entirely.

After locating his car keys under a box of old records, that afternoon he made five trips to the dump, hauling somewhere between twenty and thirty bags, the contents of which he couldn't be sure. He was fairly confident that the Klinkosch box wasn't in among the discarded things. But even if it was, what difference did it make? It was necessary to rid himself of the albatross of trying to cling to things that were never really his, be it possessions or care or love. He swore right there and then that he would never try to make another person stay with him again. Allowing his full anger to manifest, he realized just how upset he was by Tabitha's actions. For taking those necklaces, and for convincing him that it was possible that they had another chance. How was it possible for so much anger to exist simultaneously with such great hurt? Perhaps, he thought, they were just two sides of the same coin.

Unable to sleep he eventually pulled down the file that Mr. Bradbury had brought to him. He had leafed through it once already, but hadn't read it properly. The truth was that he felt quite overwhelmed by the information in there, all those letters and reports that had been written about him without his knowledge, about a time in his life he could barely remember.

The strange thing, he thought to himself as he looked at the snowy photograph slipped into the front of the file, was that all the evidence he had of his life with his mother before she left him was at direct odds with what was written in that file. When he let his mind wander back, he could remember other moments from the time they spent together. Moments like her laughing in the kitchen, and her holding him at night when he woke from a dream. Sailing boats on the stream outside and feeding a small family of ducks. Loving things they had shared. And there were many discovered photographs that could attest to that time, including those on Elsie's dresser. So why had she left him? Saved in the file was a news report, about the little boy found on the bench. A NATION SHOCKED, read the headline of a clipping from the paper. A search for the mother had ensued, and then somebody had recognized Harry, and Frances had been found not long after that. By reading the letters on file, it became clear that while social services had tried to help her, even suggesting she might be able to resume care of her son with help, his mother had remained steadfast in her stance; he could not, and should not, live with her. No explanation had been given for why.

These were not the answers his mother had promised in her letter.

Yet there was more in that file too. Turning the page, he saw a letter, an address in France. Reading the words, he could hardly believe it. It had been written by an aunt of his mother's, and she had begged the British authorities to let her take care of her great-nephew. Placing the file down for a moment, he stood up and walked to the window. He had a family? A family in France whom he could call his own, and who had wanted him all along? Brushing a tear from his eye, he returned to the file, his breath quickened and mouth dried as he skimmed the pages. There were photographs of people he didn't recognize, a farmhouse that could have been his home, and the offer of a life that had never become his.

Scanning the information, he found the name of the home belonging to his aunt. It was a painter's retreat, called La Muse. Grabbing his cell phone, he entered the name, and just moments later he was looking at the same farmhouse, still operating, and right there under the Contact Us tab was a telephone number.

Before he knew it he was entering the numbers into the phone, all along wondering whether he was doing the right thing but unable to stop himself. It wasn't courage that drove him as such, more like survival instinct, as if he was swimming toward the surface despite being caught in the tide, because the only other option was to drown. A foreign tone rang in his ear, and then after a few rings somebody picked up. It took a moment before the person spoke, clearing her throat as she did.

"Good afternoon, La Muse retreat." Nothing was planned, and words escaped him. What was he supposed to say now? Blurt it out, or dance around the subject? Determination it seemed could only take him so far. "Hello, is there anybody there?"

"Hello," he finally said, mustering the strength to do what he must. "Is that Henrietta Durand?"

"Speaking. And who is calling?"

"Erm, my name is Harry Langley, and I was calling about—" he began, but she cut him off.

"What did you say? Your name, I mean. Did I mishear it? I thought you said your name was Harry Langley."

Her voice had changed, her breath caught. "I did. I'm calling because I think we might be related. I was Frances's son."

"Oh, my good lord," she cried, before sniffling into the mouthpiece. "Harry? Is that really you? Oh, I can't believe it, after all these years we've finally found you."

And with that Harry too could no longer hold it together. His tears returned, along with the realization that while he had no idea they had existed, they had been waiting for him all along.

Although his sleep was broken by vivid dreams of being buried alive under piles of books and dusty paperwork, it wasn't until he heard the letterbox rattle the following morning that he awoke fully with a start. The room was brighter than he could remember it, the windows offering the light a clear path through. Storm clouds from the night before had cleared, and he crawled out from underneath the blankets, pushing the file aside, still smiling over what he had discovered, the plans and hopes he had made. Standing up in the space, the sheer expanse of it, he felt unable to believe what he had achieved the day before. Sometimes not thinking about things was the best way forward. Walking through to the almost clear hallway, he saw a single envelope balanced on top of one of the bags. Reaching across he found a letter addressed to him.

Back in the living room he gazed at it for a while, tried to glean information from the ineligible postmark to no avail. The last time he had received mail it had set a course of events in motion, and the truth was that he feared what this letter might be able to do. Eventually, after a big breath in, he fiddled at the corner of the well-sealed envelope and managed to get it open. Inside he saw there were several small objects in the place of a letter, so he turned it up on its side and tipped them out. Eight small rectangles fell into his lap, dog-eared edges delivering a musty smell.

Picking up the first, followed by each subsequent piece, he found that each item was a sticker, the faces of the footballers of his youth staring back at him. At first it didn't make any sense, but then he recalled that sticker album filed away for safekeeping. A sense of dread overwhelmed him then, the thought that he had perhaps thrown it away the day before. Scrambling toward his sleeping area, remembering that he had tucked it under his makeshift mattress, he searched frantically, and to his relief he found it exactly where he'd left it. Leafing through the pages, he saw that each of the stickers filled a space in the album. By the time he reached the last page it was complete. Still, it didn't make any sense, so he returned to the envelope to look for an answer. And he found it, a small handwritten note that hadn't fallen out on the first opening. Unfolding the letter, he read the words. *It's never too late to fulfill your dreams. Maybe we can help fulfill each others. Thanks for letting me stay, Tabitha.*

It didn't make sense when read alongside what had happened yesterday. How could she make such a promise, offer such gratitude, when all along she knew she was selling those necklaces in a pawnshop? How could she offer to fulfill their dreams together, when all along she knew she was here for the valuable goods? He thought of her willingness to stay with him, the husband he hadn't known about. Of the kindness she had shown, like the way she had held him when he told her all about his past. That kiss she placed on his neck that he had wanted so much to reciprocate, and how betrayed he had felt yesterday when he saw his mother's things for sale in that shop. Those little notes on the fridge, and with his trumpet, and on his pillow at direct odds with the truth he had seemingly revealed. They made him feel as if they had traveled back in time. She had given him so much space to talk, and yet when he had seen the jewelry in that shop window, he hadn't even given her a moment to explain. How could she have done all that when she knew she had stolen those necklaces and put them up for sale? There was only one explanation.

She couldn't have.

Reading the message over and over, he realized that not only was it a promise, but it was a promise that she had no reason to make unless she really meant it. By buying these old stickers, by sending them through the post, this arrival meant that even when she wasn't with him, she was still thinking about him, still planning a future in which they were together. Hope it seemed continued to exist in the most unexpected places, even those that perhaps he had already written off more than once.

He had to know. He had to give her a chance to explain. Grabbing his car keys, he set off from the house in search of something he hoped he hadn't already lost.

Chapter Fourteen

Tabitha threw the onion into the pan and watched as the chunks morphed from spiky white shards into slithers of golden translucence. The smell of hot fat stung her eyes as the sound of the television droned in the background, barely audible over the sizzle of the pan. Cutting through the din was Daniel's voice, swearing at the host of a game show when he got the answers wrong. She turned the extractor to the highest setting to drown him out, then poured herself another glass of wine. Catching sight of herself in the reflective surface of the hood, she was drawn to the bruise that darkened her cheekbone, the eye that was ever so slightly swollen. Although it had been a long time since he had struck her like that, a sudden burst of uncontrolled anger, there was a sense of disappointing familiarity about it. It had been worse in the past, but that fact didn't make her feel any better. Slow, apologetic footsteps grew louder, and moments later she felt his hands rest cautiously on her shoulders.

Gently, almost tenderly, his fingers worked against her shoulders to turn her around, before he began to inspect the black eye that he had given her the night before. It had started with nothing more than a push or shove, the sort of thing she could brush off, forget that it had even happened. Perhaps a nudge while they were in a crowd that made her question whether it was even wrong in the first place. Wouldn't somebody have said something if it was? But when had it tipped over into violence? Acts that left a mark? It was impossible to trace the source of it, but she knew her record at work was littered with sick days and poor excuses. Yet still she was here. After hurting Harry, she didn't know what else to do, but return to what she knew.

Daniel tapped at the outer edges of the bruise, but even the soft touch of his fingertips was enough to make her wince. "Sorry," she said, when she was forced to pull away. "It's just a bit sore, that's all."

Deep lines cut through his forehead, a pained expression as he used his fingers to brush her hair away from her face. It was as if the sight of her left him aching, as if it was one of *his* ribs that was likely to be cracked.

"I was just so lost without you, Tabitha," he whispered. "I got myself all worked up over the idea that you were never coming back. When I saw you, I wasn't myself." Nodding agreeably, she forced a smile. "I got carried away."

"I better see to the food," she said, turning around to tend to the pan. His presence pulsated behind her, the heat from his body too close to hers.

"Do you want me to help with anything?" he asked.

"You could chop that pepper," she whispered with a smile. His breath struck warm as it hit the back of her neck, followed by a kiss that made her freeze. But then his body eased away, and she managed to take another breath. Sometimes that was how she felt, that she needed to remind herself to breathe, as if she was no longer sure that she was even alive.

"Okay," he said. "See," he said with a smile that she once used to find so attractive. "Look what a good team we make."

Working alongside him while he was calm and sober, it was easy to feel as if things were going to be all right if she stayed, and as if this place could still be home. Even after what had happened the night before, everything she owned was here, evidence of her in this place, marking her territory. What she had come to understand each time she returned was that everybody was looking for a place to belong. To be truly alone was unbearable, went against human nature. People were supposed to form leaves of a larger tree, fit within a family, a pack, be part of some greater, more complicated picture.

After a restless night she made herself a cup of tea and sat by the window to watch the sunrise, mindlessly turning her wedding ring with her thumb. There was a beautiful view toward the park, a line of perfect trees, the chirping of birds to welcome the new day. Many a morning following a terrible night she had sat there to remind herself that every day held new possibilities, new potential. That each new day was an opportunity for a different choice. The quiet gave her a moment for thought. If she was going to go, really go and stay away this time, why not now? His resonant snore could be heard from upstairs, so what was she waiting for? She had heard a phrase once, that everything she wanted was on the other side of fear. But for her, that wasn't true. Fear was what she kept if she stayed. She didn't have to cross fear to get what she wanted, she had to choose to leave it behind. Nothing unknown could be as terrifying as a life lived like this one.

Setting her cup down, she pulled off her ring, then set it down on the table. Upstairs she found Daniel fast asleep, his mouth open wide and loose, drool on his pillow. Her jeans and white T-shirt were there on the ottoman at the end of the bed, so she carefully slid them off and snuck into the bathroom, where she dressed. Opening the door to the airing cupboard on the landing she found the bag she had packed days before. Stopping for a moment, a thought came to her, concern about what she was going to do, and where she was going to go. But she realized now that was a question for later, and that it didn't matter where she was going, only that she was leaving. Treading softly down each step she arrived in the hall and opened the front door. But to her surprise, instead of an empty road to an unknown destination, before her she saw Harry.

Gray bags hung heavy under his eyes, his hair a mess, as if he had slept badly, his finger poised ready to press the doorbell.

"Tabitha, I had to come. I had to . . ." he began, before looking up and catching sight of her eye. His voice dropped to a whisper. "What happened to you?" he said, taking a step forward. She pushed the door to cover part of the entrance, as if there was a way to undo what he had seen by keeping him out. She set the bag down at her side. "Your eye," he said then, as if there was any doubt about what he had meant the first time.

"What are you doing here?" she asked, ignoring his question. Was that footsteps she could hear, Daniel moving around upstairs? She didn't want him to find Harry on the doorstep. Harry would get hurt, so would she. Instinct told her to force the door closed, but Harry was in the way. "How did you know where I lived?"

Harry seemed to give her question a lot of thought before answering, his gaze still on her eye, and his expression one of confusion. "From the letter my mother wrote. You left it at my house. I came here to say I was sorry. Yesterday, outside the pawnshop . . . I over-reacted and never even gave you a chance to explain. I made assumptions and I think I got things wrong."

Gazing up the stairs, sure she could no longer hear Daniel's snoring, she edged the door closed as much as she could. "I should have been honest from the start," she said. "I should have told you about my situation."

Harry appeared nervous in a way she hadn't seen in a long time. "We would all like to get things right first time, but sometimes that's just not possible." And then with all his courage, fighting his inner voice telling him that he was making a mistake, he said, "Just look at you and me."

On the way over to Tabitha's house he had been trying to work out what to say. He had toyed with the idea of saying that he forgave her, that he didn't understand but that he wanted to, and even that the necklaces didn't matter. He knew that wasn't true, but he wondered if they mattered half as much as he thought they had, and certainly knew that they didn't matter as much as Tabitha. He couldn't explain why the necklaces that she took with her for valuation had ended up in a pawnshop, but there was something definite that he now knew beyond any doubt: Tabitha hadn't put them there. It was the stickers that reminded him of that. She was the kind of person who used to run him a bath on a Friday night and massage his feet before bed, bring him a cup of tea each morning, and leave notes on the fridge. Tabitha was the person who had baked him a cake on his birthday, who when he was sick went out to buy supplies, and who ordered stickers to complete albums he started when he was a child over thirty years before.

"And on top of that, I wanted to tell you I was stupid," he eventually said, and felt that pretty much summed things up. He held up the album. "I should have known better than to blame you. I should have known *you* better, and I didn't give you a chance to explain."

She shook her head. "You had every right."

"No," he said. "I didn't. I should have realized you would never have done that." He took another look at that black eye. "Tabitha, please, tell me what's going on. How did you get that bruise?"

"I can't."

"Why not?"

"Tabitha," they both heard Daniel shout then. Before she had the chance to reply she heard footsteps on the landing, definite footsteps this time, lured by the sound of voices from below. "Who is it?" Daniel called. And that was when she saw something in Harry change in a way she never had before.

"Is that your husband?" Recognizing that same look on her face as he had seen in Nook Cottage when the doorbell rang, he took another step forward. "Did he do that to you? Tabitha, please, if he did you need to tell me."

She shrugged, almost as if she was guilty, as if she had been accused of something. "This is his house. I had nowhere else to go." Moments later he was at her side, pulling open the door.

"Who the hell is this?" Daniel asked as he stood back to take a look at Harry. "Do you know what time it is, mate?"

"Did you give her that black eye?" Harry asked, ignoring Daniel's question.

"You the police or something?" He turned to Tabitha. "Did you call them?"

"No, no," she said, and Harry heard something in her voice that he recognized. He hadn't understood her fear when Mr. Bradbury came to the door, but he understood it now well enough. In his house she was so lively, so cheerful. He had assumed that was how she always was, as she always had been. Now he saw that in this place, she looked as caged as one of his birds. That just like him, the last ten years had changed her after all.

"Then who are you?" Daniel asked as he took a step closer, brushing past Tabitha. "And what are you doing in my hallway?"

"I'm Harry," he said, placing one hand against the door, and his foot in the frame.

Daniel thought to himself for a moment, and then he laughed. "This is Harry?" he said, pointing at Harry and looking at Tabitha. "And all that time I thought I had competition. This is the big love that left you? Some gangly twat in cargo trousers and a fleece. So, what," he asked, turning to Harry, "you've come back to rescue her? Too little too late, mate." He held up his left hand, flashed the ring on his finger.

Harry had to admit that the sight of Daniel was intimidating. All edges and corners, he was one of those men who was chiseled from top to toe, nothing but muscle and strength. Certainly, physically Harry was no match. But then he thought of that black eye Tabitha was sporting, and just how little courage it must take for a man of that size to strike a woman. And Harry took heart from that, found that it made him feel powerful. As if without doubt he suddenly believed he was better than Daniel. Plus, he couldn't fail to see that there was strength to be found in the fact that Daniel knew who he was.

"You don't have to stay here," Harry said, turning to Tabitha. Moving in a way that blocked Daniel the best he could, he added, "You can stay with me instead."

"Tabitha, do you want to explain this?" Daniel interrupted. "I don't expect to wake up to one of your exes in my hallway offering my wife a place to live."

Harry took a step forward. Not quite between them, but close enough, and he was surprised to find that it took less courage than anticipated. "And she probably didn't expect to get a black eye at some point over the last twenty-four hours, but you still gave her one." The audacity of it stunned Daniel, and for a moment he said nothing. It gave Harry all the time he needed to ask Tabitha to trust him once more. His voice dropped to a whisper, his words just for her, as if they were the only ones there. "Come with me. You can't stay here like this. You don't belong here."

"Harry, what are you doing?" she said.

"Yeah," Daniel said, edging toward them. "What are you doing? You think she belongs to you?"

"I don't think she belongs to anyone," Harry said, never more certain in his life. Then, turning to Tabitha. "I'm giving you a choice. A way out." He took a step closer and reached for her hand. He could feel the size of Daniel behind him but still he did it, knowing it to be right. "I let you down when I didn't give you a chance to explain. Just like I let you down before. I know you would never have tried to sell my mother's necklaces." He looked at Daniel when he said that, and for a moment Harry was sure he saw some slither of guilt or confusion cross his face.

By then Tabitha was shaking. "I'll get them back for you. I promise. I've been speaking to the owner of the shop and he said he'd hold them for—"

Daniel took a step forward then. "Tabitha, have you been seeing this loser behind my—"

"It doesn't matter," Harry said, pulling her gently toward him so he could further block the space between her and Daniel. "It's just stuff. It can't change anything. None of it can; not magazines or old baby clothes, and certainly not some jewelry that I vaguely remember my mother wearing." Daniel said something then but neither of them heard what it was. "But do you know what can change things?" She shook her head. "A little envelope filled with stickers. I should have known, Tabitha. I'm sorry. Please don't stay here. Please, come with me."

"All right. I've heard enough of your bullshit. You're leaving." With that Harry felt Daniel's hands on his shoulders. He fought against it, but Daniel was adept at manhandling others, and just a moment later he had rough-handled him away from the front door, toward the gate, his arm twisted and shoulder sore. But when Daniel turned back to the house he saw that Tabitha was behind him, a bag in her hand.

"It's me that's leaving, Daniel," she said, before she had even the time to think it through. "Seven years later than I should have." She stepped to move forward but Daniel blocked her. "It doesn't matter what you do. I'm going to leave."

"No, you're not. You're my wife."

Calm washed over her as she stepped forward again, and when he reached to grab her arm she didn't flinch, not like she usually did. After years of holding back, a decision had been made. Something was different here.

"You can't stop me."

"Damn right I can."

But just as Daniel leaned to take hold, Harry appeared behind him. Harry knew that he couldn't overpower him, but at least he had the advantage of surprise. With all his force he kicked at the back of Daniel's knees, sending him toppling to the floor. It was just enough time for Tabitha to skip past him, and moments later with her hand held in Harry's, they were together and moving past the gate.

"She does this, you know," Daniel called from behind as he staggered to his feet. "Leaves and then comes back." They stopped for a moment. The sight was an imposing one, Daniel's wide shoulders and crossed arms, barely concealing his pumped-up chest. Harry looked to Tabitha but for a moment he couldn't read what she was thinking. "She always finds her way back to me eventually. And when she can't, I find her instead. She's mine. She belongs here, with me."

Harry watched Tabitha, waiting for her response. Her lips quivered as she fought for the courage to say it. "There's only one place I belong," she said, and then Harry felt her grip firm up against his. "And it was never with you." Just moments later they were driving away in Harry's car.

Vibration from the engine was the only sound to soften the silence as they drove away. Neither of them was sure what to say, both trying to process what had just happened. But after traveling for miles, no clue where they were going, Tabitha turned to Harry.

"I'm so sorry," she said, her voice shaky with pent-up fear. "For everything, I mean. The necklaces, the disappearing, and of course today. The fact he pushed you over."

"I'm okay," Harry said, shrugging as if it was nothing. The truth was that his heart rate hadn't returned to normal for the first ten miles on the road. "I'm just glad you're out of there. I can't stand the idea that he was hurting you like that. You can't ever go back, you know that, right."

"I know," she said, although she wasn't sure where she was supposed to go. A new life had to be built on some sort of foundation, and she wasn't sure she had one.

"I don't mean that as an instruction," Harry added. "I don't want to tell you what to do."

"I know."

"I just want you to be safe." Wishing they could just slot straight back into the place they had been yesterday, he tried to bring himself to raise the idea of how much he loved her. But he couldn't do it. Not then. Not after what had happened to her in the last twenty-four hours, and for goodness knows how many years before. How long had she been living in fear? Now wasn't the time for him to make demands. He just wanted to be there for her, to help, and to protect her. What he wanted in that moment had to come second to what she needed. "I'll do whatever I can to help you. I promise I won't let you down again."

"I know you won't."

With a red light glaring in front of him, Harry pulled up at the traffic lights and watched ahead as a young mother crossed with her stroller. It choked him as he saw her reach in, adjust the blanket, before continuing to cross the road. A little further up the road he pulled into a garage and alongside the pump before killing the engine.

"Tabitha, about what we've been doing back at the house. You know, going through my mother's things has made me want to understand my past like never before. To work out who I am, and where I come from. So, last night I read the file that Steven Bradbury brought to me."

"All of it?"

"Every last page. Turns out I do have a family after all. In France. There were letters in there from my great-aunt, all of which she had written in the hope to offer me a permanent home back when I was first in care." He nodded as Tabitha's eyes widened. "I called her, and they were so pleased to hear from me." He was sure she was fighting back a tear, and he felt comforted when she reached out and touched his leg. That touch was so supportive, perhaps even more than he deserved. Soft hands slipped around his. "They want to meet me, and have invited me over. They have a huge place, a painter's retreat. It's really beautiful." He reached into his pocket, pulled out a photograph of the barn that he had taken from the file. He handed it to her.

"Wow," she said.

"And it's not just that. Everything points us in the direction of France, right? And now I have a family there. Like you said, it can't all be a coincidence." She nodded. "Yesterday I tried to convince myself that I didn't care about my history, that it didn't matter. But it does. It always has. That's why I went to live with my mother all those years ago, when I should have been living with you. I want to know where I'm from. I need to know. If my mother was in love with somebody from France, maybe that is where my story really begins."

"Your father?"

He nodded.

"Then you should go."

He smiled. "Yes, I should. I must. And I was thinking about going right now."

"Okay," she said, feeling her heart rate rise. "If you can drop me at the museum, I can . . ." she said, pausing when she saw that he was shaking his head.

"I mean we should go together."

"Are you serious?"

"Never more so in my whole life. I want to do whatever I can to understand the past, and then move on. Into a future."

"What about the Klinkosch box? Saving the house?"

"Going to France doesn't mean that we have stopped looking. If we can find out who wrote those letters, maybe even who gave it to her, then it would really help us understand who she was. But even if not, maybe there are other things I need to discover too." He left the rest unsaid, but from the smile on her face he was sure they were thinking the same thing. "So, will you come?"

"Yes," she said, without hesitation.

Harry was stunned his plan had worked, and Tabitha couldn't believe she had left that house. As they whizzed past trees on the way to the ferry she glanced at her reflection in the wing mirror. Although her eye was black and a little swollen, the weight she carried on her shoulders from that house had been lifted. The air was so much clearer after yesterday's storm, and she held her face to the open window and breathed.

Reaching over with her right hand, she placed it on top of Harry's where it was resting on the gear stick. "You saved me, you know that?" she said as she let her fingers glide over his. His skin was warm and soft, his grip loose and unthreatening as he lifted his fingers to accommodate hers.

But he was shaking his head. "No, I didn't," he said without once taking his eyes off the road. "You saved yourself. You made a choice, and stopped waiting for life to make it for you." She felt his fingers tighten against hers. "I understand now, that's the only way things ever change."

Chapter Fifteen

Mirepoix, France, Summer 1981

Sneaking to the farmhouse became part of her day
after that. Instead of waiting on the driveway
for Benoit to pass by, she would head down into the
garden, pick lavender flowers from wildly overgrown
bushes, and watch as the water in the nearby brook ran
over the rocky bed. It reminded her of home, or at least
a place she had once called as such. But had that place
ever really been home? Weren't you supposed to feel
a sense of belonging in such a place, a draw to return,
no matter how far you traveled? If that was what home
was like, that was not the place she had left behind.
The idea of leaving France next month left her cold.

Benoit had taken to leaving the house unlocked, but
most days when he arrived she was outside waiting for
him. Hearing the chug of his car excited her, the antici-

pation of his arrival something too good to miss. Sometimes they stayed in the garden where he found her, especially if he was in a rush, just enough time to kick off his shoes and have a roll about in the overgrown grass. But other times they went inside. The first time she had lain with Benoit she had felt awkward and unsure, afraid almost to move in the wrong way at the wrong moment. But with each time they were together, which had been countless since then—sometimes one right after the other and which Benoit said was as much a surprise to him as it was to her—it had become easier. On some occasions their lovemaking was calm and slow, and he would ask her if she was okay and call her *mon amour*. Other times it all seemed to be over in a flash, a rush of bodies moving to a rhythm set by him. Only a few days had passed when they had been forced to go without, when the urgency of the day before came back to haunt her each time she peed. Benoit got in a flap about it, apologizing, saying it was all his fault, before rushing to the shops to buy cranberry juice and antibiotics. That afternoon he served her like a waiter, canceled his meetings, and never left her side once. It had been easy to forget about the discomfort with that sort of undivided attention.

"What would you say to a little trip?" he asked her that afternoon. Sunlight was pouring through the windows, a trickle of warm breeze that did little to ease the humidity. It was too hot to be pressed up against each other, so he was lying with his legs stretched out of the sheets, his chest bare save his necklace and key. Any initial embarrassment she had felt about her naked form had vanished by then, so she was on her front, bottom in the air. Every so often he reached across and stroked it, and it made her feel as if they had passed some unmarked barrier, that they were no longer just two people who cared for each other, but were people playing by different rules that they themselves had made up. Nobody else could touch her like that.

"Where to?" she asked, nibbling a nail.

"I was thinking Toulouse. It is far enough away that nobody will spot us, and close enough that I can pull some strings. I don't want to spend all our time together stuck in this house, and there is something happening there that I want to show you."

"Okay."

A glint shimmered in his eye. "Can you get away for a day?"

She loved it when he asked if she could manage the details of a plan. As if she had a full, rich life with so many things going on that she had to fit him in. "I should think so," she said with a wink. "For you. And why is that?"

"Because you love me." He smiled.

"Because I love you," she repeated.

Rolling over, he used his elbows to drag himself to Frances. Just as she expected, his hand slid over the top of her behind, his lips on her shoulder. But then he slipped his hand all the way underneath her hip, before rolling her over so that she was lying on her back, tucked against his body, hair all over her face.

"Now I want to do something for you," he said, brushing her hair from her eyes, before letting his hand wander. "Something I know you'll like." His fingers settled as soft as snowflakes on her chest, stroking, circling, moving like the figure eight.

"How do you know I'll like it?" she asked, but he said nothing, only smiled. Seconds slowed to minutes with his soft touch against her, minutes to hours as his fingers and eyes roamed all over her skin. Whispers in French went unheard, until his hand reached between her legs and she went to pull away.

"Do you want me to stop?"

She shook her head.

"Are you sure? Perhaps I'm too quick. I'll slow down. Is that better?"

"What are you doing to me?" she asked, but it wasn't really a question. Closing her eyes, she let her head rest back against the pillow. How did he know she would like this? Because he was right, she really did. His breath was hot as he whispered in her ear.

"You didn't finish yet. But you will now, like this."

It was new to her, the way he touched her body, but she knew what he wanted to see. For some reason then she thought of Amélie, and what she would tell her if she could. Had Gaspard done this to Amélie? With her eyes tightly closed she felt his body moving, his fingers never once losing their rhythm. Daring to look, she saw his head was by her knees, and just a moment later he took over his efforts with his mouth. "It's different for a woman," he said, and there was that word again. A woman. A woman who was free to choose. And with that she let herself go, falling somewhere, into a place as deep as the darkest ocean, and from which after a time, she didn't want to return.

Everything was different after that, the way they were together, the way she felt about him. It had nothing to do with the orgasm either, not the first, fifth, or . . . however many it was they had tallied by then. Instead it had everything to do with how she saw herself. Even after writing letters to Benoit, kissing, and perhaps even making love the first few times, she had still thought of herself as a girl bound by her father's laws. But now she felt capable of making choices that only a short while ago would have seemed impossible.

Benoit's friendship had laid paving on a road she had struggled to see, because he, more than anybody else, saw her. During the drive to Toulouse the following week she flung her arms out through the open roof of Benoit's 2CV and let her hair chase currents in the wind.

"What are you doing?" Benoit asked, struggling to concentrate on the road. It was the first time he had looked at her with any confusion.

What could she tell him? Not what she truly wanted, that meeting him had broken the chains holding her back. That she would return home changed, if she returned at all. There was no way she could tell him that she wanted to stay, here with him, in their farmhouse home. Was there? Maybe she could. It was after all the place where she felt most like herself, where there was not a single part of her she had to hide. But whether she could or she couldn't, now was not the time to get bogged down in conversation.

"*Je vie,*" she shouted into the wind, and it had never been more true.

Leaving the fields of yellow harvests behind they drove into the city of Toulouse, parking up in a small side street. Exiting the car, her heart was racing, and as if he read her thoughts he reached for her hand and strolled as if neither of them had a care in the world.

They soon found themselves in a tunnel of oaks, high branches casting them in shade. They were near the edge of a park, but the deeper they got, the quieter it became.

"Where are you taking me?" she asked.

"You'll see."

Temporary fencing marked a barrier, and just beyond she saw workers planting shrubs. They walked together across a jade-green lawn to a small hill that he helped her negotiate because her sandals were slipping against the loose dry earth.

"What is this place?" she asked as they stood on the brow. Beyond, men and women worked, arranging plants and laying stones. Water trickled, and in the center of it all she could see a lake, the water shimmering in the gentle sunlight, a red bridge cutting a path across.

"These gardens are still under construction. Almost finished. They will be the most beautiful Japanese-inspired gardens in the whole of Europe, I am sure of it."

He went to move forward, opening a gate in the constructed fence.

"I don't think it's open yet," she said.

"I know. But that's why we are here. To enjoy it before anybody else."

Later she would learn that Benoit knew the mayor, that the gardens were commissioned under his instruction. But in the moment her thoughts were captivated by what she saw before her, the beauty of the wildflowers, the bushes that seemed to slope into the water. Monolithic stones jutted from the landscape, dwarfing the immature shrubbery snipped into perfect spheres. It was, she believed, the most beautiful place she had ever been.

"Do you like it?" he asked.

"It's stunning," she said.

"Here, *mon amour*, come take a look at these." He gestured for her to sit on the ground, and so she did, and before her he spread out some rolls of paper he had been carrying with him. An artist had rendered the missing details, the plan to be followed by the workers. "It will be like this when it is done. Quite different from now. But even when they are finished planting and the gardens receive their first official visitors, it will still need a lot of time to settle and mature. For the flowers to grow, and for the trees to put down their roots."

"I think it's already beautiful. Even before it's finished."

"As do I. But imagine how it will be in a year, two years. Perhaps ten." His eyes were on the ground, his hand brushing against the soft grass. "How it will change and grow, need more water to sustain itself, but at the same time, need less support by which to flourish. It will be quite something, *non?*"

"It will."

From a small satchel he produced bottles of juice, brown paper bags with bread and cheese. Together they sat and ate, Benoit propped up on an elbow, Frances with her head on his chest. Gazing toward the ceiling of blue, they watched the passing clouds forming shapes and countries in the sky.

"I could stay here forever," she said then.

"Wouldn't you miss England?" he asked, rolling onto his side. He picked leaves from her hair, brushed crumbs from her lips.

"I don't think so. I like it more here." Could she tell him now that she wanted to stay? Hadn't he already said as much himself, that the farmhouse would be their little home? She couldn't imagine saying goodbye to any of this. "In this place I can be myself."

Chewing the last of his bread he reached across and took her hand in his. "Are you not always yourself? Who have I been with up until now?" he asked, laughing.

"Maybe I am." She wanted to tell him then that England wasn't home anymore, not now that she had met him. That with him she felt more like herself than she ever had. That she wanted to belong to him. But that felt too big, too unruly to wrangle into words. So instead, she said the closest thing she could. "But I still think I belong here in France. This place is supposed to be my home."

He stood then, held out a hand for her to take. She did, and he pulled her to her feet. Their trip was over, and she felt disappointment swell like a pain that needed either medicine or excision. "Home is not a place, Frances. Not in this beautiful city of Toulouse, or on a mountainside in Japan. Home is not the place we shelter. Instead it is the place we are free." He placed a hand against her chest, and she felt her own heart beating against it. "Home, *mon amour*, can only exist in here. Only once you know who you are in your heart, and when you live as the person you are supposed to be, will you find the place you truly belong. It will have nothing to do with your location in this world, or which person you choose to love, or who loves you in return. But it will have everything to do with how you choose to love yourself."

Chapter Sixteen

"**D**id we arrive?" Harry awoke to the sound of the door opening, to the heat of the morning sun casting his face in a golden glow. The smell of earth filled the car, warm sun on dewy grass. Peering in, she smiled.

"Sorry, not yet. I took a little detour. I couldn't take any more driving last night, and you were sound asleep." Smiling, she beckoned him from the car. "I've got something to show you. Come on," she said, already moving away.

His eyes adjusted to the bright light as she led him toward the still surface of the water, mirroring a cloudy sky. Surrounding fields were rich with crops, the hedgerows lush and green. Just ahead, a thin, well-trodden path led them onto a grassy embankment, sloping gently until they were close to the water's edge where the water lapped gently at the riverbank.

"Isn't it beautiful?" she said. On the far side of the wide river was a small hillside town, much like any quintessential French village that might cling to the foot of a mountain. Rising high above the last line of terra-cotta roofs was a magnificent rock face, stippled and chalky white, the color of brilliant sand. Surrounded by greenery, it was as if the land had opened its mouth and they were looking deep inside the earth.

"I've never seen anything like it," he said. He watched the gentle flow of water over the edge of a weir, his reflection staring back at him. Harry thought of his young mother then, those old letters, and how it seemed she had fallen in love with a version of life in France. Perhaps a person, who went on to become a father he never knew. "What a beautiful place. How did you know about it?"

"I didn't. I was just too tired to keep driving. I pulled off the motorway and this was what I found. Guess you never know what's right there, just on the other side of a quick decision."

"It makes me want to swim in it." Sun glistened like diamonds from the mirror-like surface.

"Why don't you?"

"I don't think so." Harry shook his head, and

Tabitha reached across to take his hand. The warmth of her touch surprised him, and he was pleased to see she was smiling.

"Thank you again for yesterday. For what you did."

"You don't need to thank me." Each time he looked at her and saw that black eye, a sense of responsibility swelled inside him. Because he felt sure that if he had listened when she tried to explain, she would never have gone back to Daniel, and that black eye would never have happened. All that anger over some necklaces that he could barely remember. What he had wanted to do was punch Daniel in the face until it looked like the inside of a pot of jam, and then felt stupid about it, because he wasn't really a fighter at all. Even still, the thought kept coming to him, scaring and satisfying him in unequal measure. "It was you who made the choice to leave," he said then. "You should be thanking yourself."

"But because you were there, I found the strength to actually do it. I was going to slip away, not even a word. Like I had something to be ashamed of. You made it so that I faced up to him." Harry let his grip tighten around hers. "Daniel's face was a picture, wasn't it? I don't think he really believes that I won't go back. And I'm sorry," she said then. "That I have to meet your family with this." Catching sight of herself in the still water, she saw that despite the fact it was less swollen today, the color seemed infinitely worse. "And"—she paused—"that he took those necklaces. I didn't think he'd be there when I went home that night. I thought it was safe. I didn't even know that he had pawned them."

"Tabitha, I'm not sure it was *ever* safe to go back to that house." Yet he knew from his own experience that you could live somewhere that wasn't safe and still, each day, return because that was your only option. "Please promise me you won't go back there."

"I promise," she said, although when she said it, she wondered where on earth she *was* going to go. Months of planning to leave had set things in motion, but nothing was definite. Only the week before she had received Frances's letter she had applied for several jobs, some in London, and another at a New York auction house. Anything to get away. Looking at Harry, she wished she knew what he was thinking. Before they had seen those necklaces in the pawnshop window it had felt to her as if they had both admitted how they really felt. Only now, those confessions felt a million miles away. Since then Harry had discovered she was married, living with an abusive husband. How was she supposed to explain to him that those facts didn't change how she felt about him? That it was the love she felt for him that changed everything else, not the other way around.

"Good. That's all that matters right now, that you stay well away from him. He doesn't deserve you."

"No, you're right. He doesn't."

"So, when we get back, I'll help you find somewhere to live, if you like. I mean, I'll be looking for myself anyway." Part of her had hoped he still thought of their future together. Perhaps he felt differently now. Perhaps the fact that those necklaces had disappeared really did matter after all. Perhaps it was the black eye, or the fact it wasn't the first. "I'd do anything to stop you going back there. You could even continue staying with me if you wanted to. What are friends for, and all," he said.

Friends. That hadn't been what she was hoping for, but perhaps his friendship was all that was on offer now. "Well, let's not think about it just yet," she said. "After all, we're in France now. At least I hope we're in France. I've not really got any idea where we are. The GPS was dodgy and we lost signal." She handed him a brown paper bag and a coffee in a takeaway cup that she had brought back from the nearby village. "Let's have this and get back on the road. Okay?"

"Okay," he said. "Sounds like a plan."

After some time in the car, the Pyrenean mountains growing larger in the distance as they cut a path through the open countryside, Tabitha noticed Harry nibbling on the edges of his fingers. His silence was excruciating. "Are you okay, Harry?" According to their route planner they were no more than a few kilometers from his aunt's farm, and as the distance decreased, his fidgeting had escalated.

Air stuttered through his lips as he sucked anxiously for breath. Currents of warm breeze streamed in as he wound down the window, before reaching up to wipe his brow. A handkerchief came away wet. "I'm not sure," he said, pulling off his fleece. The temperature had crept up slowly, and now, just minutes away from the farm, it was an uncomfortable eighty-eight degrees. A bend in the road housed a little white sign, their destination of Mirepoix announced as lying just ahead. Harry let out a sigh. "We're just so close now. I don't know what I was thinking, coming here like this." Turning to Tabitha, he said, "I'm not sure I can do this."

"You can," Tabitha said. "If you don't, you'll never know the truth."

"Maybe that's for the best."

"You know that's not true."

Rounding the final turn in the road they headed straight, over a river bridge, the land around them green and lush. A medieval market town appeared ahead, and by the time they reached the village square, with buildings propped up on ancient wooden stilts, it was beginning to feel undeniably French. Muted pastel buildings rose all around him, and the scent of fresh bread and warm lemons drifted in through the window. Harry pulled the car over, his breathing urgent and knuckles bone white as he gripped the steering wheel.

"Harry, what's going on?"

"What if they don't like me?" he panted. "Or think I'm strange?" He patted his pockets looking for his inhaler. Eventually he found it and took a puff. "I'm not exactly normal, am I?"

"Don't say that," she said, although she knew as soon as she said it that he had a point. He wasn't typical, never had been really, although that was always why she'd liked him in the first place and had felt relieved upon their reunion at the realization that the last ten years had done little to stifle those idiosyncrasies. "But if you feel uncomfortable, I guess we can turn around and drive all the way back just as easily as we drove here."

"All that way?"

Reaching over she placed her hand on his, and with her touch she felt his grip soften. This was going to be one of the biggest moments in his life. Meeting family, the people to whom he belonged. While she wanted to know what he felt about her, whether it was different now, whatever they were to each other had to wait. "There's no decision that can't be undone, Harry, no matter how undoable it seems."

Tall trees lined the dusty road that wound away from the main road and led all the way down to the gate that marked the entrance to the painter's retreat. The wide branches cast pleasant shadows, and here the cooler air felt comforting. It took only a moment for Harry, stepping down from the car with his chest thundering along, to realize that he had arrived to a king's welcome.

They must have been waiting for him, because when they drove through the gate he saw a woman jump up from a bench and begin running to the car. Parking the car, Tabitha killed the engine, and then Harry opened the door.

"Oh my goodness, you look just like her," his aunt Henrietta said as she reached for him. Hot skin pressed up against his, his body softening against her curves. With tears in her eyes she took his face in her calloused hands, regarding him so closely that Harry wondered if he'd ever been looked upon with such scrutiny before. Her fine blond hair was nothing like his, and she had to stretch to reach, either because she was so short, or he was too tall. But her actions made him feel as if he belonged. "You are so handsome. Look at him, Alistair," she said, and Harry noticed a tall man with scruffy hair and a kind face smiling at her side. "He has her hair, her blue eyes. It's so . . ." Aunt Henrietta began, before pausing to find the right words. "You are so . . ." she tried again, before the tears spilled over and streamed down her cheeks. "You are finally here," she said, pulling him close again. Held in his aunt's embrace, his head against her hair, he reached across, his fingers finding Tabitha's, and after twelve hours of mounting panic, he finally began to relax.

The retreat was even bigger than the photos suggested. The driveway meandered through green pastures, surrounded by tall trees on either side. The farmhouse almost seemed to ease from the ground, like the distant mountains in the west. An open barn on the far side of the house looked set to collapse, and yet it was full of people working diligently at their canvases. Lavender grew among roses, and gravel crunched underfoot. Cicadas chatted in the trees. As he stepped inside the building he had the most peculiar feeling, something he had never really felt before. There was a smell he couldn't place, yet instantly recognized. It was almost as if he was home.

Beyond the initial greeting, his welcome continued

with a large dinner, and it was the kind of family get-together of which he had always dreamed of being a part. Harry told them about the Klinkosch box, although it seemed as much of a mystery to them as it remained to Harry and Tabitha. Yet it was easier than he expected to put that aside for the evening. Because dinner reminded him of those provincial cooking shows, the kind Rick Stein and Keith Floyd used to make, when they would visit some native land and meet the locals, attend a feast of unrecognizable delicacies as if they were a contented familial adjunct. The amount of food made it seem as if his aunt and uncle had begun cooking the moment he hung up the phone over twenty-four hours before. His emotions seemed enjoyably childish, a sense of joyous selfishness that made him feel as if everything was about him. He had never been the center of all things, but on that night he was the traveler from afar who had news and stories to share. Who had returned, to a place he had never yet been. The painters who were staying at the retreat shared in the festivities, succumbing one by one to the lure of their beds until it was just Harry, his aunt and uncle, and Tabitha. Throughout the night he watched Tabitha, how she sometimes seemed lost in thought, like she wasn't quite there with them. He had wanted to tell her that nothing had changed, but he thought it presumptuous and intrusive in light of what he had learned. Perhaps she wasn't ready to hear how he felt about her. They were there together, and in that moment, that was all that mattered. Anything more than that could wait.

"It is getting late now," his uncle Alistair announced when the final painter retreated. "Or early depending on your perspective," he said, glancing at his watch. "You both need to get some rest. Tabitha," he said, standing up. "Why don't I show you to your room?"

"Okay," Tabitha said, joining him in the doorway. "Are you coming, Harry?"

"Just let me hang on to him awhile longer, won't you, Tabitha?" Henrietta said. "Now he's here, I don't want to let him out of my sight. Come," she said to Harry, once Tabitha and Alistair's footsteps could be heard on the stairs. "Let's go outside for a moment."

Silver moonlight picked out the silhouette of the distant Pyrenees as they stepped onto the terrace, clouds traveling past the summits, which seemed to be there one minute and gone the next. From the unrelenting way his aunt looked at him, Harry got the impression that she might have been waiting for him just as long as he was unknowingly waiting for her.

When the quiet got too much, he searched for something to say. It was the first thing that came to mind.

"I think I might love this terrace more than any other place I've been in my life. The smell, and the view . . ." He paused to appreciate both. "There's nothing like this in England."

"It's the lavender and the fresh air," said his aunt Henrietta. "Your mother loved it too, you know. Oh yes," she said, when she saw his shock, answering as if he had moved to disagree. "I often used to find her sitting out here, thinking and contemplating as she did. On this very bench." She smiled, pointing toward a distant tree line. "And tomorrow you might want to have a walk along that track just through those trees over there. It leads to the river. If she wasn't sitting here, she was usually down there."

Even the thought of following in his mother's footsteps, albeit years later, seemed like a gift to Harry. "I feel close to her somehow. Perhaps closer than we ever were in real life." His aunt nodded as if she understood. "Did she really love it here?"

"This was undoubtedly her favorite place. My brother and his wife, your grandparents I mean, well, they were good people, but they were both very different from your mother. I don't think they quite knew how to deal with her. They were academics, people who strived for success. Goodness me, they were determined when it came to their careers, and I don't think they understood when their daughter wanted something different. Don't get me wrong, they loved her. They just wished she was different, and that created a lot of tension."

"I can understand that."

"I should imagine you can, my love. Your mother found peace here, could relax in a way she couldn't at home. Your mother, you see, well, it wasn't just what she wanted to do with her future that was a problem. There were other things too. She was, well, she was different, I suppose."

"In what way?"

His aunt Henrietta sat back for a moment, folded her arms. "She was an old soul in a young person's body. She was mature in some ways and a baby in another. Your grandfather was a doctor, your grandmother a lawyer, which when you think of their generation was quite something." It was incredible to him to think of this, whole stories he had never heard. Ancestors and histories that belonged to him. Doctors, lawyers, painters, all part of the fabric of his life. "They expected things of her, good things, but not necessarily what your mother wanted. She loved the past, anything old, and wanted to be," she said, before stopping herself. "No, that's wrong. She *was* an archivist. Wanted to preserve what had come before. She collected and documented everything and anything. The things we used to find in her room." He couldn't help but smile at that. "It makes me so sad to think of what you told me on the telephone, of how she was living. Of all that mess. My poor little Frances."

"You really loved her, didn't you?"

"She was like a daughter to me, Harry." The thought of her belonging here made him so glad he had come, to meet this person who had loved his mother so much. "Her parents loved her but they had her pegged to follow in either of their footsteps, as if the choice between two careers was enough to be satisfied with. That's why she liked it so much here. She relished the freedom I gave her. Freedom to be herself." Ice clattered in the glass as his aunt took a sip of a long, transparent drink. "But I suppose it was also that freedom which ultimately kept her away from us in the end."

"What do you mean?"

Smiling, she shook away the thought. "Oh, don't mind me. I'm just an old woman lost in the past. Life changed for your mother. You came along, and she couldn't spend her summers in France anymore. She had other responsibilities."

"I suppose I did change her life."

"For the better no doubt. All children bring great joy, no matter the circumstances or difficulties. And your mother certainly had some difficulties. We could all see it, and tried to do what we could. None of us did enough."

To his surprise, that idea came as a comfort. He wasn't the only one who had failed. "Did she ever tell you anything about my father?" The wristwatch, tighter on his skin in the heat, felt cool as he let his hand fall to it. "I mean who he was."

"She never told you either? I'm afraid not, Harry. Her being pregnant came as a shock to all of us."

"And nothing about somebody whose name started with *B*?"

"*B*?" Gazing to the sky, she thought for a moment. "No, I can't think of anybody. Why do you ask?"

"It doesn't matter."

"What about you and Tabitha. Any little ones?"

"Oh, no." He laughed, but it was tinged with an audible sadness. "We're not a couple. At one point, a long time ago, but um . . ." And he found he lost his words then. "No, we're not together now."

"Oh, I see." She took another sip of her drink. "And that eye of hers? It looks pretty nasty."

"It was her husband." That confused her. "She left him, very recently. We were together ten years ago, so I'm trying to help her now. She needs somebody to be there for her. To care about her."

"We all need that, my love," she said. "But I could have sworn you were a couple." Harry shrugged, wondered what to say, and whether he had done something wrong to give a false impression. "Well, good on you for helping. We all need friends like you. But I'm afraid that does cause a bit of a bother. You see, I'm afraid we might have made a bit of a mistake," she eventually concluded.

"Why's that?"

She sighed heavily. "Well, it's August, my love. We're full. We only had one room left that we don't normally let out, so we have put you in there. Together."

He thought of all those nights they had shared a duvet, of how close they had come to confessing the true extent of their feelings, and wondered if just a few more nights would be all right. Sitting there with a person who was loving, yet essentially a stranger reminded him of all those times when he had arrived at a new home as a child and tried to show his approval and thanks, no matter how shoddy his new room was, or how many people he was sharing with. Now was no different. He wanted them to keep him. "It won't be a problem," he said, hoping that Tabitha would go along with it. "As long as you don't mind."

His aunt Henrietta smiled to herself. "This is an artist's retreat, my love. I don't want to cast aspersions, but who sleeps where and with whom is none of my business." Chuckling, seemingly relieved to have discovered the cause of the black eye, she stroked him fondly across the shoulders. "Maybe social services were right all along, and this wasn't the place to raise a child after all."

Darkness filled the house as he crept up the stairs, the cicadas unrelenting in the trees outside. At the top he had to squeeze past a large dresser, but he stopped to look at a selection of photographs displayed upon it, quickly identifying his aunt and uncle at various stages of their lives. Although he wasn't in the pictures, he somehow now felt as if they were part of his history, even if he hadn't known it before then. Just before he stepped away, he saw his mother. Just a young girl, smiling, alongside his aunt.

"Tabitha?" he whispered when he came upon an oak door branded with a number nine. He knocked lightly against the wood.

"Come in," she said without hesitation.

Pushing the door open, it was as if he was looking into his past. Sitting on the top of the bed in what he could only assume was her effort at nightwear, a Rolling Stones T-shirt that barely skimmed her thighs, she smiled as he stood in the doorway. Tanned legs were curled up in her lap, and her strawberry blond hair tumbled over her shoulders, a kink through the middle where she had scraped it back into a bun earlier on that day when the heat made her neck damp. The T-shirt was old, he knew that. She had been wearing it since they first shared a bed twelve years ago.

"I'm afraid that my aunt and uncle made some assumptions. This is supposed to be my room too." He realized then that these conditions were quite different from those under which they had shared sleeping space in his house. That was a makeshift affair, an act of convenience. This was a proper bed, and a proper life. "I can sleep in the lounge, or on the floor if you'd prefer."

She seemed confused for a moment and then looked to the door, which was still open.

"Just close the door, won't you? I think we'll be all right."

He shook his head. "No, this is different. Anyway, my bag is still in the car. I'll need that."

"Harry, will you just relax." Patting the empty space on the bed, she beckoned him over. It was a bed just as he imagined a French bed should be, the head- and toeboards in a classic chateau style, the gray blue of a winter ocean. The floorboards were bare and the curtains gauze. He closed the door, then everything creaked as he moved, the mattress complaining as he sat with his hands on his knees, in clear view. "Please tell me why the idea of us being here together is such a problem?"

"I just thought you might need your privacy, that's all. The last forty-eight hours have been a bit full on, haven't they?"

"Yes, they have," she said, pulling one leg underneath her so she was angled to face him. "But I'd much rather stay in here together than on my own. I'd rather be with you. Don't you realize that yet?"

He nodded, quietly thinking. Eventually he said, "Can I ask you something?" She gave no indication that he should not, so he lowered his voice, as if that might make it somehow easier to ask. "Why did you stay with him?"

The sigh that left her made him regret being so forward. Surely, he had no right to ask such a thing. He was about to tell her that it didn't matter, even though it did, and that she didn't need to answer, even though he really wanted her to, when she began to speak.

"Haven't you ever wanted something more from life, Harry? Haven't you looked back into the past and wondered what might have been if just a few small moments had been different?" Her eyes were wide, her gaze not quite focused on anything tangible. After a moment she looked to him, waiting for an answer.

"You know I have."

"When I was younger, Harry, I wanted to be an artist. Not the kind with paints or canvases, but with makeup and special effects. Like the stuff on TV. Did I ever tell you about that?" Harry shook his head. "I had all these plans, lists and lists of things I would need to buy, and makeup artists with whom I should try and intern. I wanted to move to America, work in Hollywood. I could picture it all, even down to the studio I'd rent in Little Armenia because it was cheaper there, but still close to the studios. I had it all worked out. Do you know why I never did that?"

"No."

"And neither do I. We were together for two years and I never even told you about that dream, yet it was all I thought about for years. Sometimes, Harry, life swallows you up, then spits you out on a different path from the one you intended and somewhere along the way you get lost, and can't find your way back. That's what happened with us. With me. Most people are lucky, end up on reasonable paths. Might even think they intended to get where they end up. Other people like us end up in a place we would never have chosen, and from which we have no idea how to leave."

For a moment he wondered how she might be able to compare their lives with such ease. After all, what did he know about domestic violence? But then he began to wonder whether the violence in her situation was even the worst thing. Perhaps what really hurt was knowing that you wanted something but had no idea how to get it. He had lived his whole life feeling that way. As a child he had wanted his mother, and then when he found her, he had spent ten years alongside her wanting something more than what he'd found. He had asked why she abandoned him, and who his father was, only to be met with the same blank response. Perhaps he understood why Tabitha had stayed with Daniel after all.

While he was still sitting on the edge of the bed, she slipped under the sheets. Although the day had been warm, the air had cooled, the chill of the Pyrenean peaks drifting down the valleys and up through their open window. That night he slept on top of the covers, still dressed in his clothes. But he stayed. He told himself that he stayed because she didn't want him to leave. But as the night deepened and the black sky began to fade into the pastel blue of the dawn, he realized that he hadn't wanted to leave either. There was only one place he wanted to be, and that was with her.

Chapter Seventeen

Harry awoke to the sound of slippers shuffling against the floorboards. With his eyes still half closed he assumed it was Tabitha, so was surprised to find himself rolling into her body as he turned over in bed.

"I thought as much," said his aunt Henrietta. Dressed in a Breton stripe T-shirt and what looked to be a pair of baggy linen trousers, she was the epitome of what he thought of as a French woman. A paint-brush held her hair in place, piled loosely on top of her head. "You looked absolutely exhausted yesterday, and we rushed you straight into a party with a houseful of guests." Speaking in hushed tones, she balanced a tray of food precariously on her lap as she sat on the edge of the bed. The sight of the pastries, juice, and mugs of coffee made him salivate. From the deep smile on her face, and the soft way she gazed at Harry, he assumed that she was totally at ease to have woken them, two strangers, one of whom was in a state of undress with her leg half out from underneath the quilt. He supposed that happened if guests funneled in and out of your house on a near constant basis. Or perhaps, he heard a quiet voice whisper in his head, because he was family. "Didn't even make it out of your clothes, did you," she continued, chuckling to herself. "I'm still not quite sure I can believe you're really here. It's like looking into the past, seeing somebody in this bed again."

Last night, unable to sleep, he had lain awake for hours, listening to the sound of insects and the distant chime of a cattle bell as animals began to wake. Light softened the dark of night, and only when the birds were marking the start of another new day did his eyes fall shut. Over his aunt's shoulder, through the open window he could see the muscular bulk of the mountains, which reminded him that he really had made it to the south of France. Reverting to his aunt, he still couldn't believe she was real either.

"Did we oversleep?" he asked, wondering how he might rectify it if a mistake had been made. "I'm so sorry if we did."

Using his hands, his limbs shaky with fatigue, he

pushed himself up in the bed, anxious that he had taken a liberty that he wasn't quite due. He remembered all those first mornings in new homes, unsure about the way of things. In some he was supposed to be up and ready, downstairs, and set for action. In others he was supposed to stay out of the way. It never mattered how warm the greeting, the rules were always there, and last night, lost in excitement and disbelief, he had forgotten to check what they were. He never did get used to that feeling of waking up in a strange place, no matter how many times he had done it. The discomfort was physical, like a chronic illness, something palpable in his body.

"Of course not," she said as Harry felt Tabitha stirring at his side. Aunt Henrietta let her hand rest against his, glancing over at Tabitha with a smile. "No such thing as oversleeping here, Harry. You sleep as much as your body needs. How many times do you think I delivered a tray like this to your mum when she slept in? All I can say is that this must be a very comfortable bed." Was that really intended how he had heard it, that he was sleeping in his mother's room? "Oh yes," Aunt Henrietta added then, as if reading his mind. "I didn't tell you last night, did I? You'll still find her books on the shelves and some of her clothes in the wardrobe. I never let this room out. It's just for family." Sighing, she suddenly seemed burdened by an unexpected memory. "I suppose I always hoped that one day she would need it again. I still can't believe she's gone. When you told me it came as such a shock."

"Neither can I."

"But," she said, straightening her clothes as she stood up, brushing a tear from the corner of her eye. "Sometimes life throws up something unexpected. I might not have my Frances anymore, but here you are. And what a wonderful surprise you are." Reaching to move Harry's bag aside, his aunt set the tray on the ottoman at the end of the bed. "You just take it easy this morning and come down when you're ready. We'll be waiting for you when you do."

As he watched his aunt retreat from the room, tiptoeing so that she didn't disturb Tabitha, Harry thought how her words brought him a great deal of comfort. The easy way she spoke of their connection, and the joy his arrival had brought to her made him feel welcome in a way he had never felt before. Springs groaned underneath his weight as he shifted in bed, sitting up so that he could see the tray of food. There was even a little bud vase with a sprig of lavender poking out from the top. Cut that morning from the garden? What an effort to make. It was as if his aunt's care stretched all the way back through his lonely years to hold the hand of the boy he once was. Would he go through it all again, the loneliness and pain, if it meant he got to wake up here, alongside Tabitha, in a house that belonged to his family? He thought perhaps he would.

"Who was that?" Tabitha let out a small grunt of sleepy satisfaction as she stretched her arms above her head.

"Aunt Henrietta," he said. The sound of the name rolling from his lips was still a bit surreal, but without doubt in a good way. Tabitha noticed his reaction, and she smiled too, her eyes still partly closed from sleep. "She brought us breakfast in bed."

Harry averted his eyes as she stretched over to pull it toward them, exposing the back of her legs and the lowest part of her behind as her T-shirt rode up. Then he let them drift back. Her body had changed, and he knew that if he touched her in the ways he once did she would feel different. In the place of the soft curves of youth jutted chiseled, sculpted edges. But whatever it was that a woman needed to register his interest, Tabitha had it in abundance, just as she always had.

"I guess this is mine then," she said as she sat back down, pulling the tray and its little legs over hers. "After all, I'm the only one who is actually *in bed*." Adjusting the pillows, she wriggled about until she was comfortable, then bit into a croissant. After a quick look at Harry, she passed him the rest. "I guess it must have been a bit overwhelming yesterday to meet your family along with everybody else who is staying here. There's quite a few of them, aren't there?"

"Yes. Just a few."

"Imagine if you had lived here growing up, like they wanted. You'd be French now."

The idea settled in his mind, the possibility that in his past were scattered versions of his potential self that never came to be. Gazing at Tabitha, he wondered whether the man he was at one point with her was just another possible outcome destined to lead to nowhere.

"I would never have met you, though, would I?"

"Well, you never know. Maybe it was fate that brought us together. Perhaps we were always destined to meet."

"Do you think so?"

"I don't know." She shrugged. "Maybe." Taking another bite from a second pastry, she spoke with a full mouth. "I know yesterday was a bit overwhelming, but everybody seemed really nice." She motioned to the tray. "And very keen to get this right."

"They do, don't they?" In the space of twenty-four hours he had gone from having no family at all to a whole new family he never knew about who he could legitimately call his own. Over dinner his aunt had insisted on showing him old photographs of his mother; one where she was sitting at an easel, painting in the nearby fields; another where she was swimming in the river with an old friend; buying books in the market-place; and reading in a little café. Aunt Henrietta showed him an inventory she used to keep in an old notebook, like those they had found in the house. Titles of books she had read, bought, or borrowed. Part of him was glad to see those items. But he felt another part of himself closing off when he saw the evidence of the life she lived here; that girl seemed so unlike the sad character to whom he had become accustomed in the recent past. When had that vibrant young girl disappeared? Was he the reason for the change?

"Guess what Aunt Henrietta told me," he said as they ate a slice of toast.

"What?"

"That this was actually my mother's room." Gazing out the window he took in the view, doubting it would ever get old, knowing that he was enjoying something that had once been witnessed by his mother. "Look at this." He leaned over the bed and pulled up the old notebook that his mother had written in. On the front she had etched her name and decorated the stems of the letters with delicate drawings of lavender flowers. He watched as Tabitha depressed the filter on a cafetière of coffee and poured them both a cup, splashing in a little cream and one sugar, the way she knew he liked it. It amazed him, little things like that, how observant a person could be, and how much they could remember. It was never the big gestures that stirred connections, but the simple things, the intricacies of everyday life that tied two people together.

"Books?" she asked, leafing through the pages.

"Yes. Titles that my mother read. Seems like she was collecting for a long time." He pointed to the shelves alongside the bed. "My aunt said she wanted to be an archivist, and I'd hazard a guess that what's written in here matches what's on those shelves."

"Just like in the cottage. She must have recorded everything. Even the date she read it, and when it was published," she said, running her finger down the list. Then she stopped, gasped. "Shit," she said, tapping the page. "Look at that."

"Look at what?" Harry asked, reaching for the notebook. But before she offered him an explanation she was slipping from the bed and crouching before the bookshelf. One by one she let her finger trip across the spines, until she stopped to pull one out.

"Harry, would you look at this. It's a first edition," she said, opening the cover, her mouth widening before curving into a smile. "And there's a dedication to your mother," she said, slipping into the bed once again alongside him. "Signed *B*, just like the letters. Do you know how much a book like this would be worth at auction? At least if somebody hadn't signed it like that."

"It's still priceless," he said, and Tabitha set the book down, embarrassed that she had focused on its potential monetary value. She decided not to mention the money again, even though it would have been worth thousands.

"I'd say our best chance would be to ask your aunt if she knows who this was." Tabitha curled her knees up and pulled the sheets up to get cozy. Harry sighed. "What is it?"

"I already asked her last night. She doesn't have any idea. Nor anything about this *B* person."

"Okay. That's a shame, but it doesn't mean we can't still find out the truth. Somebody in this place must know something."

What was he looking for here in this remote French village? The truth about his origins? His father? An explanation for the decision his mother took when she left him on a bench in the shopping center? The Klinkosch box? He wanted all of that, but he also wanted something for himself. A moment to enjoy this place, as his mother once had.

"I want to know the truth, I really do, but I also

want to do more of this," he said, pointing at the note-book. "I want to hear about her life and the things she used to do. Enjoy the places she enjoyed."

"Maybe we could start by going into the village we drove through on the way here last night. It looked really pretty."

"It did, didn't it." Warmth filled him as he sipped his coffee, let himself rest against the headboard. The weight of Tabitha's body beside him seemed to pull him in, and he let his body sink into the space between them, until their legs were touching. "You know, I need to be honest with you about something." He took another sip of the coffee. "While you weren't there, I sort of gave up a little bit. I had arranged to go in and sign the transfer documents, let the house be sold. I stopped trying to save it. And I threw a huge amount of stuff away without even searching for the box."

"You stopped searching?"

"It all started to feel a bit hopeless. I think I was scared to try and got a bit overwhelmed." His whole body ached with weariness, but it was as if each time he verbalized his thoughts it relieved him of some of the burden he had been carrying all his life. "I don't think I came across it. But even if I had found it, what-ever answers I get, it's not going to change anything about the past, is it?"

"No, it won't," Tabitha said. "But it might change the future."

After that, those first few days at the farmhouse were something unexpected, and yet altogether exactly what they both needed. They spent their time walking into the village, enjoying the steady pace with little else to do but learn how to be still. Because while he had spent a lot of time sitting over the last ten years, he learned in those first few days that he had never once learned how to be at peace. All that time his mind had been busy, trying to work out what he could do to put things right, how it might be that he could find a way back to his mother in mind as well as presence. For the first time in years he learned how to sit in a chair without thought or intention, how to take in a view, and live in the moment he was in. At his aunt's insistence he took an easel into the fields and attempted a painting of the mountains, and when he returned with a poor effort and little will to try again, he savored his aunt's laughter.

"Like mother like son," she said.

Armed with the information from the *Le Monde* article, they asked around after the Ellison family, although came up with nothing. They searched the *Pages Blanches* too, but there was only one Ellison registered anywhere close by, and one phone call later they had excluded that one on the basis that they were a couple of expats who had moved to France from the USA two years before. They tried Paris too, but neither of the people they spoke to admitted having any knowledge of a Klinkosch box.

Sometimes Tabitha would say she was going for a walk while they were in the marketplace, and he always understood that at those moments she wasn't looking for company. It was the first time in his life that he realized with compassion that sometimes people were dealing with their own problems, and although her bruise was fading, he knew from the fact she always wore her sunglasses that she was still coming to terms with what had happened in her marriage. He knew that sometimes the worst situation could still hurt, even when it was over. He also knew the best support he could give her was the freedom to heal herself.

Yet he felt out of sorts when he found himself alone, concerned at first that she might not return. He would gaze anxiously at the crowds, wondering if they were judging him for sitting in a café alone. At times it felt like he was still there in the shopping center, abandoned and adrift with nobody to call his own. It made the world feel small and yet simultaneously too large. Often he would watch the men who seemed to be in their fifties, wondering if they could be his father. Often, he liked to think that for his father, time had stopped too, paralyzed by an absence that could never be rectified. That he was looking for him. But he knew now that nothing was ever that simple. Not even a reunion was guaranteed to correct the wrongs of the past. History could no more easily be explained in one sentence than the future could be conceived in a single thought.

It took only a few instances to realize there was no risk that Tabitha wasn't coming back. Sometimes she arrived with little gifts, like a bag of warm nuts, or a small bird statue from Bonnets Galerie, a curiosities shop that was nestled in the medieval cloisters just a little way up from their favorite café. Yes, they had a favorite now. Something they shared, just the two of them. It was the same café in which his mother had once had her photograph taken, and something about that made him feel as if he was exactly where he was supposed to be. It came as both a surprise and a relief to learn that it was possible to sit alongside another person and have them say nothing at all and be totally at ease with that. He had never got used to his mother's silence. Yet Tabitha's was something he was gradually learning to cherish.

He thought a lot during those quiet moments about what he was going to do when this adventure in

France reached a conclusion. Neither of them had discussed a return date, but he knew he couldn't be away
from River View Care Home for too long, and there
was the little matter of the orchestral performance
he had committed to. He had let John the bandmaster know why he wouldn't be there, but he knew
if he didn't get back soon that being part of the performance would be impossible. Not to appear in that
show would be to let Tabitha down again too, and
he was glad that he had brought his trumpet along
to practice. In the early evenings he stepped out into
the barn, ran through the songs he was meant to play
with his sheet music propped up on an easel. Only last
night he had finished his set to hear applause coming
from behind him. His aunt was there, along with his
uncle, both listening in.

"Simply wonderful," she said. "Like a miracle."
That evening he hadn't been able to stop smiling, and
when Tabitha asked him what he was grinning about
he had shrugged and said nothing.

But what felt more complicated was the situation
between him and Tabitha. He wanted so much to put
right the things he had got wrong by telling her just
how he felt, but then he would catch her in a moment of
quiet contemplation and wonder how he was supposed
to tell a person who had come through so much hurt

that he wanted so much from her. They had teetered on expressing themselves back in England, but that seemed like a long time ago, and a lot had happened since then. Tabitha seemed distracted the more time went by, going for more and more walks on her own, making work-related phone calls at funny times of the evening, and had become somewhat distant. Those first nights they had fallen asleep holding hands, but now when they slept, she turned away, whispering good night without looking into his eyes. Was she regretting it? Was this second chance already running its course? When they got in bed on one of the evenings following a late dinner and too much wine, he decided to ask her.

"Is there anything wrong, Tabitha?" By then there was little friction between them, and they both comfortably slipped under the sheets. She was already moving to turn away, so he placed a gentle hand on her shoulder, against the bird tattoo, and motioned for her to face him. She did, and they rested on the pillows with their hands tucked under their heads. Light from a full moon cast a silver sheen across her skin. It had been a boiling-hot day, and that afternoon they had paddled in the river and her cheeks had become lightly burned by the sun. Still she looked beautiful to him, perhaps even more so than before.

"Yes, I'm fine. Why do you ask?"

"I don't know, it's just, you seem a bit quiet, as if there's something on your mind."

As she rolled onto her back the moonlight caught her cheekbone and he wasn't sure whether the sheen on her skin was from warmth or whether a tear had bled from her eye.

"I was just thinking about the past. Whether if once somebody leaves it's really over."

Was she thinking about Daniel? Did she fear the return to normal life as he did, albeit for different reasons? Harry had hoped she was as wrapped up in thoughts about them as he was, but of course she had other, much more pressing matters to resolve. He knew he had to reassure her.

"Yes, I think once it's over, it's over, Tabitha. When somebody leaves it's the purest indication that they don't want to go back." He said it quickly, wanted to ease her fears. "You never have to go back to Daniel again."

"You think?" she asked, her voice quiet. "He keeps sending me messages. He is saying terrible things. Threatening me and saying that he won't let me leave him. Threatening to hurt you."

"I won't let him hurt you, Tabitha. He doesn't have a choice about this. If you say it's over, it's over."

Sighing, she touched the edge of her eye. "I hope

you're right, Harry, but it's never been that simple before."

The bruise was almost gone but he could see the pain of what she had been through had not. It took courage on his part to let his fingers brush her cheek in that moment, for them to slip down and mingle with her hair. Moving into his touch, she smiled, but still she turned away. There were so many things he wanted to say, promises he wanted to make, but the words failed him, and he thought in place of saying the wrong thing, perhaps it was better to say nothing at all.

When he awoke the following morning it was to an empty bed, yet after a moment of disorientation he realized that he could hear Tabitha's voice in the kitchen, chatting with his aunt Henrietta. They had spent the best part of a week doing the best part of nothing, but he was aware that something had changed in the last twenty-four hours. Something in the dynamic of the conversation had caused a shift on the tide and now he found himself floating in what felt like the opposite direction from Tabitha. Each day they had woken up and she had been there, already awake, waiting for him. Once she had kissed him on the nose, and he had thought how wonderful it was to wake in a world where his life was lived in her vision. On a couple of occasions he had found notes, one on his pillow, the other in his shoe. But today she was gone, and that simple difference felt seismic. For the first time since their arrival, he felt acutely aware that the life he was living in France wasn't really his. This was nothing more than an interlude to reality, both on holiday from who they really were.

A few moments later he saw his aunt and uncle walking away across the driveway. He checked the clock; later than he had expected. They had mentioned the need for supplies the night before, both food and paint, and that they were heading into Toulouse the following day. All the painters were busy in the barn with yet another nude, this time a middle-aged man with long blond hair. More were scattered like cats through the grass, gazing up at the mountains. He recognized the blond man sprawled out on a rug. He had been there several times, always seemed to be watching Harry in a way that Harry wasn't entirely sure he liked. But as his aunt's car drove away, Harry's attention was drawn by Tabitha heading from the house, taking up a seat on the veranda. Setting a plate of breakfast on the table alongside a mug of coffee, she dialed a number on her telephone then held it to her ear.

"Yes, hello, is that Lucian?" Pausing for a moment, Harry listened. He told himself to pull back, but when he started to walk away he stopped, returning to the open window. "Yes, yes, it is, good morning." She waited while the person on the other end spoke. "I know, I'm so sorry. It's just that something came up, and I was unexpectedly delayed." Again, she waited. "Well, it was looking that way for a time, but I've made a decision. I'd like to tell you that I can accept your offer, and that next month will be fine." Harry was lost for a moment. What offer? Who was Lucian? "Shall I book the tickets, or is that something you'll organize?" He listened as she waited. "Okay, that's great." A pause. "Yes, I'm really looking forward to it. I know, I can't wait to start either. Working in New York has always been a dream of mine. I can't wait to get there and make a start."

After the phone call ended Harry sat on the edge of the bed unable to process what he had just heard. If he wasn't mistaken, she had just accepted a job on the other side of the world. She had said nothing of the possibility during their time together, and even now as she was having the conversation, she was trying to keep it secret. All this time he had been biding, waiting for what he thought was the right moment. Now it had passed, or perhaps never existed in the first place, because she had agreed to go to New York, an ocean away for crying out loud. When they went back to England, she would be gone. At least now he knew why she had been distracted. He felt foolish for his offer to help her look for a place to live, his efforts to get this right. How stupid could he be.

"Morning," she said as he sat down at the breakfast table a short while later. It was quiet out on the veranda that morning, just them. The only sound was that of a few bees busy at the lavender, and the painters working in the barn a few meters away. "You were sleeping so soundly, I didn't want to wake you."

He nodded although it was at odds with what he was thinking, so sure that the truth was that she had wanted to avoid him. Anger simmered, hurt too. "I must have been tired," he said, reaching over and taking a small pastry from the plate in the center of the table. He would miss those when he returned to England. He took a bite, realized he couldn't eat, and pushed the rest away. "I've been awake for a while actually, just getting a few things ready."

"Oh," she said. "Ready for what?"

"Going back home."

"What?" Neither of them moved as what he said sank in. "You want to go back to England? We haven't even been here for a full week yet. I thought you were enjoying yourself? We still have to ask your aunt about the letters too."

"It doesn't matter now."

"Of course it matters."

"I said it doesn't," he snapped, sharper than intended. Temptation to say that she was right, that indeed it wasn't necessary for them to leave so soon, festered within him. God, it was so easy to linger in something that wasn't right. Because the truth was that he wanted to stay, wanted to eke every last moment out of this experience with her before she left. But he also knew that the longer he waited, the harder it was going to be when it ended. And it was going to end, a certainty agreed to as soon as she had accepted the job in New York. At some point in his life he had to learn to say goodbye to all the things that were never really his in the first place.

"Okay," she said, holding back, sensing that something was wrong. "So when do you want to leave?"

"As soon as possible, I suppose."

"What?" she asked, bewildered. "Why so suddenly?"

"We have to leave at some point, don't we? And I have a lot to sort out, as do you I'd hazard a guess. I have to get rid of the cottage, and before that I have to finish clearing it out." Her gaze flickered like the bumblebee's flight around the lavender flowers. "Plus," he said, and he had to swallow hard before he could get the words out. "I need to find a place to live. And while we're talking about that, I know I mentioned the idea of you staying with me on our way down here, but I've been thinking and I'm not sure that it would really work."

"Oh?"

"No. You need your space. I mean, your marriage has just ended."

"Erm . . . yeah, I guess." It was just a beat before she spoke, but in that silence, he heard his own words again, and thought how hurtful and insensitive they were.

"I'm sorry," he said then. "That didn't sound right. I just mean we both have a lot to sort out. New lives to build. We can't linger here."

Softening, she shrugged her approval. "I suppose you're right. There are some big changes to make. In fact, there's something I need to tell you about."

"Oh?" he asked, trying not to sound as desperate as he felt for her answer.

Nibbling her lip, hesitating for a moment, Harry silently begged her to have already changed her mind. To tell him that she loved him, and that New York was a stupid idea. "I have a lot on with work too. I suppose

I have stayed longer than I should have, so yes, whenever you want to go, we should go."

"I thought you wanted to tell me something," he pushed.

She shook her head. "Only that I agree. We should leave as soon as we're ready."

For a moment he didn't know what to say. Why couldn't she bring herself to tell him the truth, and why couldn't he bring himself to tell her that he already knew?

"We can leave today if you like," he said in lieu of what he really wanted to say. "Here in France we are just wasting time."

"Yes," she said, not looking up. "I suppose that's all this is. A great big waste of time." For a moment there was silence, neither sure what to say. Then, as if she couldn't sit there a moment longer, she stood up to leave. "I'm going into town," she said.

"I don't fancy it," he said.

"I didn't ask you to come."

Shaking his head, he stood to leave, not having touched his breakfast. "No, that's right. You didn't. I'll make a start with the packing. We can leave as soon as you get back."

Chapter Eighteen

Mirepoix, France, Summer 1981

F rances couldn't concentrate on anything but Benoit after Toulouse. That trip had brushed away any lasting haze over how she might have felt, and any lingering concerns about whether what they were doing was right or not simply disintegrated like stone in the path of a volcanic eruption. When she wasn't with him, she was thinking about the next time they would be together. Lost in thought about a future that was as exciting as it was unclear, she had forgotten about Alex's comments about Paris, regarding Benoit looking for some sort of box. His absence, and the reasons for it, seemed trivial in comparison to how she felt while she was in his company.

"What are you daydreaming about now?" her aunt

asked as she passed through the hallway one morning. "It's as if you've been in another place for days."

Perched on the bottom step, pulling threads from the edge of a runner of carpet, Frances shrugged. "Nothing."

Aunt Henrietta brushed her arm against her damp brow and sat alongside her niece. Dust swirled as she shifted, before wrapping her arm around Frances's shoulders. "Darling, you know you can talk to me, don't you?"

"Yes, I know."

"Well then I wish you would, because when I see you like this, gazing into thin air, it worries me. Are you having an episode, Frances? Please tell me if you are."

"What?"

"If you are starting to feel like you were in England, then I can call the doctor. Doctor Dupont is very kind, and he—"

"No," Frances said, laughing. "I'm fine. I'm not having an episode, and there's nothing wrong." Despite her laughter, Frances didn't like the reference to her English self. Coming to France was a way to get away from that girl who lived through periods where life felt impossible, where sometimes putting one foot in front of the other was a step too far. In those moments her father worried himself into drinking and her mother cried a lot, but those episodes never happened in France. It made her uncomfortable to think that people assumed the girl she was here was that same girl back home. To her they were two lives, two separate people. Those problems didn't exist while she was here. Not while she was with Benoit.

"Are you sure? I could call him to come over if you—"

"I said no, Aunt Henrietta. I'm fine. I'm just thinking, that's all. There's nothing wrong."

"Okay," Aunt Henrietta said, taking a big breath at the same time as she let her palms slap against her knees. "Then that's all I'll say on the matter." Taking her word for it was something that her aunt Henrietta did when it came to matters like this, and it was one of the things Frances treasured, her innate trust in the things she said and did; her parents never listened to or believed her in the way her aunt did. When people realized that you had a problem, often that was all they could see. "But that does beg the question, for what possible reason are you staring at my blank wall?"

Sunlight cast a bright shard of light across the wall as Frances stared at the white space, wondering what it was she could tell her. Maybe one day she would be able to tell her aunt about Benoit, but it was not that day. Certainly, she hated the blankness of that wall. She didn't like space; her logging and archiving practices were testament to that.

"I'm wondering why you never hung anything there."

Her aunt gazed at the wall, and then to her niece. Before she spoke, she looked down to her hands, and the thumb of her right hand brushed the golden band on her ring finger. "I suppose I've just never found the right piece. There are lots of decent paintings out there, but you don't just settle on the first one that takes your eye. It's got to fit for a long time, see you through different stages of your life, and you have to look at it every day. Such a decision must still seem like the right choice years down the line."

"You could just change it later."

"Get rid of a piece of art? Oh no, my love," Aunt Henrietta said, her chubby cheeks trembling as she began to laugh. "Paintings are like men. Once you choose them, you are stuck with them. Even if you get rid of it, you will always remember the place it once occupied in your life."

"Maybe you should hang something from the visiting artists," Frances began, but her aunt was shaking her head.

"I'm very specific about that, Frances. Not a single piece on the walls of this house was created by a guest. I can't be seen to show preference. All the painters who come here must trust that I am impartial." As she raised an eyebrow, she also lowered her voice. "Which of course I am not, but the less said about that the better."

Frances smiled and they continued to sit on the lower steps of the oak staircase, solid and strong under her weight. It seemed to her that her aunt was infinitely wise, even though her father called her a relentless hippy, which Frances understood was not intended as a compliment. In that moment of quiet she found herself thinking of Benoit. What would her aunt think of her decision to be with him? Was there any version of reality in which she might understand? Frances doubted it, but the desire to talk of him in the open was too great to deny.

"You know," Frances began, her lips dry, "I went to that old warehouse the other day. The one with all the antiques on the road out of the village."

"The one that belongs to Monsieur Bonnet?" Frances nodded. "What were you doing out there?"

Frances saw something cross her aunt's face, the fine lines that remained white around her eyes shrinking away as she squinted. The look made her think of last summer, the night that she first saw Benoit at the book festival, and when she noticed her aunt watching them.

"Alex took me there," she lied, which seemed to go some way to settle any anxieties her aunt might have had. "He had some lovely things. Big paintings that would look great here."

"Yes," she said, but it sounded anything but definitive. "But how long would they stay on my wall?" Frances didn't know what to say, wasn't sure what had just been exchanged. Her aunt stole a glance her way, and then as if contemplating whether her niece could be trusted, sighed as a conclusion was reached. "Not a word about what I am about to tell you, right?" Frances nodded, eager for whatever it was she had to say. "But it would appear that nobody is very certain where Monsieur Bonnet's paintings come from."

Frances wanted to scream what she knew: Austria, Paris, and Copenhagen. It was a truth she knew because Benoit himself had told her. Place names whispered over her shoulder as his fingers traced the outline of her chest. Since that first day in the farmhouse they had become riskier, as if he couldn't stand to be apart from her. Within moments of being together his hands were on her body, skirts lifted and belts loosened. Their lovemaking had spilled over from the farmhouse to his car, the shop, the toilets of a restaurant in Toulouse, and even the barn on her aunt's property, and that didn't even have a proper door. It seemed anything they did could turn him on. But to share anything of this knowledge would have been no less than a confession of what they were, so instead she played ignorant.

"What do you mean?" she asked instead. "He's an art dealer. He buys them."

Aunt Henrietta seemed disappointed in herself for starting the conversation, but also resolved to finish it now that she had. "Perhaps. But perhaps not. You see, Alex is a bit of a blabbermouth, and claims to have seen a painting by Van Gogh in his warehouse. If it's what he says it is, it would be worth a lot of money. And I don't mean enough to renovate that farmhouse of his. I mean big money, Frances, the likes of which you and I would never even dream of seeing. Art dealing is one thing, but art *theft* is a big business, you know."

"Art theft?" Frances asked, still not following and almost shouting. Up on her feet at the very idea he was a thief, she couldn't accept that Benoit was involved in something like that. Although as the moments passed and facts found their place in her mind like pieces in a jigsaw, she realized that there was something less than certain about how he conducted himself in business. She should have asked more about Paris, and that box.

"Maybe he's rich and he buys them? That's not inconceivable is it?"

"Rich he may very well be, my love, but just how rich do you think you need to be to buy a lost artwork of Van Gogh? Much more likely he's got sticky fingers, I'd say," Aunt Henrietta whispered, standing up and heading toward the kitchen to suggest the discussion was over. But Frances wasn't ready to leave it there, and followed her along the corridor.

"You can't just go around telling people he is a thief," Frances said, following her aunt to the sink. Aunt Henrietta handed her a tea towel and a wet cup, but when Frances took them, she placed them on the side. "Even if he does have a Van Gogh, it doesn't have to be stolen."

"Oh, really," Aunt Henrietta said, dropping her hands in the sink. "And why do you care so much?"

Her aunt's gaze was intense, and it spoke of things she wasn't ready to discuss. This whole conversation was leading her down a rabbit hole, a trap from which she wouldn't be able to escape.

"It's just unfair, that's all," Frances said, picking up the cup and towel. "To make assumptions like that."

"Is it really, now?" Aunt Henrietta rolled her eyes, more at herself than anything. "Well, let me tell you something. From the way Alex described it, a self-portrait of Van Gogh walking through a field with his easel in hand, it is a painting that has been missing since the Nazis took it during the Second World War. Now, if Alex is right and Monsieur Bonnet really does have it, he's either a thief or a Nazi, and I can tell you something for nothing, I know which of the two I'd prefer for a neighbor."

After a moment of silence as what her aunt said sunk in, Frances did something she didn't even see coming herself. She laughed. "That's the most ridiculous thing I've ever heard. Benoit's not a Nazi. He's Jewish."

For a second her aunt did nothing, only stand very still. But when Frances's laughter died down, she said, "Benoit? Not Monsieur Bonnet?" Nothing seemed funny anymore, not even the idea that Benoit was somehow connected to the Nazis. "And how would you know that he is Jewish?"

The image of a Magen David pendant glinting against his chest came to mind, but she doubted her intimate knowledge of his body or beliefs would ease the flow of the conversation.

"I . . . I . . . I just thought. I'm not sure. I just don't think that he's, um," she said, stumbling. "I just don't think he's a Nazi. That's all."

Plates clattering in the water gave Frances the idea that perhaps she had managed to smooth it over, watching carefully as her aunt returned to her task. "Well, I dare say you'd be right, but that still doesn't mean that the things that pass through his hands aren't as hot as the pavement outside." Reaching forward, she opened a window and a breeze drenched in warm summer florals seeped through the window. It brought with it dust from the baked earth that somehow reminded Frances of Benoit's farmhouse. "Word is that beyond that warehouse he has a secret room somewhere, filled with stolen artworks." Frances stifled the laughter this time, but she couldn't conceal the smile. "Oh, I know. Probably all seems very silly to you. But rumors come from somewhere, Frances. There's usually some slither of truth in them."

The toot of Alex's horn as he pulled up on the driveway broke her concentration.

"I better get going," she said.

"Have a great day," Aunt Henrietta replied, reaching with a wet hand for Frances's arm as she went to leave. "And just be careful if you go out there again. Thieves make all sorts of promises they don't have the authority, or even the intention, to keep."

Since the day in Toulouse they spent less time holed up in the farmhouse. Although he was still bound by working commitments, Benoit had begun to carve more and more time from his schedule to see her. Business lunches were rushed or postponed, and whole afternoons were spent together with the locks turned and shutters pulled down, where the air would stagnate with their sweat. Sometimes being with him made her feel so untethered it was as if she was floating, lost in space and unable to breathe. Yet she craved those moments, when all she could hear was his breath in her ear, his whisperings of devotion, and where the paralysis she felt in normal life was temporarily stifled by the sheer weight of his body lying heavily on top of her.

Most afternoons were spent at his warehouse, a second property he had outside of town, and in which he kept most of his stock. Although Alex was often there with them, it didn't matter to her. She might as well have been alone. Lost within the sheer scale and number of artifacts, she felt right at home. The place was an Aladdin's cave and Pandora's box all rolled into one. There were paintings hung and stacked, ancient horse saddles crisp around the edges, the leather thick in scent and heat. Boots too, all lined up in a mix of unmatched sizes. Panels of stained glass that looked to have been lifted from a church, and more costume jewelry than she could ever wear in her life. One wall seemed almost entirely dedicated to Christmas baubles, and in the spaces between them were photographs, some framed, some on shelves in boxes. There were books and furniture and glassware sprinkled between everything. A globe the size of a small planet stood at the center of all things. But what there certainly was not, was a door that led to a hidden room. It was one giant space with a small office at one end. There was no secret to be uncovered here.

With the exception of the secret that she was keeping herself.

Alex pulled on the handbrake as they pulled up outside the warehouse that morning. It was a quiet place away from the life of the village, the barn far from any other property, sitting in a dusty patch of dry soil. It was the kind of place you could hear the movement of trees, the bleating of nearby sheep. Beautiful and sprawling, the surrounding land was green and lush as it crept toward the Pyrenees. Two conifer trees stood proudly like gates to an ancient city, which roused thoughts of Tuscany and places she was yet to visit.

"Are we not heading into town?" she asked. They didn't usually come to the warehouse in the mornings.

He shook his head. "Benoit asked me to bring you here."

"Oh, okay." Stepping down from the car she was

surprised to hear the engine still running. "Aren't you staying?"

"I suppose he wants you all to himself." Disapproval infected his tone, and Frances wondered from where it came. Her love for Benoit, or Benoit's love for her? Perhaps he would have approved more if she had chosen him over Benoit. His little glances her way, the way he watched her, spoke of the same desire she had for Benoit. But she saw little benefit in worrying herself about that. Jealousy was an ugly trait as far as she could see; if it wasn't yours to covet what was the point in craving something? Anyway, she had her own eyes, and she had chosen Benoit, just as Alex had chosen Amélie. Only yesterday she had seen them holding hands, sharing a kiss. Alex turned off the engine and turned to face her. "He told me to tell you to go inside and wait for him. The side door is open." Dust kicked up in little clouds as she walked around the car and headed toward the door. As she reached for the handle, Alex spoke again. "Unless you want me to take you somewhere else."

"What?" she asked.

"I mean, I will, if you want. I'd take you anywhere you asked. Because what you're doing in there with him is a mistake, Frances."

"What would you know about it?"

"You don't know him like you think you do. He's

not," he said, pausing to think. Whether it was to find the right words or the correct translation she wasn't sure, but whatever it was that came to mind it clearly pained Alex to express. "He's not the kind of person you think he is. I saw you with that broach. It wasn't his to give. Do you know where it's from?"

"It's from Benoit," she said, and turned to open the door. "It was a gift."

"I know that, but it was supposed to belong to somebody else. What you have together, it can't become anything, Frances. You are going to get hurt."

"Benoit would never hurt me. He loves me, and I love him."

"Yes," Alex said. "That's what I'm afraid of."

"This is none of your business, Alex. You're just jealous. You can't stand to see me with him."

"Yes, I am. I like you, Frances, I won't lie. But can't you see that I care? I am trying to help."

"I don't need your help." As she stepped inside, she heard the whir of an engine, and moments later the tires skidded on the gravel as Alex sped off.

Alex's words were still on her mind as she entered the warehouse. Her breathing was labored, her cheeks flushed. Each time she came here she wanted to touch everything, smell it, use every little item in the way it was intended and how it had been before. Only today she wanted to shrink. What Alex had said had made her feel stupid, as if she was silly, when only days ago Benoit had made her feel so special. He had locked the doors after she arrived that day, and as he guided her around the warehouse he had dressed her in all the jewelry he could find. Draping her in emeralds, diamonds, and beautiful polished amber, he decorated her until she was dressed up like a carnival queen.

"I look silly," she had said to him then, sitting as she was on the surface of his desk.

"You mean beautiful," he'd told her, and then he had peeled away her clothes until she was little more than skin and jewels. "You are the most precious thing in my hands right now," he had said, and she knew right there and then that she truly was. She had never felt more worthy than she was in that moment, despite how silly she had felt dressed at first in all those jewels. Now, waiting for him to finish making his calls, she realized that she had never felt so foolish as she did then, waiting for a man who didn't even know her real age.

"Frances," she heard him calling from the office. "Is that you?"

"Yes, it's me."

"Come through," he called. "I have a few things to finish here."

The deeper she moved into the warehouse, the stuffier the air became. It licked at her damp skin, unusually humid for the region. With the door ajar he could see her coming from some distance, so she couldn't help but smile when she saw the pleasure on his face at the mere sight of her, and her early fears dimmed a little.

"Hi," she said.

Blowing her a kiss, he motioned to the table in the corner. "Pour us something to drink if you like. It is ridiculously hot in here today. I've got a few more things to sign off here. Paperwork," he said, rolling his eyes. "But then I'll be done."

From the little table at the side of his desk she poured them both a glass of lemonade. A ring of condensation formed as she set his down on the desk, her fingers wet with it by the time she sat on an easy chair in the corner. Those sorts of moments, quiet in each other's company, were the ones she enjoyed the most. His presence was all she really needed, and she liked watching him work. Her father used to take her to the hospital where he worked when she was small, but that had stopped a long time ago. Benoit was a kindred spirit, and in him she had found herself a home. He would never tell her that her presence was a distraction or try to exclude her in the way her father often did now.

"Right," he said, shuffling some paperwork together

in a way that suggested he was done. "What would you like to do today? We have all day together, so what do you think?"

Part of her wanted to stay there in the warehouse, riffling through stuff. He had told her about many of the objects, their value, and the story behind them, but she was sure there was still lots more to uncover.

"We could go for a drive?" She knew he hated staying at the warehouse.

"Or go straight to the farmhouse?" he said with a wink as he joined her in the chair made for one. He squeezed in, shuffled about until he was comfortable, pulling her weight into his lap. "But why wait until we get there." His top lip was bigger than the bottom, pronounced more so now as he leaned in, bringing his mouth to rest on her neck. One of his hands slipped under her dress, and before she knew it he was rising to his feet, carrying her onto a nearby table. Miscellaneous items shifted under her body as he set her down. Peeling away the straps of her lilac dress, her skin came alive as his stubble brushed against her. "You taste of summer," he said, but this time she didn't let him continue. Something about what Alex had said had stuck with her.

"Benoit, somebody might come in."

"I locked the front door."

"There's still the side door."

He smiled, kissed her forehead. "You want me all to yourself, *non*?" She felt his hands curl around her back.

"I do, yes." Guilt rose in her then, swelling in her chest and blocking her throat. Why, if they were so right for each other, were they sneaking around like this? It always seemed as if he was so straight with her, telling her when and where he could meet, and how he had never loved another woman like he loved Frances. Yet she had no say in the matter. She did only as he told her. Benoit was the one with the choices, and yet she craved so much more.

"Then where?" he said with a glint in his eye. "You want to go to a hotel?"

"No," she said, pushing him away. Stepping back, he seemed hurt, his hands held out as if to protest his innocence. "I want us to talk about something."

"Okay," he said, straightening his shirt. "What do you want to talk about?"

"About this, this thing between us. I don't want it to be like this anymore." Her lie was right there at the forefront of her mind. If she wanted them to be something more, she had to tell him the truth. "We are just a secret. Nothing more than a secret."

"Frances, where is all this coming from? Have I upset you? Have I done something wrong?"

"No, Benoit," she said, which she supposed was sort of true.

"Good, because I would never forgive myself if I had. What has upset you so much today?"

Sighing, she resigned herself to the truth. "We're not honest with each other."

"What?"

"This is all a lie. You and me, it's not real. Even when we go out, it's to a city where nobody will see us. To a garden that isn't even open to the public. It's like we're nothing."

"How can you say that?"

"Because I know it. And it's my fault. It's all my fault. I have to tell you something. Something I should have told you before."

"Okay, then tell me."

"I don't want to go home to England. I want to stay here, with you."

"And I want that too, but . . ."

"No, wait. Let me say this. I want to stay, and I know you want me to stay too, but I can't stay with you if I'm lying." This situation wasn't ideal for her confession, but it had to be now. If they were to be what she wanted them to be she had to be honest. Teetering on a precipice, it was as if she was about to jump, with no idea what was at the bottom of her fall.

"Lying?" he asked. "Who is lying?"

"I just said that. I've been lying, Benoit. About something you need to know." That was enough to stop him trying to kiss her for a while. "Something you must know before we can be together. Before we can live together at the farmhouse."

Adjusting himself, straightening the edges of his jacket, his whole body seemed to tighten. "Before we what?"

"Live together. In the farmhouse. I can't go home without you, but I can't stay here until I tell you the truth."

It was, for a moment, as if she was watching a painting fade in the sun. His face became a pale gray, his lips shriveled, losing their moist pink fullness that only moments ago had been traveling along her neck. The soft scar on his cheek twitched. His wandering hands slipped into his pockets, then one came up to his face, stroking at his stubble. "You mean, you and me together, Frances?" She nodded. "Living in the farmhouse?"

"Yes," she said. A telephone rang out in the background, and they waited until it cut out. "Isn't that what you said you wanted?"

"It doesn't matter what I want, Frances. What about your studies? Hum? You can't just stay in France and forget about your degree. Where did you get the idea that we would live together in the farmhouse?" The ringing started up again.

"That's what you said you wanted," she said then, realizing that this was not going the way she hoped. "You said you wanted to share everything. That you wanted to share it with me. That I would know in my heart what was right. And I do," she said, stepping toward him. "You and me, that's what's right. You said the farmhouse would be our home. They were your words."

"Yes," he said through difficult breaths. "Perhaps I said that, but I meant it metaphorically." He sighed, brushing his hand across his mouth. "I meant for now, while you are here. While we are together."

"*While* we are together?" she said, and Benoit closed his eyes. "You said you couldn't live without me."

"I said a lot of things, Frances, when we were together in bed," he said, sitting back on the edge of his desk. "But, Frances," he began, his tone changed, more desperate. "*Mon amour*, it was something I meant in that moment. Because of the passion. I felt so close to you, it was as if real life did not exist. It was something I wanted, but—" He paused, shaking his head. "But, Frances, I . . . I . . . the um, *sacre dieu*," he suddenly bellowed. "I can't think straight with this phone ringing all the time." He snatched it up. *"Oui, qu'est ce que c'est?"* he said.

It took only a moment before she realized that whoever was on the other end of the phone was frantic. The person shouted a few things and then Benoit hung up, slamming the phone on the desk. Sweat glistened on his brow. Something was wrong, and from the way he was looking at her she knew it involved her.

"What is it?" she asked, suddenly frightened.

"Quick, quick," he said, motioning for her to stand.

"Benoit, what's going on?" she asked as he pulled her behind the desk. "Benoit what is it?"

On his knees, he fumbled for the key that he wore around his neck. A button popped from his collar as he yanked the key loose. "Now is not the time for questions or explanations," he whispered. "Afterward, I promise that I will tell you everything. Now, please, just do as I say."

She nodded, and with that he used the key from the necklace to open the cupboard door on the side of his desk. Reaching in, he pulled a small shelf free and beneath it she saw a narrow stairway that led to what looked to be a room underground.

"What the . . ." she muttered to herself.

"I said no questions, Frances. Go, get in." Hesitating, everything her aunt had told her seemed to flood her thoughts. He said again, quieter this time, his voice changed. It reminded her of her father. "Come on, hurry up." And then softer as he touched her face, "I'll be right behind you." His face was changed too, whiter than the summer clouds in the sky. It was possible to understand fear, she realized then, even when you didn't understand the threat. For that reason alone she did as he asked, and descended down a set of ramshackle wooden steps, only just maintaining her balance as they creaked beneath her. After just four or five steps she found herself in a small dark room that was no more than a few meters squared, chiseled from rough earth and held back with what looked like an unstable wooden frame. Darkness consumed her as Benoit descended into the space, blocking whatever sliver of light there was before. For a split second the light returned as he cleared the opening, but she had never known anything as dark as when he pulled the door from the other side and locked it behind them. Replacing the shelf, she felt his body move in close to hers.

"Benoit, what is . . ." she began.

"Sshh," he said, and although she wanted to protest, she didn't ask anything else when she heard the unmistakable sound of breaking glass coming from the room above.

Chapter Nineteen

Much to his aunt's disappointment Harry announced the decision to leave while Tabitha was visiting the town. Their regret was reassuring, because although he was leaving France he felt sure that he wasn't also losing them. But just over an hour later with his bag on the bed and little packed inside it, he heard the slap of Tabitha's sandals against the floor. Bursting through the bedroom door she found him sitting on the edge of the bed with one of his mother's inventories in his hands. Beckoning him to stand, her cheeks were flushed with effort. "Why don't you answer your bloody phone," she said, panting and out of breath. "I've been calling and calling." When he didn't move, she waved him forward. "Come on," she said, hurrying him to his feet. "You've got to see this. I can't believe we never saw it."

"Never saw what?" he asked, but she was already gripping his hand, leading him down the stairs. Moments later they were in the car, heading into the town. Just a few minutes later they pulled up on the side of the road, parked haphazardly outside the church.

"Why won't you tell me what this is about?" he asked as they stepped down from the car. Her face glistened with sweat. Weaving through a tourist crowd she pulled him along, before pushing open the wooden doors to enter the cathedral. Dodging lit candles and shafts of light that cut through the high windows that punctuated the walls, they moved toward the back of the church. They stopped in a chapel behind the nave, and before him he saw just a table with a couple of candles burning, sending drifts of smoke up an already blackened wall. "What are you showing me?" he asked, but even as he was finishing his question, he saw what she had brought him there to see. A photograph of a beautiful box on a small stand, exactly like the one he was searching for in his mother's house.

"It's the Klinkosch box, Harry," she said, too excited to control herself. "It says here that it belonged to the Bonnet family. I don't know anything about that, but I do know this. Come on," she said, taking his hand again and marching him back out from the dark atmosphere of the church. Outside sunlight blazed, making him squint as she pulled him toward the market square. "Look over there." Pointing proudly, as if she had just solved the mystery of the Holy Grail, he brought up a hand to shade his eyes.

"What am I supposed to be looking at?"

With greater purpose she pointed again across the street. "Open your eyes, for once in your life, Harry. Where did I buy that little bird statue from?" Across the square, at the Place des Couverts, where the shops hid behind the cloisters and where the air was always cooler, he saw what she was so keen for him to see. Right alongside the bookshop was a small gallery of curiosities called Bonnets Galerie. "Come on, Harry. Think about it. The Klinkosch, the name Bonnet, which starts with a *B*. The French letters from the year you were born. This is all linked, Harry. I know you're scared, but this is your chance to discover the truth."

And he felt it then, as all other worries seemed to crumble away. Possibility simmered in his chest, making his heart thrum. "Yes, it does," he said, his voice shaky. Even the upset he felt for her lies about New York seemed to fade then. "If there's a way to know, then I want to."

"Then let's go," she said, holding his hand tightly in

hers. Her touch steadied him, and he was grateful for it. "Let's solve this once and for all."

Harry pushed open the door and a little bell above chimed to announce their arrival. It tinkled once more when Tabitha followed. Packed walls closed in on them, the smell of dust and mildew strong and heady. There was a sense of familiarity about it, the scent rousing memories of his mother, the lack of space a déjà vu. From behind the counter a figure rose. He was older than they were, closing in on sixty perhaps, with straggly blond hair and a well-weathered face. Harry realized that he recognized him as the life model who had been in and out of his aunt's retreat over the course of the week they had spent there. He smiled, and then frowned as if there was something on his mind. Beside him a woman stood up from a creaky chair, stepping forward.

"*Bonjour,*" she said. "*Puis-je vouz aider?*"

Harry looked to Tabitha for support, and she gave him a nudge forward.

"*Bonjour,* hello," Harry said, mixing up his words. He wasn't sure where to begin. "Er, *je ne pas parler . . .*" he began, pauses littering his efforts. Turning to Tabitha, he whispered, "I've forgotten how to say it."

Setting an old book on the counter, the woman

stepped forward. Older than Harry, her face was lined by the sun, her eyes framed by spiderweb wrinkles. But her face was soft, an open smile of youth putting him at ease. "You do not speak French, eh? Never mind. Tell me, how can we help you?"

"Ah," said the man, drawn into the conversation. "I recognize you. You are the English woman who bought the little bird. I remember you. And you?" he said, nodding to Harry. "You must be the man who received it."

"The bird ornament," Tabitha prompted as if Harry didn't know. "But we're not here about that."

"You are the couple from the farm, *non*? Madame Henrietta's great-nephew."

Harry nodded.

"You probably don't recognize me with my clothes on."

Harry found himself looking for familial characteristics in the man's features, the plump lips and wide eyes, but found none. "No, I recognize you," Harry said. "You model there, right?"

"Yes, that's right."

Sitting down on the edge of a small wooden table, the woman folded her arms and looked at Harry, then back to the man in the shop. "You were right, Alex. He looks exactly the same."

"The same as who?" Tabitha asked.

"His mother," she said. "We knew each other back then. I'm Amélie, this is Alex. We were friends."

"Really?" Harry asked, inching closer. "You knew my mother?"

The woman nodded. "We grew up together. Summers at least. She was a sweet girl, whose company I liked very much. Alex too, if I remember correctly." Turning to Alex, she winked, and he rolled his eyes.

The man called Alex came out from behind the counter and offered his hand. Harry took it and they shook. "Amélie here is getting off topic. What can I help you with?"

"We wanted to ask you about something," Tabitha said then. "About a box. You are Mr. Bonnet, yes?"

Alex and Amélie laughed, and he shook his head. "No, no, no. I work for Monsieur Bonnet. What box is it that you want to ask about?"

"The one in the church," she said. "The one that's not there."

For a moment Alex said nothing. Turning to Amélie he whispered something inaudible in French, before his gaze moved from Tabitha to Harry. After a moment he smiled.

"The Klinkosch?"

"Yes," said Tabitha excitedly. "You know it?"

"I most certainly do." His gaze was fixed on Harry.

"But what is it that you want to know about it? It is . . ." Alex stopped mid-sentence, his gaze shifting, his mouth wide. *"Tu te fiches de moi?"*

"I beg your pardon?" Harry asked. "I don't understand. Tabitha, what did he say?"

"He thinks you're kidding him about something."

Amélie took a step closer to Alex. *"Qu'est-ce qui ne va pas?"*

Shaking his head, ignoring Amélie, Alex said, *"Pas possible. Non, non. Pas possible."*

"What's wrong?" Tabitha asked. "We don't know what you're saying."

Alex took a step toward Harry. Reaching up he touched his chin, moved his face left and right, gazing at him in profile. "Now I see it. Now it makes sense."

"What makes sense?" Harry asked.

Stepping behind the desk, he picked up a small piece of paper and a pencil. He drew a rough sketch that they quickly understood was the village with a long road leading out of it, all the while Amélie asking questions that neither Tabitha nor Harry could understand. "Monsieur Bonnet works from the warehouse nowadays. It will take you about twenty minutes on foot, but I think you should make the trip." He patted Harry on the shoulder and moved toward the door. "He usually breaks for lunch at one, so you better get a move on. Come on, don't waste time. Everything you want to know he will be able to answer."

It took them half an hour and considerable protest on Harry's behalf before Tabitha would accept that they were lost. As it happened it was easy to confuse your *á droite* from your *á gauche*, but once they doubled back to a T junction where they had turned right instead of left, it was only a short drive to the nearest farmstead. Staked outside in the crusty earth they saw a small sign, the paintwork distressed by years of weather funneling down from the Pyrenean peaks. The sign read *Antiquités Rares*. They stopped at the head of a dirt track, cicadas buzzing loudly in the trees to remind Harry that he was in a place so far from home.

"Do you think this is it?" she asked. She looked down at the sign and studied the foreign tongue. "It says they are open."

"I don't suppose there are two antiques warehouses around here. I still can't believe we came here on the words of that man, though."

"Why not?"

"Because we have no idea who he is."

"He was Alex," she said and shrugged, as if that should allay their concerns. "And he said that Monsieur Bonnet would be able to answer our questions.

Anyway, we're here now. We might as well go in and find out." Harry gazed down the dirt track toward a door in the farmhouse at the other end. What truth lay beyond that door?

"I'm nervous," Harry admitted, hesitating. "What if this is just another dead end?"

"Well, it might be," she said, reaching out to take his hand. "But I'm here. I'm not going anywhere." He thought back to that overheard phone call, the knowledge he was already losing her. It made him incredibly sad that what they had, as simple a connection as it was, would soon be over for good. "Come on, let's do it together," she said, and with that they began to walk down the track. Just ahead lay the door. Before they arrived, she turned to him and smiled, feeling as if some of the tension from earlier that day had dissipated. "What would you ever do without me?"

"I don't know," he replied, unable to look at her then. "I really don't know."

Chapter Twenty

There was something comforting to Harry the second he stepped into the old warehouse. It was the familiarity of what lay before him, the stockpiles of old, the things people had discarded or forgotten all corralled together for safekeeping. Even the smell was something to which he could relate. It was the scent of old books, sweet and musty, and he realized with a sense of sadness that it sparked a memory of the home he had known for the last decade. The longest time he had ever stayed anywhere.

Tabitha was already rummaging through the goods, kicking up a bit of a dust cloud. She was searching for something it seemed, although from the frenzied movements nobody would have guessed what. Urgent fingers moved over glassware, crockery, old dolls. Then she stopped as they heard movement in a back office, the scrape of a chair, and footsteps on the wooden floor that steadily grew closer.

An aging man stood before them, slim and tall, his hair receding yet still long on top. The man spoke in French, and then converted into English when his two guests didn't understand. "You are in the wrong place," he said. "This is a storage warehouse. My shop is in the town."

Harry looked to Tabitha, who was dusting off her hands. But Harry was transfixed by the man, trying to work out if he had seen him before, and how old he might be. Mid-sixties he thought. Maybe seventies. Although he seemed familiar, it was clear that he didn't recognize either Harry or Tabitha; he did not look in the least bit pleased to see them.

"I'm sorry," Tabitha said, "but Alex from the gallery directed us here. I'm an enthusiast, you see," she said, nodding toward the tables. "The collection that you have here is wonderful." The man stopped and turned to face them, and Harry couldn't help but be impressed by Tabitha's tenacity. "Isn't that a Pairpoint?" she said, pointing to a lampshade set on what appeared to be a solid brass stand. Soft, muted colors decorated the shade, a motif of flowers and foliage.

The man was quiet for a moment, before his whole

body seemed to shift into an altogether softer pose. In the silence, the building seemed to creak around them. "Yes," he said, moving closer, smiling for the first time. "You know about glassware?"

She shook her head. "Not really. It's not my specialty, but my father was a big fan of Pairpoint glass. We had a few pieces in our house. Still got them, probably."

The man was nodding, and after a moment he approached. "Well, you have an eye for it, that's for sure. This is a very rare example. Worth quite a bit, I'm hoping. It goes to auction next month." Setting down some paperwork on the nearest table, he held out his hand. "Benoit Bonnet. Pleasure to meet a fellow *enthusiast*, as you put it." He turned to Harry. "And you are also in the antiques business?"

"No, no. Not at all," he said, holding out his hand. "I'm just Harry. Tabitha is the expert here."

"An expert?" he said, smiling. "What is it that you do?"

"I work as a museum curator," she said, picking up a small china dish and inspecting its markings on the underside. "I specialize in twentieth-century art and its restitution."

"Restitution?" The man sat back against the table and folded his arms. "I have a keen interest in that myself. Have you worked on any big pieces?"

This was the first Harry had heard of it, and he wondered if perhaps it was an elaborate fable to direct the conversation toward the Klinkosch box. As far as he knew she was curating a show about Chinese ceramics. But Tabitha nodded, totally convincing. "A few. A Picasso, and a Degas. Some smaller, lesser-known pieces."

"That is most impressive."

She set the little china dish back down among the litter of goods and Harry watched Benoit's eyes follow it. "I believe every piece should be returned to its rightful owner, don't you?"

"I do." Harry could feel his heart racing. "If I may, which Picasso did you work on?"

"*Buste de Femme*." Her gaze followed as Benoit gripped the table. "A few years ago, if I remember correctly."

"Yes," he said, hurrying forward. "Really, you worked on it?"

"Loosely. Those responsible for its recovery are friends. I did very little myself."

"Anything you did garners you good favor with me." As the two smiled, both understood a truce of trust had been won. "So," Benoit continued. "You are not from around here, I take it. You are here on holiday, no?"

"We are staying nearby. At the painter's retreat."

"Ah," he said with a sigh. "Madame Henrietta. I do believe she cooks a wonderful breakfast." Harry noticed Benoit smiling at him, perhaps trying to lure him into the conversation. He nodded to show willingness, although inside his thoughts were all over the place, like a tangle of wires at the back of a television. "We used to be good friends, a long time ago. Many years have passed since then." His gaze drifted, as if revisiting something or somebody from a distant time in the past. His eyes settled on Harry again, and then, as if somebody pressed a button, Benoit shook the memory away and got himself back on track. "Well, I don't suppose there is any harm in you browsing what we have here. Please, take a look around, as long as you like. Can I tempt you with an espresso, or some tea while you are here?" He shrugged as if it was no bother. "I was just about to make some."

While Benoit made tea for Harry and coffee for Tabitha she continued to rummage, cooing to herself as she came across items that took her fancy. Imagining his mother might have shared a similar joy when her collections began, when her logging of each item was a carefully managed inventory, sympathy grew inside him for her then. Joy, he realized, could go either way. Feelings needed expression, but they also needed to be shared. There was no joy in isolation, otherwise it could lead you down a path from which it was very difficult to return. That was something he had learned now. He stood up and wandered over to where Tabitha was sitting on a tea chest, flicking through a box of old postcards.

"Do you know," she said, "there is probably something like the value of a thousand pounds in this one box. Some of these could go for fifteen, twenty pounds each, and look how many there are. This is all treasure," she said, her eyes still on the box, her arm motioning behind her in the general direction of the shop.

"That may be so," Harry whispered, "but we're not here for all this, are we? We're supposed to be finding out what he knows about my mother."

"And we will," she hissed in response. "But we can't just blurt it out, can we?"

Just then Benoit arrived alongside them with a small tray carrying three cups.

"She is right, you know," he said to Harry. "We have quite a lot of nice things at the moment. Like this." Benoit handed Harry a necklace and as he held out his hand it fell like a silk thread into his palm. "Eighteen carat, diamond links. It's a Van Cleef and Arpels."

Tabitha dropped the book she was leafing through and rushed toward them. Her eyes widened at the piece. "Oh my goodness, is it really?"

"It is," Benoit said. "You know the maker?"

"Yes. I know their pieces well. It's beautiful."

"And quite rare," Benoit added, removing the piece from Harry's grip. Benoit set it back on the side and turned to the small tray, picking up and handing them both a cup. "Let me show you around. Just"—he stopped, a sudden and urgent fear—"please do be careful. I really don't have things stored as safely as I once did. I don't get many visitors now."

Benoit gave them a tour of the shop, showed them some of his favorite items. Shelves showcased paintings and books, first editions and rare copies, jewelry more beautiful than either of them had ever seen. Harry listened as Benoit and Tabitha discussed dates and painters and felt simultaneously impressed by Tabitha's knowledge, and bewildered by the fact he knew so little. It was in a moment of contemplation when Harry realized that Tabitha was raising the idea of the box.

"We saw it in the church," she said. "The photo in the chapel." Benoit was nodding. "The placard said it was still lost."

"Since the war, my dear." He shook his head and let go of a heavy sigh. "A terrible shame."

"And it belonged in your family? Your name is Bonnet, but I thought it belonged to the Ellison family?"

"You are a remarkable historian," he said with a

smile, "and also quite right. My grandfather was Jacob Ellison. He gave it as a gift to my mother when she married my father. But where it is now, we could never hope to know."

Harry saw something on her face change, a bitten lip that couldn't contain whatever was coming next. "What if we knew where it was?"

Benoit sat back against the side, folded his arms slowly across his chest. He set down the small trinket that he had been holding in his fingers, looking from Harry to Tabitha and back again. "Well, first off I'd say you were lying, and then if you persisted, I'd ask you what you wanted, and what exactly you were doing here."

The mood had changed, each now suspicious of the other. Tabitha was shaking her head. "We're not lying. Not exactly."

"Not exactly or not at all?"

Tabitha slumped against a wooden post. "The Klinkosch box is somewhere in his mother's house."

Benoit stood up. Harry could see the small hairs on Benoit's forearms standing on end, and a bead of sweat tracking down a crease on his face. His eyes darted around a little before landing on Harry. "Your mother's house?"

Harry's body shook, and a strange taste flooded

his mouth. He couldn't remember feeling so nervous before in his life. It was as if he was on the cusp of a confession, although he had no idea what it was. Slowly, Harry nodded. "Apparently so."

For a moment Benoit was dumbfounded. He sat and stood several times. His breathing had changed. It was almost as if he had just gone for a quick run and come back red-faced and out of breath. "And who is your mother?"

Harry spoke quietly, the sound of the name bringing back a whole host of memories, many of which he wished were different. But some, he now knew, thinking of the photograph of him sitting in front of the small igloo, were good. "Frances Langley."

Both Harry and Tabitha saw the shift in Benoit's mood. He sat for one final time, but it was an entirely passive moment, his body slumping under the weight of what had been said. It was as if somebody had just told him that he was the president of his country and that they were on the brink of war. The information had taken the breath right out of him, visibly deflating right before their eyes. His hand found the countertop and some of the knickknacks went awry.

"Frances," he said, but he wasn't talking to either of them. "My Frances."

"Are you okay, Monsieur Bonnet?" Tabitha asked.

"Fine, fine." He batted her hand away, appearing anything but. "I have these dizzy spells," he said, wafting air toward his face. "It's hot in here." His gaze weaved its way across items until it settled on Harry. "Your mother? Frances was your mother?"

"Yes."

Benoit was quiet then, his eyes unblinking as if looking for an answer and not wanting to miss it, fleeting as it might be. "And she told you of this box? Of its location?"

"She asked me to find it, and said only that it was in her house. It was after she died."

"What?" In that moment he became even more desperate. "Frances is . . . is gone?"

"A few weeks ago." And that was when they noticed that Benoit was crying. "I'm sorry, I've upset you," Harry said, trying the best he could to recover his composure.

"You knew her, didn't you?" Tabitha probed.

Benoit wiped his eyes on the handkerchief from his top pocket and nodded. "She spent her summers here when she was younger. I cared for her a great deal. A very sweet girl." The confusion clouded his thoughts. "But she is too young to have died," he said, and the thought seemed to lead him to some unknown place neither of them could have pictured. "Too young to . . .

too young for . . . Please," he said, eventually looking up. "Tell me how?"

"A blood clot formed in her leg, traveled to her lungs."

Tabitha still wasn't sure what they had uncovered here, but she was sure it was something both as painful as it was pertinent. She looked at Benoit, whose limp face appeared red and puffy, and then to Harry, who looked as lost as a small boy on his first day of school. What was it that had moved Benoit so? Why was he so upset to learn of the death of a girl he once knew so many years before? And it was then she realized, finally seeing the facts before her, that everything made sense. She recognized the look on his face, and realized she understood it as something from her own past. It was the look of a person who had just lost the love of their life. It was her own reflection when she lost Harry.

Tabitha stood up, moved a little closer to the two men who were still not saying or doing anything.

"Benoit," she said. "It's you, isn't it?"

"What is me?"

"You weren't shocked that his mother had the box, only that we knew she had it. You gave it to her, didn't you?"

Benoit seemed to compose himself then. He stood up, his damp forehead creasing at the idea, his face wrinkled and puckered. "I've no idea what you're talking about."

Tabitha was smiling. She sat next to Harry and held his hand. "I thought he was too old at first, but it makes perfect sense. The letters. The book. *B*." Harry understood where she was going with the idea. Tabitha gazed at Benoit. "It's you. You loved her."

"I said I don't know what you are talking about," Benoit protested, but Tabitha knew from the way he couldn't meet her gaze anymore that he was lying.

Tabitha turned to Harry. "Don't you see?" It took a moment to process the implication of everything she was saying, all the loose connections finding their complementary half until the picture was complete. He was trying to reconstruct a history he had no idea about, and the strangest thing was that, despite all the gaps, it didn't seem so implausible.

"But he's . . ."

"Old," said Tabitha for him. "Yes." She stood up then, moved closer to Benoit, who despite all appearances of wanting to flee seemed rooted to the spot. "That's why you never signed your name on the letters, isn't it? Why nobody ever knew who his father was." She reached back, pulled Harry toward Benoit. "Don't you see it?" she asked Harry, looking from him to Benoit. "Don't you see what Alex saw? This man is your father."

Could he see it? The man before him sure was older than he had ever anticipated his father to be. But he couldn't deny that it made sense, that the links in the chain seemed logical. But before he could answer Benoit broke the silence. "You don't look like me. You look like her," he stuttered, another tear forming in his eye. Muttering his apologies, he ran from the room, tipping a table and a box of greeting cards as he fled. The sight was so plaintive that neither of them tried to stop him or said anything in return. They watched as he slammed the door and then heard the clunk as he locked the office from inside.

"Are you okay?" Tabitha asked after a moment, both standing there watching with hope that Benoit might return. When Harry didn't answer she didn't push it. Not at first. But then she heard the whistle of his breath as he gasped for air. "Harry, do you need to sit down?"

"I'm going to have an asthma attack," he said, before he staggered forward and pushed the door to the warehouse wide open. Rushing onto the gravel driveway, he fell to his knees. Tabitha joined him, rubbed his back until he managed to pull his inhaler from his pocket. With the inhaler against his lips he went to breathe in before pausing, pulling back slightly to regard the device. After a moment's thought, he remembered what the doctor had said at the hospital, and tossed it to the ground.

"Harry, you should take it." Kneeling beside him she reached for the inhaler, and with a smile and soft movements she brought it to his lips. "Just one puff. You'll feel better."

"No," he said, pushing her away. "I don't have asthma." Leaning in, Tabitha appeared confused. "They told me at the hospital. It's just a panic attack. It's all in my mind."

Tabitha chose not to question him, only held on to his hands, and after a while, sitting together, his breathing returned to normal and he could bring himself to speak. Warm sunlight caressed his face.

"Are you okay now?"

He felt his face flush. "A bit embarrassed, if I'm honest."

"Well, you have no reason to be. There's no shame in having a panic attack. It was pretty big information you just got delivered in there."

"I don't know. I can't really believe that man is my father. He's so old. I think I just want to go back to the farmhouse. Can we please go?"

"Of course we can," she said. "Let's take a steady drive back. There's no point staying here right now. He obviously needs time. Come on," she said, reaching for his hand. "Let me help you up."

Driving back to the farmhouse, slower than their journey there, they didn't speak of what had just happened. All the way her hand cupped his, holding him close to her side, and despite the recent revelation concerning her departure for New York, he found comfort in her presence. There was a certainty to it that he cherished, and he knew he would continue to revere that connection even once she was gone. While they hadn't quite solved the mystery of the box, it felt as if they were almost close enough to touch the answers. Even the possibility of having found his father didn't seem as farfetched as it once had. All the clues were there. Was it possible that Benoit had loved his mother and fathered a child? It seemed not only a possibility, but more likely than anything he had ever considered before.

"Harry, I'm only going to say this once, so make sure you listen to me," Tabitha said as they arrived back to the quiet of their bedroom, bags half packed on the bed. "We can't, under any circumstances, leave now." Their skin was damp with sweat. The sounds of the painters chatting over lunch thrummed through the heat of midday. Harry was sitting on the edge of the bed, still in shock. Tabitha was pacing back and forth, fired up and ready to dig. "It all makes sense. We have to go back another time and talk to him again."

But Harry didn't hear her. He wasn't listening to anything but the thunderous sound of his own thoughts, raining down on him like a torrent. "Even then he would have been, what, thirty? Thirty-five? Mum was sixteen when she got pregnant with me."

"It would explain everything, Harry, including why she never told you. She loved him, so maybe she was protecting him." A memory came to him then, of a holiday they had once shared in Greece, the way her nose tanned deeper than the rest of her face, and how she got freckles in a small patch on her left cheek. The little moped they'd hired, the day on the beach where they found a stone in the shape of a heart. Where was that stone now? What had happened to those hopeful people? What had happened to him? "We have found your father, Harry. We must stay. You can't let it go now you're this close."

His weight shifted as she sat beside him. Harry watched as her hand slipped over his. "He didn't look very happy about it though, did he?"

"He was in shock. Your aunt said that your mother left France in a rush, so maybe he never even knew about you." Harry felt her fingers grip his. "He didn't know what to say to us, that was all."

Harry found himself thinking about the man they had met just an hour before. He didn't know him of course, had no idea about his life or beliefs or the things he liked. But he had warmed to him. He had seemed familiar, as if perhaps he had met him before. But perhaps it was not Benoit he recognized, but instead himself in Benoit's features. Could they have that conversation? Could Harry finally have the answers he had always hoped for?

"You really think he'd want me to go back?"

"Yes, I do." She knelt on the floor before him, resting her arms on his legs. Lowering her voice, she spoke as she once had in the past, when it was just them, as close as skin, watching her eyes glisten in the dark. "Who wouldn't want you in their life?"

Their time together that morning had made him forget that France was coming to an end. That she was leaving him, as he had once left her. Remembering now, it was as if it was happening all over again.

"You, Tabitha." For a moment she was confused, but he had to tell her he knew. "I'm going to lose you, aren't I? I overheard you this morning. I know about the job in New York."

She sat back on her heels, rubbed her hands across her face. "So that's why you wanted to leave? Get it over and done with?" He shrugged. Scrunching up her eyes, she shook her head. "You think I'm leaving because I care more about a job in New York than I do you?"

"Don't you?"

Fingertips pinched at her eyes as if it was all too much. "Why do you always do this, Harry? Of all the times to raise this, you raise it now. If you knew, why didn't you ask me about it? You always make decisions based on your own thoughts without even talking to the other people about how they feel first."

"Tabitha," he said, amazed that somehow, he was to blame in this. "You took a job in New York. I heard it with my own ears."

"And on your own you decided that meant I didn't care about you? After coming here with you, staying with you at your house? You really think that's what this boils down to?"

"What does it boil down to?" He was feeling nervous then, could tell that she was on the verge of tears.

"I applied for that job before all this began. I was looking for a way to get away. But you still have no idea how I feel about you, do you? I'm going to protect you. Because I'm scared that if I'm with you Daniel will get to us both, that he will hurt you."

"I'm not scared of Daniel."

"You should be." Sinking to the bed, her head dropped into her hands. She began to half laugh, half cry. Harry wasn't sure which it was, but knew there was nothing funny to be found in what was happening. "But that aside, I wasn't even sure whether you still wanted me in that way."

"How can you not know that? I was just trying to give you space. I thought that was what you needed."

"Harry, I've never needed space from you. Ten years ago you walked away from me, and I tried then, really tried to forget you. I didn't want to still love you ten years later."

"So, what, you do still love me?"

Shaking her head, she said, "I can't believe you still have to ask."

He knew it was now or never. There was never going to be another chance for him to get this right. "Tabitha, I still love you too. I was just trying to do the right thing. I wanted to give you space to get over Daniel, and what he did. And, I guess, a chance to leave if that's what you really wanted."

Picking up the hem of her skirt, she wiped her eyes. "You've been giving me the space to leave, while all along I've been trying to work out how I can stay. But I can't, Harry. I can't stay. It wouldn't be fair to either of us."

Words hovered on the tip of his tongue. Just a simple request, one wish, and it would be done. *Stay with me.*

But he also knew that it would be selfish. How could he ask her not to go now? Daniel had been controlling her for years, making decisions on her behalf, and he didn't want to step into his shoes, despite the fact he knew he would be lost without her. He didn't want to hold on to something just because he could. For years he had been trying to hold on to people he loved, and it hadn't got him anywhere fast. From the moment his mother left him on that bench, he had been begging for somebody to keep him, always looking for somebody else's love to define exactly who he was. But he didn't want to be that little boy on a bench anymore. He didn't want to define himself or measure his worth by whom he had managed to hold on to. And he certainly didn't want to hold Tabitha back. He'd had his chance, and he'd blown it over a decade before. They both wanted the same thing, but there was no way to achieve it.

"I do love you, Tabitha, but I know what it's like to live in a situation that hurts, and I can't do that to you. You need something different now."

When he felt his own tears coming, he leaned forward and held her close, their foreheads pressed together. "What if I told you that ten years ago all I ever needed was you?" she whispered.

He shook his head. "Then I'd tell you I don't believe you. Nobody could ever need just that."

That night his great-aunt Henrietta prepared another feast. A family get-together, she called it, just his aunt and uncle and him and Tabitha. It wasn't easy to sit alongside Tabitha knowing that what they had was coming to an end, but their confession of love had brought them closer, and they held hands the whole evening. Harry still hadn't decided whether he was going to leave as planned the next day or whether he was going to try to talk to Benoit one last time. But by then his aunt had confirmed her own suspicions about what went on between his mother and Benoit, although when questioned she said his mother had always denied it.

"I'm sorry I didn't tell you about Benoit," she said as they finished eating. "You see, he often had trouble following him, dodgy types on the hunt for stolen art, and I didn't want to expose you to it. I was never certain that he was your father, but I do admit I had my suspicions."

"I wish you'd have told me anyway."

"I should have," she said, staring at the table. "But I didn't want you to get hurt. I felt sure that he was the reason your mother would never come back here. I didn't want him to be the reason that this was your one and only visit too. There's not much more I can say, other than I just really didn't want to lose you."

A smile crossed his lips at that. "You won't, Aunt Henrietta. I promise you won't."

They climbed the stairs silently after kissing Harry's family good night. Harry was about to suggest he sleep elsewhere when Tabitha opened their bedroom door a little before midnight and prompted him to go inside. After closing the door, she moved to be close to him. Just as it always did when she was so close that he could feel her breath, his mouth ran dry, his muscles tightened, wondering what she was going to do next. The moment was so alive that he could feel its heartbeat. It could just have been his own. Then, hooking one of her thumbs under the strap of her summer dress, she brushed it down, away from her shoulder. She did the same on the other side and the dress fell away, leaving her in just her underwear. Her body was slim, her tummy rounded, full of food from the meal they had just shared. His gaze followed the curve of her hip, then back again, to her chest, and finally to her face. To see her again like that made it hard to breathe for anticipation. Blushing as she removed the rest of her clothes, she took his hands in hers, and placed them around her waist.

"Look at me, Harry." Eventually, after a moment of hesitation, he looked up. "How did you never try to kiss me during one of those nights we slept under the same duvet?"

Fear was the simple answer, but how could he tell her that? How could he explain that his fear of being unwanted was still greater than his fear of being alone?

"I wanted to," he said. "I wanted to so much."

"But you never did," she whispered.

With nothing left to say, no mutual conclusion upon which they could agree, she pushed herself against him, and placed her lips on his. For a second it was like it had been the first time, when he couldn't believe how perfectly they fit, how she knew just where to kiss him to awaken his desires. In her arms he found the comfort of home, of a place he truly belonged. With her, with the person whose body fit against his as if she was a part of him, he felt as if there was nowhere else he was supposed to be. Edging him back to the bed she pushed him to the mattress, climbed on top. Their bodies moved against each other, rocking together, sometimes fast, then slowing down. When it was over, he lay against her, her hair rough in his face, their legs pressed together like clay in a mold. Her fingers stroked against his thigh as he shivered.

"Tabitha," he whispered, his lips against her neck.

"Yes?" she asked.

Part of him dared believe that what he had found

with Tabitha could last forever. All he had to do was say the words. *Stay with me. Please don't leave.*

"I never stopped loving you, you know," he said instead. "Not once since the day I left."

Patting his hand, she pulled him close. "I love you too, Harry," she said. But even then, in that perfect moment, he knew that love wasn't enough. But what he didn't know was that by the time he woke up, what they had shared together would already be over.

Chapter Twenty-One

Mirepoix, France, Summer 1981

Muffled words filtered to their hole in the ground while her eyes began to adjust. It didn't sound like French to her, or English. If she had to guess, she would have suggested German. Maybe Polish. Benoit was calm and held her tightly, whispering in her ear that everything would be okay. One of his hands was clamped over her mouth, the other stroked her hair. Every now and again his lips found the cold skin of her shoulder, slick with the sweat of fear. Her body trembled to the rhythm of goods being toppled on the floor above.

How long they remained there, she wasn't sure, but it was certainly long enough for her vision to adjust to the underground light. Slowly, items in the room bled like watercolors into view; a stack of paintings to her left, some framed and some rolled up as canvases on the floor. Once the footsteps from above faded, she shifted from Benoit's hold.

Watching her with the expression of a small boy with his hand caught in a biscuit barrel, she leafed through each frame. Some seemed familiar to her, and then the sixth frame contained what she thought looked to be a work of Van Gogh. It was of a man walking, his shadow long and lazy under a dappled sun. The subject carried an easel, surrounded by trees and pastureland. Was this the stolen painting that her aunt had warned her about?

At eye level there were shelves, stacked full of jewels and silver, watches whose makers mark she couldn't see but whose values she didn't doubt. The stones in the items of jewelry were so large that they gleamed even in the dark. And then she saw it, the beautiful silver box that Alex had shown her and that had taken Benoit from her just a few short weeks ago, the piece that she had been told would go into his new home, one that she now realized she was never intended to share.

It had gone quiet above them by then. She dared a whisper.

"You're a thief, aren't you?" she said. Benoit was quiet, still. "My aunt was right. This is all stolen."

He shook his head. "You cannot steal something that already belongs to you, Frances."

"You're trying to tell me that this all belongs to you. I'm not stupid." The weight of the broach hung on her dress, pulling a dimple in the material. Reaching up she unclipped it and set it on the side; she didn't want something stolen. Then she held back the frames to point to the painting she believed her aunt had referenced. "This must be worth thousands," she said. "It's a Van Gogh."

He sighed then, shook his head. "Millions, Frances. And no, you are certainly not stupid. In fact, you are so wonderfully smart. What other person of your age would have such knowledge?" Cupping the back of her head with his hand she was reminded of his strength, and also how gentle he could be as he kissed her forehead. She let him, despite the mention of her age, which she knew to be a lie. "These things cannot be moved quickly. They are safe here, while we wait."

"Wait for what?"

"Restitution. These are all stolen works, yes, but not stolen by me. I recovered them. I am giving them back." Even the minor doubts she harbored seemed to fizzle away then. His care for the work was great, his efforts not driven by selfish need, but an altruistic desire to preserve them for future generations. "I return that which is stolen to its rightful place in the world." In that moment, she had perhaps never loved him more.

"And the men upstairs?" she asked, thinking of how Alex had told her that Benoit's work made people unhappy. The silence ushered in by their departure had emboldened her.

"They want something they believe belongs to them. But it doesn't, I swear it."

"This?" she said, pointing to the Van Gogh.

He shook his head. "They would want it if they knew about it." He removed her hand from the frames and set them aside. "That picture has been missing since the war from a beautiful German museum and will be returned in due course. No," he said, reaching above her head. "They are here for this." He pulled down the silver box, the same one she recognized from the photograph that Alex had shown her. "Isn't it something?" Moments ago, she had him down as a common thief. But now, as he spoke with love for the object in her hand, she realized he was so much more. He dared turn on a soft light, and as the room came into view, she saw that it hadn't been crudely gouged from the earth as she had first thought. Instead, it had been carefully constructed, gauges on the wall for temperature and humidity, soft cloths on the floor to protect the ancient canvases. He might have acquired the goods dishonestly, but he cared about what happened to them. He worked for the pieces, not himself. Letting her fingers run along the cool silverwork of the box, appreciating the rippling of the cherubs, the smoothness of the elegant plinth, she felt so foolish for misjudging him. The box was heavy, larger than she had anticipated. She found herself wondering who the men upstairs really were, and what they would do if they got their hands on something as special as this piece.

"Who were they?"

Anger laced his words. "Common thieves. They would rather see this piece destroyed than carefully preserved." He looked to the paintings. "Each piece here has been taken because it belongs somewhere that it wasn't. But this box, this beautiful silver Klinkosch box belonged to my mother. I was not yet born when this was taken from our home in Paris. My mother was just married, May nineteen forty. For years after she cried about that night. They took what they wanted, all the paintings my father had collected, the fine gifts he had bought my mother. Can you imagine how scared my mother must've been?" There was such anger in his voice, but not directed at her, only the injustice of what happened. "But this was perhaps the most special item of all that was lost, a gift from her own father, Jacob Ellison, who had died years before. Frances, this box you are holding belongs in my family, not in the collection of a descendant of some wartime thief." He sat down then, his knees spread wide, his elbows resting upon them. "All of these pieces have their homes waiting for them. Each taken by me in the name of restitution. But I fear that I may not have enough time to get them to where they are supposed to be if those men come back." He looked once again at the box. "I fear that once again this box will be lost from my family."

"What do you mean?" The fear she held for herself only moments ago had been replaced by a concern for the item she was holding. What would become of it if it ended up in the wrong hands?

"They know where I am now. They will be back, no doubt about that. I might just have time to ship the rest of this out, but where can I send something like this? Who could I trust with it when I have no other family to help me care for it?"

"And everything upstairs," she said somberly. "It sounds as if they destroyed it."

But he shook his head. "All rubbish, Frances. A ruse. Everything on that floor is there to detract from what you see before you here."

She realized that the implication was that everything he had told her until that point had been a lie. But she also understood that some lies were told to protect.

Maybe not her, but other precious things that needed to be saved.

"You can't let them get it back."

"Then where will I send it? You can't recruit just anybody, Frances, surely you must understand that. Who could I trust with such a piece? Something with such value. An item that people would kill for." Then he looked up, at her. "Unless." He paused, thinking to himself. "No, I couldn't ask that of you."

"Ask it," she said, already knowing what he was going to ask, and knowing that she was going to say yes. There was no other choice, because despite it all, in face of the doubts, she knew she would help him in any way she could. Because he loved her, and she loved him. There was nothing more important than that.

Although they left their underground hideaway, it was another hour before they left the barn. They didn't speak much during that time, their focus mainly on the damage, which was significant. But not even the precious books that had been torn apart could raise Frances's interest, for her mind was stuck on what she had realized. Although she was going to keep the box for Benoit, she knew now that they had never been what she thought they were. A future for them was not about the long term. Even before they stepped out into the sunlight Frances could feel the clouds that normally followed her in England returning. The place she had found in the world was shrinking away from her, and she too was shrinking along with it.

Benoit didn't try to comfort her as they drove away, the silver Klinkosch box heavy on her knees. When they pulled up at the gate of her aunt's retreat he smiled at her, but it was a smile she didn't recognize. Usually his joy was clear to see, his mouth wide and confident, but this time it was timid and cautious. Perhaps, she thought, it wasn't real. Or then again, perhaps this was the real smile, and everything else had been fake.

"Benoit," she said, one hand already on the door. Clouds had begun to form low in the sky, promising a summer shower, but she could feel rivulets of sweat running down her back. "Before I go, I need to ask you something."

With a heavy sigh he turned to her. Lines covered his face, a pained expression that felt so alien to Frances. Something fundamental had changed about him, and he was no longer the man who had placed that stolen book on her bed. Then, to her surprise, and despite the fact they were in full view of the farmhouse, he reached up, touched her hair. Brushing it behind her ears, she wondered if she would ever feel something as generous as that touch again.

"Anything, my love."

The words were the same but the tune was different. Hearing him call her his love hurt no less than a physical pain, but she pushed on through it, knowing there was harder still yet to come.

"I was wrong about us, wasn't I?"

Part of her wanted him to deny it. He had the good grace to pause, but it wasn't enough to stop the truth. "I thought you understood what we were. How could we ever be anything more than this, Frances? We are at different stages of our lives. You have a whole life in England, and I a life here. You were always going to return to complete your studies, and I am, well . . ."

"You are what?" she asked, every last shred of hope thrown into that final chance.

"Frances, I never told you because I thought it didn't matter. Not in the face of how I felt about you. And what I'm about to tell you doesn't change anything about what I said. When I said I loved you, Frances, it was the truth. But I am . . . Frances, I'm sorry, but I am married," he said, stumbling over his words. His shoulders curled in on themselves, his hands, usually so free and wild, retreated into his lap, a love redacted. His gaze flickered around the car as if even his surroundings were unfamiliar to him now. Frances sat with her mouth hanging wide open. A whole other life that she had known nothing about.

"You are married?"

"From a young age. I married a woman who I was expected to marry. She lives in Nice. We share no love, Frances, not at least as I love you. But I could never leave her. I wish we had met in a different time. Because I do love you, Frances. Perhaps you doubt that now, but it's the truth. I so wish things were different. Everything I said about my feelings for you was true, remains true, but our lives have different paths mapped out for us. And I promise, once you return to university this year you will never think of me again. Perhaps," he said then, his lip quivering, "perhaps that makes this even sadder for me. You will move on, meet a man who can join you on your journey, but I will always be stuck in this age, in this car, here with you."

Looking down at the box, the cold metal on her skin and the weight of it on her knees, she knew that wasn't true. Every time she saw it, she would be here too, in that very moment, being let go. Being set free into what felt like subjection at her own hands. The truth that she had wanted to tell him was still right there on the tip of her tongue. Only in telling him could she know that he truly loved her for exactly who she was. But where was the sense in telling him about her age now? All it would do was introduce doubt about her own part in this, where there was no place or need for it. So instead she told him another truth, one that held much greater importance.

"I would have given up everything, you know. I would have stayed here with you, if you had asked me to."

A tear skimmed his cheek as he reached across, held her head in his cupped hand the way she liked. Lips hot against her skin, he placed a tender kiss on her forehead. "I know you would have," he said, a strain in his voice. "I felt it. And it is because of my love for you that I never asked you to stay. It is because I love you that I must give you up. Not for me, but for you."

Leaving her aunt would be just as hard. Aunt Henrietta held her close as she cried, said it wasn't possible to understand how she could decide to leave with such urgency. Frances gave the same excuse she had given to Benoit, about realizing she still had a huge amount of reading to do before her A levels began— although with Benoit it had been before her final year at university. After packing her bag she sat down on the bed with the stolen copy of *The Great Gatsby* in her hand. The thought of leaving it behind made her head hurt with sadness, especially knowing she would never come here again. That was another decision she took then. Everything about this place was finished for her. Glancing over at the box on the bed, she knew she had another job to do. If the love they had shared meant anything, protecting that box was the most important thing she could do. Every day she kept it safe was proof that what she had shared that summer was something more than a lie. Placing the book back on the shelf, she picked up her bags and didn't look back.

The goodbyes were nearly over, Aunt Henrietta's soft body still pressed against her own, when she saw Benoit's 2CV blazing down the driveway only moments before she was due to leave. They had said their goodbyes already, so she had no idea what he was doing there, driving so fast that at one point it looked as if the little car might topple over on its side. Screeching to a halt, the skinny wheels skidded across the gravel, cutting tracks in the ground as plumes of dust encircled the car. Frances thought of how many times he'd done that before, how he had done it purposefully for her. Was he doing it for her now? This time, blinking through the cloud, all she could think was how the dust was stinging her eyes.

"Benoit?" Henrietta asked, stepping forward toward his car. "What are you doing here in such a rush?"

Benoit hurried from the driver's seat, his hair a mess, his cheeks red. Were his eyes swollen? Had he been crying too?

"Ah, I am in time," he panted.

"What is it?" Frances asked, nerves pricking across her skin like static. Never expecting to see him again, the sight of him standing there brought sweat to her palms and sapped the saliva from her tongue. Looking as disheveled as he was made her fear that the thieves were back, and her eyes flicked to the road to see if somebody was following, the bag with the Klinkosch box heavy in her hand. When she spoke, her words came out like the gravel from the ground. "Is everything all right?"

"Yes, yes," he stuttered. "All is well, I suppose." Laughter slipped from his lips, but it felt unnatural, without resonance or heart.

"Then what's the hurry?" Aunt Henrietta asked. "What are you doing here in such a rush?"

"Well, I heard my assistant is leaving." He tried a smile, but Frances could see it took all his effort.

"Your assistant?" Henrietta said as he took a step closer. "Frances?"

"I was helping him," Frances said.

"I asked her, you see," Benoit added. "She has been helping me catalogue all manner of items in my warehouse. A proper little archivist, this one."

Henrietta looked as proud as she was surprised as she turned to Frances for confirmation. "You didn't say?"

"I was just helping out. It was nothing."

"No, no. It was not nothing, Frances. I hope you know that. You must continue to do this work. You are very talented," he said, reaching forward and taking Frances in a tight embrace. It was the first time he had touched her in view of people they knew, and something caught in her throat as he spoke into her ear. Hot lips brushed against her skin. "You must never give up this calling of yours, you hear me? Never give up."

"I won't," she said, pulling away. An invisible link tried to pull her back, but she couldn't give in to it. He was in there somewhere, that person who loved her, who she had once expected to give up everything for her. Who would ask her to do the same. But the longer she stayed there searching for him, the harder it would be to leave. "I have to go otherwise I'll miss my train. Alex is driving me to the station."

"Good. Very good," Benoit said, stepping back. "Then let me help you with this bag." Before she could say no, he had slipped it from her arm and was guiding her toward the car. "Alex, could you open the boot," he shouted, and as they arrived at the vehicle, he pulled Alex close. "Please, Alex, stall them. Whatever it takes." Pulling Frances's passport from the pocket of the bag, he slipped it into Alex's hand. "Say this is lost, and give me a minute with her."

Alex turned to the crowd and Frances heard him say something about a lost passport and each one of them headed into the house to look for it. Benoit turned to her once they were alone. Her heart was racing.

"You think everything I have said is a lie, and that I am sending you off now to cover my tracks. But I want to tell you that you would be wrong. You think badly of me, I know it, and perhaps you have every right. You think I have used you, but I hope one day you look back and know that everything I said in those letters, and since, was true." Sunlight glinted from his eyes, wet with unshed tears. "I never told you what the broach was called, did I? The one you left in my safe." She shook her head, and then followed his hand to see him pull it from his pocket. "Les Inséparables. It represents an indomitable love, something that nobody could have stopped or subdued. These are not just lovebirds," he said, gazing down at the jeweled piece, "but us. I gave this to you because it is us. I don't want you to leave here doubting how I felt about you. You were always more to me than what you think you were today." He approached, seeking approval, and when she didn't stop him she felt the warmth of his fingers against her skin for what she knew would be the last time. Pinning the broach back in place, he looked up, and for a moment their eyes met. "When I can, I will come to take back the box. Until then, protect it, and everything you know about it, including me. Hide it away, and never let it be seen, as safe as you would keep your own child. There are no lengths you wouldn't go to in order to keep such a thing safe, right?"

"Right," she confirmed. "Whatever it takes."

They both heard Alex calling in the background. "It was on the stairs," he shouted, holding the passport above his head. Cool air encircled her as Benoit pulled away, but he held on to the tips of her fingers as long as he dared. And then, just a second longer, just before they were in view of everybody else, he let her go for good.

"Well then, Frances," he said, still at her side, his tone changed now that her aunt was back. "I wish you well. Going into your final year at university is a big one. Go forth and change the world."

Her aunt Henrietta laughed, was speaking before Frances could cover it up. "University? Well, we hope so in a couple of years, Benoit, but she's got to do her A levels first."

Benoit looked at her, then Henrietta, and then back to Frances. "What did you say?"

"I said maybe in a couple of years. Once her A levels are done."

Much in the same way it had when he explained his underground stash of paintings, the color drained from his face. "You are still at school?" And standing there with Benoit at her side, listening to his silent, desperate plea that her aunt was somehow inexplicably wrong, she realized that she had perhaps deceived him in a no less painful way than he had her. "Frances," Benoit said, almost shouting. She realized her aunt and uncle shared a look of concern, and then their eyes fell to the broach. She felt herself covering it up. "Did you not tell me that you were at university?"

She stalled, before eventually saying, "I don't know what I told you." But she did know. Perhaps her words had been different, but she had implied it for sure, and allowed him to believe that very thing. And why had she withheld the truth? Because she knew if she hadn't, she would have lost him before he was even hers to lose.

"Monsieur Benoit," Henrietta said, more forceful than she had ever spoken before. "She is only sixteen." And that was when she felt her aunt's gaze fall upon her, begging answers to all the questions swirling around in her head. Then she felt her aunt's hand on her shoulder. Frances looked up, and saw the disappointment, and yet still the kindness on her face. "Frances, darling. I think you better get in the car. Amélie," she said. "You go with her."

It was only a moment later that they pulled away. The sound of the gravel driveway faded under the burr of the tires, the green of the trees disappearing as they neared the entrance gate. Turning around for one last look, Frances saw her aunt with her hands raised in the air, Benoit rushing back to his car.

"At least it is over now," Amélie said then from the front passenger seat. "Now you are apart, it will be easier."

Reaching to the broach, Frances pulled it loose from her dress. "We will never be apart," she said. Pulling a notepad from her bag, she wrote, Archive book 1, before opening the cover and continuing inside.

Les Inséparables. Maison Van Cleef and Arpels. Paris.

Scoring a line under the first entry, she began a second, thinking of the box in the boot of the car.

Silver Klinkosch jewelry casket, detailed with cast cherubs and foliage, lid in the shape of a plinth. Two handles at the side with lions and olive branches. Box is lockable and comes with a key. Origin, Ellison family Paris. Date unknown.

"Frances," Amélie said then. "Frances, please. Are you going to be all right?"

"I don't know," she said, placing the notebook back in her bag. "I really don't know." Closing her eyes, she made a promise not to love anything again as greatly as she had loved Benoit. In those moments before she left, she knew she had shattered the trust he had in her. Now, safe in her bag was the most valuable thing he owned, entrusted to her. She would hide it away, do as he asked, and hope it was never found. That was all she could do now, become steadfast in her task in the hope one day it might bring Benoit back to her. Because although he had lied about certain things, he had done it to protect her, to protect the box and other valuable items. She had lied to be with him, lied to her aunt and friends too, and it was those lies that had destroyed what she had once shared with Benoit. Was that how she treated the people she loved, the people and things most precious to her? That truth made her realize that despite her commitment to seeing it through, she would never be able to trust herself with anything as precious as the box or Benoit again.

Chapter Twenty-Two

A few hours after Tabitha slipped from the farmhouse, Harry awoke with a start when he heard a fist hammering against the front door. In the fissure between sleep and wakefulness he heard the mumble of harried French, voices raised and hushed all at once. Disoriented, he was still confused when he heard his uncle's footsteps as he stumbled down the stairs. Harry was sweltering, the atmosphere thick with damp nocturnal heat. Freeing himself from the tangled sheets he reached for the phone on his bedside table to see that it was just before four in the morning.

Only then, as his eyes began to acclimatize to the faint gray light of predawn, did he realize that Tabitha wasn't there. Assuming she must be in the toilet, he thought of the night before, the things they had done.

Even then he could smell her, the earthy scent of her skin. Never once had he dared to imagine that one day they would be reunited as they had been here in France. He was still smiling about it when he heard the knock on his door, and the click of the latch as somebody entered.

"Harry, my love." Something must be wrong for his aunt Henrietta to wake him in the night. Sitting up with some urgency he moved to step from the bed, stopping himself only at the last minute when he remembered that he was naked.

"What is it?" he asked, reaching for a T-shirt.

"I'm sorry to wake you. But I'm afraid you have a visitor." He must have looked as confused as he felt. "I know, I know. I did ask him to come back first thing, but he insists. Why don't you get yourself dressed, and head down into the kitchen. I'll be waiting in the lounge if you need me."

Stumbling from bed, a little delirious, he grabbed the rest of the clothes that had been scattered on the floor the evening before. A throbbing headache troubled at his eyes, too much wine at dinner. For the last week he had been skirting around the bulk of the oversized dresser, yet now, still unsteady with sleep, he maneuvered around the corners without thinking, and the intrinsic familiarity of that sparked a sadness that he was leaving so soon. Through the half-open door to the lounge he could see his aunt and uncle. Sitting by the fireplace they smiled as he passed, but it appeared to him to be a look of concern. Was this something to do with Tabitha? Where was she? Hurrying into the kitchen, his eyes dazzled by the blinding lights, he was overcome by a need to find her.

But on the other side of the table sat Benoit. For a moment it was like staring at a teacher away from school, the strange realization that they wore casual clothes and had a life outside of work. Dressed in poorly fitting clothes, a baggy white T-shirt, with hair that looked fresh from bed, he stood up, fidgeting as Harry entered the room. In his hand he was holding something, an envelope perhaps.

"Please," Benoit said, motioning to the table. Sweat glistened on his brow. "Take a seat, so that we can talk."

After a glance to the door, Harry moved toward the table, and with a scrape of wood against the flagstone floor as he pulled out a chair, he sat down. The scent of cassoulet lingered in the air from the evening before, and four dirty wineglasses remained on the table.

"You realize the time?" Harry asked.

Benoit nodded. His breathing was labored, and Harry thought of the inhaler that he wasn't supposed to need anymore. "I do, and I'm sorry. But this couldn't wait. Not after everything that was said before." Benoit appeared lost for a moment, his gaze fixed on the paper in his hands, which Harry noticed were gripping too tightly, as if he was doing everything in his power to hold on. "And also, after everything that wasn't. After I ran off. I'm so sorry. I should never have done that."

"It's okay," Harry said. With his hands shaking, he slipped them under his knees. All those conclusions he had reached with Tabitha were stoking his nerves. *Are you my father?* he found himself thinking. Taking in the characteristics of Benoit's face, the way he held himself, the hunch in his shoulders, he looked for similarities, roots mapped in DNA. Did he bear any resemblance? Maybe, he thought. It was possible.

"I had to talk to you. I wasn't sure when you were leaving, and I was afraid if I didn't speak to you before you left, I might never have got the chance again. Either that, or perhaps courage might fail me. One of the two." With an air of desperation, he brushed his flopping hair away from his eyes and sucked at breath that seemed in short supply. "If I'd known you were here before I would have made more of an effort. I'm sure I would have." From the timbre of his voice Harry thought he sounded anything but certain. The two or three whiskies Harry suspected he had downed before coming here seemed to have done little to settle his nerves. His cheeks gave off that ruddy shimmer of Dutch Courage, the ficklest kind there was. "I would have," he continued, more certain this time. "I would have tried to do something. To talk to you, to explain, to do . . ." He shook his head as if trying to rid himself of a thought, or perhaps the fear that this was not going as well as he'd hoped. He was rambling. In a sudden movement that made Harry jump, Benoit stood from the chair. Opening cupboards, he moved through the kitchen until he found a bottle of what looked like brandy. He grabbed a beaker and poured himself a measure. Raising it to his lips, he hesitated, and then as if he suddenly remembered that Harry was there, he held the glass out to him. "You want one?"

Harry shook his head. "No thanks."

Benoit knocked the liquor back before returning to the table. Pouring himself another measure, he sipped, slowly this time. Harry hadn't taken a breath in what felt like forever as he waited for Benoit to speak.

"You know," he began, licking his lips and sipping again at the liquor. "Your mother loved my old warehouse. Anything to do with it. Spending time there, cleaning items, cataloguing things that didn't need cataloguing." After removing a handkerchief from his pocket, he mopped his brow. "Your friend, the girl you were with. She reminded me a lot of your mother, in the sense that she wanted to touch everything, sort of swoop through, fingers on whatever she could find." A memory stirred a smile. "She wanted to feel it all, smell it. She was very passionate about the things she loved. Do you know that she wanted to be an archivist?"

"She became one. Sort of, at least," Harry said. "Didn't want to let anything go."

"That doesn't surprise me." Benoit took another sip of his brandy. "Did she ever tell you anything about me? Ever mention a man in France called Benoit?" Harry shook his head. Benoit let out a quiet laugh, laced with sadness and disappointment. "I suspected not. Your mother was a very strong and loyal person." Harry tried not to let that idea upset him. Pain silenced him as he bit hard against his lip. "I met her at a book fair in the town. She was younger than me, but we were both drawn to old things. I gave her a book. *Gave* perhaps is not the right word, but that is how we met. And then you see, the truth is, I grew very fond of her. We used to write to each other after she left for England." Harry remembered the letters that Tabitha had been reading. "When she returned the following summer, we became close. I cared for her a great deal, Harry. It was wrong of me, because I was a lot older than her, and at the time I was also married. But I loved your mother. Very, very much. Unfortunately, the circumstances under which she left were not good."

"What do you mean?"

For just a moment Benoit closed his eyes. Resting his head in his hands, he struggled to find the words. "When you came to me, you were looking for a box. The Klinkosch box, *non*? The one you saw in the church?" Nodding, Harry was surprised when Benoit began to smile. "I haven't spoken of that box in close to forty years. You see, nobody is supposed to know where it is. Except for two people. Me, and one other."

"My mother."

"Yes. When she left, she took it with her. It had only recently come into my possession, but it was in danger. Eh, no," he said, his face wrinkling as if he had to rid himself of a bad taste. "A box cannot be in danger. Not even a Klinkosch. I was the one in danger because I took it. I took it from somewhere it wasn't supposed to be. I reclaimed it, because that box belongs in my family. It was taken from us when Paris fell during the Second World War. My parents were wealthy, and unfortunately for them they were also Jewish at a time when the expression of such faith set you apart. Made you a target. When the German forces entered the city, my father refused to believe that the French would not put up a fight. A resistance, if you will. And we did, in many ways, but still the city fell, and many people lost a great deal. My parents escaped eventually, but not before things were taken from them. Their wealth, their belongings. And also, many works of art."

"Who took it?"

Benoit pulled a cigarette from a pack. Harry didn't take one when offered, but Benoit eased into his chair, seemingly more at ease.

"I do not know. My mother spoke of soldiers as if they were one, you know? They had no face, no smile or frown, no feeling or emotion. No identity other than that of Enemy. Perhaps they were just young men like you, probably even younger, who regret what they did. Sometimes it is hard to find our own way, so I do not blame the thieves themselves. But I always remember the pain of that injustice in my parents' lives. It wasn't that they had lost the valuables, but it was as if they had lost part of themselves. Something had been stolen from them, and I grew up wanting so much to be able to give it back. To place a full stop at the end of an ugly chapter. Can you understand that, Harry?"

"I think so, yes."

"And the more I learned about things taken during the war, the more I realized that my parents weren't alone. Many people lost things in the same way, and by the time I reached adulthood I fancied myself as a bit of a hero." He shook his head at the memory, laughing. This time Harry saw a glimpse of who Benoit might have been in other circumstances. His face was kind, soft around the edges. Handsome once, he thought, with a little scar on his cheek. "As it turns out I was good at tracking down things that people wanted to hide, arrogant enough to dare take them back. Because these items were already stolen, I thought nothing of trying to return them to their rightful owner. In the case of the Klinkosch box, it was to be returned to me."

"So how did my mother get it?"

"Harry, you must understand that to retrieve stolen goods, you must first negotiate with people who live in a different world. A dangerous world. People you wouldn't dream of dealing with under different circumstances. I thought people were following me in order to retrieve this box. As it turns out, it was something else entirely, but in a moment of desperation I gave your mother the box, and she took it back to England. I always thought I would go back to get it, but I never did. I even had people follow her, to make sure she was okay, placed a car outside her house to watch over her. I wanted to go to her, but I couldn't risk putting her in danger."

Remembering Elsie's words, Harry couldn't help

but feel anger at the irony of it. Benoit sent a car to watch over his mother, and the very presence of those people following her might have been the impetus she needed to give him away. "You knew it wasn't safe, and yet you left a sixteen-year-old girl to hide such a valuable asset that people might hunt her in order to get it back."

"Yes, but I thought she was safe. Especially with the people who I had following her." There it was again. Snapping his eyes shut, he wasn't sure he even wanted to hear anything else. "But when I heard about what happened to her parents, dying as they did, I was so sure that it wasn't an accident. After that I was too scared even to communicate with her."

"You were a coward."

"Yes, I was. But then people would stop at nothing to get that box back. They came for me, hurt me. They only stopped because I crafted some story about it being in Munich. I had to do something, and I knew as long as nobody knew your mother had it, then nobody would hurt her."

"And what are you here for now? To make excuses? Or perhaps you want the box back?"

Benoit laughed a sad little laugh. "Perhaps at some point in the past I have thought about that box." Memories stirred within Benoit, a quiet moment of consideration. "I felt very sad that this piece was lost to me again. It was as if I had failed my parents. But no, I did not come here because I want it back. It is not mine anymore."

"Then what do you want?"

Taking his handkerchief, he wiped his brow. "It was quite a scandal then, for me to love a girl so young. I didn't know her age at the time, and you would never have guessed. She did not look sixteen, Harry."

Harry thought of his mother, young as she was, how impressionable she must have been. Had Benoit taken advantage of her? "Did she look thirty?"

For a man of such stature, such wide shoulders and oversized limbs, regret seemed to shrink him then. "No, I admit she did not. But I thought she was a young woman, free to make a choice. She even told me that she was at university, I think. Perhaps I was wrong to love somebody who I knew to be young. Certainly, most people would see it that way, including a few people who had their suspicions, and others like your aunt who worked it out for themselves. But by then, by the time I realized how I felt, I was quite powerless to stop it. And because of that I am ashamed to say that I was pleased when she left. Her presence was overwhelming. I loved her, but I knew she was too young for us ever to be anything more than what we were. I knew we could not have built a future together. I suppose I tried to tell her in my own way, thinking she understood. I was naive, and wrong. But I could not forget her when she left, and I promise that had nothing to do with that box. You see, she took something else that was even more precious to me, although I didn't know it at the time."

"Which was?"

"You." He paused, swallowed hard. "She took you, Harry."

So, there was the truth. Harry sat back in his chair. While he had considered the likelihood, to have it confirmed was a different matter altogether. Harry thought of all those times he wondered about his father, where he was and what he was doing. Why he wasn't there with him. Anger surfaced, unreasonably perhaps, but regardless it was there.

"What I have said is a shock," Benoit continued. "Perhaps you don't even believe that I could be your father, but here, I have proof, see." Reaching across the table Benoit retrieved the tattered envelope, handed it over to Harry. Lifting the flap Harry pulled it out, his fingers moving across the page very carefully. It was written by his mother in a script he recognized, according to the date etched at the top in the year that he was born, telling Benoit he was to be a father.

"I tried to be there for her, really I did. But I have already explained that dangerous people were looking for me, and I couldn't risk them looking for me when I was with her. With you. I had to keep you safe. That's why I never tried to get this box back. I left it there to protect you both. Please," he begged after a moment's silence. "Say something."

It took Harry a while to filter through all the thoughts running around his head. But when he finally snatched at an idea he knew it was the only thing that he could say. "You should have risked it all. At least that way I would have known that you cared. She would have known that you cared. That way, she might have been able to keep me."

"Keep you?"

Harry scoffed. "Don't tell me you don't know."

"Know what?"

"That she abandoned me."

A look crossed Benoit's face, an expression that told Harry the truth looked very different from the picture Benoit had painted for himself.

"You didn't know, did you?" Harry asked. And in realizing that truth, that every one of them had muddled through the best they could, it somehow did more to ease the pain of the past than anything had before.

They spoke for some time after that. Harry was mostly quiet, but when Benoit asked whether he would like to hear more about how he met his mother and Harry said he would, Benoit found he was able to speak at length about a time long ago that he had tried to forget. It seemed almost a relief to him that he had found a person who wanted to hear their story, of how he had loved Harry's mother with such might. And for Harry, to hear of another version of the mother he never really knew came as both a relief and burden; for his arrival not only ended her love with Benoit, but also served as the turning point for the shift in her life, something from which he now knew she had never recovered.

But all the time talking with Benoit had also left him with one more unavoidable conclusion. In all that time, the hour or so that they were sitting together, Tabitha never once made an appearance. When Benoit finally left and Harry went back up to the room it took only a moment for him to realize that her bag was gone, and when he checked the drawer where he knew she had stored it, he also saw that her passport was no longer there. All that was left as evidence that she had ever been there at all was the smell on his skin and the small bird statue that she had brought him from the Bonnets

Galerie. It left him with an emptiness, built of regret, of inevitability, and he thought perhaps he understood then, just how much he had hurt her when he had left.

As day broke, he collected his things and thanked his new family, promising that soon he would be back. But now he knew he had to move forward into a new life; his life, something he had never really done before. Walking up the driveway to the waiting car as the birds began to sing and as the mountains breathed into view, he turned to take one last look. They were waving, his aunt crying and smiling. Gazing back at himself when he reached for the handle was his reflection, through a window glazed thick with condensation. A smile crept onto his lips, least expected and most welcome. This time, although he had lost Tabitha, for the first time in his life he had a place to which he knew he would one day choose to return. As he pulled away from the village, Benoit's barn came into view. For a moment Harry wondered about stopping, saying a final good-bye. But would it be goodbye? Would he ever see his father again? Time would tell, he realized, but this time he felt sure that his absence would no longer plague him as it once had. Things were different for Harry now, and perhaps, he dared to hope, that with time, he would learn to be different too.

Chapter Twenty-Three

The Cotswolds, England, 1981

The weeks following her return were character-ized by whispers. It was obvious to Frances that her mother knew something of what had happened in France, and Tabitha suspected that Aunt Henri-etta had been on the telephone, sharing information she believed to be true. Annabella had always had her concerns about letting Frances travel alone, expressed freely before the event, so that when she was quiet and friendly upon Frances's return it felt unnatural and out of place. Seeing her mother waiting in the train station, their shared characteristics implying that Frances was home, only served to increase her disappointment at her early return.

That night when she stood in her old room, sur-rounded by her childish collections, she wasn't sure what she wanted to be anymore. She had left that house so certain of her future as an archivist, but that summer had changed everything. How could what she had shared with Benoit be over, she thought, as she looked at the Klinkosch box? Had he really loved her, as she had loved him? Lifting the lid, finding the little broach, Les Inséparables staring back at her, she felt for a second as if she was still there with him. Nothing that good could be a lie, could it? Surely you couldn't feel as if you belonged somewhere with such certainty if you did not. But whatever it was they had shared, if it had meant anything to her, she had to honor what he had asked of her. Perhaps if she could get this right he would come back, claim what was rightly his as he said he would. But the people who had come for the box had left a real trail of destruction and danger. Benoit had told her he was going to disappear for a while, and she knew that the box too must become undiscoverable. So, she hid it as well as she could, just as she had promised.

The last weeks of summer passed without much ado. From the couch to her bed, she spent her days escaping into fiction instead of reading her schoolwork. It was as if she was paralyzed, unsure how to move forward into a future, and yet utterly unable to return to the life she had lived before. Last year it was easy to return.

Well, not easy perhaps, but manageable, because she was always sure that she would be going back. Now the dream was over, stuck in England. What didn't help were the strange phone calls that the house had been receiving, always hanging up before her parents had a chance to inquire who it was. Then there was the blue car that had been sitting outside the house. Who was that? Had she been followed? Were they here about the box?

A letter from Benoit had arrived not three days after her return, unsigned of course, but she knew it was from him. Just to know he was thinking about her came as a comfort, that in her absence she had left a space in his life, one that would grow as he did, and which could only be filled by her. But the thought of his regret did little to settle her despair of being away from him, because the void that his absence had created in her life was equally destined to remain unfilled. All those mini episodes that her parents had panicked about, those quiet moments her aunt had tried to avoid; they were the collective precursor to what was coming for her now. The fog was stirring, coming to claim her, as black as the night descending.

It was only when her exam results came in, when she thought about how much she would like to tell Benoit that she had done well, that she realized how long it was since they had been together. Six weeks had passed since her return from France, twelve weeks since she had first arrived at the retreat. All those days she had spent in his old farmhouse, uninterrupted by the rhythms of her body. When was the last time that she had been forced into bed by debilitating stomach cramps, the type she always got during her menstrual cycle? That afternoon she went to the doctor, and they took a small vial of blood from her arm. Three days later they gave her the results. When she had wondered what she wanted after coming back to England, the answer had never been a baby.

Fueled by a sense of desperation she wrote and sent a letter to Benoit that same afternoon telling him the truth. If she didn't say it right there and then she thought she might not be able to tell anybody at all. Weeks went by without a response, so she tried to call the warehouse, but not even Alex picked up. It was as if Benoit had disappeared from the face of the earth. Two months later and tired of shouldering the burden of truth, she stood in front of her mother and whispered the words.

"Mum," she said, and watched as her mother looked up from the legal paperwork she was working on that night. Frances had chosen the time carefully, an evening when her father was at work overnight. Convincing the family doctor to give her a few days to tell her parents hadn't been easy, but she knew if she didn't tell them now, the doctor would do so on her behalf. It must have been the heat or something, because her eyes already appeared glazed over. "I'm having a baby."

Immobilized by her daughter's words, Annabella said nothing at first. But as the truth of the statement sank in, she rose from her seat, walked to her daughter, and took her in her arms.

"Just thank god you've told us. We can help you now. We promise. We will do whatever it takes."

Frances wasn't so sure about that, and was hesitant when it came to her mother's promises and faith in the concept of we. Her father was going to kill her. Gone was the promise of university, the journey to become a doctor as he wanted so much for her. But that night when he came home at her mother's request, he sat alongside her, and following a sustained silence in which he seemed to make and unmake plans a thousand times over, he too promised her that everything would be all right.

"We can get through this," he promised. "We can help you with whatever you need and support you with whatever you choose."

None of the anger she had expected came forth, and that night when she heard their low mumbled voices as they spoke on the other side of the wall, she realized that even though Benoit was gone, they had in some way returned to her. He might have let her go, but she had been recaptured by her parents, where for years she thought they were lost. And true to their word they let her make all the important decisions. There was minimal pressure. Anything was okay by them, they said, although they suggested she needed to decide quickly if an abortion was what she wanted. Would her father prefer that? she wondered. Would Benoit? Perhaps life could go on as planned if the baby was out of the way. But when she chose to keep the child growing inside her, they were there for her too, just as they said they would be.

The months of pregnancy passed slowly, and her stomach grew. Her mood lifted. She felt her baby kick, and Christmas came and went as brisk as a December snowstorm. Settling on a name, her mother said they didn't need a nursery just yet, that babies were the safest when they were kept alongside you. So instead of decorating one of the spare rooms they cleared out the old archives from her bedroom and placed the cot alongside the old chimney stack where it would be warmest. They painted the room in a fresh white, and her mother ordered linen from her sister-in-law in France. Although she missed her things, her father had agreed to let them be kept in the dining room while she focused on the imminent birth. Never once did they ask who the father was, but Frances never imagined it could have been because they already knew.

That April was showery, the petrichor strong, and while she slowed to a snail's pace it reminded her of her early days in France. She was folding baby clothes and blankets when the pains began, and not half an hour later her legs were wet with amniotic fluid. The rains were heavier by then, her parents uncontactable at a work dinner for her father's department. With no other way to go to the hospital, Frances called an ambulance. They wove through the streets, the hard foam of the trolley underneath her. When they arrived at the hospital a kind nurse with cold hands offered to contact her parents just once more, and this time she found her mother. They were on their way, she said, urgency in their voices. Yet three hours later when her baby boy arrived in the world they were still not there. It was an hour after that, when a police officer came into the ward and sat on the edge of her bed with a doctor and a nurse alongside him, that she would learn what had happened. All the conditions were against them, and they had been so busy of late that the car service had been put off. They didn't suffer, the police officer reassured her as he handed over her father's damaged watch, but neither the promises of help nor the broken timepiece brought her any comfort.

Once the funeral was over, although her aunt and uncle tried desperately to get her to go to them, she knew she couldn't. Not because of the box, because then it paled in comparison to the need she felt to care for her child, but rather because Aunt Henrietta told her that Benoit had moved into the farmhouse. When Frances asked when he had returned to Mirepoix she had replied simply enough; he had never left. He had told her of the need to disappear, to leave Mirepoix for a time, but all along it had been a lie, designed to keep her away. Frances understood then; despite her letters and telephone calls he had made his decision, planned his future. Frances, and without doubt a baby, were not part of it.

Because Benoit didn't want them. Even that idea had taken her by surprise. She was no longer her, no longer alone. They were each other. Mrs. Gillman from next door had been there every day to help. Frances wasn't quite sure what she would have done without her, and no matter how hard it was when it was just the two of them at night, her baby was all the reason she needed to get through this. Only when she looked at him, that tiny, perfect, wrinkled face, when she thought about how precious he was, it wasn't just love she felt. She also felt frightened. She had loved somebody else once, with everything she had at the time. She had given it her best, and it hadn't been enough. What she and Benoit shared had been something precious, and she had ruined it with her lies. Looking down at the beautiful little boy she had decided to call Harry, she wondered even then whether her best would ever prove good enough for him.

Chapter Twenty-Four

Pulling away from the motorway, Harry turned into the services and parked his car alongside a small garden planted with roses. Taking out his phone he took a deep breath before making the necessary arrangements. Despite the fact he wasn't ready, it had to be now. Shielding his eyes from the sun pouring in through the window, he arranged for the clearance firm to be there the next day. A dry-edged sandwich of ham and cheese from the café filled a hole in his stomach, while he waited for the necessary documents to be faxed over to Mr. Lewisham. When he spoke to the lawyer to confirm receipt, Harry was sure he had never heard such relief in all his life.

Despite the long journey through the open French countryside on so little sleep, he didn't feel tired at all when he pulled onto the ferry to cross back to his home country. Even the disappointments of the trip, of the way it ended and returning alone, failed to dampen his sense of calm as he stood on deck with the wind in his hair and the taste of salt on his lips. Although he didn't want to have lost Tabitha, for the first time he realized that love was capable of stretching across distance, its power greater than the miles between two people. Benoit hadn't seen Harry's mother since she left France with the Klinkosch box in her bag, yet it was clear to Harry that Benoit loved her no less today than he had then. Perhaps even more, for Harry understood that regret could often sharpen the blade of longing. Watching England bleed into view as he crossed the Channel, he felt for the first time as close to ready as he could be to face whatever was coming next.

As he pulled up outside Nook Cottage the initial impression was one that things had changed. Curtains hung loose on the other side of the window, no longer constrained by goods. The square of grass at the front of the house had been cut that morning, just as he had arranged. Inside he was overcome by a strange sort of comfort, the sight of clear floor space. Moving outside he checked the pigeons and cleaned them out one last time.

"Not long now," he told them, a promise for himself as much as it was for them.

That night he slept on the floor in the corner of the room as he always used to, unable to bring himself to sleep in the place he had once shared with Tabitha. Covered with a thin blanket, the air cool and the sky clear, he thought about Tabitha. Where was she now? What was she doing? Knowing that giving her the freedom to live her life was the right thing to do, he couldn't bring himself to regret losing her. After eventually falling asleep she formed the brickwork of his dreams, their time together in France playing out in his mind. But those dreams were interspersed with images of her returning to Daniel, and when he woke early, drenched in sweat and fears for her safety, he drove to her old house and knocked on the door.

"Nobody in, mate," said the man from next door as he looked to be leaving for work.

"You haven't seen Tabitha?" Harry asked.

"Not for the best part of a couple of weeks."

"And Daniel?"

The man shook his head as he descended the steps and unlocked his van. "Not likely to come back here, I think. Had a few characters knocking the door a few nights ago, and they made some promises I wouldn't mind betting they'd be more than happy to keep. Owes them money, looks like."

If she wasn't here, where was she? "You're sure that nobody has been here over the last couple of nights?"

"Not that I've seen."

Harry watched as the man climbed into his van and drove away. Just to see her, to know that she was okay, would have been enough. Even to know that she arrived back from France. It would have to be enough to know that she wasn't with Daniel. Only the dial tone could be heard when he called her. Perhaps he had to accept that now she was gone for good. He had set her free. Wasn't that what he wanted?

Heading home he picked up some takeaway coffees and muffins from a little café on the outskirts of town, and when he arrived back at Nook Cottage the clearance van was waiting. Goodness knows how the driver had managed to maneuver such a big truck down the narrow lane. Smoke chugged from the exhaust, the engine idling. He let the men in, distributed the drinks and snacks, before showing them the picture of the Klinkosch box.

"So just to be clear," he said, holding them all to court while they ate their muffins and sipped on coffee too hot and bitter. "This is what you're looking for.

Everything else goes, but if you find this, I want it."
They nosed in, their burly frames and overworked
shoulders casting him in shade as they gazed at the
Klinkosch box he desperately hoped he hadn't thrown
away in his moment of stupidity. He thought of Benoit,
and his size. How, in some way, he wasn't so different.
For most of his life he had felt small and insignificant,
but he wondered if perhaps other people had seen him
as something quite different.

"Why's it so important?" one of them asked.

There were so many things he could have said. Before
leaving France Benoit had disclosed its approximated
value, but not even that explanation seemed enough.
He decided on what he wanted to say. "Because it's all
I've got left of a person I lost."

Watching the clearance team was like observing
a colony of termites rip through his home. After just
an hour the downstairs rooms were clear of rubbish.
Throughout the process, Harry spent most of his time
in the back garden with his pigeons, unable to watch as
they tore through the remaining possessions, working
in teams as they moved upstairs. Only once did one of
the men come outside for an update.

"Downstairs is clear. No sign of it so far."

A while later Harry went inside, listened to them
working overhead as he paced the empty rooms. All

that was left now was his sleeping bag. The auction was set for tomorrow. Placing a full stop at the end of an ugly chapter, as Benoit had put it, was not always as easy as one hoped.

A little over two hours later he was handing over three hundred pounds to the clearance firm, and as he watched the van pull away with the last of his mother's possessions, he let go of a breath he had been holding for most of his life. The box had still not been found.

"I guess that's it then," he said to himself, but also to his mother. "Sorry we couldn't find it." With a sigh he headed back to the front door. "Just one more job to do."

His pigeons cooed at the wire of their coop as he approached. He had always thought the birds were the only real thing in this house that belonged to him, but now he realized that just because he had caged them, cared for them, and called them his own, it didn't mean that they were ever really his. It was just one more thing that Tabitha had shown him; connection had nothing to do with possession. That was merely a state of existence. Connection was about a choice, a desire to be together. It had to be a two-way thing, and he realized now, it spanned time and distance in a way possession never could. Letting something go was the only real way to know whether it was yours in the first place.

"I hope you guys haven't forgotten what to do out there." He half expected, half hoped there would be some hesitation. But as soon as he opened the coop and stepped back from the door the first bird flew out, shortly followed by the second and then the third. It took only a moment before all six birds were in flight. That was it. The day was over, his birds gone. It was time, he knew, to say goodbye.

With the house cleared, drafts crept in where before they had been thwarted, and the lure of the fireplace was too much to bear. He stepped into the garden and snapped off some branches from one of the dead trees, and with a few scraps of paper for kindling he soon had a fire growing in the downstairs grate. He pulled his sleeping bag over to the hearth and bedded down. It was warm and cozy, and strangely enough, felt homelier than the place ever had before. He dozed off within minutes, his body and mind exhausted.

The sirens woke him, piercing through the dark. Blue light flickered through the window, then urgent feet hurried closer. Then a smell, something he recognized. Instinct took over and he got to his feet. Because it was smoke. Fire. Pulling his shirt up over his mouth as coughing overtook him, he ran from the room. As he arrived in the hallway, he saw thick smoke billowing down the stairs, clinging to the ceiling in sickening drifts. Wood cracked as the front door swung open, and seconds later the firefighters flooded in. Most headed toward the danger, but one held back to guide him to safety. Stumbling from the house, Harry turned to see black smoke rushing from the windows upstairs. Elsie Gillman was out there, dressed in little more than a robe.

"Oh, love." She moved close, held his arm tightly. "I couldn't make you hear me. Thank goodness they didn't take long to get here."

Stunned by what was happening, Harry stood back, staring at the roof as it cracked and spat. Falling onto the cool grass with the heat from the fire on his face, he thought of his mother as the downstairs window shattered. There really was nothing left for him there now.

It took less than fifteen minutes for the fire service to get the situation under control. By then other neighbors had turned on their lights, many of whom were outside trying to be helpful. Mrs. Gillman made tea, strong and sweet with too much milk. A man whose face he recognized as a neighbor from a few doors down brought him a coat and some shoes. Others were there with no discernible task, yet seemed unable to leave. An ambulance arrived, checked him over, then hooked him up to some oxygen. The paramedic, a skinhead with hands the size of dinner plates and a bird tattooed onto one, insisted on taking him to the hospital.

"I can't leave," Harry said. "That's my house." To leave it in the hands of the firefighters felt criminal and cruel. He was responsible for this fire, as unintentional as it was, and the least he could do was to be here to oversee its salvation. Or demise. Perhaps to witness that was just as important.

The paramedic seemed to be weighing up the options. Harry felt the surprisingly tender touch of his massive hands as he assessed the reaction of his eyes. "Well, you do seem to appear unscathed. Lucky bugger, mustn't you be? We can wait a little while until one of the firefighters comes and talks to you. But then you're off to hospital, all right? They'll need to keep an eye on you overnight."

Firefighters streamed in and out of his house, dragging water pipes and opening windows that remained closed. It didn't take long until he saw the paramedic talking to somebody who seemed to be in charge. Moments later they were walking over to him.

"How are you doing?" the firefighter asked. Peeling her mask away she revealed a blackened neck, her face sweaty and red.

"I'm all right, I think." Harry looked to the paramedic, who nodded.

"I'm looking after him," Mrs. Gillman added.

"It certainly looks like you are. Now, sir, was it you who lit this fire?"

"In the downstairs grate. It was chilly, but it must have got out of hand."

"You could say that. In future, you might want to check your chimneys before lighting a fire. Found all sorts stuffed up there." Harry hung his head. Of course there was.

"What did you find?" he asked hopefully.

"The remains of a lot of paperwork by the looks of things. Still can't really get access to it. Looks as if the smoke had nowhere to go. The damage is surprisingly minimal, save the thatched roof. You won't be able to stay here tonight."

"No concerns there," said Mrs. Gillman. "He'll be staying with me."

"I'm afraid he won't be, my love," the paramedic said, stepping forward. "Now he's spoken to you, he's off to A and E."

"Oh," said Elsie, a little disappointed. "But when will you be back?"

Harry patted her hand. "I don't know. But I will be, I can promise you that."

With a wave of thanks, the paramedic and his colleague slammed the backdoors closed, and moments later, with the blue siren blaring they were en route to the hospital, leaving the house, his memories, and his past behind.

Not an hour after arriving in A and E he found himself on a ward full of patients; all bar one appeared to be asleep. The man who was awake was reading under the glow of a small yellow light, and they shared a moment of acknowledgment, a welcoming wave to a stranger. It made Harry feel remarkably lucky. Only now did he stop to appreciate the danger. The smoke alone could have killed him, if Elsie hadn't noticed and alerted the fire brigade. For years he had thought that his life was worth little, but now it had been brought into question, he realized just how much he valued it. But what he also realized was not just that he cared, but that other people cared too. Glancing down at his borrowed coat and shoes, he realized that he had always had more support and friendship than he appreciated. All the little jobs he used to do for them; they had needed him just as much as he had needed them.

An hour later, the only one still awake, he suddenly heard voices at the nurses' station. Sitting up he glanced across, saw one of the firefighters from earlier talking to two young nurses. There was laughter and a lot of hair twirling, and the idea of the nurses flirting with the firefighter made Harry smile. It also made him think of Tabitha and the night they had shared. It made him wonder what had really happened between them, and whether he hadn't been just a little bit stupid to let her go like that. Why didn't he just ask her to stay? Was it really so important to prove a point? A moment later the firefighter was standing before him, something tucked under his arm.

"Didn't wake you, did I?"

Harry shook his head. "Not at all. Don't think I'll sleep tonight."

"Yeah, pretty lucky escape, eh." His uniform rustled as he took a step forward. "Anyway, I can't be long as I've got the engine parked up outside and it's blocking an entrance. But we found something we thought you might not want to lose." And then from under his arm he produced the Klinkosch box. Calloused hands set it on the bed. "Found it stuck up the chimney in one of the bedrooms. People often hide things they don't want to lose somewhere they think is safe. Probably not something you want to let slip through your fingers again, though."

Harry watched the firefighter leave, then took the

box, turning its blackened body around in his hands. The metal was still warm, the key, strung to a chain along with a simple Magen David star, was still in the lock. This was everything his mother hoped he would find, the search that was supposed to reunite him with Tabitha. Turning the key, he lifted the lid.

Inside, he saw a red velvet lining, as perfect as the day it was stitched in. Next, a small white baby sleeper, and on top of that a little white box, the type that might once have held a ring. He opened it and inside he saw a lock of curly blond hair. There was a small silver rattle in the shape of an owl, and a pair of blue knitted booties. A silver knife and fork, and a Christmas bauble etched with the name Harry. Underneath all that he found a crusty-looking black nugget that he couldn't explain, a dry sprig of lavender that he could, and a hospital band in blue plastic with his date of birth and name written on it. His mother's hidden treasures, the most valuable things she owned, were all mementoes from his birth.

"Are you all right?" He hadn't heard the nurse creeping up on him. A kindly face stood to his side, and he realized he was crying.

"I think so."

Reaching across, she handed him a tissue. "That's a beautiful box," she said, nosing inside. "Baby stuff. Oh my god," she said, pointing. "You've even got a bit of the umbilical cord there," she said, pointing to the small black chunk of what he now knew to be a part of him. And her. "Thank god it survived the fire."

"Yes," he said. "Otherwise I would never have known."

"Never have known what?"

He thought of the firefighter's words, the idea of this box being stored for safekeeping. Then of Benoit, telling him that people had been looking for him, and how he stayed away to keep his mother safe. That she refused to let him live with Aunt Henrietta. Was it possible to believe that she had left him in order to protect him? Instead of the belongings in this box, was he the most precious thing that she kept hidden? He was beginning to think that just maybe he was.

"Never known what, Mr. Langley?" the nurse asked again.

"Just how much she wanted to keep me safe. That," he said, pausing, before finding the certainty within himself to say it aloud. "That she really had wanted me all along."

Chapter Twenty-Five

Cheltenham, England, 1986

Watching from as far away as she dared, she held her breath and told herself not to go back. That she was doing the right thing, even though every bone in her body seemed poised to undo what she had just done. But still she could hear that quiet voice, the same one that had whispered this plan to her in the first instance, reminding her that with her, he wasn't safe. Meters away her little boy, her Harry, was sitting exactly as she left him, doing exactly what she had told him to do.

That was the thing about Harry. He was such a good little boy, so smiley and happy and content. Even on those days when the house was cold or the food in the fridge was limited, he was always there to brighten her life. Never before had she known a person so capable of detecting her mood, of being able to offer a simple touch, a loving stare, when things were getting hard. How many times had Harry pulled her back from the brink? Too many to remember. But she also knew that was no life for a little boy.

Although he had arrived in a world she couldn't understand or comprehend, somehow his presence made her new world bearable. Easier perhaps, than it ever was before. Because instead of waking up on what should have been a horrible wet morning as an orphan, she woke up as a mother. The need to care for him kept her going. But only just. It was harder in practice than it had felt on that day, when all he did was sleep and feed. Aunt Henrietta came for a while, but she couldn't stay indefinitely, and Frances knew she couldn't go to France. Mrs. Gillman was way more than a friend, but still the fog came back, and then it felt impossible. Especially with the men following her. That was what forced her to act today. This was for him. She was doing this so he could have a normal life, even if it meant that his life would be forever without her.

It would have been easier if Benoit was there. Perhaps with him things would have seemed possible. Even close to four years after he failed to answer her letter, she still thought of him when she felt alone, imagined him circling the room at night with Harry in his arms when she needed a break. To imagine them as a family. Sometimes she thought he was there, that she could sense him, but it must have been her mind playing tricks. But she didn't let herself think of him too often, couldn't allow herself that luxury; to do so was to consider everything that she and Harry lacked. Benoit's promises had always seemed so special before, but lately they had started to feel empty. Had he ever loved her? She wasn't sure anymore, not even when she looked at that broach. It no longer felt as if they were inseparable. And now there were people watching them, following them everywhere they went, and Benoit was nowhere to be found.

She knew it was about the box. Benoit had made it clear just how precarious its ownership was. Somebody must have discovered its whereabouts. What if she just pulled that box down from the chimney and went outside to take it to the men who were watching her? Once she even got the box down, was on her way to hand it over, when she wondered if handing over the box would be enough. What if they wanted revenge, or couldn't risk leaving her alive once she'd seen their faces? It wasn't possible just to get rid of the box. She couldn't do it; she had to keep Harry safe.

That was when she knew she had to do something. She thought about calling social services, but what good would that do? They'd be in her home, trying to fix things, and fixing things was no good while there was a blue Ford Escort parked outside day and night, testing handles and attempting a break-in. Taking photos. At some point they'd get in. She couldn't understand why they weren't acting, and somehow that made it even worse. What was it that they were waiting for? No, if she called for help eventually they'd trace Harry back to her. She had to be smarter than that. She had to hide Harry away, just like she had hidden the box. But how was she supposed to hide a little boy, one that she loved, and couldn't bear to be without?

The idea came to her only moments before she did it. It was something about the security guard on duty that day in the shopping center. His face was kind, his shoulders broad, reminding her of Benoit. For a while she watched, wondering whether he was capable of watching over her boy. Whether he'd do the right thing. Then, as if the world was conspiring for her, a little girl fell right in front of them and she observed as the guard dashed to help, picking her up and offering a tissue for her tears. Safety lay behind that smile. It had to be him. This was what she had to do, for Harry, even if it was the worst possible thing she could imagine in the whole world for her.

Harry didn't question her, not for a moment. It was a

cool day, a frost on the ground, so she did up the zipper on his coat. A scrap of paper from her bag was enough to write on, and she placed that note folded tightly in the palm of his chubby little hand.

"Harry, I need you to be a good boy for me now, okay? Hold on to this bit of paper for me." Frances kissed his head as he took it, drank in his smell. "Mummy will be back soon. Everything will be all right, I promise. Do you know how I know that?" Little shoes swung back and forth as he nodded.

"Because you love me," Harry said, as he had repeated a thousand times before, just as she had taught him.

"Yes, that's right. Because I love you so, so very much. And what are we, you and me?" Tears wouldn't break free, so they pooled in her throat, making it hard to speak. "What does Mummy say we are?"

"Insepable," he tried, still unable to say it.

"That's right. We're inseparable." His hand was warm as she held it. "No matter where we are, we're always together. Don't you ever forget that."

After one more kiss she placed his hand on his knee, before steeling herself to walk away. Three times she had to stop herself going back. But she had done the hard part, or so she told herself, even though something inside her disagreed. Harry got down from the bench at one point, went to walk away, and that almost changed everything. But moments later the security guard wandered over. Calling to a lady from the nearest clothes shop put things in motion, and just ten minutes and one gifted ice cream later, the police were there. Harry wasn't crying, so she stayed, watched a little while longer until she saw somebody read the note in his hand. With a heavy heart and wet cheeks she left him then, knowing that her boy was finally safe, away from the men who were following her, away from the box, safely hidden in the protective embrace of strangers.

Chapter Twenty-Six

M r. Lewisham held his head in his hands across the other side of the oversized wooden desk. Covered in paperwork and dusty textbooks, he seemed to lose everything from his pen, to his glasses, to the place he was at on the page. This was his third apology since Harry arrived in the office twenty minutes earlier.

"I'm only sorry that we couldn't get more. The damage was, I'm afraid, just too great to bear."

"It's all right, really," said Harry, shifting in the uncomfortable Chesterfield chair. "There was nothing more that could be done."

"If they'd saved the roof then maybe we could have pushed it, but all we had to sell were walls and a tile floor. Better to sell it as it was, and when the insurance monies come in, we can clear the rest of the debts."

Taking a magnifying glass from the desk, he scanned the page. "Now sign here and I'll get whatever monies are left over transferred to you in due course. Plus, that insurance policy to which Steven Bradbury relinquished his claim. Yes, that's it, just there where there's a cross."

The auction had taken place a few days before. Since then, Harry had been back twice to see Elsie, leaving with a promise to return as often as he could. He didn't want to leave her wondering, as his mother had left her wondering once before. Having people in his life who had loved him across the years was something to be cherished. He had also delivered the coat and shoes back to Mr. Wright, with whom he was scheduled to have cake the following Thursday.

"Thank you," Harry said then as he set down a pen. "I'm just glad to have it all finalized. Sorry it took me so long."

"That's no problem at all. It couldn't have been an easy search. Did you find the box your mother was searching for?" Mr. Lewisham asked as he opened the front door onto the busy treelined St. George's Place in Cheltenham city center.

"I beg your pardon?"

"Oh, I know all about it. She said it was some sort of family heirloom. A jewelry box, wasn't it?" he said. "Did you happen to find it?"

"I suppose so, Mr. Lewisham. Yes, I did."

"Well, that's good. At least now it's back where it belongs. Your mother, God bless her, can rest in peace."

Although he wasn't sure about Mr. Lewisham's final statement, by the next morning, with the house sold and the box safely recovered, he felt unburdened in a way he had never expected. Waking early, he ate breakfast and drank a coffee, before opening the box for one final time. The items in the box told a story he had never known before, one in which he was cherished right from the moment of his birth. Carefully taking each item out he told himself that it was all right to keep some things, especially those that were special to him. But this time, as he removed the items from the box, he found that one of the lower levels also lifted out.

Underneath the false bottom he found a series of what looked to be tattered envelopes, all with her mother's name and address on them. Opening the first, he found a letter from one of his foster carers, those people who had given him life and experiences, and who had offered him what he now realized was love. He read each subsequent letter, one for each year, detailing a different stage in his life, the things he was doing and the things he liked. They told of his immature loves, like yo-yos, hiking, skateboards. Encyclopedias,

National Geographic magazines, and the trumpet. Bowling, naval ships, and heavy metal music. And as he read, he built the picture in his mind of the past he had lived, all that exposure to novel hobbies, interests his guardians had introduced him to, then written about in agreed annual letters to his mother. These letters were documentation of the life he'd lived, and the person he had been throughout his years.

And as he thought of his old home, the one he had shared with his mother, he realized then that the things she had collected were not for her at all; instead she had been collecting things for him, for a possible life that neither of them was living. She had collected things that she had been told he liked. It had all been his all along.

He could look upon the way she lived differently then, with a kinder more generous eye. It made sense somehow, in a way it never had before. In the absence of what you truly love, you keep the next best thing. She had relied on material objects to remind her that she had a son whom she loved. Letters that could take her back to the man she loved, and items that once belonged to parents whom she lost too soon, which perhaps could transport her back to a time when she was safe and loved. Her passion for collecting and preserving history mutated into a pathology, brought into existence by too many losses and periods of hurt. How could Harry not forgive her failings after realizing that? Reaching back into the box he pulled out the final object, the last thing to be buried under the false bottom. It was a small broach in the shape of two birds. It was covered in diamonds, or something similar, and quite beautiful. It reminded him of the bird painted on Tabitha's shoulder, wings mid-flight, ready to take off. *Spread your wings, Harry,* he thought. Perhaps he was finally ready to do so.

When he called his boss, Victor, and arranged his return to work, he had not expected to find a new place to live. But after hearing about the fire Victor said he would have it no other way. Moving into Victor's house came as a relief, as did being able to slip back into the routines he knew at work. He saw a couple of apartments for rent, and decided upon a small garden flat with large doors that he could open up and let the world in. It would be ready the following month. Polly said how pleased she was to see him back at orchestra practice, and even John seemed relieved by his presence. Busy at work, his days were filled with activities, people who wanted to hear of his travels, and others who just wanted him to read the newspaper aloud. But when he slipped into bed at night, he always found himself thinking about Tabitha, and exactly what he was supposed to do now that she was gone.

During one wakeful night at Victor's, he logged onto the internet to search for her in the capacity of her new job in New York. And there on the website of the auction house, under the tab NEWS, was an article announcing her imminent arrival. There was a photograph, black-and-white, and in it she looked proud and strong. It felt as if she was moving a thousand leagues further from him. Yet he didn't resent it. The sight of her moving forward made him feel as if he didn't want to live in the past anymore either.

The following evening he sat in the orchestra looking out at the growing audience. It was incredible to him that so many people had come to see them play, and he was so thankful to be there. Smiling at the noise, the hubbub as people found their seats, he was shaking with a sort of nervous exhilaration. Although he wished there was somebody in the audience to play for, he also realized that this time he was happy to play for himself, keeping a promise he made to the person he wanted to be. As the show began, he forgot all about the crowd as he played through the repertoire. As the notes vibrated through his body, he vowed to himself right there and then, as his lips stung and his lungs throbbed from effort, that he would always strive for life to feel as good as it did in that moment.

It was during the final song, a rendition of "Unchained Melody," when he saw her moving through the crowd. That flaming hair was undeniable even in the dark of the theater. Tabitha, right there, still in the UK. Before he could think he was on his feet.

"Tabitha," he shouted, but she kept on moving. Certain that he was on his feet as part of the performance, the rest of the band stood up for a rousing finale. John was loving every minute of it, his arms waving about to the climax of the show. "Tabitha, wait," he called, trying to push his way forward. But he couldn't move for brass instruments, and found himself stuck behind the trombones to his left and the percussion section to his right. Kettle drums too big to pass, and too heavy to shove out of the way. Just moments later the show was over. Cheering and applause flooded the auditorium. Trapped onstage, he watched as Tabitha slipped through the doors, his free bird lost once more.

When he woke up the next morning, his original plan for the box seemed uncertain now that he knew Tabitha was still around. They had searched for it together, and he knew the value she placed on it. It wasn't monetary, the true value it's preservation and discovery. Staring at the box, packaged with Benoit's name written on it, it didn't seem right to send it without even letting Tabitha know it had been found. Perhaps it didn't belong with him as Mr. Lewisham and his mother had implied, but perhaps it also didn't belong to Benoit either. The value of this box was about more than one family, or one person. It was about a wider wrong being rectified. It was about truth being set free. Unwrapping the box, he reached in and took out the broach, and quickly wrote a letter to Tabitha. Sealing the broach inside an envelope, he grabbed the box, stuffed it in his rucksack, and left Victor's house.

Moving quickly through the streets, he was desperate to reach the museum, a grand old building with a stucco frontage and columns holding up a portico. He had never seen where Tabitha worked, but he felt sure this was the right place. Stepping into the reception, a large, echoey space with a marbled floor, silence all around save the beat of his own feet, his hands suddenly began to shake. What was he doing? Was this a mistake? But then a young woman with shiny black hair who was sitting at the only desk waved him over. She smiled as he approached.

"Hello there," she said. "Can I help?"

"Er, yes. I'd like to leave something for Tabitha Grant."

"Okay," the receptionist said, taking the bag as

Harry handed it to her. "I'll just give her a call to come down."

"No, no, it's okay," Harry said as she reached for the phone. "There's no need. She's not expecting me. But along with that bag, could you please just give her this."

Setting the envelope down on her desk she nodded her head. "If that's what you want. Would you like to leave a name?"

"No," Harry said, already moving away. "Everything I need to say is in that note."

Tabitha couldn't believe it was him as she saw him walking across the street away from the museum. What was he doing there? Pushing back her chair she headed from her office, past the boxes packed with textbooks ready to ship to New York. After charging down the stairs she crossed the foyer, breaking into a sweat as she rushed to Jenny at reception.

"Oh, I was just calling you," Jenny said. "Somebody just left you a package."

"I saw him. That was Harry."

"Oh god!" Jenny said, her hand cupping her mouth. "That was him?" Then she smiled. "He's very sexy, in a sort of *let me rearrange your bookshelves* kind of way."

"I know." Tabitha sighed, taking the envelope. Watching his performance the night before had been torture, never more so than when he stood up and called her name. It had only made the fact he wasn't part of her life harder to bear. But she had to leave. She had to keep them both safe.

Tabitha tore the envelope open. The little broach dropped into her hand. Recognizing it instantly as something of value, she knew it was a Van Cleef and Arpels design from the unmistakable craftsmanship and the tiny inset jewels. It was almost identical to the one Benoit had in France.

"Wow," Jenny said as she stood up to look at the broach. "Isn't that a Van Cleef?"

"I think so," Tabitha said. But she was more interested in the letter. It was short, and sweet.

This broach is for you. It's worth something I'm sure, but that's not why I'm giving it to you. It reminded me of you, the little tattoo on your shoulder, the love you had for the birds in my cages. I've let them go now, Tabitha, just as you wanted. You see, finally I understand that to know whether something is truly yours, first you have to let it go. What is in the bag is not for you, but it is for you to deal with. I know you will do the right thing.

"Give me the bag," Tabitha said then, and without taking her eyes from the computer screen, Jenny handed it across the desk. Opening the clips, Tabitha peeled back the lid. Within a split second she knew what it was.

"Oh my god," Tabitha said, closing the lid again. He had found it. He really had. Now he was leaving it with her. "I can't believe it."

"I know," Jenny said, turning the screen to face Tabitha. "Look what it's called."

"I know what it's called," Tabitha began as she looked up. But Jenny wasn't talking about the Klinkosch box. On the screen was the very broach that Harry had left for her. It was an old photograph, taken years before. "Is that the same one?"

"Sure is," Jenny said. "Les Inséparables, made in nineteen forty-one by Van—"

"What did you say it was called?" Tabitha asked.

"Les Inséparables."

Did he know the name of the broach? Was that why he gave her this? Suddenly, she realized, it didn't matter. All her life she had latched onto people, tried to be their everything. But this time, just like his birds, Harry had set her free to be whatever it was she wanted. Only now she was totally free, she knew the thing she wanted the most was the very thing she had let slip away.

"Do not show anybody what's in that bag until I get back," she screamed, before flying from the museum.

Racing through the streets, at first she couldn't see him, didn't even know which direction to look. But suddenly there he was in the crowd ahead. Too many bodies lingered between them, hindering her progress to reach him. Running as fast as she could, the sheen of desperation shone slick across her brow.

"Harry," she screamed, running some more. After a moment she had to stop to catch her breath. "Harry," she called again. There was too much noise, he couldn't hear her. Strangers glanced her way, wondering what was wrong with her. If she didn't make him turn around soon, he was going to be gone for good. Seeing an opportunity she climbed on top of a nearby bin, rising her up above the crowds. Just about to turn the corner, she called once more. "Harrrrrrrry," she shouted as loud as she could, and just a moment later, along with several other people, he stopped.

Jumping down from the bin she charged through the crowds. Pushing just as hard to reach her, they were reunited. Reaching forward she grabbed his body, pulled it close. Holding him as tightly as she could, his arms enveloped her.

"You saw it?" he asked.

"Yes. I can't believe you found it."

He nodded. "I did." His eyes were glassy as he smiled. "I thought you'd know what to do. I thought you would know what is right. You'd be able to find out where it truly belongs."

"I do, and I will."

"I looked for you, you know," he said, stroking her arm. "I went to your house and the neighbor said you were gone."

"I went to my parents' place," she said, unable to hide her smile. "I couldn't leave without working things out with them first."

His hand held hers, fiddling with her fingers as if he needed to make sure she was real. But his mind was elsewhere, on the very real facts as he knew them. "When do you leave?"

"Next week." She closed her eyes like a small child trying to make something different from reality. "I have to go. But you know something? It doesn't matter."

"It doesn't?"

"No. Because no matter where I am, I'm yours,

Harry. Nothing can change that. You don't belong to me, and I don't belong to you. But we do belong together. We're inseparable, aren't we?"

All his life he had tried to hide how he really felt, scared to make demands of anybody. To try to be what people needed him to be, yet all the while scared to push himself into their lives for fear of not being wanted. He wasn't scared to risk things anymore. Now he understood that he deserved something more, so there was no longer any reason to be afraid.

"We are," he said, taking a shaky breath. It was now or never. "Which is why I was thinking that maybe we should leave together."

"Harry, are you serious?"

"Nothing matters if we leave. Not Daniel's threats, not the house, or the past. It would just be me and you, and a fresh start. If you want me to, I'll come."

Reaching down she took his hand in a grip so tight it almost hurt. "There is nothing I want more."

As they walked away, her head resting against his shoulder, he realized that for the first time in his life he had given up everything that he had been clinging to, let everything go, and despite his worst fears, he was still there to live another day. In letting things go he had now only that which had come back to him. Now he wasn't alone. Gazing up at the sky he saw a chink of bright blue struggling for space between two black clouds. Some things, he realized, important things that felt truly lost, were really there all along, safely hidden, just waiting to be found.

Acknowledgments

S o many thanks come at the end of writing a book. To my agent, Madeleine Milburn, and her wonderful team. Thank you for championing my work and making me feel as if I am in such safe hands.

To Lucia Macro, my editor at William Morrow in the US, and Sam Eades at Orion in the UK, thank you so much for your input into this book.

To the other editors around the world who have put their faith in this work, I am truly grateful. There might be no greater buzz than receiving a book I have written, but which I cannot read.

Thank you to the publishing, marketing, and sales teams who get this book into the hands of readers.

Thanks to the many people whose names I will

never hear, who play a part in turning my manuscript into a book.

Thank you to Stasinos, Theo, and Themis, who listen to endless "what if" scenarios, early chapter drafts, and rambling synopses. I love you all so much.

And lastly, thank you to Lelia, surely the greatest gift I was ever given. My love for you and respect for our story, and all those involved, played no small part in the creation of this book. I hope you know what a treasure you are. I am yours, forever.

About the Author

MICHELLE ADAMS grew up in the UK and now lives in Cyprus with her husband, stepchildren, and young daughter. She is also the author of *Little Wishes* and two psychological suspense novels, *My Sister* and *Between the Lines*.